Praise for Sarra Manning:

'These return chick lit in the vein of *Bridget Jones' Diary*'
Heat

'Deliciously addictive tale of
Marie Claire

'A sexy, modern read'
Glamour

'This brilliant story is classic chick lit with plenty of laughs'
Closer

'We were superglued to the pages of this book, and you'll
be hooked too . . . this sexy, gritty tale is Sarra Manning's
first novel and she's nailed it'
Heat

'Wonderfully written, the story is a laugh-out-loud page-
turner with believable characters'
News of the World

'Superior, old fashioned chick lit'
Heat

'A fab read – you'll be hooked'
Closer

'Manning knows a good modern romance when she sees
one'
Daily Mirror

www.transworldbooks.co.uk

Sarra Manning is an author and journalist. She started her writing career on *Melody Maker*, then spent five years on legendary UK teen mag *J17*, first as a writer then as entertainment editor. Subsequently she edited teen fashion bible *Ellegirl UK* and the BBC's *What To Wear* magazine.

Sarra has written for *ELLE*, *Grazia*, *Red*, *InStyle*, the *Guardian*, the *Mail On Sunday*'s *You* magazine, *Harper's Bazaar*, *Stylist*, *Time Out* and the *Sunday Telegraph*'s *Stella*. Her bestselling young adult novels, which include *Guitar Girl*, *Let's Get Lost*, the *Diary Of A Crush* trilogy, *Nobody's Girl* and *Adorables*, have been translated into numerous languages.

She has also written three grown-up novels: *Unsticky*, *You Don't Have To Say You Love Me* and *Nine Uses for an Ex-Boyfriend*.

Sarra lives in North London.

For more information on Sarra Manning and her books, see her website at www.sarramanning.co.uk

Also by Sarra Manning

YOU DON'T HAVE TO SAY YOU LOVE ME
NINE USES FOR AN EX-BOYFRIEND
UNSTICKY

and published by Corgi

It Felt Like A Kiss

Sarra Manning

CORGI BOOKS

TRANSWORLD PUBLISHERS
61–63 Uxbridge Road, London W5 5SA
A Random House Group Company
www.transworldbooks.co.uk

IT FELT LIKE A KISS
A CORGI BOOK: 9780552163279

First published in Great Britain
in 2014 by Corgi Books,
an imprint of Transworld Publishers

A CIP catalogue record for this book
is available from the British Library.

Addresses for Random House Group Ltd companies outside the UK
can be found at: www.randomhouse.co.uk
The Random House Group Ltd Reg. No. 954009

The Random House Group Limited supports The Forest
Stewardship Council® (FSC®), the leading international
forest-certification organisation. Our books carrying the FSC
label are printed on FSC®-certified paper. FSC is the only forest-
certification scheme supported by the leading environmental
organisations, including Greenpeace. Our paper-procurement
policy can be found at www.randomhouse.co.uk/environment

Typeset in 10.25/13 pt Meridien by Falcon Oast Graphic Art Ltd.
Printed and bound by CPI Group (UK) Ltd, Croydon, CR0 4YY

2 4 6 8 10 9 7 5 3 1

MIX
Paper from
responsible sources
FSC
www.fsc.org   FSC® C016897

Dedicated to the memory of Gordon Shaw who was always the most exemplary of fathers.

Thanks

Thank you to my bestie, Kate, who talked me down from so many ledges this year, and Lesley Lawson, Sophie Wilson and Sarah Bailey just for being there. Thanks also to Sam Baker, Sarah Franklin, Anna Carey, Julie Mayhew and my Twitter friends, who keep me sane and hooked up with cute pictures of doggies.

I have meant to say thank you to Leanne Forrester for an unconscionably long time, so, Leanne, thank you so much for all your support. And I would also like to give big, big, BIG thanks to Sue Goodyear, who has waited patiently for over two years to have her name in this novel after she very generously bid in the Authors for Japan auction. Sue, I hope you like your namesake!

As ever, I owe a huge debt of gratitude to my wonderful agent, Karolina Sutton, and Catherine Saunders, Helen Manders, Alice Lutyens and all at Curtis Brown. I'd also like to thank my editor Catherine Cobain and Sophie Wilson (yes, I know two Sophie Wilsons), Madeline Toy, Sarah Roscoe, Sophie Holmes, Vivien Garrett and all at Transworld.

twitter.com/sarramanning

www.sarramanning.co.uk

It's very difficult to keep the line between the past and the present. You know what I mean? It's awfully difficult.

Edith 'Little Edie' Bouvier Beale

Camden, London, 1986

He was the most beautiful man Ari Underground had ever seen.

'I could eat him for breakfast,' she said to her friend Tabitha as they stood at the bar of the Black Horse. 'He looks like a cross between James Dean and Serge Gainsbourg.'

'He's married,' Tabitha said flatly. 'Even if he wasn't, he's bad news.'

He might be married but he was also brooding and dark, and Ari wanted to lick the sneer right off his pretty face.

And if he was married then he had no right to be staring back at her.

Afterwards, when she'd come off stage in the tiny room above the bar, still high on the applause, the buzz, the sheer thrill of playing songs that hot-wired people's hearts, and was packing her amp and her guitar into the back of the van that Chester had borrowed from his dad, she suddenly felt a pair of eyes painting pictures on the back of her neck.

Ari turned round and he was there, *right there*. Didn't say a word, just took a step nearer, and another one, until she was pressed between the van and his hard body. This close she could see how long his eyelashes were, and the sneer disappeared because they were close enough that she could purse her lips and blow it away. It was a lot like kissing without actually kissing.

They weren't touching either, though his body hustled her against the side of the van. When Ari panted a little because he was so intense, so silent, and she'd never been so turned on, it was as if he caught her every breath.

A door banged behind them, then she heard Chester say plaintively, 'I've got to have the van back by midnight or my dad'll kill me,' and the spell was broken.

In the time it took to blink, Billy Kay wasn't there any more.

Chapter One

Camden, London, The Present

It had rained hard that lunchtime. There was still a damp, peaty smell rising up from the undergrowth in Regent's Park, but the sharp scent of wet grass was fading as Ellie Cohen walked home from work. There was a luminescence to the early evening; soft and light, no crispness in the air. Ellie slipped off her jacket and hoped that the good weather would last until the end of the week when she was off to Glastonbury. Spending three rainy days battling the elements and trudging through squelching fields of mud with the risk of getting trench foot would not be fun.

Ellie would spend most of the week anxiously clicking refresh on the Met Office website, but now it was Monday evening, which was household chores night. Then, as a reward for their hard work, Ellie and her flatmates would watch trashy TV and eat like queens, courtesy of Theo, owner of the Greek restaurant downstairs, who needed to get rid of any food left from the weekend. The thought was enough to have Ellie quickening her pace as she left the park by Gloucester Gate and hurried towards Delancey Street.

Five minutes later she was outside her flat but before she could pull out her keys, the door opened to reveal Tess and Lola. For two women who had hummus, lamb kebabs, stuffed vine leaves and back-to-back episodes of

The Only Way Is Essex in their immediate future, they didn't look very happy.

'Why are you both looking so grim?' Ellie asked, as they made no effort to step aside and let her in. 'Is it the thought of the pre-cleaner tidy-up? Come on, you know the thought of it is worse than the actual doing of it.'

'We need to talk,' Lola said soberly, and Tess nodded, not looking Ellie in the eye. Instantly Ellie was suspicious.

'Why? What have you done? Have you broken something? Have you broken something of mine?' Each thought was worse than the last. 'Did you borrow something without asking and break it? Please don't say it was my new hairdryer!'

'It's not about your new hairdryer. We haven't broken any of your things,' Tess added quickly as Ellie opened her mouth to fire off a new round of questions. 'It's about, well . . . first of all you should know that we're not judging you. We love you, but it's a case of loving the sinner, not the sin, you know?'

Ellie didn't know, and couldn't imagine what heinous act she'd committed that might warrant an intervention. 'You're going to have to give me a clue because I don't remember sinning lately. Anyway, I'm not a Catholic, don't they have the monopoly on sinning?' she asked brightly to lighten the mood. It didn't work.

'Yeah, and you have the monopoly on bad boyfriends,' Lola said. 'After what happened on Saturday night, enough is enough.'

'Richey is bad news. He's the zenith of bad news,' Tess elaborated, as she finally stopped blocking Ellie's way and pushed her into the living room, then marched her over to the IKEA sofa. 'Sit!'

It was the tone of voice tweedy women of a certain age used to discipline unruly dogs. Ellie sat. 'OK, maybe things got a little out of hand on the weekend but Richey is not bad news, he just had a bad Saturday night.'

'Not as bad as our Saturday night was having to deal with his crap,' Lola said in a tight voice. They were both standing over her, hands on hips. It was Ellie who had brought the two of them together but they still hadn't quite made the transition from roomies to friends. In fact they argued a lot, so how ironic that they'd finally bonded over the shortcomings of Richey.

Richey, Ellie's latest boyfriend, was shaping up to be a fine boyfriend. A great boyfriend. He was very good-looking, almost model standard – not that Ellie was shallow – was gainfully employed as an assistant at a film production company in Soho, had a good sense of humour, didn't feel emasculated that Ellie earned more than he did, and generally Ellie was starting to feel that the two and a half months that she'd been seeing Richey were turning into something. Maybe even quite a serious something.

'. . . and really, Ellie, he's awful. He's not worthy of you. Not even close,' Tess insisted so shrilly that Ellie stopped mentally listing all of Richey's considerable plus points and frowned at her best friend.

Ellie loved Tess, and often referred to her as 'my sister from another mister'. She'd bought Tess her first bottle of Chanel No 5 for her twenty-first birthday and had once endured three hours in Topshop as Tess tried on jeans and cried every time she swivelled round and looked at her bum in the changing-room mirror. There'd also been tough love, like the time she'd nursed Tess through an affair with a married man, or when she'd finally persuaded Tess to get her brown hair highlighted and to soldier through growing out her over-plucked eyebrows, and *this* was how Tess chose to repay her?

'I've already said I'm sorry about Saturday night at least ten times and you know I'll get your dress dry-cleaned.'

Lola sat down next to Ellie and gently patted her knee. Lola never did anything gently so it was a measure of just how serious they both thought this was; this *fuss* about Richey.

'Sweetie, it's not about the dress. It's about you failing to see what's blatantly clear to all the people who care about you,' Lola said softly. 'We don't want to see you in a relationship with a smack addict or a meth head, or whatever horrible shit Richey is into.'

Ellie couldn't believe what she was hearing. So, there'd been half an hour during an admittedly wild Saturday night that she hadn't been with Richey and in that time he'd apparently gone on a drug-fuelled bender? This didn't equate with the Richey that she'd been seeing. He held doors open for her. He gave her back rubs when she'd had a bad day at the office. He was always sending her funny, sweet little texts . . .

'You're blowing this whole thing way out of proportion. Yes, he smokes dope, but more people smoke dope than go to church on Sundays.' Ellie had read that in the *Guardian*, so it had to be true. 'And maybe he caned it a bit hard on Saturday night, but really, Lola, you don't exactly live a blameless life yourself, and Richey's been going through a rough time . . .'

'Yeah, like he was going through my drawers. Probably to find stuff he could sell to fund his habit,' Tess revealed, and Ellie's heart plummeted, as it did from time to time. Usually when she was seeing a guy and it was all going well, until all of a sudden it wasn't. Then her plummeting heart was the precursor to many nights of not sleeping, and drinking too much wine, and wondering why, when everything else was turning out just as she'd planned, right on schedule, the relationship area of her life was piled high with emotional debris.

But the thing was that you had to get back on the horse. Keep on trying. Give potential new boyfriends the benefit of the doubt because the alternative was to become one of those embittered women who sat with other embittered women in bars and said embittered things like, 'All men are bastards. You can't trust any of them. Better to be on your own than to be with some waste of space who makes you miserable.'

Ellie didn't want to end up like that. Half her mother's friends were like that. She had to stay positive, though sometimes staying positive was really hard. 'I'm sorry, I really am. I don't know how many more times I can say it, but we were *all* pretty out of it on Saturday night. There were Jäger shots—'

'That doesn't excuse him trying to steal from us,' Tess said. She had every right to sound upset – Ellie was upset on her behalf – but there could be a perfectly rational explanation for Richey rifling through her sock drawer, although Ellie couldn't think what it might be.

'I'm sure Richey doesn't have a habit,' she said emphatically, though she was going to be having words with him later. Serious words. 'It's not as if I've only just met him. I've been seeing him for nearly three months now and anyway, how bad can he be? My mum introduced us!'

'We're getting sidetracked here.' Tess sat down so she could put an arm round Ellie's stiff shoulders. 'Sweetie, this is coming from a place of love. Not a place of judgement.' Ever since Tess had read *How to Win Friends and Influence People*, in the hope it would lead to a promotion from freelance dogsbody to permanent researcher on the TV morning show *On The Sofa*, where she worked, she always used calm, modulated tones when faced with a difficult situation or truculent housemate. 'Also, I have to point out that Richey is the very worst in a long line of crap men you've dated.'

'I don't date crap men!'

'Lame ducks, then,' Tess countered, like that made it even better. 'Oh, Ells, you must have noticed that you always end up copping off with men who are, well, challenging and diff—'

'What Tess is trying to say is that you go out with total

17

losers who hang around the flat with all their neuroses and hang-ups until you straighten them out and then . . .' Lola took a deep breath, either for dramatic effect or because she needed oxygen . . . 'and then instead of thanking you, they dump you!'

That was a very harsh way of summarising her previous relationships, and, Ellie thought, a complete twisting of the facts.

'I'm twenty-six, and yes, I've dated a few men and it hasn't worked out. Big deal.' Ellie folded her arms and glared at her flatmates mutinously. 'I'm really sorry that I haven't settled down with my one true love, but then again neither have you, and while we're on the subject of exes with severe emotional disorders, two words, Lola: Noah Skinner!'

Lola flushed at the mention of the dissolute fine artist who'd made her life sheer misery for eighteen months as he slept with other women, tried it on with all her friends and had repeatedly ponced money off her even though his family owned half of Shropshire. 'Everyone's allowed a couple of bad boyfriends, but you're stuck in a bad boyfriend loop. It needs to end now.'

Ellie wasn't going to give up without a fight. She even opened her mouth to remind Lola that the two of them had first spoken only after Noah had come on to Ellie in the hope she'd persuade her boss at the gallery to represent him, but Tess got there first. 'Mark, your very first boyfriend, had all those issues with low self-esteem. He couldn't even walk into a room without genuflecting. Then you encouraged him to talk through his issues with a responsible adult, and his parish priest persuaded him to accept Jesus Christ as his personal Lord and Saviour, and he entered a seminary instead of coming to Ibiza with us after A levels,' she said in a furious burst.

'Doesn't prove anything,' Ellie ground out, even as she remembered that awful week after A levels when she should have been excited about going to Ibiza and, well, the rest of her life, and instead she'd stayed in her tiny bedroom, curtains drawn, listening to her mother's Smiths albums as she began to understand that heartache wasn't just a word used in sad songs; it was an actual tangible thing and it hurt like hell.

Tess continued to list Ellie's past boyfriends: including Alex, the cross-dressing performance artist she'd dated when she was studying at Central St Martins, who she'd caught wearing her underwear and who was now one of Australia's most celebrated drag queens, and Jimmy the alcoholic, until he'd spent a night drinking with Ellie's mother and her friends. He'd woken up two days later in a skip, minus his shoes, trousers and wallet. Then he'd decided to go straight edge and dumped Ellie for being a bad influence.

Then there'd been Andy, the compulsive gambler, who'd once pawned Ellie's TV but, buoyed up by her belief in his gift for numbers, left her to study for a degree in Applied Mathematics at Edinburgh University.

Even her attempt at a friend-with-benefits arrangement during her final year at Central St Martins had ended in absolute unmitigated disaster when Ellie broke Oscar's penis during a particularly vigorous sex session. Or that's what she thought until the A&E registrar said that it was just a bad sprain.

'Don't forget Danny,' Lola said to Tess, as she finished regaling Ellie with this list of lost loves. Not that Ellie needed any reminding. She remembered all of them. Not just the way things had ended, but the way each relationship had begun, with a smile, a joke, or a surreptitious look across a bar. Ellie remembered the good bits: lazy Sunday mornings with tea and toast, and wild nights out in Soho and Hoxton, as well as the bad bits: the rows and accusations and inability to reach a compromise.

Now Ellie listened as Lola hit the highlights of Ellie's

two-year relationship with lovely, geeky Danny, who she'd been planning on moving in with despite his lax personal hygiene and failure to turn up on dates because he was engrossed in *Call of Duty: Black Ops*.

Then Ellie had bought him a birthday consultation with a personal shopper at Selfridges and he'd fallen heart first for his birthday present, Sophie – they'd just become the proud parents of twins.

Yes, Ellie's love life was perfect to serve up as bite-sized anecdotes on a girls' night out when everyone moaned about how rubbish men were, but just as she remembered the good and bad bits of each relationship, she also remembered how they'd ended and that the heartache had never got any easier. On the contrary, it had got worse and had become her special friend, threatening to drag her under, and it had taken all of Ellie's considerable self-control to pick herself up each time, set her shoulders back and try again.

At least Tess and Lola appeared to have reached the end of their intervention because they each took hold of one of Ellie's hands.

'You're a smart, lovely gorgeous girl,' Tess told her, holding up her phone to show Ellie a photo as proof. It had been taken on a girls' weekend in Brighton last summer. Ellie was posing on Palace Pier and, yes, she was quite pretty. Or rather she thought of herself as a bit of a blank canvas. She was five foot seven, and slim because she worked hard at it, with long, straight shiny brown hair, though her mother and grandmother both insisted her best features were her big brown eyes and her smile. But the raw material had been shaped with some subtle warm-toned highlights, not to mention the Brazilian blowdry every three months to transform her Jew-fro into sleek and shiny perfection. The brown eyes were made more remarkable by lash extensions and her eyebrow threader's skill with cotton, wax and dye, and the smile was a result of several years of painful orthodontics. She wasn't going to be giving Alexa Chung any sleepless nights, but Ellie was perfectly satisfied with how she looked, apart from her 34As and the sign on her forehead that read, 'All your problems solved, stop and ask me how,' which apparently could only be seen by men with severe behavioural disorders.

'I don't have bad taste in men,' she said hotly, though admittedly the evidence was pretty damning. 'Everyone has some kind of issue they need to work on so it's completely unfair of you to act as if my exes were Care in the Community case studies. They might have been fixer-uppers but—'

'No, this is way beyond ironing out a few flaws on an otherwise decent boyfriend,' Lola argued. 'You're an emotional fluffer, Ellie.'

'What's a fluffer?' Tess asked.

'It's a girl on a porn shoot who gets the men all hard and primed for action, then after doing all the heavy lifting, as it were, she has to watch while all her good work is enjoyed by another woman.'

Tess looked appalled. 'Oh my God, that's exactly what you do, Ellie!'

'No, I don't.' Ellie yanked her hands out of their grasps so she could fold her arms, her head lowered so her chin was almost on her chest. 'Danny was the only one who went off with another woman.'

'And you stay friends with all of them,' Tess added accusingly, like that was a bad thing.

'What's wrong with that?' Ellie demanded. 'What's wrong with being the bigger person and keeping in touch with your exes? It's a sign of maturity.'

'It's a sign of you not being able to cut the cord. If I'm into some guy and he treats me like shit and dumps me, then no, I'm not going to banter with him on Facebook or invite him to my birthday parties. Look, we just want you to find a nice, normal man instead of these lame ducks you always manage to bring home,' Lola said, patting Ellie's knee again, even though Lola, who looked like a 1940s pin-up girl with her dark auburn hair styled in a slinky Veronica Lake do, tight wiggle dresses and tattoos, would never, ever entertain the idea of finding a nice, normal man.

Ellie slowly shook her head. 'Sometimes lame ducks appear nice and normal. It's not until you're at least seven dates in that they reveal themselves and by then, well, it just seems rude to make your excuses and leave.'

'She can't dump people,' Tess explained to Lola over Ellie's head. 'Never could. When we started secondary school, we were all assigned people to sit next to until we made friends and Ellie got this horrible girl called Laura Mulkenny, who had BO, the most pustular acne I've ever seen . . .'

'Which wasn't her fault. She had a hormonal imbalance.'

'. . . she copied Ellie's homework and left grease stains over it because she was one of those girls that ate her packed lunch in registration, and teased Ellie for being flat-chested. Ellie was far too chicken to come and sit next to me, even after we bonded about how much we loved Westlife.'

'I felt sorry for her. No one else wanted to sit next to her.'

Lola smiled knowingly. 'How long did you sit next to her for?'

'It's neither here nor there.'

'Five years,' Tess replied. 'Then Laura failed most of her GCSEs despite copying Ellie's homework, and wasn't allowed to stay on for A levels.'

'Well, you're going to have to dump Richey,' Lola said. 'He's more than just a lame duck. I know his type from way back, and his type is big, fat trouble. And once you've

22

sent him packing, unless you find a decent bloke who isn't a complete freak of nature then you're forbidden from bringing any men back to the flat.'

'I'm sorry, Ellie, but that's how it has to be,' Tess added. 'I know it sounds harsh but it's for your own good. You have to get rid of Richey.'

'I don't have to do anything on the basis of your flimsy circumstantial evidence,' Ellie argued. 'It might all be a simple misunderstanding, and if it is then I'll have broken up with Richey for no reason. He might be the One.' They both snorted. 'But he might be! I'm not going to throw that away on a load of hearsay.'

'It's not hearsay. It's your two best friends who witnessed your current boyfriend off his tits on class-As and we're not doing this to be cruel, Ellster, we're doing this for your own good.' Tess had the sanctimonious note to her voice that brooked no denial.

'I'll talk to him,' Ellie conceded. 'But it's Glastonbury this weekend and he's booked time off work. I can't get all heavy and issue ultimatums then head off to Somerset with him like nothing's happened.' The injustice of their demands made Ellie clasp her hands to her heart. 'You can't expect me to do that!'

'Don't care when you do it, just that you do it.' Lola stopped with the knee-patting. 'He's not stepping foot in this flat ever again. End of. Now, can we get the pre-cleaner tidy-up over and done with?'

There was no budging them. Tess and Lola refused to discuss the matter further because Tess was too busy snapping at Lola, who spent the entire pre-cleaner clean moaning about the pointlessness of having a cleaner if you spent the evening before she came tidying up. 'It's so middle class,' she complained.

'You *are* middle class,' Tess told her. 'I don't care if one of your grandfathers was a coal miner, your parents live in Reading and your dad's a GP. We wouldn't have to do a

23

pre-cleaner tidy-up if you didn't have a dirty crockery mountain in your bedroom and you never rinse the sink after you've brushed your teeth.'

It seemed as if the row would descend into hair-pulling until Tess played her trump card and threatened to get rid of the cleaner altogether and Lola was forced to admit that paying ten pounds for her share of the cleaner was money well spent.

They had the same argument at the same time every Monday evening and it ended only when Theo brought up a bag bulging with takeaway containers, as he did this evening, so the three of them could pick their way through a selection of stuffed vine leaves, lamb souvlaki and assorted dips while they caught up on trashy TV. Every time they skipped through an ad break, Lola would shake her head and sigh. 'Jesus, I can't believe I'm living with two people who used to like Westlife.'

Then Tess would bop Lola with a cushion and Ellie would smile faintly, while on the inside she was in turmoil; not sure whether she should be angry with her friends or angry with her boyfriend. She was already steeling herself for the talk she needed to have with Richey. Past experience had proved that these kinds of talks always ended with her boyfriends having some kind of epiphany, then heading off into the sunset without her.

Chapter Two

The next morning Ellie was pulled out of sleep and fitful dreams of being followed around by a family of fluffy ducklings, who had a nasty habit of falling off kerbstones into the path of oncoming traffic, by the chirp of her phone.

She opened one eye. It was only six fifteen, three-quarters of an hour before her alarm. The number of the Mayfair gallery where she worked was flashing on the screen. Her boss had no respect for an eight- or even a nine- or ten-hour working day. If he was paying your wages and a hefty sales commission on top, then he owned your arse.

'Hello? Is there a problem?' Ellie hoped she sounded vaguely alert.

'You have to come in right now. I'm in a world of trouble.' It was Piers, her boss's hapless assistant, so, no, she didn't have to come to the gallery right now.

'Give me one reason why you felt it necessary to wake me up at such an ungodly hour,' she demanded, because, contrary to popular opinion, there were lots and lots of people who Ellie could say 'no' to, and Piers was at the top of the list. 'It had better be a really, really good reason.'

'Oh, please, Ellie. I've been here all night trying to fix it and I've just made it worse.' Piers sounded shrill and hysterical. 'There's a virus on my computer and somehow it's spread to all the other computers.'

That got Ellie's attention. She sat up. 'What kind of virus?'

She heard Piers swallow hard. 'Penises,' he whispered. 'There are pop-up penises on all the computers.'

'Have you been looking at porn? Again? You were warned about this.' She was already throwing back her duvet. 'I'll be there in an hour.'

Piers moaned. 'It's an emergency! Just this once can you not walk to work? I'll order you a car.'

Ellie always walked into work. She walked through heatwaves, torrential rainfall and even the occasional blizzard, and although pop-up penises on the gallery server were serious, they didn't warrant extraordinary measures. Besides, since their boss had got married he'd become boringly fixated about his own work/life balance – not that of his employees – and his wife got very pouty if he left for the office before eight thirty, so there was plenty of time.

'I don't need a car. But I'm going to need copious amounts of coffee when I get to work,' Ellie said, phone clamped between ear and shoulder as she rifled through her summer work dresses, which ranged from taupe to white to pale blue to show off her tan, and also because anything brighter (or, God forbid, with a print) tended to clash with the art. 'Also, I'm planning to smack you repeatedly with *Davenport's Art Reference & Price Guide.*'

Fifteen minutes later she was stepping out onto Delancey Street, showered, dressed and wearing really big sunglasses because it was an emergency and there wasn't time for a light I'll-apply-my-proper-make-up-later make-up.

Regent's Park was deserted apart from a few dog walkers and dedicated runners, but there was no time to appreciate the almost preternatural stillness of the early morning, as if the trees rustled in the breeze and the water rippled on the boating lake only when there were people around to appreciate these selfless acts.

There wasn't even enough time to pop into Le Pain Quotidien on Marylebone High Street. Ellie crossed Oxford Street, which was just starting to come to life, and headed for the rarefied thoroughfares of Mayfair and instantly, the bustle was muted. The hedge fund managers had been at their desks for at least an hour but it was too soon for the imperious-looking girls who worked in the luxury stores to start work and it was far, far, *far* too early for the ladies who still lunched to be heading for Miu Miu or Moschino or Marc Jacobs for a quick retail hit before their roast chicken, saffron, almond & parmesan salad (without the parmesan) and a bottle of sparkling water at Cecconi's.

Ellie didn't even dare dawdle for a little window-shopping as she walked past the hip boutiques on Dover Street and arrived at Thirlestone Mews, a pretty cobbled street just round the corner from Berkeley Square, at thirty-one minutes past seven. Piers hurried towards her. He was tall, thin and effete-looking, which made people automatically want to look after him, which was fortunate as his greatest talent was for getting himself into serious trouble.

'I thought you'd never get here,' he cried, grabbing Ellie's hand and tugging her towards number seventeen, which was identical to all the other stucco-covered houses in the mews, its door wide open.

'You must never leave the gallery unattended,' Ellie gasped as she was yanked through the door. 'Someone could already have had a painting off the wall.'

'Don't even joke about things like that,' Piers snapped, as they both turned and looked across the reception area into the main gallery to make sure there were still fourteen paintings by an obscure yet collectable British Pop artist. There were.

'See? Things could be worse,' Ellie said brightly, though she didn't feel bright and Piers didn't seem to have delivered on the coffee front. 'Now shall we sort out this penis infestation?'

It was just as well that Ellie hadn't had breakfast because the sight of so many angry red, tumescent cocks multiplying every time she pressed a key on any of the gallery's computers made her feel bilious.

Piers twitched behind her. 'Oh my days! I never want to see an erect penis again.'

'If you hadn't been trawling the internet for erect penises in the first place this would never have happened,' Ellie told him sternly, though she knew they'd laugh about this, probably in a few short hours. Right now, it was Penis Apocalypse. 'I don't know what you've done. I can't fix it. We have to call IT.'

'You can't! They'll log it and he'll know. He'll fire me for absolute certain this time.'

Ellie doubted that. Anyway, it wasn't as if Piers needed to work when he had a private income and trust funds. This wasn't even as bad as the time he'd put his foot through a painting when he'd been mucking about in the packing room, though that time he'd got his long-suffering mother to buy the painting. So Ellie ignored Piers and dialled their IT service's emergency number.

She was put straight through to Danny, her ex, who happened to be on-call. Ellie always prided herself on remaining on good terms with her exes, but now having to speak to Danny after last night's conversation with Tess and Lola made her feel raw and exposed. Maybe staying on speakers with all the men who'd done her wrong, hurt her heart and made her cry was just another example of her total pushoverdom.

'Ellie? How are you?' At least Danny sounded pleased to hear from her, which was nice, even if there was the sound of a baby squalling in the background.

'I'm good, except we have a porn virus on the computer

system,' Ellie said, deciding it was best to get straight down to business, because Piers was now huffing on his asthma inhaler.

Danny chatted away as he took control of their servers by remote access and painstakingly removed each and every penis from the system. He and Sophie had just got back from their first weekend away without the twins, who'd been left with her parents, and were teething and refusing to sleep through the night.

'Anyway, enough about me,' Danny said when the last penis had magically melted away and he was doing something with their firewall to make it penis-repellent in future. 'What's your news?'

Now that the crisis had been averted, Piers, inevitably, was nowhere to be found.

'Oh, nothing much. Work is busy and I'm going to Glastonbury this weekend. You know how my mum feels about Glastonbury.'

'It's like her Christmas, birthday and all other major holidays rolled into one,' Danny said, and he chuckled and then suggested that they should get together for lunch or, even better, she should come round for dinner and some twin-cuddling time because Sophie was saying only the other day that they hadn't seen her in ages.

Ellie finished the call in much better spirits. She'd also come to a new conclusion about her past relationships. Yes, she'd been involved with men who'd been challenging, and yes, they'd become a lot less challenging thanks to her support and guidance, but that was what she brought to a relationship. The fact that they stayed in touch proved that she was a person worth having in their lives. How could that be bad?

She was only twenty-six. Of course she was going to rack up a few failed relationships. It didn't mean she was addicted to lame ducks. What it meant was that every time her heart got broken, it healed and was stronger than it had been before. Like her grandfather said, 'Broken hearts make the best vessels.'

Ellie wasn't ready to write off Richey because of half an hour on Saturday night. Richey liked a good time, and there wasn't anything wrong with that, but he also liked talking quietly for hours over pizza and beer about everything from French New Wave cinema to climate change to how they could both see themselves buying a dilapidated house near Deauville and doing it up on long weekends, as the restaurant staff pointedly kept wiping their table down because it was well past closing time. Ellie and Richey had a connection and Ellie wasn't sure how deep it went but she owed it to herself – to them – to get Richey's side of the story before she walked away.

Anyway, nobody was perfect. Not Tess, who was always jumping to conclusions, and especially not Lola, so they could get off her case.

'So . . . is everything all right? Is my nightmare over?'

Ellie swivelled round to see Piers standing behind her, asthma inhaler poised. She gestured at the computer. 'Do you see any penises? Danny is going to log the job as a non-specific virus and system reboot, so you're off the hook.'

Piers still looked as if he was about to burst into tears. 'Are you really sure that there isn't some great big todger that you've overlooked that's going to pop up and it will start all over again and never end until I'm fired and I'll have to explain to Mummy why I've been fired and then she'll tell my grandfather and he'll—'

'Piers, shut up,' Ellie said very gently, as she levered herself out of the chair. 'Just stop talking.'

She took hold of his elbows and gave him a tiny shake. Up close he had the sour smell of someone who'd stayed up all night awash in his own fear, and his elfin face was puffy and sallow. He was still gibbering about his grandfather and the very real possibility that he might get cut off from his trust fund if he couldn't stay gainfully employed and prove he was a worthwhile member of society.

'You need to go home . . .'

'I can't! It's almost nine and I promised that I'd have all the customs declarations finished and on his desk this morning.' Piers looked at her pleadingly. 'I don't suppose you could—'

'If I were you I'd go home, have a shower and a shave and change your shirt,' Ellie said quickly before Piers could completely take advantage of her good nature. 'You'll feel much better, and don't worry about the customs declarations. The courier company aren't coming to pick up that shipment until the end of the week. It's only Tuesday. You can do them when you get back.'

Piers surreptitiously sniffed an armpit, then agreed to Ellie's plan of action. After setting the alarm, she walked out with him as far as the nearest Leon for a triple skimmed latte and granola with strawberry compote.

By the time she got back to the gallery, Muffin and Inge were waiting for her. Neither of them was trusted to have her own keys, because they were just two more posh girls in a long line of posh girls that Ellie had seen come and go in the five years that she'd worked at the gallery. As far as she could remember Muffin and Inge were Posh Girl Ten and Posh Girl Eleven respectively, though after a while all the posh girls seemed to merge into one posh girl composite of shiny hair, expensive clothes and strident voice, who lived in Chelsea and was morbidly fascinated by the fact that Ellie lived in North London, had gone to a state school and didn't know anybody called Bunny.

Still, most of the posh girls were perfectly nice and friendly, and both Muffin and especially Inge looked pleased to see Ellie as she rocked unsteadily over the cobbles because she hadn't had time to swap her toning trainers for the Bloch ballet flats she had stashed in the bottom drawer of her desk.

'Oh my, your natural look is looking very natural today,' Muffin said by way of a greeting. Inge muttered something that might have been agreement or dissent but it was hard to tell with Inge because she never said much of anything, but sat behind the reception desk dreamily staring into space for most of the day. 'It's odd, you really do have *quite* a good complexion.'

It was a bit of a headspin for Muffin, who'd been raised in the country on food grown on the home farm and lots of untainted fresh air, that Ellie, born and bred in Camden, wasn't riddled with rickets and tuberculosis.

'It's not a natural look, I just haven't had time to put any make-up on,' Ellie said and as she unlocked the door and they began to go through the morning ritual of turning off the alarm, switching on the water cooler and sorting through the post, she gave them a brief account of Piers's latest mishap.

'He's such a silly boy,' Muffin said, even though Piers, unlike Muffin, had never mistaken a very famous conceptual artist for the window cleaner. 'I'd go and put your face on if I were you. Don't worry, we can hold the fort.'

Ellie doubted that very much because Inge had already abandoned the onerous task of opening the post to assume her usual position behind the reception desk so she could gaze into the middle distance while Muffin was glued to her iPhone, fingers skating over the screen.

'Let me know if we have any walk-ins,' Ellie said, just as she did every morning, because every walk-in was a potential client and every potential client meant potential commission and she refused to mount even one stair until she got a verbal commitment from both girls. Then, and only then, was she able to head upstairs for the sanctuary of her office.

Camden, London, 1986

It wasn't like Ari saw him everywhere she went after that, but she saw him often enough that it was more than a coincidence.

Billy Kay didn't usually slum it in Camden. He was part of a louche Ladbroke Grove set of jaded rich kids with coke habits who all pretended to be living the hard times but looked down on anyone whose parents didn't own half a county or a merchant bank, as Billy's father did.

Ari's parents might be the dry-cleaning moguls of North London but they'd started out in Hackney and dragged themselves out by their bootstraps. They weren't too happy that their youngest daughter pulled pints and worked on a second-hand clothes stall to fund the amazing thirty minutes when she was on stage, but Ari didn't much care what Sadie and Morry Cohen thought.

She got it. Nice Jewish girls weren't in bands, but maybe that was what intrigued Billy Kay – that besides him, she was the only other cool Jewish person in London. Yeah, there might be a whole coterie of artsy, liberal Jewish types in Hampstead all descended from Sigmund Freud, but they couldn't tell one end of a guitar from the other so they didn't count as far as Ari was concerned. That had to be why Billy stared at her when she was ordering a drink in a grimy Camden pub or flicking through the racks in the record shops on Hanway Street. He pretended to ignore her, but when she pretended to ignore him right back, Tabitha would hiss, 'He's staring at you.'

Or he could have been staring because every other girl in a

band or in a club or in a record shop in 1986 wore fifties summer dresses, white ankle socks and lace-up brogues, and they all bobbed their hair and carried their stuff in leather satchels and tried to look gamine and coy. Ari hated coy.

She dyed her hair black and backcombed it into a gravity-defying bouffant, applied lashings of thick black liquid eyeliner and red lipstick and wore her dresses leopard print and skin tight. Sure it was hard to work a fuzz pedal in a five-inch-high winklepicker but it wasn't impossible.

And when you were married to a girl called the Honourable Olivia Chivers, whose parents owned a fucking stately home and had probably got down one of their shotguns when you knocked up their daughter, a not-so-nice Jewish girl had to be the last word in exotica.

Chapter Three

Ellie loved her office. Not just because she was twenty-six and already had her own office – it was the only place in her world that was exactly how she wanted it.

It was airy and light. It was minimalist. She had a big desk, which was actually a Le Corbusier dining table, with nothing on it but her telephone, laptop, a white Roberts radio, and a small white Eames elephant, which she'd found heavily reduced in a little shop in Margate that was going out of business.

There was one splash of colour from a reproduction art-deco rug in soft shades of blue. Her books and reference guides and box files were neatly arranged on her modular shelving and everything else was hidden from view in the cupboard below.

Ellie strived to achieve the same clean minimalism at home but it was hard with two flatmates who liked to traipse into her bedroom to borrow clothes, books and make-up, and to spill drinks or, worse, nail varnish, on her floor and even her bedclothes as they hung out in her room to escape the noise of bouzouki music and plate smashing from Theo's restaurant when he did special ladies' nights on alternate Wednesday and Thursday evenings.

It was little wonder then that her pristine work environment was so pleasing. Calmness and order reigned, and every time Ellie walked into her office she felt like the best version of her that there was. It was a feeling that she could never get used to. Like this morning, as she sat down on her Arne Jacobsen swivel chair, her bum nestled lovingly on over two thousand pounds' worth of white lacquered, laminated sliced veneer, which had been languishing in her boss's storage facility in King's Cross until Ellie had liberated it, and sipped her latte as she read the morning's emails. It was at moments like this that Ellie felt like a proper grown-up, though most proper grown-ups probably didn't have to remind themselves they were proper grown-ups.

She worked steadily for half an hour but was replying to an email from her grandmother who wanted her to go to John Lewis in Oxford Street and buy vacuum cleaner bags because the Brent Cross branch were out of stock when her office door, which had been ajar, opened.

'Cohen, where's Piers?'

She didn't pause.

. . . and I can pop them in the post or bring them when I come round for Friday night dinner in a couple of weeks, if you can wait that long.

Lots and lots and lots of love
Ellie xoxo

Then she looked up at Vaughn, her boss, who was waiting with a querulous expression on his face. To be fair, he spent ninety per cent of the time looking querulous. It was just the way his face was.

'He had some errands to run,' Ellie lied, trying to sound harried and glancing down at her laptop as if she was busy with important gallery business.

'What kind of errands were more pressing than the customs declarations that I needed on my desk first thing?' Vaughn wanted to know.

He sounded properly annoyed now. Ellie decided to give him her full attention.

'He had to take an invoice to the printers because they forgot to sign it, then he had to go to the post office.' She frowned. 'Something to do with the customs declaration. He did say, but I wasn't paying much attention.'

'You're lying, Cohen,' Vaughn said. He always called her 'Cohen' because he said her first name was too insipid to be said out loud. Ellie didn't take offence. He also refused to call Muffin anything other than Alexandra, which was the name she'd been christened with. 'You always give everything your full attention so you must be covering for him.' He sighed and almost cracked a smile, so he was obviously in a good mood. 'Dare I even ask what he's done now? Has he put his foot through something again?'

For the briefest moment, Ellie considered telling Vaughn about the penis epidemic, but his moods were mercurial and she didn't want to talk about penises with her boss. She liked to maintain some professional distance. 'Nothing like that,' she murmured non-committally. 'Just errands.'

Vaughn wasn't convinced but Ellie managed to distract him by giving him an update on the Emerging Scandinavian Artists exhibition she was curating and soon he was leaving her office with an uncharacteristic: 'Looks like you have everything under control. By the way, Grace says that Copenhagen is the new Berlin, but then she's always saying something is the new something.'

Grace, Vaughn's much younger wife, was fashion editor on *Skirt* magazine. In the two years since he'd got married, Vaughn was much easier to deal with, apart from when he and Grace rowed (which they did frequently), when he was much worse. Luckily, Piers was tight with Grace and Lola knew her socially, so Ellie got the nod when Vaughn and Grace had been fighting and could stay out of his way.

Besides, Vaughn could never be as scary as he'd been the first time that Ellie had met him. His name had been mentioned in awestruck whispers all the way through her degree course in Criticism, Communication and Curation. There had been a huge furore in her second year at Central St Martins when he'd mounted a successful coup to have the creative director of the Institute of Contemporary Arts fired. That same year he'd swept into one of the studios before the Fine Art undergraduates' final show, bought every single piece from a German student called Frans and made him sign away the rights to everything he produced for the next ten years.

Then came that awful fateful day in her final year when Ellie had been tasked with curating the Conceptual Arts undergraduate degree show. Theoretically she was meant to be *assisting* but it had been a very weak crop of under-graduates that year and when the actual salaried curator had seen the badly executed, poorly conceptualised fruits of their labours, she'd washed her hands of them. It was left to Ellie to write the exhibition brochure, drum up what publicity she could, contact dealers, agents and museum muckety-mucks and beg them to attend.

It had been an absolute, bloody disaster, which had counted as thirty per cent of Ellie's final mark. On opening night, the art critic of the *Evening Standard* had even refused to enter the gallery. 'Far kinder that I say nothing at all,' he'd told Ellie when she pleaded with him to stay for a glass of really indifferent Chardonnay.

Ellie had then spent the next two days being shouted at by Conceptual Artists and Conceptual Artists' parents and significant others, who blamed her for the lack of interest. She'd been feeling pretty despondent on a Thursday after-noon, three days into the exhibition, and was standing in the gallery wondering if it might help in the slightest if she repositioned some of the pieces when Vaughn had walked in. He looked just like his photo on artpedia.org: tall, grim and utterly formidable.

Ellie had simply stood there, face aflame, as Vaughn had slowly walked round the space. Finally he'd walked up to her and she'd tried to smile but gave up when he said, 'This is the worst undergraduate show I have ever seen. Every single one of these artists, though I hesitate to use that word, should be shot for crimes against aestheticism. You should be ashamed for having any part of this.'

Then he'd gone. Ellie had made sure that he was really gone and wasn't coming back to say even more mean things, then she'd burst into tears.

It wasn't until she'd scrubbed her eyes with a piece of toilet tissue, and phoned her mum and her grandma and her grandpa and her mum's friends, who all assured her that it wasn't her fault and she'd done the best she could in the circumstances, that Ellie had the best idea of her life. Ever.

She'd cobbled together a press release, then emailed the *Evening Standard* critic, the critics at *The Times*, the *Guardian*, the *Independent*, the *Financial Times* and every art blogger she knew with the scoop that she, according to the most feared and influential art dealer in London, was curating the worst ever undergraduate show to take up gallery space. She'd quoted Vaughn verbatim, then added a few flourishes about the hard lot in life Conceptual Arts graduates had and how the industry had to support them or there'd be no art industry left.

Somehow it had worked. The gallery was packed with critics, dealers and scenesters eager to see what all the fuss was about. Ellie had given countless interviews, coined the phrase 'The New Ugly' (she was still particularly proud of that), and sold every single vile piece and installation.

When the Dean of Undergraduate Studies asked to see Ellie, she knew no fear. The students curating the Fine Arts undergraduate degree show had done a pretty poor job and props were due but when she was shown into the Dean's office, Vaughn was sitting behind his desk.

Ellie had looked imploringly at the Dean but he'd pushed her onto a chair and headed for the door. 'I'll let you two sort this out,' he'd blustered, and left her with Vaughn, who wielded enough power to get some big kahuna from the ICA fired, so ruining her nascent career wasn't going to tax him unduly.

They'd sat there in silence for an agonising while. Ellie knew what Vaughn was thinking: she was a nice Home Counties girl who'd crack under pressure. That was what most people at Central St Martins thought of her because she'd never cultivated a mockney accent or tried to disguise a privileged upbringing by dressing as if she'd just done a trolley dash in Oxfam. If that was what Vaughn thought too, then he was in for a nasty surprise, because she'd been brought up on a rough Camden council estate and had regularly stepped over the slumbering bodies of itinerant musicians who were kipping on the living-room floor as she got ready for school. Hell, she'd once been taken to the park by the late Ruby X, so if Vaughn thought he could start shouting at her and that she'd just sit there and take it, then . . . well, she'd probably cry but on the inside she'd be giving him the finger.

'I did a little digging on you,' was what he'd eventually said in a calm voice. 'I know exactly who you are. I used to know your mother . . . and your father.'

It hadn't exactly been a shock, though Ellie felt herself pitching forward. When she'd mentioned her predicament to her mother, who knew absolutely everyone, she'd shaken her head. 'Jimmy Vaughn,' she'd mused. 'Always thought he'd end up in prison or, well, dead.'

But to hear Vaughn mention her father, who was never, ever mentioned, wasn't what Ellie had been expecting and the shock threw her for a second. But only for a second, until she'd forced herself to raise her head and look Vaughn directly in the eye. 'Yeah, Mum says hi, by the way.'

Then she'd waited for him to start with the shouting and the threatening and the 'I'm going to ruin yous', but he'd offered her a job instead.

'As my general assistant, then we'll see how things progress once you're house-trained,' he'd said. 'I do like to have someone poor and hungry on staff. They tend to have more of a work ethic than the children of the aristocracy.'

Ellie had lasted six months as Vaughn's general assistant. He'd shouted at her every day; threatened to fire her without references every day; sent her scuttling to the loo every day so she could cry angry tears in private, but she'd learned more in six months than she had in her three years as an undergraduate.

When she'd picked a degree course it had been a compromise between her mother's desire for Ellie 'to do something really creative and rock 'n' roll with your life' and her grandparents' belief in a solid recession-proof career. Ellie knew all about the major art movements, could differentiate between good and bad brushstrokes and could understand why investing in art was a safer bet than hedge funds or stock options, but she didn't really 'get' art. It turned out that not getting art wasn't a huge obstacle to success if you worked for an art dealer and she did have great interpersonal skills.

So when a Premier League footballer had arrived to buy some art for his new Epping Forest mansion, Ellie was entrusted with the care of his wife, a nice girl called Carlie, who she'd taken up to Vaughn's office so they could talk about handbags and shoes and all the other things Vaughn had told her to talk to Carlie about.

Carlie had been more interested in the catalogue on Vaughn's coffee table. She'd done History of Art A level and, 'I adore Fiona Rae. You got anything by her?'

Ellie hadn't but she sold Carlie two alabaster seahorse sculptures by a Japanese figurative artist from the catalogue at list price. Vaughn had bawled her out for not sending Carlie down to him and hadn't spoken to her for two days, but then he'd sacked Minty, one of the posh

41

girls, so Ellie could start working front of house and knocked fifty per cent off her pitiful salary 'because it will give you an incentive to make up the rest in commission.'

Ellie now had her own office, a small but perfectly formed roster of young artists and even though she earned only seven point five per cent commission and Vaughn took the other seven point five per cent, she'd paid off her student loans and was now saving up for a deposit on a flat. Vaughn also let her pick two pieces of art every year for her own personal collection, as long as she didn't go mad and ask for a Damien Hirst or a Tracey Emin, because she was indispensable. Being indispensable was a good thing. It meant that people were stuck with you.

She was pulled back from the undignified gloat about her successful career trajectory by a beep from her phone.

Hello sexy. Fancy lunch? I can come to you. Rich x

Ellie smiled as she felt that anticipatory rush course through her at the thought of seeing Richey. He was always so spontaneous, so in-the-moment, in a way that Ellie longed to be but couldn't. Then the anticipatory rush was replaced with a feeling of despair. If she had things out with Richey as she'd been instructed, then a spontaneous lunch date might be the last time she saw him, which seemed crazy when she'd been imagining that they might have a future together.

Sounds great. Victory Cafe at 1? Ellie xoxo

Richey was only ten minutes late to meet her, which was a personal best. Ellie had already snagged the last free table in the fifties-themed café in the basement of Gray's Antique Market in a little mews behind Bond Street station. She looked up from the menu to see him walk in just as two people were leaving. He stood to one side to let them out and Ellie let herself relax ever so slightly.

If Richey were such a bad person, then he wouldn't

have such good manners. 'Manners maketh the man' was what people, especially her grandparents, said. It made Ellie smile and wave with more enthusiasm than was strictly appropriate when they needed to talk about his alleged problem with class-A narcotics.

Richey smiled back. He wasn't tall, only a couple of inches taller than Ellie, but he was a little dangerous-looking with his shaven head and the tattooed sleeves inked on his arms, shown off by his tight white T-shirt. He had good muscles too; being a runner for a film production company involved a lot of heavy lifting, and there was something about the way he smiled, how the light in his eyes became more of a glint, that made Ellie want to blush and duck her head. She did neither but tilted her face so Richey could kiss her cheek as he reached her side.

Finally Richey was sitting opposite her, knee brushing against hers and Ellie had to think of a way to lead into a serious discussion that wouldn't result in a big fight. They'd been seeing each other for eleven weeks exactly, only slept together a handful of times, so serious discussions were new territory.

'You look so buttoned up in your work gear,' Richey commented, as his eyes swept over Ellie's hair, which had had a quick encounter with her office hair straighteners, as had her grey cotton tunic dress, so it was at its optimum uncreasedness. 'Bit different to how you looked on Saturday night.'

On Saturday night Ellie had cuffed her boyfriend jeans and worn them with an old Sonic Youth T-shirt she'd borrowed from her mother, and white Converses; her hair had been tied back in a ponytail. It had been the perfect outfit to see Lola's friend's band in Soho and go to the aftershow party in Hoxton. Then Lola had invited everyone back to their flat, where the night had quickly degenerated into mayhem when Richey had supposedly done a few lines of coke on the breakfast bar and it transpired that doing a few lines of coke turned Richey into a belligerent tool.

Ellie pushed away the panini she'd barely touched, because Richey had given her the perfect opening gambit, but before she could open her mouth, he reached across the table to take her hand.

'That reminds me,' he said. 'Look, about Saturday night, I'm really sorry about what went down.'

'Yeah, well, I wanted to talk to you about that,' Ellie said carefully. 'Tess and Lola are quite annoyed with you.'

Richey pulled a face to indicate that Tess and Lola and their feelings towards him weren't weighing that heavily on his mind. 'But are *you* annoyed with me?'

'Well, I wasn't there for your big rampage. I'd gone down to the High Street with Laetitia to find her a cab and when I got back you were passed out in the bath.' Ellie paused to gauge Richey's reaction so far. He was nodding and his eyes were fixed on her intently. He had lovely eyes; they were dark and slumberous, and he had such long lashes that Ellie half suspected he'd had eyelash extensions. 'But I saw the broken plates, and Lola told me what you called her when she, you know, saw you doing coke in the kitchen.'

'Oh God,' Richey said, and he cradled his face in his hands. 'What else did I do?'

Ellie's heart was galloping at a rate that couldn't be healthy. 'Tess said that she caught you rifling through her drawers. Like you were looking for something.' Richey's face was still hidden and she took a deep breath. 'I'm sure there's a simple explanation but Tess is convinced that you were hunting for something to sell to fund your habit. You weren't, were you?' she added anxiously.

Richey groaned, which wasn't a no or a yes. Then he lifted his head and he looked so stricken, so ashamed that Ellie couldn't help but feel sorry for him. And then she felt sorry for herself because she'd seen that look before on other men's faces just before they confessed to getting their jollies from dressing up in women's underwear or that they'd just put their entire month's pay on red, and black had come up instead.

Not again, she thought. Not a-bloody-gain.

'The thing is, Ellie . . .' Richey faltered, and Ellie gripped the table top and said nothing, though she was sure everything that she was trying hard not to say was written all over her face. '. . . well, it's all a blank. I remember going back to yours and I remember waking up in the bath and stumbling round in the dark and tripping over when I tried to find your room, but the bit in the middle just isn't there.'

'So you don't recall buying any coke?' Ellie asked sceptically. 'It just fell into your pocket, did it?'

Richey flushed. 'I did a favour for my boss on Saturday. Helped him shift some gear and he gave me a couple of grams as a thank-you. It wasn't like I could refuse. He's my boss and I don't normally do the hard stuff.' He looked at her pleadingly. 'I do a bit of spliff and it was Saturday night so, yeah, I sunk a skinful of booze but I don't usually do coke. I really don't.'

'Yeah, but—'

'Oh, come on, Ellie! I'm a glorified runner. I'm on minimum wage. I couldn't afford a raging coke habit and if I did act like that on Saturday night, then I'm never touching the stuff again.'

He was certainly talking a good game and Ellie wanted to believe that he wasn't just another headshot in her own rogues' gallery, but she had to be certain.

'I can't be around someone with a drug habit,' she whispered fiercely, because the jukebox was switching between tracks. 'I've seen enough of my mum's friends get really messed up. If you need help, I will absolutely support you . . .'

Oh God. Any doubts Ellie might have had about this whole lame ducks business were gone now. Ten minutes into a serious discussion with Richey and she'd reverted to type. She really was an emotional fluffer. There was no hope but to head for the door as fast as she could and swear off dating.

'Hey, Ellie, don't look at me like that.' Richey gave her hand a little squeeze. 'I promise it was just a one-off. I don't have that kind of problem and I'd hate it if I've screwed things up before we've even got started.'

'Really?' Ellie still wasn't convinced. But maybe she was amenable to being convinced.

'I know it hasn't been that long since we started hooking up, but I think we could be something special,' Richey murmured, and he was looking her straight in the eye and Ellie would know if he was lying. She would, she was sure of it. 'I'll make this up to you and I'll apologise to Tess. Not to Lola, though; she's fucking scary.'

Ellie was as convinced as she could be without demanding Richey take a drug test. He wanted to put things right, not just with her, but with her flatmates too (at least Tess, because Lola really was fucking scary until you'd known her for a minimum of six months). He must think that they had a future together.

It was her turn to squeeze Richey's hand. 'I don't want this to end either,' she mumbled. 'I'll talk to Tess and Lola, and explain that this whole thing has just been a huge misunderstanding.'

Richey smiled crookedly; it made him look like a little boy who'd been caught stealing from the sweetie cupboard. 'I bet you're wondering what you did to get landed with an arsehole like me.'

'You're not an arsehole. You've just made some bad decisions,' Ellie insisted. 'Look, let's just draw a line under this and move on.'

'But you do know that I'm sorry, right? I don't want you to spend all your time at Glastonbury worrying I'm going to get high on crystal meth and wreck our yurt.'

Ellie didn't want to spend her time worrying about that either. Not when she was worried that it was going to rain. Worried about having to get backstage to meet clients. Worried that she wouldn't pack the right clothes. Worried that she might not be able to charge up phone, laptop, iPad, or plug in her hair straighteners. Worried about so many things that she didn't have space in her schedule to worry about Richey as well. 'I really wish I didn't have to go to Glastonbury,' she blurted out as she'd been blurting out at regular intervals for the last few weeks.

'Yeah, sucks to be you.' Richey grinned at her, and Ellie grinned back because now his thigh was pressing against hers and he was giving her a look from under his lashes that was making her feel decidedly hot in a way that had nothing to do with it being unseasonably warm for late June. 'I don't suppose you fancy bunking off for the rest of the afternoon?'

She sighed and moved her leg away. 'I do fancy it but I have to be in King's Cross in . . .' She glanced at her watch. '. . . half an hour. Can we take a raincheck?' She was already standing up and bending down to kiss Richey's cheek. 'Sorry, I'm going to have to run. I'll pay on my way out.'

'No, I'll get this. It's the least I can do.'

Ellie beamed at him, because if you took Saturday night completely out of the equation, which she planned to do, then Richey was a very good boyfriend. He might not be the normal boyfriend that Tess and Lola thought she should be dating, but normal was boring and normal definitely wouldn't pinch Ellie's arse as she got up to leave.

Brighton, 1986

Chester drove them down to Brighton to see Spacemen 3. Tab and Tom said it was because he still fancied Ari, even in the face of zero encouragement.

At the gig, Chester kept getting closer and closer, as if he was going to lunge at any moment. Ari said she was going to the loo but sidled down as close to the front as she could get.

The music was loud and hypnotic, the beat getting right inside her, and as she leaned in to let the sound swallow her whole someone pulled her back. Pressed a glass of something cold against her shoulder blade where her dress dipped down low, low, low because she didn't care if anyone saw her black bra strap.

Ari sighed, turned round, ready to let Chester down kind of gently because she wanted a lift back to London, and there was Billy Kay. 'Gin and tonic, right?' he said, and he handed her a drink. Stood next to her, the sleeve of his leather jacket brushing against her arm. Lit her cigarettes. Steadied her when someone slammed into her and she teetered on high heels.

After the band had finished and Ari had just stood there for five minutes because she hadn't noticed the music had stopped and the lights had come on, he took her hand.

'Come on,' he said. 'I know a place where we can go.'

They walked along the esplanade, wind whipping in from the sea and making Ari shiver, neither of them speaking, until Brighton was almost Hove. Their destination was a square of elegant Regency townhouses. Billy had a key to one of them.

Said it had a sea view as Ari followed him inside, up a sweeping staircase and into a room.

A room with a bed in it.

Billy was on her and then he was in her, hadn't even kissed her yet, just pulled up her dress, pulled down her black lace panties and thrust inside her, his hands tight on her arms so she could feel the bite of his fingers.

Ari got excitement just standing close to him, but she wasn't excited enough and he was hard and demanding inside her and she . . . 'Stop! Just stop, OK?'

Billy's eyes glinted but he stilled, and Ari brushed back the lock of thick dark hair that always fell over his face, and God, she just wanted him to say something, acknowledge her, who she was, not just a random girl he'd picked up at a gig.

'You don't just shove it in without asking,' Ari told him, thumping his shoulder so he eased away and pulled out of her. 'Fuck! You haven't even kissed me!'

'Do you want to be kissed then?' he enquired lazily. 'How . . . sweet.'

He was one of those guys who liked playing games. Liked collecting broken hearts as bitter trophies. But Ari wasn't going to be one of those girls.

Ari eased down the tight skirt of her dress, then leaned over to place a finger on that cruel, pretty mouth. 'I want some of this, before I get some of this.' Her hand slid down to his cock, wet-tipped and hard beneath her fingers, and he shivered. Billy Kay shivered like a schoolgirl.

He kissed her then and Ari had expected something fierce, angry, but the kiss was gentle, almost reverent, and though she didn't have the kind of hair a man could run his fingers through, he stroked the wispy strands along her hairline where the lacquer hadn't taken hold, then rubbed his cheek against hers.

'Oh, Ari, you're going to destroy me, aren't you?' he said, and before she could deny it or come up with a sassy, snappy reply, he was easing down the zip of her dress, placing kisses over every inch of flesh he laid bare.

49

When Billy started moving in her again, Ari was ready for him. She wrapped her legs around him, buried her mouth against the salt-slick of his skin and hoped he wouldn't destroy her first.

Chapter Four

On Thursday morning at precisely ten fifteen, Ellie was waiting patiently on the corner of Delancey Street and Albert Street with her matching Orla Kiely wheeled duffle bag, humungous tote and laptop case, and her beloved Mulberry handbag clamped to her chest.

Her mother had said to be ready at nine sharp, but Ellie knew her mother from way back, and there was probably still time to nip to the newsagent to buy more tissues because you could never have too many at a festival, and she might just as well check that the weather forecast was still predicting blue skies and sunshine, even though she wanted to go easy on her phone's battery because God knows when she'd have a chance to charge it again.

For one reckless minute Ellie thought about dragging her luggage back home and locking the doors, but her mum had a spare set of keys and anyway, she was being silly. She should stop thinking of Glastonbury as a weekend spent outdoors with rudimentary toilet facilities and a lot of unwashed people wearing ridiculous hats, and think of it as a mini-break. Ellie loved mini-breaks.

She heard the toot of a horn, then Chester's van was pulling up alongside her. Before it had even stopped, Ari jumped out.

'Give Mama some loving,' she demanded as she pulled Ellie and her handbag and laptop case in for a hug. 'How's my best girl?'

'I'm fine. How's my favourite mother? Apart from being shockingly late as usual.'

'Darling, have you ever known me to be on time for anything?' Ari asked, stepping back so she could survey Ellie's luggage with a slight frown. 'Planning to move to Glastonbury permanently then?'

'This was my fifth attempt to whittle everything down to essential items only,' Ellie said. 'I have to have options.'

'Of course you do,' Ari agreed, but when Ellie opened the van's sliding door she saw the battered leather holdall held together with ancient 'Access All Areas' and 'Artists Only' stickers that contained her mother's clothes, toiletries and make-up. Ari managed to achieve a high-maintenance look with a lot less product than her daughter.

Even without her cat's-eyes sunglasses on, Ari could pass for thirty-five in direct sunlight. Not that she ever ventured out in direct sunlight without slathering herself in sunblock to protect skin so pale it was positively vampiric. With her long London bus-red hair and the huge tattoo on her left arm of her beloved Les Paul Melody Maker guitar, it was hard to believe that she was going to be forty-nine on her next birthday. Ellie might have been biased but she thought Ari looked incredible and never mutton-y, not even in her fifties sundress, adorned with poodles, and Converse high tops. Ellie felt positively frumpy in her Topshop shorts, stripy Sonia Rykiel T-shirt and . . .

'Wellies? Why are you wearing your wellies when there's a big shiny yellow orb up in the sky? It's called the sun, darling.'

Ellie looked down at her green Hunter wellingtons, then back to Ari's amused face. 'I don't want to end up with trench foot if it rains torrentially all weekend.'

There was a hearty chuckle and, 'You owe me a tenner, Ari,' from the driver's seat, and Ellie scowled at Chester. It wasn't much of a scowl because she loved Chester.

That was why when she got into the van, sitting in the middle seat between Ari and Chester – because that was where she always sat – she let him gather her up into an enthusiastic hug. Chester was all ribs and elbows and the smell of Creed Green Irish Tweed aftershave tickled her nostrils and made Ellie want to sneeze but it was Chester and she'd known him her entire life, and a hug from Chester always made her feel everything was all right in the world.

'That's enough, Chester,' Ari said, as she climbed up next to Ellie and slammed the van door shut. 'Girl needs to breathe.'

An hour later, after picking up Richey, Ari and Chester's friends, Tom and Tabitha, and enough alcohol to see them through the weekend, they were on the motorway with the windows wound down and happily listening to a Stax compilation if only Ari would shut up.

'I'm just saying, Ellie, that luxury yurts aren't what Glastonbury is about. It won't be the end of the world if you can't straighten your hair for a couple of days.'

'It will be the end of my world,' Ellie said, and she fingered some sample strands of hair to make sure they were still straight and silky smooth. 'If God had wanted us to sleep in tents, he'd never have invented luxury yurts, and I take it you won't be coming round to borrow my hairdryer and charge your phone, then?' she added slyly.

'Of course I will, but I've earned my Glastonbury stripes.' Ari smiled smugly.

'If you're going to behave like a brat all weekend, then no yurt privileges for you,' Ellie told her mother sternly. Ari opened her mouth to argue the point but Chester rapped on the dashboard to get their attention.

'Hey, do you think it's going to be as hot as it was in 2010? Do you remember, Ells, you nearly passed out during the Pet Shop Boys set?'

'I don't know,' Tom piped up from the back of the van. 'It was pretty hot in 1999 too.'

Chester nodded. 'Manic Street Preachers.'

'And Blondie!' Ari and Tabitha chorused, because Deborah Harry was like a god to them, and they were off.

Someone would shout a year and someone else, usually Chester, would reel off a long list of bands that had played that year, with other fun facts ('and wasn't that the year Mad Glen fell over and broke his foot in the healing circle?') being thrown in from the cheap seats.

'Then there was 1993 and 1997,' Tabitha announced. 'Very special years because . . .'

'Ninety-seven was the year of the mud,' Ellie reminded everyone with a shudder.

'Yeah, but it was still a good year and so was 1993 because those were the years that I played Glastonbury,' Ari said with a slightly injured tone.

'Did you really?' Richey asked. He'd been quiet up until then, but every time Ellie had turned round to make sure he was all right and that the stories of Glastonburys past weren't boring, Richey had grinned like he was enjoying himself. 'You've played Glastonbury twice?'

'Well, not on the main stage,' Ari admitted sadly. 'But yes, in 1993 I was in a Riot Grrrl band called The Beauty Queens and we played one of the smaller stages, and by '97 it was all Britpop and I was playing guitar with these muppets called Bloomsbury.'

Richey gave a long, low whistle. 'They got quite big, didn't they?'

'Yeah, just after they kicked me out because they decided they'd be better with an all-male line up.' Ari sighed. 'Story of my fucking life, isn't it?'

There were murmurs of agreement. Although Ari was an amazing guitarist and a pretty good singer (and that wasn't Ellie cutting her some slack, there were actual reviews, even one from the *Guardian*, supporting that

54

claim), success had always remained just out of reach. Sooner or later, usually when whatever band Ari was in was on the verge of signing to a major label, Ari would be told it wasn't working out. 'Musical differences' were usually mentioned, but Ari had forgotten more about music than most of her band-mates would ever know and she'd been on the scene – on countless scenes – for so long that A & R always wanted to go with a fresher face. Or a face that wouldn't call them on it when they were acting like corporate, soul-sucking twats.

Ari would rage for a couple of weeks, then dust herself down and scout around for another band to join, always hopeful that this time it would be different, that this time she might get a shot at the fame that had always eluded her, that this time she'd finally get her dues.

It still hadn't happened, but Ellie hoped she'd inherited just a fraction of her mother's grit and determination. 'I loved The Beauty Queens,' Ellie declared, though they'd been very shouty. 'They taught me about third-wave feminism and bought me loads of Hello Kitty stuff. I think Glastonbury was their best ever gig.'

Ari beamed at her. 'We did rock it out, didn't we? And that was one of the best Glastonburys ever anyway because the Velvet Underground headlined, and I wanted you to see them once before they all started dying.'

'Have you been to every Glastonbury then?' Richey asked, interrupting the mother–daughter bonding.

Ari had been to every Glastonbury since 1984. 'Well, apart from 1996.'

There were murmurs of agreement, as they'd all boycotted that year too in solidarity, but Richey wasn't to know why they'd been a no-show or what Tabitha meant when she said, 'Well, that was the year you-know-who was headlining.'

Chester made a sound in the back of his throat that conveyed exactly what he thought about you-know-who, because again, apart from Richey, everyone else in the van knew that only Voldemort and Ellie's dad were the two names that you never, ever mentioned.

'Have I missed something?' Richey looked perplexed. 'Who headlined in 1996? Shall I google it?'

'No!' Ellie turned round again so she could glare at Richey, then at Tom and Tabitha for good measure. 'Can we please change the subject?'

'Honestly, Richey, it's not worth talking about,' Ari assured him. 'Though I like to think that Ellie was a gift from the angels, she does actually have a father.'

'Mum!' Ellie wrenched herself round, so she could now glare at her mother. But Ari was immune to Ellie's glares.

'So, yeah, Ellie's dad is . . . well, kind of a big deal. Elder statesman of rock. The godfather of cool. You know the type? But he wasn't that famous when I knew him.' Ari's eyes were hidden behind her shades, but Ellie knew she was rolling them and she knew that Ari wouldn't say much on the topic because she never did, so it was best just to let her mother say what she had to say. 'I'm not knocking him; he's shifted a metric fuckton of units and raised millions of pounds for starving children, and I can't argue with that, though he only organised that global concert because he had an album to plug, but whatever . . '. Anyway, we fell madly in love back in the day, then we fell madly out of love, *then* he became household-name famous, and I certainly wasn't going to pay good money to see him do his tired old man of the people shtick . . .' Ari drew a deep breath. 'So that's why we didn't go to Glastonbury in 1996.'

The silence was absolute. Even Richey had stopped asking questions because anyone with a passing knowledge of the British music scene could work out who Ellie's father was, and Richey had a lot more than a passing knowledge. After all, the album that her father had released six months after he left Ari, *Songs For A Girl*, was the eleventh best-selling UK album ever and always topped the 'Greatest Records Of All Times' polls in the Sunday supplements. And the most famous single off that album, 'It Felt Like A Kiss', was one of those songs as instantly familiar as 'Hey Jude' or 'Dancing Queen'. It was embedded into the national consciousness, had been used to advertise everything from lipstick to cars, and the man who'd written it was known only by his first name. Since he'd been knighted two years ago (though, as Tabitha and Tom continually pointed out, David Bowie had been cool enough to decline his knighthood), he was also known as Sir. So, there was no doubt about it, Richey could confirm who her father was with one click in the Google search box.

'Just one more question?' Richey asked timidly. Ellie sank down in her seat. They hadn't had the Dad conversation, other than to establish that neither of theirs had stuck around, so why couldn't he just let this go? 'How come you're so straight, Ellie, if your parents are so rock 'n' roll?'

Ellie grinned. 'I think the rock 'n' roll DNA skips a generation. You'd know that if you'd met my grandparents.'

'Ellie is not straight,' Ari argued. 'She just pretends to be straight when she's working at that stuffy gallery, don't you, dollface?'

'Well, I am a little bit straight but it's OK because you're rock 'n' roll enough for the both of us,' Ellie said, and it was time to shift the mood. She reached forward so she could jab at the iPod hooked up to the dashboard. 'I'm sick of this compilation. Any requests or shall we listen to Magic FM?'

There were good-natured howls of dissent, then a fierce debate about what constituted the perfect road trip soundtrack and soon they were all sucking on lemon sherbets and nodding their heads in time to a Doo-Wop playlist.

*

Two hours out of London, they stopped at a service station. Ellie saw everyone off to purchase coffee and snacks while she stayed behind to check her email.

Chester came back with her Diet Coke as Ellie was frowning over an unintelligible message from Inge. 'Everything all right, princess?' he asked. He called Ari 'duchess', but as far as Chester was concerned, Ellie would always outrank her.

Ellie frowned a little harder. 'I can't get a 3G signal.' She held her phone out like she was divining for water. 'It's very frustrating.'

'You shouldn't have to work over the weekend.'

'If I refused to work over the weekend, Vaughn would sack me and then I'd be poor,' Ellie said, as her phone decided that it would send her email into the ether with a whooshing sound.

'They'd never fire you. You run that place single-handedly,' he said proudly. 'But I actually meant is everything all right with you and Richey?'

It was no surprise that Chester knew about Richey's misdemeanours. Ellie told Ari everything and Ari usually fed the information back to Chester because they'd been friends for thirty years. 'He's like a faithful family pet,' Ari had once said to Ellie. 'I love the guy to death, but he's not what my heart wants, you know?'

Ellie thought that Chester's dogged devotion had to count for something. He'd stuck by Ari through thick and thin. Even after one of Ari's attempts to cook had hospitalised him with the worst case of food poisoning the A&E doctor had ever seen. That was why Ellie still held out hope that Ari would one day finally realise she'd never find a man who was worth even a fraction of Chester.

'Richey's fine,' she said with conviction. 'We had a talk and it was all a fuss over nothing. He promised it would never, ever happen again.'

'It better not,' Chester said grimly and predictably. 'Otherwise me and Richey are going to have to have a little man-to-man chat.'

'You don't have to do that,' Ellie assured him quickly, because even though Richey had twenty years on Chester, Chester had his own roofing business and was wiry, street-smart and tough. Ellie could still see the scar that bisected his eyebrow after an altercation with a scaffolder and a crowbar. 'Really, he's been on his best behaviour ever since we talked about it,' she added.

'Well, if you're sure . . .' Chester didn't sound as if he was and he watched intently as Ellie opened her can of Diet Coke in case her face gave her away.

'I am sure,' she said after she'd taken several icy gulps. 'Stop doing your heavy-handed dad routine, or I won't get you a Father's Day present this year.'

'We go through this every year,' Chester said, but he ducked his head and tried not to smile. 'It's not like I'm your real dad.'

'But you're my faux dad so you get a faux Father's Day present,' Ellie said. She shrugged. 'Deal with it.'

'Well, if I must.' Chester sighed and played along. 'As long as you haven't made me aftershave out of crushed-up bay leaves and hot water again.'

'I was nine. I had a lot to learn,' Ellie said and there was just time for a faux father/daughter hug before they heard Ari's voice calling to them and they were done with their special moment.

Glastonbury, as ever, was the best and worst of times. On the Friday, it had almost been Ellie's best Glastonbury ever, though a lot of her good cheer was down to the luxury yurt. It had a proper door and walls covered in billowing white cloth and, best of all, a proper bed with duvet and pillows. It would have been absolutely perfect if there'd been an en suite, but at least there were luxury toilets and showers in the gated yurt enclosure, which was patrolled 24/7 by security guards, and a restaurant providing meals made from locally sourced ingredients. It was like Ellie had never left North London.

Even Richey had wondered aloud if they could stay in and around the yurt all weekend, but the sun was shining so they decided to venture out among the riffraff who weren't lucky enough to be staying in a luxury yurt enclosure.

It was impossible to stick to a schedule at Glastonbury, but sometimes not having twelve hours of your day diarised was fun. Mostly Ellie and Richey ambled along, saw some bands they wanted to see, but not all of them, hung out with some people they'd planned to hang out with, but not all the people they'd arranged to meet, and spent a lot of time entwined on the grass behind the Healing Field working on their tans when they weren't engaged in mild PDAs.

But on Saturday there were stormclouds. Not actual stormclouds rolling across the duck-egg-blue skies, but metaphorical stormclouds. They'd started before ten on Saturday morning when Ellie and Richey had had a slight contretemps because she didn't want a pint of lager with her breakfast burrito. It wasn't like she minded if Richey wanted to start drinking before lunch, it really wasn't, though she did think that he should pace himself. Then Richey had called her uptight, and if there was one thing Ellie hated, it was being called uptight. She worked very, very hard never to give off an uptight vibe.

They'd separated for a few hours, and while Ellie hung out with Lola, whose friends were appearing in the cabaret tent (though Ellie also thought it was a bit early for a full burlesque show), Richey had texted her to say that he was sorry. Then he texted her to say that he was with his friend Spencer but he'd meet her at five at the entrance to the Acoustic Tent. Ellie was unmoved. She was also suspicious because Spencer was less a friend and more a partner in crime. Maybe she should have listened to Tess and Lola; not allowed herself to be swayed so easily by Richey's easy charm and easier smile, she thought as she watched one of Lola's friends shimmy her nipple tassels. But then Richey had texted her to say that he loved her. They'd never said that to each other before, and Ellie thought that it might also be too early for 'I love you' but it was just what she needed to make her feel better, and why she waited at the entrance to the Acoustic Tent with an expectant smile.

The expectant smile was long gone when Richey stumbled towards her twenty minutes later than scheduled.

'Sweetheart! Sorry! Maybe I've had a little bit too much to drink,' he slurred in her ear when he reached her side, and then he'd made a grab for her arse, which made Spencer, his leather jacket unzipped to reveal a pallid pigeon chest, snicker.

Richey was drunk. Very, very drunk. Maybe not just drunk because his pupils were pinned, his top lip was sweaty and he kept rubbing his thighs and licking his lips and talking absolute bollocks about things that he patently knew nothing about, in this case the God particle, and got really aggressive when Ellie challenged him.

'I don't know what you've been doing, I don't even want to know, but can you snap out of it?' she'd demanded, and Spencer had snickered again.

Richey had pointed at himself with an exaggerated 'who me?' face. 'Babe? Babe! Don't be so fucking uptight.'

It took two hours, a spliff and a portion of Thai noodles before Richey was back to mellow. 'Too much booze and too much sun,' he insisted. Ellie wasn't that naïve but she didn't want to fight in the middle of a field on a Saturday night when they were meant to be sharing a luxury yurt for another twenty-four hours. She also didn't want to confront her dating demons when she was so far away

61

from any of her comfort zones, so she'd had a few puffs on the joint too (which totally didn't count as giving in to peer pressure because she never, ever inhaled) before they headed over to Ari and Chester's traditional Saturday night Glastonbury cocktail party. The dress code was festival glam, which meant swishy dresses in bold prints for the ladies and Hawaiian shirts and drainpipe trousers for the men. They'd rigged up a sound system to play Dean Martin and Frank Sinatra and somehow, some way, they were able to serve ice-cold Martinis.

When she'd been little, Ellie would waltz around on Chester's shoulders or stand on Tom's feet as he tried to do a quickstep, but now she was all grown up and quite capable of foxtrotting under her own steam with Allison, the bassist from The Fuck Puppets, or doing the salsa with Lola, who kept asking her if something was wrong, ''cause you're looking kind of pissed off, Ells.' She *was* kind of pissed off, especially when Richey went AWOL again, but drinking quite a lot of ice-cold Martinis took the edge off her irritation.

Ellie could remember staggering back to the yurt compound at an ungodly hour, via a long detour to the Tipi Field where she got lost. Then collapsing on her double bed in a drunken stupor only to be woken up after what felt like five minutes by Richey. Or more accurately, Richey 'and a few friends'. It had felt as if there were fifty people all crowded into the yurt although, in reality, there were no more than six, but they were very drunk and very loud. Spencer had started chopping out lines on Ellie's laptop case and when she'd asked him what the hell he thought he was doing, he and Richey had shared a conspiratorial look, then Spencer had said, 'Stop being so fucking uptight.'

The two girls and the other guy with them had all laughed and Richey had made this big deal out of giving Spencer a bollocking. 'You shouldn't do coke, Spence. It's not big and it's not clever, and it makes Ellie mad at me.'

It was true, Ellie was mad at him. Furious. Fists clenched so tight she could feel her nails digging into her palms. She hated feeling so helpless and out of control, but there was nothing she could do right then. Whatever she did, short of hoovering up the coke herself, would have her labelled as uptight yet again and it wasn't the time or place for a serious discussion with Richey. Not that he'd take any notice when he was starfished on the bed and kept nudging Ellie with his foot.

'Cheer up,' he stage-whispered. 'You're bringing everybody down.'

Just as Ellie decided that she could take no more and she was going to throw everyone out, even if they did think she was uptight, they were interrupted by the yurt compound's crack security team, who removed the gatecrashers, though Spencer refused to go until he'd attempted to knock down the yurt, and screamed a string of obscenities at the stars.

It wasn't until the security guards came back to warn Ellie that if she sneaked in anyone else, both she and her possessions would be forcibly ejected from the compound, that she realised that Richey had left with Spencer and the two girls, who couldn't have been older than nineteen.

Now it was ten o'clock on Sunday morning and the alarms on her phone, iPad and MacBook were beeping to remind Ellie that she had a brunch meeting in an hour. An hour to repair the ravages of last night when she'd stared up at the billowing white folds of the yurt and begun to grieve the end of another relationship. They hadn't officially broken up and she hadn't actually got any proof that Richey had done anything harder than some weed, but she couldn't think of a way that they'd come back from this.

Yes, they were at Glastonbury and the normal rules didn't apply, and yes, she was sometimes a little uptight, but if Richey wanted to really be with her then he was going to have to lose his loser friend with the coke habit. But Ellie wasn't good at issuing ultimatums, especially not when Richey was MIA and she needed to take a meeting in one of the backstage restaurants with a hip-hop mogul in an hour. In Ellie's experience, moguls were usually at least thirty minutes late, but she daren't risk it.

Ellie showered and frantically blowdried her hair straight as she went over her talking points, tried to remember the names of the hip-hop artists the mogul represented and work on her poise, which was currently nowhere to be found. Then she piled on concealer and tinted moisturiser to try to hide the fact she'd had no sleep. Oh, and if she tied her vintage Hermès scarf round her head, it would offset any potential frizz and her Nars Orgasm highlighter would make her look perky even if she didn't feel it.

It was a point of pride that at exactly five minutes to eleven Ellie was sitting down at an empty table in an organic restaurant backstage. It was also a point of pride that she was wearing a pristine white, broderie anglaise dress, nipped in at the waist, with a full skirt.

It was a trick she'd learned a long time ago – when all around you was chaos, you needed to find some area of your life that you could control and let that define you. It didn't matter that she was on free schoolmeals and had a mother who wore leopard-print catsuits and dressed her in charity-shop clothes, when Ellie had the neatest hand-writing in her class and was homework monitor five years in a row. Or when she had a tidier bedroom and better manners than her many cousins, who all lived in two-parent, semi-detached splendour in Belsize Park. When your boss was giving you hell and your flatmates were fighting and you'd been dumped again, there was some-thing cathartic and peaceful in spending the afternoon in your pristine, minimalist office, rearranging your reference books by height and colour. So, a girl who could parade around Glastonbury in a spotless white dress was a girl who was calm and in control. Sometimes you had to fake it to make it.

She *was* back in her Hunter wellies because it was rare to get through a festival without being rained on, but there were lots of girls wearing wellies – it was accepted festival chic – and secure in the knowledge that her outfit passed muster on all counts, Ellie could settle down and wait for her hip-hop mogul.

Ninety minutes later Ellie was still waiting, still trying to appear calm and in control as she gazed at her laptop screen as if she was diligently working and not staring blindly at her email inbox in the hope that a message would suddenly arrive from the absent mogul apologising profusely for his no-show and promising to turn up in the next five minutes. Ellie tried to ignore her misery, her hangover and her urgent need for coffee. She knew that if she had coffee, she'd then need to pee and *of course* he'd turn up while she was braving the loos.

The longer she waited, the more tearful Ellie became. How dare Justin E. Peary keep her hanging for nearly two hours? Did he think that her time didn't matter, compared to his time? That she might have better things to do than sit in a glorified canteen and listen to the members of a mid-level American rock band at the next table boast of last night's sexual exploits? Why did people think they could walk all over her, treat her like shit and that she'd be OK with it?

Just as Ellie was biting her lip hard to stem the first wave of angry tears, there was a flurry of activity at the restaurant entrance and a skinny young man in red trousers, white shirt and a truly astounding pair of snake-skin loafers walked into the restaurant flanked by several minders, who were each the size of a small outbuilding and equipped with lots of chunky gold jewellery and walkie-talkies.

Ellie thought that maybe her eleven o'clock had arrived one hour and fifty-two minutes late. She stood up and mustered a big smile and a half wave.

The man and his entourage changed direction. 'Sweetheart! Do you hate me very much?' Justin E. Peary seized Ellie's hands as soon as he was in grabbing distance and clasped them to his chest. 'Sorry I'm late. Here, let's sit. Bono and Jay-Z were meant to be flying in so we had to land the helicopter in a field right out in the boonies. Cows and sheep everywhere. I mean, what the fuck? And there was no cellphone reception and you've been waiting all this time. Have you ordered? You should have ordered. All English food sounds really fucking rude. Bangers and mash. Toad in the hole. Spotted dick – I don't even want to know what that is. Shall we have a bacon butty? Do they do decent coffee?'

It was a verbal onslaught. All Ellie could do was nod, shake her head and smile. She and Justin E. Peary had been emailing back and forth for a couple of months because he wanted to leave his current art dealer (''cause I work with rap artists he thinks all I want to buy is graffiti art. For fuck's sake. I've got a degree in History of Art and Visual Culture from RISD, and yeah, I blew my first few mill on bling and Bentleys but I'm not a fucking philistine') but they'd never actually spoken before.

Not that they were really speaking now. Ellie was still nodding and shaking her head and smiling while eating a bacon butty, which was either going to be kill or cure on her hangover, while Justin did all the talking.

Ellie suspected that once you stripped away the brashness and the bravado, there was a sharp operator who could sniff out bullshit at fifty paces. So it wasn't a surprise when she finally and hesitantly began to talk that they had an in-depth discussion about Rashid Johnson and post-black art. Then she showed him the pieces she'd picked from their roster of artists. Justin didn't go for the big names or the flashiest pieces for his new Tribeca penthouse but honed in on the photo collages from a young artist Ellie had only just signed.

He looked at the fifteen images. Asked Ellie to get the guy on the phone, then pinned her with a look. 'What kind of discount for a bulk buy?'

'Ten per cent,' she said as decisively as she could.

'Twenty-five,' countered Justin. Now he decided to go quiet on Ellie to unnerve her. It was kind of working.

'He's only just starting out so you're already getting him at a bargain rate.' She hated negotiating. It always made her feel nauseous, even when she didn't have a hangover. 'I could do thirteen per cent and then he's just breaking even.'

'Or you could waive your commission if you're that worried about him.' Justin allowed himself to blink. 'Twenty-two per cent.'

Ellie could waive her commission but she wasn't going to. 'I can*not* go any lower than fifteen per cent, but I will let you have first refusal on any new work and I could probably get him to do a one-off personalised piece if you wanted to sit for him next time you were in London.' She folded her arms and tried out a flinty-eyed look of her own. 'If I went any lower than that, then I wouldn't be representing the best interests of my artist.'

Justin tried his best to stare Ellie down. The effort to resist made her eyeballs throb, then he shrugged. 'OK. Fifteen per cent, I get first look at any new pieces and we'll make arrangements to fly him to NYC. Shall we shake on it?'

They shook on it, though Ellie wished that her hands weren't quite so sweaty, then it took five minutes to arrange a wire transfer and they were done.

'It's been great, Ellie. This could be the start of something really beautiful,' Justin called over his shoulder as he was spirited away by his entourage. 'Let's diarise soon.'

Ellie sank back down on her plastic chair and willed her hands to stop shaking. As soon as they did, she called Nathan, the artist, to tell him the good news. Then, with the help of the calculator on her phone, Ellie worked out her commission, which was nearly three thousand pounds after tax, and if she hadn't been in such a public place then she might even have allowed herself an air punch. She settled for a slow, luxurious stretch, realised it was nearly three o'clock and leaped to her feet.

Right on cue, her phone beeped with a plaintive text message from Ari: *Awful hangover. U 2? Fancy getting head massage? Am @ John Peel stage. Where U @?*

There was no way Ellie was letting anyone touch her hair with fingers coated in oil, even an essential oil, but she'd have a shoulder massage to keep Ari company as she got some advice about the Richey situation. Just thinking about him made her stomach clench into a painful knot.

Coming to find you, she texted as she hurried out of the restaurant. *Been backstage. Let's meet @ phone recharge place halfway between. Hangover almost go . . .*

She looked up momentarily to see where she was going and her gaze was immediately riveted to the two girls on her right. They were both dressed in floaty tops and teeny, tiny denim shorts that showed off long, tanned legs, as they were interviewed by a TV crew. Just as her father was never mentioned by name, his two daughters – his *other* daughters, Ellie's two half-sisters – weren't mentioned either. Ellie thought about them often, though. It was hard not to when she saw their pictures every time she bought a magazine. And there they were, twenty metres away from her.

Ellie could feel her mouth hang open, the shock of seeing them like a sudden but vicious punch to the gut. They both suddenly tossed back long, blonde hair in unison and smiled at each other, and it felt like another blow aimed directly at her solar plexus. She'd never had anyone smile at her like that; with affection and acceptance and a little bit of resentment, the way that sisters did.

She needed to look away and start walking because she was causing a bottleneck, but even as she took a step forward, then another and another, she couldn't tear her eyes away from Lara and Rose and . . .

'Oh!' Ellie gasped, as she cannoned into someone and a hand shot out to steady her.

Chapter Five

Ellie jerked, because that simple, incidental touch, a hand on her arm just below her elbow to guide her, steady her, still her, sent tingles racing through her.

Not tingles – that was ridiculous – but it was as if her skin had just sat there, covering her arm, not really doing much and now it felt fully alive for the first time. All it had needed was the right kind of touch to wake it from a long slumber.

So, *so* weird, but then the last twenty-four hours had been one hellish event after another, so it was no wonder that Ellie was so overwrought. 'Careful!' a voice said. A deep pleasant voice that Ellie didn't recognize but which still sounded familiar. 'It's dangerous to text and walk at the same time.'

'I'm sorry,' Ellie said, looking up from her phone, which she'd been staring at without even seeing it, into a kind, clever face and a smile that she'd have wanted to get to know better if she hadn't still been aware of Lara and Rose just outside her line of vision. She shook her head slightly so she could focus on his hand, which hadn't left her arm and, oh, it was on the move, cupping her elbow.

'We're causing a jam.' The man with the tingling fingertips gave Ellie another devastating smile as he steered her to the right so they were standing against a fence and not blocking any major thoroughfares. 'That's better.'

'I'm really sorry,' she said again. 'I'm not normally quite so feeble-minded.'

'Not feeble-minded,' he demurred, and he was smiling again, showing two rows of beautifully even, beautifully white teeth. 'It's so easy to get distracted. Yesterday I had to take a work call and I found myself deep in something called the Field of Avalon. It took hours to retrace my steps.'

'Oh, so are you camping, then?' Ellie asked, because he was wearing navy-blue chino shorts that ended just above the knee, with a short-sleeved blue and white checked shirt and dark blue Converses. He looked box fresh, not as if he'd spent the night in a tent.

'God, no! I can't imagine anything worse than that. I'm staying in a bed and breakfast a few miles away and taxiing on and off site. I'd rather have a decent night's sleep in a proper bed than collect cool points and insect bites,' he said a little defensively, but he was in luck because Ellie was one of the few people at Glastonbury who wouldn't think ill of someone with the good sense to stay somewhere that had hot and cold running water.

'I stayed in a B and B last year,' she told him. 'It was great, but my friends threatened to disown me. This year I'm staying in a luxury yurt.'

He was wearing shades but now he lifted them up to reveal blue eyes. 'I've heard all sorts of stories about the luxury yurts,' he said, and Ellie thought that he might just be flirting with her.

Not that she was going to flirt back because she already had a boyfriend. But she didn't want to think about Richey right now, not when all she wanted to think about was the man in front of her and how the colour of his eyes reminded her of the deep, deep peacock blue of her favourite Mac eyeshadow, which had been discontinued a couple of years ago. 'Stories about proper beds and duvets? And really soft rugs?'

'Is there an en suite?' he asked eagerly.

Ellie shook her head. 'No, but there are luxury bathroom facilities and twenty-four-hour security so I forbear.'

'It sounds wonderful,' he said, and Ellie wanted to keep him talking, to stay here with him for just a little longer, and also she liked the shapes his mouth made as he spoke. It was only looking. There was no harm in looking.

Think of something to say. Keep him here. Something funny and interesting and cool. 'I put my wellies on because I was sure it was going to rain and now my feet are getting horribly moist,' Ellie said, and it was the single worst thing she'd ever said to anyone. Even worse than the time when Tess had introduced Ellie to her new boyfriend and Ellie had laughed uproariously and said, 'Yeah, right. New gay best friend, more like,' and actually Alastair had been as straight as they come, though Ellie and Lola still had their doubts. Or the time that Ari had asked her to be honest and Ellie had said that the new song she'd been working on for nearly a month sounded like a really shit version of 'Agadoo'.

It was as bad as that.

But this man, this beautiful man, looked down at Ellie's green Hunters, then back at her face and smiled. 'But if it does rain, at least your feet will be dry. Well, dry *and* moist.'

'And I think the luxury yurt is rainproof,' Ellie said, because she was destined to spout utter crap for the duration of this conversation. There was nothing she could do about it and he was going to walk away any minute now and she didn't even know why the thought of him walking away made her feel panicky and bereft but she touched his arm and she felt that brushfire tingle again – in her fingertips and in her heart, and even in the insistent pulse between her legs.

He ran his fingers through his dark brown hair, a short back and sides topped off with a riotous mass of curls. God, if they had children, they'd have the curliest hair in the world, Ellie thought, even though she had never been one of those sad, sad girls who imagined their wedding dresses and table decorations and the names of their four children seconds after being introduced to a man. She really wasn't. He wasn't even her type. He was tall enough that Ellie could wear heels, but he was thin. Too thin. Skinny. She liked her men with some heft. And in so many other ways he also wasn't her type because it was obvious from their shared loathing of tents and their neat, freshly pressed appearance that maybe they were too alike. Opposites attracted and all that and Ellie preferred her boyfriends to take more of a walk on the wild side so she didn't have to, though that approach didn't seem to be working out so well for her. Anyway, she hadn't even been introduced to this man, so why was her hand still on his arm because it felt like it belonged there?

It didn't. She stopped touching him and folded her hands behind her back where they couldn't get into any trouble. No wonder he was eyeing her with a look of disbelief too; then she saw his lips twist.

'It's not just my imagination, is it?' he asked Ellie, leaning closer as his voice was in danger of being drowned out by a heavy bassline suddenly emanating from the stage nearest to them. She could feel his breath caressing the side of her face. It felt a lot like being kissed and she shivered. 'This isn't just a line, I swear, but I feel like I've known you before.'

He didn't say 'met', like they'd been at the same party or got their morning latte from the same coffee shop, but 'known', like there was a connection between them. Like he felt it too.

'It's odd, isn't it? Did you get the tingles?'

It was an audacious thing to ask, but Ellie had to know.

He held up his hand, glanced at his fingertips, then nodded. 'All the way down my spine.'

Ellie smiled uncertainly and he smiled back. She had the strangest feeling, another strange feeling to go with all the other strange feelings she'd had in the last five minutes, that he was going to kiss her because he was leaning in again, staring at her mouth. Ellie could feel her body straining towards him even though they weren't even touching any more. She also felt short of breath, light-headed but—

'Babe! I've been looking everywhere for you. Are you still mad at me?' Someone grabbed her around the waist. Ellie's first reaction was to squeak, which she did, because the person who'd grabbed her round the waist was pulling her back against his bare and clammy chest and trying to nuzzle her neck.

'Get off me,' she hissed at Richey, at least she hoped it was Richey and not some loved-up random. Richey! For all of ninety seconds she'd forgotten about him while she talked to a complete stranger who felt a lot like a kindred spirit. Now Ellie flushed with guilt and embarrassment, and had to use her elbows to extricate herself as Richey clung even tighter.

'Oh, don't be like that, babe,' he slurred in her ear. 'We're at a festival. You really need to chill out.'

Ellie couldn't be sure, because Richey now had his tongue in her left ear, but she thought she heard the other man snort. She succeeded in wriggling out of Richey's hold and allowed herself to shoot him one positively malevolent look before she turned her attention back to the fantasy father of her imaginary curly-haired children and tried to mitigate the circumstances.

'Well, nice bumping into you,' she said. 'I guess I'll . . . um, see you around.'

He opened his mouth, probably to say something equally noncommittal or demand to know why she'd asked him about the tingles when she already had a boyfriend, but Richey was pushing Ellie aside so he could step up to the other man.

'Who are you anyway?' he asked belligerently when there was no need to be aggressive, even though the other man was looking at Richey, stripped to the waist and sweating exceedingly, with distaste. 'Are you bothering my girlfriend?'

'Oh my God. Shut up!' Ellie grabbed hold of Richey's arm, which was as sweaty as the rest of him, and tried to tug him away. It was like trying to move a forklift truck without the aid of a forklift truck. Ellie caught a whiff of the stale ethanol fumes oozing from Richey's pores as if he'd fallen into a vat of vodka after he'd left her last night. He kept working his jaw too, even when he wasn't opening his mouth to say ridiculous things, and she was going to have it out with him at Glastonbury, whether she wanted to or not. Despite what Tess and Lola might have thought, she had bad-boyfriend limits and Richey had pushed hers to breaking point. 'Go and stand over there,' she ordered, pointing at a nearby bottle refill point. 'Please.'

'It's fucking rude to come on to someone else's girlfriend,' Richey told the other man, as though Ellie hadn't even spoken. Then Richey jabbed his finger at his chest. The man stared down at it but it was impossible to tell what he was thinking because he'd put his sunglasses back on. 'Not when I'm standing right in front of you.'

The man took a step back, brushed his shirt with the back of his hand and allowed himself a little grimace. 'I was helping your, er, "girlfriend",' he made the word sound like it should have sarcastic quote marks around it. 'She was texting and walking. Nearly fell over, didn't you?'

Ellie nodded and nodded like a little nodding dog on a windy day. 'Right. That's exactly what he was doing,' she agreed as she grabbed hold of Richey's wrist again for a second attempt to pull him away, but he side-stepped out of her grasp so he could throw an arm around the shoulders of the man, who stiffened like an angry cat. 'Sorry, mate,' Richey said. 'Way out of line. Been caning it a bit hard, you know.'

Ellie shielded her eyes from the sun's glare with her hand as she peered up at Richey's face. Then she reached out and lifted up his huge mirrored aviator shades. As she suspected, his pupils were pinned, his face pale. She knew exactly what that meant, and it had nothing to do with falling into a vat of vodka.

'You promised me,' she said, wagging her finger accusingly. 'You promised.'

Richey ignored her in favour of pulling the man's stiff body a little closer. 'You in the music biz, then?' he asked as the man pulled away, his mouth set in a grim, forbidding line. 'Do you want to buy some charlie?'

'No, he absolutely does not,' said an icy voice from behind them. Ellie whipped round to see a woman standing there. Richey took a step back so the woman could slide her arm round the man's waist and they exchanged a look. If they weren't both wearing sunglasses, then Ellie would have sworn it was less of a look and more of an eyeroll. 'Darling, I was wondering what was taking you so long.'

Of course they were together, because men like him – handsome and charming – weren't going to be flying solo. And of course he'd be with a woman who was lithe and slender, with the kind of naturally shiny, sleek hair that Ellie aspired to but could never achieve – not even with a £150 Brazilian blowdry every three months – and who was wearing a draped top and blindingly white jeans. Snowy white jeans at a festival trumped a white broderie anglaise dress, which had now crumpled in the heat, every time.

76

Compared to her, Ellie was just a grubby, hungover girl in a wilted white frock and wellies. She was something less, a lot less, especially when she was accessorising with a boyfriend who was nothing but trouble.

'I got held up,' the perfect boyfriend was saying, except he wasn't a boy. He was in his mid-thirties, but this wasn't about his age. It was about the way he held himself and the way he looked, and the air of capability and control that he possessed. He was a man in a way that Richey would never be. Even if he lived to be a hundred – which was unlikely, given his lifestyle – Richey would always be a boy, a Jack-the-lad, a one-way ticket to heartbreak. 'Shall we find somewhere quiet to have a cold drink? Well, somewhere quiet-ish anyway.' He turned to Ellie even as his arm settled round his girlfriend's shoulders. 'It was nice to meet you.'

'It was nice to meet you too,' Ellie said because it had been, until Richey had rocked up and ruined everything. Though there wasn't much to ruin if he already had a girlfriend and Ellie had Richey, who now slung his arm round her shoulder like a dead weight.

'Babe,' he said, ruffling her hair with a hot hand. 'Babe, let's go somewhere quiet too so we can fuck.'

Ellie went from always giving even her most challenging boyfriends the benefit of the doubt and never having the guts to dump them, to putting her hands on Richey's perspiration-soaked chest and pushing him hard. Pushing him away from the man she'd had a weird, tingling moment with and his supercilious, absolutely perfect girlfriend, who were the last people she'd ever want to have a ringside seat to her utter humiliation dealt out by her lying, drug-taking, drug-dealing boyfriend.

'How could you?' she shouted at Richey, who looked more bemused than anything else. 'No! No! NO! This is not something I can work with. This is an absolute deal-breaker. I shouldn't have to put up with this sort of crap! We are finished. I never want to see you again!'

She couldn't even risk looking at Mr What If or his girl-friend. Who knew what he thought of Ellie now? She'd become one of his stories, an anecdote, a 'this time I went to Glastonbury and met this insane girl and her drug-addled boyfriend'.

'Babe!' Richey spluttered. 'Babe! Babe! Don't be so fucking uptight, babe.'

There were no words, so Ellie settled for shoving Richey so hard that he cannoned into the golden couple and she could start running, stumbling through the crowds, almost falling over her wellies in her determination to get as far away from him as humanly possible.

Chapter Six

Ellie had left Glastonbury early in a dark, despairing mood. It set the tone for the rest of the week.

Her mood wasn't improved by the fact that Muffin had flown out to St Barts for two weeks with ten of her closest friends who all had names like Tiger and Flick (one of them was even called Poo), which meant that Inge was supposed to take over Muffin's workload. Not that Muffin's day-to-day duties were heavy, but Inge preferred to sit behind the reception desk daydreaming, when she wasn't fending off pale young men who came into the gallery just to gaze adoringly at her.

'Inge is lovely,' Piers would say as he passed Ellie's open office door on his way to find out why Inge had just cut off one of his calls, 'but I wish she'd learn how to work the bloody switchboard.'

Ellie was also fed up with asking Inge to send out catalogues or order flowers for clients only to discover that she hadn't done it. 'Sorry,' she'd sigh, waving a languid hand about to convey her dismay and generally looking as fragile as her celebrity *doppelgänger*, Mia Farrow in *Rosemary's Baby*, 'I haven't had time to get round to it.'

Inge's father was a famous portrait painter – painted-HM-The-Queen famous – and her mother a Swedish countess who'd once come to the gallery to take Inge for lunch and spent two hundred thousand pounds on an avant-garde sculpture while Inge was fetching her coat and scarf, so Vaughn wasn't going to sack her. Not that Ellie wanted Inge to get fired; she just wanted her to develop a work ethic.

Vaughn would have no compunction about sacking Ellie, though. In fact, he came pretty close to it on the Wednesday morning when a sale she'd been painstakingly working on for months had fallen through at the eleventh hour. Not even at the eleventh hour, but when she phoned to ask if there'd been a problem with the bank transfer and was told the deal was off.

'Give me one good reason why I don't fire you!' he'd roared. His personal assistant, Madeleine, who worked on site only two days a week, had stood behind him shrugging helplessly and pointing at the picture on Vaughn's desk of his wife Grace, which was office short-hand for 'they had a row on the phone not five minutes before you walked in'.

Of course, after lunch, which Ellie had eaten at her desk with a martyred air, Vaughn had poked his head round her door.

'I've been through the proofs of the catalogue for the Scandinavian exhibition,' he said. 'Don't spell "fiord" with a j; it looks common. Apart from that, it will do.'

Obviously Vaughn and Grace had made up from their fight and her job was safe, but it was still irritating.

She was irritated with the weather, because it was hot and muggy with no promise of a good thunderstorm to ease the stickiness. Irritated with superfood salads and almond milk because she was detoxing after Glastonbury. Irritated with Tess and Lola, who were so overjoyed that she'd dumped Richey they kept trying to high-five her and were busy making plans to vet all her future boyfriends.

But mostly she was irritated with Richey for being her lamest duck yet. Once again, she was on her own after another relationship turned into a catastrophe. She was also regretting the what-might-have-been with a tall skinny man with really curly hair and deep blue eyes, whose name she didn't know. Even if that woman he'd been with turned out to be his sister, pining for him was pointless. The incredulous, appalled look on his face would probably stay with Ellie until her last moments on earth.

When Richey did finally call late on Thursday night, Ellie tried to swallow down her bitterness and disappointment so she could graciously accept his apology.

'So, like, I need to come round tomorrow morning to pick up my stuff,' he said without preamble. 'You going to be in around nine, then?'

'I'll be at work,' Ellie said tersely, though the terseness took a lot of effort. Her natural inclination was to launch into a lecture about the dangers of hard drugs, then gently ask Richey to seek professional help. 'Anyway, what stuff?'

Richey's stuff amounted to a couple of T-shirts, a can of shaving foam and a six-pack of Stella, four of the cans already consumed by Lola.

'I need my stuff,' Richey insisted when Ellie asked why he had to collect it by nine tomorrow. 'Those T-shirts have sentimental value, and it's *six* cans of Stella, and I don't get paid until next week.'

Richey couldn't make much of a profit from dealing class-A narcotics.

'You should have been honest with me and maybe I could have helped you,' Ellie said reproachfully. 'I wouldn't even have been angry – well, not much – but to behave the way you did in front of those people was unacceptable. You humiliated me.'

'Look, none of this was a big deal until you made it one,' Richey muttered. 'So, yeah, I do a bit of coke every now and again, and if I have a bit spare I try to make a profit on it. It's what everyone does . . .'

'I don't! My friends don't, because it's wrong.'

'Yeah, but you stress out about everything,' Richey explained, though Ellie didn't think she stressed out about everything. Only some things, and not all the time. 'Look, there's no point in dragging this out. I just need my shit.'

'Fine,' she said thinly, though it wasn't at all fine. 'Whatever.'

It took some tense negotiations but Lola agreed to deal with Richey at nine the next morning because she was currently working in Tabitha's vintage clothes shop in Spitalfields and didn't start until eleven. Ellie would leave Richey's pitiful collection of 'things' by the front door and he wasn't to be allowed in the flat.

Lola even got up early the next day to make sure Ellie left for work at her normal time because 'I know you. One whiff of his cheap aftershave and you'll be begging him to give it another go, and all the progress you've made will count for nothing.'

Ellie was sure that she'd do no such thing but at least it would all be settled. She could put a line through Richey. Get on with getting over him, then get on with the rest of her life. So she set off for her breakfast meeting with the arts critic from the *International Herald Tribune* with a spring in her step. Or a half-spring, because she wasn't over Richey yet, not by a long shot, and at quarter to eight it was already hot enough that the boating lake in Regent's Park seemed to shimmer in the heat and her pale blue Zara dress was wrinkled before she'd even arrived at the Riding House Café on Great Titchfield Street.

By the time breakfast was over and Ellie had prised the last bit of gossip out of the critic and seen him into a taxi, it was almost ten o'clock.

'Hey, it's me. Did it go all right?' she demanded as soon as Lola answered her phone. 'Has Richey been? Did he get his stuff? Was he an arse about the Stella?'

'Hello to you too,' Lola rapped back. 'And yes, yes and

yes. He was a total arse about his bloody Stella but I told him that the cans of Stella were compensation for the emotional distress he's caused. He wasn't too happy about that.'

'I'm not surprised,' Ellie said, but she still couldn't unclench. 'He didn't take anything he shouldn't? Like, he didn't come in, did he?'

There was a pause, which made Ellie's blood pressure rocket because Lola never paused before speaking. Usually she just said whatever she had to say without letting tact cramp her style. 'Well . . . maybe he did come in for a little bit,' she said at last. 'Something about a CD or DVD he lent you.'

'What?' Richey had listened almost exclusively to dubstep so there had never been a time when Ellie had asked to borrow any of his CDs, though he had bought her a Justin Bieber DVD as a joke and if he wanted the present back – and not even a good present, but a present that had cost two quid from a bloke in a pub selling DVDs out of a carrier bag – then Ellie really was well shot of him. 'I can't believe he'd be that petty. You didn't leave him in my room alone, did you?'

'Of course I didn't,' Lola snapped indignantly. 'Except, when he came round I was in the middle of washing my hair and I had shampoo in my eyes, then the postman rang the bell because Tess has been buying more of that home-made crap from Etsy.'

'Lola! You didn't!'

'Look, he was on his own in there for five minutes. OK, OK, maybe ten, but I checked and nothing's missing. TV, DVD player, jewellery box, it was all there. I can't guarantee that he didn't go through your knicker drawer for a souvenir but what's a pair of pants between friends?'

Quite a lot actually, especially if they were from Agent Provocateur, but there wasn't much Ellie could do about it when she was due back at work to personally take delivery of a light installation that had been overnighted from Brazil.

She always left work early the first Friday of every month to go to her grandparents' for dinner, but as Vaughn was on a yacht somewhere near Monaco with a Russian oligarch, Ellie left work even earlier so she could race home, fly up the stairs and burst into her room.

It looked the same as it had done when she'd left that morning. All consumer durables were present and correct. The bed was still neatly made. All the potions and make-up and beauty accessories were still in an orderly fashion on her dressing table and her knicker drawer, thank God, was firmly shut.

Ellie opened it just to be on the safe side. All appeared to be in order. Even the twenty-pound note for emergencies was still there. She sat on the edge of her bed and breathed deeply in and out until her pulse slowed to a manageable rate.

The panic had made Ellie hot and sweaty. She thought longingly of having a quick shower but made do with a damp flannel and a lot of body lotion. There was just time to change into a loose cotton dress and flats, then she was heading out of the door to get even hotter and sweatier as she walked up the hill to Belsize Park.

'Ellie, Ellie, you make me shake like jelly,' Morry, Ellie's grandfather, sang to the tune of 'Jeepers Creepers', when he opened the front door. 'Ellie, Ellie, you should be on the telly.'

Then he took Ellie in his arms and they waltzed down the hall. They ended up as they always did, in the kitchen with her grandmother shooing them out of her way as Morry kissed Ellie's forehead, then cupped her cheeks, exclaiming, 'What a beautiful *punim*. Oooh, I could just eat it all up.'

He did the *punim* routine with all of his granddaughters

but only Ellie got serenaded and some nifty two-step action.

'Morry, let the poor girl go, you're crushing my flowers,' her grandmother exclaimed sharply, elbowing her husband of sixty-odd years out of the way so she could take the freesias that Ellie had bought and demand a cuddle. Sadie Cohen was so short that Ellie could rest her chin on the top of her tinted strawberry-blond head. Not that she dared. Sadie got her hair shampooed and set every Friday morning after Pilates, and she'd have been furious if it didn't hold for the weekend. 'You're getting so thin, my darling, I can feel every one of your ribs.'

Ellie backed away warily. 'I'm going to leave this house at least seven pounds heavier,' she declared, gazing round the stainless-steel and frosted-white fitted kitchen that was her grandmother's pride and joy. Her eyes came to rest on the six-ring hob. 'Not chicken soup, Grandma! It's too hot.'

'We have to have chicken soup for Friday night dinner,' Sadie stated, as if on the sixth day God had stuck a boiling fowl in a huge saucepan, covered it in water and left it to simmer all afternoon. 'The BBC said it was going to rain tonight and then the temperature will plummet and you'll be glad of a nice warm drop of soup.'

The French doors that led out into the garden were open, which made no difference because it was still oppressively hot. The kitchen was steamy with the fragrant smell of chicken soup, the sweet onions that had been thrown into a dish with the chicken fat and rendered down into schmaltz, and lurking just underneath were warm base notes of apple and cinnamon because Sadie always made strudel for pudding.

'My darling, would you like to give me a hand with the chopped liver?'

Ellie pulled a stricken face as she always did. 'Can't I lay the table instead?' she asked, and predictably her grandparents chuckled indulgently, because Ellie didn't cook. Ari had been adamant that women who could cook never had the time to achieve greatness. Then she'd laugh hollowly when Ellie mentioned Julia Child, Nigella Lawson or the two women who'd founded the River Café. Now, Ellie left Sadie to finish making the chopped liver while she laid the table.

As she set down the heavy silver cutlery, Ellie could hear Sadie and Morry through the hatch. Morry was intent on taking Sadie for a quick spin around the kitchen and she was intent on batting him away with a tea towel. 'You'll break a hip, you silly fool, and then you won't be able to get up on the bima for little Daniel's bar mitzvah.' She turned her head and tutted at Ellie. 'Not the good glasses, darling, and take the salt off the table. It's bad for Grandpa's heart.'

'There's nothing wrong with my heart, Sadie. It still beats faster at the sight of you,' Morry said, and got another swipe with the tea towel for his trouble.

Ellie smiled. When she put all unhappy thoughts of Richey to one side along with the rest of her lame ducks, what she really wanted one day was a relationship like her grandparents'. A relationship built on mutual affection, humour, hard work and a hell of a lot of love.

Her grandparents had grown up together in a Samuel Lewis Trust building on Dalston Lane in Hackney, but lost touch when they'd both been evacuated during the war. They had found each other again on the dance floor of the Lyceum Ballroom on a Saturday night in 1952 and married four months later, a week after Sadie's eighteenth birthday.

They'd started married life in a back bedroom of Sadie's parents' rented basement flat in Fremont Street, Hackney. Morry worked as a tailor in Savile Row; then when his father died, he took his small inheritance and used it to buy the lease on a tiny shop off Marylebone High Street and opened a dry-cleaners frequented by his old Savile Row customers. Morry had looked after front of house, Sadie had done the books. Then the Savile Row customers' wives had started sending in their ballgowns and cocktail dresses. Sadie and Morry took the lease on the premises next door and moved into a tiny attic flat in Hampstead. They'd been the first members of either of their families to buy their own home.

Fifty-five years later they lived in a huge house in Belsize Park, had sixteen grandchildren, ten great grand-children, and had passed their fifteen-shop dry-cleaning empire to their two eldest sons when they'd retired. Morry and Sadie hadn't liked being retired very much so they'd opened a small alterations shop in Golders Green. Now they had ten shops in North London, but still joint-chaired the synagogue's social committee, fund-raised for Jewish Care and hosted Friday-night dinners for their family on a four-week-rota basis. Tonight was the turn of the unmarried grandchildren, and just as Morry finally persuaded Sadie to join him in a very sedate waltz, there was a ring at the door. Ellie rushed to answer it.

It was her cousin Tanya, closely followed by sisters Emma and Laurel, the three of them falling on Ellie with cries of excitement and kisses. Bringing up the rear was Louis, who managed the family's original dry-cleaners in Marylebone (frequented by the *Vogue* and *Skirt* girls). He wrapped the four girls in an extravagant group hug.

'My favourite unmarried cousins,' he exclaimed with a wicked grin as Sadie bustled into the hall to find out why the front door was still open.

Half an hour later they were all seated round the big table in the morning room. The proper dining room was only used on High Holy Days, and the second Friday of each month when it was the turn of married grand-children with offspring.

Sadie waited until after the blessings and the lighting of

the Shabbat candles, when everyone was eating the chopped-liver starter, before she sighed long and hard, 'My unmarried grandchildren. So beautiful, so talented but so unattached. I don't understand it.'

'It's not for want of trying, Grandma,' Emma said. Laurel nodded in agreement and Ellie knew what was coming next. They finished the chopped liver, choked down a bowl of soup and were picking at the chicken and Emma and Laurel still hadn't finished lamenting the lack of suitable Jewish men in their lives. This was despite attending charity balls, speed-dating evenings, nature walks, casino club nights and every other event organised by any Jewish-affiliated group in North London, Middlesex and the less tacky parts of Essex.

'Don't even talk to me about weddings,' Laurel spat as she received a plate heaped with chicken, savoury lokshen pudding, tzimmes – a sweet stew made with carrots and prunes – and a couple of sugar snap peas because Ellie and Louis insisted on something green on their plates. 'We've been to six weddings so far this year. All the good men are taken and the ones that are left are . . .'

'. . . Mummy's boys or total losers who've never even touched a woman, let alone spoken to one,' Tanya, who'd been silent up until now, added darkly.

'Try being Jewish and gay,' Louis offered glumly. 'Talk about a small dating pool. I should emigrate. Everyone and his mother is Jewish and gay in New York.'

'So true,' Ellie agreed loyally, but Sadie and Morry were having none of that kind of talk. They didn't mind Louis being gay – it gave them a certain social cachet – but they weren't having any of their grandchildren move from North London. After she'd graduated, Ellie had considered living in Hoxton but Morry had summoned her to his office and told her gravely that Hoxton was for 'ladies of easy virtue and gangsters'. He refused to believe Hoxton was now full of poncy bars, art galleries and lots of young people in distressed clothing with hedge-trimmer hairdos.

Sadie sighed again. 'There was never a problem finding nice Jewish boys when I was your age.'

'Sometimes I think it would be so much easier if we still used matchmakers,' Ellie said feelingly. She gestured at Morry and Sadie. 'You could find me a nice boy from a good home, we'd get married and simply have to make the best of it.'

Sadie and Morry shared a hopeful look. 'Is that really what you want, darling, because there's always ads in the *Jewish Chronicle* for those kinds of services?'

Ellie almost spat out a mouthful of chicken. 'No! I was only saying.' But for a moment she was distracted by the thought of a nice Jewish boy – kind, solvent, who always put the toilet seat down – until Sadie reached across the table to prod her with the bread knife.

'Are you not seeing anyone then, *motek*?' she asked.

'Not right now.' Ellie grimaced. 'I was but he turned out to be a very, very bad person.'

'He wasn't Jewish then?'

'You can't cross yourself, Grandpa! It only works if you're Catholic!'

'What about Marilyn Simons' son?' Sadie looked round the table hopefully. 'Lovely boy. An accountant. Whoever heard of a poor accountant?'

For a second, Ellie was almost tempted. A Jewish accountant sounded like the dose of normal she needed to get the bad Richey taste out of her mouth and to stop her fevered dreams about tall, dark strangers, but then Tanya said doubtfully, 'Justin Simons?' and Ellie shuddered because she remembered Justin Simons from Hebrew classes. He'd always smelled of really eggy farts.

'Think I'll pass, Bubba,' she muttered. 'But he sounds like he'd be perfect for Laurel or Emma,' she added, and that led to a good-natured argument that took them right through a game of kalooki over coffee and apple strudel.

It was gone ten by the time the cousins were lined up in the hall, all feeling slightly bilious and in need of fresh air.

'I've got something for you,' Sadie told Ellie, who was slumped against the wall, because the food baby in her belly was giving her backache. 'Leftovers and a few things I had knocking about in the fridge.'

She handed over a cool bag straining at the seams, not just with leftovers but fishballs, potato latkes, salt beef sandwiches and an apple cake – all of Ari's favourite foods.

'Thanks, Bubba,' Ellie said, bending down to kiss her grandmother's cheek.

'If there's too much for you, you could share it with Ariella,' Sadie said casually. 'I'd hate for good food to go to waste.' It wasn't like mother and daughter were on no-speakers, but Sadie's other children were always popping in for coffee or to show off recent John Lewis purchases while Ari only ever came round for the first night of Rosh Hashanah and Christmas lunch. Much as she loved Ellie – and Ellie was in no doubt of that love, not ever – Sadie would never forgive Ari for giving birth to a child out of wedlock or getting tattooed.

'Well, I'm seeing Mum on Sunday so if I haven't eaten it all by then, I'll share it with her,' Ellie said just as casually, and there was time for one last hug and a quick two-step with Morry before she staggered home.

Camden, London, 1986

Billy was gone when Ari woke up the next morning. Hadn't even asked for her number, but left her to do the walk of shame up to the station.

Left Ari to fixate and obsess and agonise for two whole weeks and just when she'd worked through it, Billy Kay was back. Propping up the bar of the Lizard Lounge off Bayham Street where she pulled pints on Monday and Tuesday nights when she didn't have a gig.

Ari still wasn't going to be *that* girl. Anyway, he was married, for fuck's sake, and he was a dick who thought he was too cool even to smile or say hello to her, or join in with the latest barroom gossip about that band who sounded like a tenth-generation copy of The Stooges that had signed to EMI for over a million pounds.

When it came down to it, no one was that dangerous or intense. Especially not Billy Kay, not when he'd been on *Top of the Pops* in a paisley shirt with really bad hair in his really shit former band who'd been dumped by their record label after they delivered their second album.

But Ari still somehow ended up going home with him most nights. Not *home*, because he lived in Powis Square with his wife, the honourable Olivia, and child. And not her home because she was illegally subletting a flat in a grim council tower block in Mornington Crescent with Tabitha and Tom, who'd made their feelings about Billy Kay really clear, and their feelings could be summed up in three words: 'fucking poseur bastard'.

But it was OK, because Billy knew someone, Billy always knew someone, and this particular someone was a playwright who lived in Chalcot Square in Primrose Hill and Billy had squatter's rights to the summerhouse in his back garden.

Sylvia Plath had once lived in a flat on the other side of Chalcot Square and Ari didn't think that was a good omen. Still wasn't enough to stop her, though.

Chapter Seven

After Friday-night dinner, there was always Hair Dye Sunday. Always. Ellie would go round to Ari's to assist in the monthly session with bleach, a box of Manic Panic Rock 'n' Roll Red hair dye, and to share her spoils from Sadie.

'I can't believe you went out in public in a tracksuit,' Ari exclaimed when Ellie walked through the front door of her tiny flat and took the four steps that led into the kitchen. 'Are you really my daughter?'

'Yoga pants and a Uniqlo vest do not look like a track-suit,' Ellie said indignantly. 'They look like I've been exercising. Tess got a voucher for a place in Islington that does that Pilates where they stretch you on Reformer machines.'

Ari looked up from her bowl of bleach solution. 'Really? Sounds painful.'

'Well, I don't recommend it on a hangover,' Ellie said as she slumped on a stool. Ari's décor style could be summed up as rock 'n' roll kitsch meets Victorian clutter. The flat was stuffed full of paraphernalia, from assorted taxidermy including a pair of ravens, a one-legged squirrel and a motheaten fox to Mexican Day of the Dead masks on the shelf over the cooker, three ceramic hula girls dancing above the mantelpiece in the living room, and posters, flyers and photographs of Ari's musical past and present covering the walls. There were also amps, guitars, an accordion and other pieces of musical equipment stacked wherever there was space. Ellie lived in dread of a frantic phone call from Ari to say she was trapped and unable to get to the front door because there was so much crap in the way. 'Your Mexican Day of the Dead masks are looking at me funny.'

'You're so cranky when you have a hangover,' Ari said. She tossed something at Ellie. 'Put on your turban. It will make you feel better.'

There were certain rituals that had to be observed on Hair Dye Sunday, and one of them was that Ellie had to wear a maroon velvet turban of the sort favoured by chic Parisian geriatrics. Then, once she'd applied bleach to Ari's roots, they sat on Ari's bright pink Chesterfield and watched the *Grey Gardens* documentary. They'd both seen it so often that they could recite the lines from memory with only one eye on the screen. Ellie was Little Edie, Ari was Big Edie, and when Ari said, as she always did, 'Do you think we'll end up as two mad old women living in a big, decaying house full of feral cats?' Ellie would tell Ari that she planned to stick her in a care home before that could ever happen.

They also doggedly ate their way through Sadie's food parcel. Eventually all that was left was the apple cake, which they were saving to have with a cup of tea once the dye had been washed out. Ellie felt as if the worst of her hangover had receded and she could tell Ari about the night before.

Tess and Lola were adamant that Ellie shouldn't waste a single night crying about Richey so Lola had dragged her to a Blitz-themed party in Shoreditch. They'd dressed in vintage frocks with stocking seams drawn down the backs of their legs with eyeliner, ordered cocktails from a menu designed like a ration book, danced to Glenn Miller tunes and tried and tried and tried to find a normal bloke for Ellie to hook up with.

'I don't think normal blokes hang out at Blitz-themed club nights in Shoreditch,' Ellie said, her feet propped up on Ari's lap as Ari painted her toenails a glittery red. 'I know you're probably not down with me going out with some normal guy who wears a suit and has a pension plan but I really need normal in my life right now.'

'I'm down with whatever makes you happy,' Ari said. 'But you should know that there's no such thing as a normal person. What you need is a man who'll make you feel normal, even when you feel like you're the biggest freak in the world.'

'Is that how my dad made you feel?' Ellie asked. She didn't even know what had prompted that question, because it wasn't something they ever talked about. Ari occasionally ranted about how he'd sold out as a musician, but she never talked about him as her lover, or about the year they'd been together, and the little Ellie did know had been gleaned from Tabitha, Tom and Chester (who would clench his jaw so painfully that Ellie had stopped asking him). 'Did he make you feel normal?'

Ari didn't answer at first. She applied a second coat of polish to the little toenail on Ellie's left foot, screwed the top back on the bottle and only then did she look up. Even with a carrier bag tied around her head so she didn't get red dye everywhere, she looked sad and pensive. But mostly sad. 'God, normal was the last thing he made me feel,' she said quietly, and before Ellie could apologise for dredging up painful memories, Ari patted her leg. 'Come on, Little Edie, help me wash this crap off my head. It's starting to itch.'

All the way through the rest of the hair-dyeing process, which involved some hardcore conditioning, Ari kept up a stream of inconsequential chatter about The Fuck Puppets' next gig and the guitar class she was running at a rock 'n' roll summer camp for girls in the school holidays. She even talked about the weather, or rather speculated if it was ever going to rain again 'because this relentless sunshine is going to give me a tan and you know how I feel about tans'.

It meant that Ellie didn't have the opportunity to ask any more questions Ari couldn't or wouldn't answer. Ellie understood. She'd never had her heart broken quite like that, but there had been times when her heart had taken a beating, and even getting out of bed, much less talking about the person responsible, had made the ache almost unbearable. Still, her curiosity was piqued and when she got home and started to organise her outfit options for the coming week, 'It Felt Like A Kiss' was playing on the radio. It was a sign from God to stop what she was doing so she could sit on her bed and rummage through her Dad box.

Even without fetching it from its hiding place and opening it, Ellie knew what was in the pretty art-deco tin, which had once contained some *sablés au beurre* Tess had brought back from a school trip to Brittany. Originally it had been a safe place to store her birth certificate, and the results of the DNA test, requested four months after she was born. Slowly she'd added to its contents. There were a couple of black-and-white photos of her dad and a heavily pregnant Ari, with black hair in a truly monumental beehive, snuggled up on a bed. A *Melody Maker* interview with her father conducted in someone's back garden in Primrose Hill with Ari throwing in a few comments from the sidelines that had made it onto the yellowing pages. A flyer from a gig at the Black Horse in 1986, when his old band, The Incognitos, had headlined and Ari's group, the Saturday Girls, were third on the bill and legend (and Tabitha) had it that that was the night they'd first connected. A few pictures of him torn out of magazines, not that Ellie slavishly searched for her father's likeness but if she came across a photo or an article she usually added it to her box.

The most recent cutting was from the *Evening Standard*'s

party pages a few months before. Her father and his wife had been photographed at the opening night of a play. He was dressed in a sharp black suit and though he was fifty-five and starting to look a little weatherbeaten around the edges, it was easy to see why he was featured whenever a women's magazine did a feature on silver foxes. Ellie always scrutinised his face for clues to see if there was any family resemblance, but Sadie and Ari were both united in their belief that Ellie got her looks from the Cohens.

The last item in the box, buried under all the scraps of paper purloined from newspapers and magazines, was a CD of her father's first and stratospherically successful solo album, *Songs for a Girl*. He'd dedicated it to his wife; the wife he'd left for Ari and the woman he'd gone back to when the affair was over. It was the record that had made him famous. Ellie had never listened to it, couldn't bear to, but the songs were woven into the fabric of British life and she was pretty sure that she knew all the words to at least half of them.

It wasn't much of a Dad box, but then he'd never been much of a dad. Ari had tried to ensure that Ellie never really felt his absence. Between them, Chester, Tom and her grandpa had turned up for sports days and carol concerts, been the happy recipients of ineptly made Father's Day cards and, much later, had been the ones to lecture Ellie on the perils of underage drinking and teenage boys who were only after one thing, and would come and pick her up in the wee small hours from the other side of London when she didn't have enough money for a taxi.

Ellie had always had so many people in her life that the lack of a father shouldn't have bothered her, but she'd still wondered what her life might have been like if he'd been in it. It had been a recurring but secret theme when she was younger. Every birthday, at Chanukah and Christmas-time, whenever she had a part in a school concert, Ellie would hope that this time her father would turn up, even though Ari said that he was really busy or that things were complicated and that Ellie would understand when she was older. Ellie had especially wanted her father to suddenly appear during the year when Ari had been getting up at five each morning to clean offices and had also worked until midnight as a barmaid to save for the deposit to join a shared ownership scheme and buy a flat, and Ellie had had to go and live with Sadie and Morry.

There had been so many times when money was tight and there'd been bailiffs at the door. They'd always turn up on a Friday afternoon, preferably the Friday afternoon of a bank holiday weekend when Ari could do nothing but hide behind the sofa with Ellie, both of them quiet as the quietest of mice. Then Ellie would wonder why her father wasn't coming to their rescue because he had lots of money and he could make all the bad stuff go away.

That was back then, and now Ellie didn't really wonder about her father any more. It was clear that he didn't wonder about her. But sometimes, like this evening, her curiosity about this man she barely knew even though she had his DNA coursing through her veins (or whatever it was that DNA did) got the better of her. So Ellie kneeled down on the floor and stuck her arm under her bed, fingers ready to close around the edge of her Dad box, because it was always there beneath the right-hand side. Always. Unless she'd knocked into it when she was vacuuming, because she knew for a fact that their cleaner didn't bother with the bits that couldn't be seen. Ellie lay flat on the floor, and peered into the shadowy recesses.

There was a plastic crate with her winter hats, gloves and scarves in it. Three long cardboard boxes where her winter boots nestled on boot trees. The concertina file containing all her important papers and another plastic crate housing all her *Malory Towers*, *St Clare's* and boarding school books, which Ari had tried to ban with little success. There was even her Mason Pearson flat hairbrush, which Ellie had been looking for everywhere, but no Dad box.

Keep calm, keep calm, she muttered. Maybe the cleaner had moved it. Or she'd moved it herself when she'd reorganised her room a couple of months ago. Ten minutes later she'd rifled through her wardrobe, checked under the chest of drawers, done a second sweep of the wardrobe and searched through suitcases and travel bags. Each time she came up empty.

Ellie stood in the middle of her room and looked around. Maybe the Dad box was hiding in plain sight, but if it was then she couldn't see it.

There was a muffled thud on the stairs, then the sound of a key in the lock and she was scurrying out into the hall to greet Tess with an anguished, 'Have you seen a French biscuit tin? It's usually under my bed but I can't find it anywhere!'

Tess couldn't even remember the French biscuit tin that she'd once given to Ellie. After taking precious minutes to be brought up to speed, Tess dutifully searched all the places that Ellie had searched, opened every drawer and created havoc where once there had been neatly folded clothes arranged by season, texture and colour. Then, mainly to humour Ellie, Tess even hunted through her own room.

'Sorry, Ellie, but it's not here,' she said at last, as she finished shoving her own underwear back in its drawers. 'I don't know what's happened to it.'

'Oh, I do,' Ellie growled. She marched into Lola's room without knocking, and anyway it was seven o'clock and Lola had been mouldering in bed all day and Ellie had no sympathy for her. 'This is all your fault!' she snapped at a barely conscious Lola. 'I told you not to let him into the flat. That was all you had to do. Just stand in the hall and pass him his stupid, bloody stuff and now he's taken my Dad box. That's the only explanation. Unless you have it. Do you have it?'

Ellie's eyes swept over the mess that was Lola's living space. There were heaps of clothes and dirty crockery everywhere and, quite frankly, Lord Lucan and Shergar could have been stashed in Lola's room and no one would be any the wiser. As it was, Lola was struggling out of her fugue state and trying to sit up on the mattress that she slept on ever since she'd lent her bed base to a friend for a conceptual art piece.

'What the fuck?' she mumbled. 'Why are you shouting?'

'I'm shouting because Richey must have taken my Dad box when he was in my room, even though you made a big thing about how he wasn't even allowed into the flat. How could you do this to me?'

'What the hell is a Dad box? You don't have a dad!' Lola could go from catatonic to roaring in thirty seconds. 'And don't come into my room when I have a hangover and start screaming at me. What's got into you, Ells?'

Panic and fear and the feeling that the end of the world was coming were what had got into her, but Ellie thought the words might choke her. In fact, she did make a choking sound when she tried to speak, so she settled for storming out of Lola's room and slamming the door behind her. It was the first time in her life that Ellie had ever felt the need to slam a door.

It was the warning she needed to put herself on a time-out in the bathroom so she could calm down and stop doing out-of-character things like shouting and slamming doors. She stayed there for ten minutes, though that was mostly spent pulling everything out of the pot cupboard where they kept tampons, razors and a huge range of Korres toiletries, from whenever they did a TK Maxx run. The Dad box was not there or hidden behind any towels and it was obviously too big to fit in the cabinet over the basin, but Ellie still checked to be sure.

Ellie emerged from the bathroom, a lot less panic-stricken, because now she was resigned to the awful truth that the Dad box was gone. She also needed to apologise to Lola, who was in a foetal position on the living-room sofa.

'Dude, it's already forgiven,' Lola said. 'Sorry I shouted at you, but I can't believe you've been holding out on me all this time. So, tell me, who's your daddy?'

Ellie shot Tess a grateful look for not blabbing her darkest secrets. Ari's affair and subsequent heavy-with-child-ness had happened before her father went from obscure purveyor of substandard mope rock to mega-famous, stadium-playing purveyor of anthemic mope rock, and also the internet hadn't been invented then. Life had, apparently, been simpler when it was much, much harder for the whole world to get all up in your grille. Besides Ari wasn't the type to sell her story, 'because it's no one else's bloody business and I am not going to be a sad cliché of the wronged woman'.

Ellie had kept quiet too. Her father had never acknow-ledged her so there was no reason to acknowledge him. And even though she and Tess were bestics and had known each other since they were eleven, Ellie had still waited until the summer after they'd done their A levels to confess all. Lola had only been in her life for four years and for two of those years they'd glared at each other at parties, so she hadn't yet earned access to Ellie's secrets.

'I can't tell you that,' Ellie replied. 'It's nothing personal, but you're rubbish at keeping secrets. It would be on Twitter in the space of an hour.'

'It wouldn't!' Lola made a hurt face, then Ellie saw her scroll back and reconsider. 'Well, I can keep a secret until I get drunk, *then* all bets are off.'

'Anyway, he's only my father in the biological sense of . . . Why are you looking at me like that?'

Lola was staring at her as if she was seeing Ellie for the very first time. 'Is it Paul McCartney? You do look a bit like him around the eyes.'

'No, she doesn't!' Tess gasped indignantly. 'She's much prettier than Stella McCartney.'

'I guess.' Lola gave Ellie another appraising glance. 'I can't see Ari doing the nasty with Macca anyway. Is it Bono?'

'No! And it's not David Bowie or Shaun Ryder or any other bonkers suggestions you're going to come up with,' Ellie said quickly, because if they started this game, sooner or later Lola would hit paydirt. 'Listen, is there any way that my box might be in your room?'

'I don't think so but let's have a look,' Lola said, and she even moved off the sofa and didn't get mad when Ellie and Tess ransacked her room. Although they found the DVD remote control that had been missing for months, there was no Dad box.

The three of them trailed back to the living room. While Tess and Lola sank down on the sofa, Ellie stood there, hands hanging limply down by her sides.

Tess gave her a stricken look. 'What are you going to do, Ells?'

Ellie knew that she should take charge of the situation: find a solution or, at the very least, a silver lining, but all she wanted to do was climb into bed, pull the covers over her head and stay there indefinitely. 'Well, I need to call Richey,' she said heavily. 'See if he took it. Why he took it. What I need to do to get it back.'

'Why don't I ring him?' Lola offered. 'That way he won't see your number if he's screening his calls.'

Ellie waited for a tension-filled minute as Lola made the call but she'd known even before Lola shook her head that it would do no good. 'It just says, "The number has not been recognised",' Lola reported. 'If I were you, I'd call Chester. Get him to go round and have a word.'

Ellie was already reaching for her phone. All it took was two garbled sentences, and Chester was cutting her off. 'Where do you think he'll be? Dublin Castle? Spread Eagle? I'll also try The Mixer and The Monarch. Give me his address too.'

'He might not have the box any more. Or maybe he never took it and I've just misplaced it,' Ellie ventured.

'You don't misplace stuff, Ellie. Not you.' He paused. 'Let's not tell Ari about this. Wouldn't want to worry her. I'll sort this out and I'll give you a ring once I've tracked down the little shit.'

'Don't get into anything with him. Just get the box back,' Ellie pleaded.

'Sweetheart, leave it to me. I won't do anything that will get blood on my Trojan Records T-shirt,' Chester said calmly, which didn't exactly allay Ellie's fears.

It wasn't the funnest Sunday evening ever. The three of them had originally planned to have a *Come Dine With Me* marathon, as they had over twenty episodes taking up valuable space on the TiVo, but Ellie found that her eyes kept straying to her mobile phone. Every now and again Tess or Lola would say something like, 'Are you sure you checked in the airing cupboard?' or 'Did you pull out everything from under your bed?' Then all three of them would get up, rush to the place in question and every time Ellie would get her hopes up and dare to believe that this nightmare was over, only to have them cruelly dashed, and return to her vigil on the sofa.

Chester eventually rang back just before eleven. He'd been to every pub, club and drinking den in NW1 and NW5 but Richey was nowhere to be found. None of his friends or drinking buddies or the three stoners he shared a flat with had seen him since last Friday morning.

'Do you think I should call his lawyers tomorrow

morning? My dad's, I mean,' Ellie asked Chester as she sat on her bed and surveyed the wreckage of what had once been her beautifully tidy, almost minimalist bedroom. 'Just to give them a heads up. Maybe Richey just took the box to piss me off and he'll turn up in the next day or so to give it back? Or he might have just dumped it in a bin. Or—'

'Couldn't do any harm to give the lawyers a call,' Chester said quickly, as if he couldn't bear to listen to Ellie's torturous explanations of what had happened to the box, when the only logical explanation was that it was currently the subject of a bidding war between several tabloid newspapers.

'But it's not like my father's had an album out for ages, is it? He's not exactly newsworthy right now, and I know his daughters are always in the papers but that's not the same,' Ellie insisted. She'd never had to contact the lawyers before – had no reason to – and it felt a lot like opening up a can of worms best left tightly shut and buried underground.

She and Chester agreed that there was no point in doing anything but sleeping on it and reconvening in the morning but Ellie abandoned any hope of sleep in favour of imagining Ari's fury and hurt if the story hit the papers. And God! What horrible things would Richey say about her? That she was really uptight and it was impossible to believe she was a rock star's daughter. He'd probably tell them that they'd been seeing each other for weeks before they'd actually slept together. So when she thought about it, as rationally as she could when it was four in the morning, Ellie decided she wasn't really tabloid fodder.

For a start, she had a regular job, rather than being a model, actress or singer. She'd never dated anyone remotely famous. She'd never let a boyfriend take dirty pictures of her. She'd certainly never made a sex tape, and apart from smoking a few joints, she'd never taken drugs.

The tabloids would laugh in Richey's face. Although Ellie didn't think she was that boring, not when you got to know her, she was boring on paper. Who knew that being boring could be a good thing?

It was enough to lull Ellie to sleep for a few fitful hours. When she woke up, she was still sure that she was a non-story, and once she got to work she'd phone Chester and tell him that. She was desperate to get her Dad box back but at least she didn't have to ring some faceless legal drone. Ellie didn't want the only contact she had with her father in twenty-six years to be an email forwarded by his lawyer about her thieving scumbag of an ex-boyfriend.

With a renewed sense of purpose, Ellie even bought flaky pastries from the fancy French patisserie in Marylebone on her way to work so everyone at the gallery could start the week on a sweet note. Though if she kept stuffing her face and drinking ruinous amounts of alcohol, another detox beckoned, she thought, juggling pastries, coffee and purse as her phone began to ring.

'Hello?' she said, after she'd balanced coffee and carbs on a handy bollard.

'Ellie Cohen?' said a voice that she didn't recognise, and every molecule in her body stiffened in alarm. 'Sam Curtis here. I work on the celebrity desk at the *Sunday Chronicle*. Have you got time for a quick chat?'

'No!' Ellie yelped. 'You've got the wrong number.' It was the best she could come up with when all the blood in her body had rushed to her head and was making it hard to see or speak or think clearly.

'We'd love to run a story about you and your dad,' the Sam person continued as if he hadn't heard her. 'Great human interest piece. Can't wait to hear your side of it. We'll take some nice photos. How does that sound?'

It sounded . . . Ellie wasn't even sure. She was clawing at her throat because it felt like she couldn't breathe. She forced herself to take several juddering breaths, to focus on her Styrofoam cup of coffee until she was lucid again and able to make decisions. Not that there was anything to consider.

'No,' she said very forcefully. 'Absolutely not.'

'Look, love, this story is going to run with or without your cooperation. It really would be better for you if it was with your cooperation.'

'You don't understand! Any evidence you might have is actually my personal property. You're in receipt of stolen goods. That's a crime,' Ellie explained calmly. Or she was trying to stay in the same ballpark as calm. 'I need you to return these items to me by courier immediately. I'll give you my work address.'

Sam Curtis chuckled. 'Yeah, so anyway, darling, I'd love to meet up for a chat. When's good for you?'

'Never. I need my box back. Are you going to give it back to me?'

'It doesn't work like that, sweetheart.'

'Right. OK. Well, I'm going to call the police then.' Ellie hung up and she was all set to call 999, one quivering finger even hovering over the '9', but then she recalled the gory details of the phone-hacking scandal. The police all took backhanders from the newspapers and they'd do nothing to help. There really was only one other option, though it was the very last thing Ellie wanted to do. The very last thing. She'd rather have rectal surgery without an anaesthetic.

'You've reached Wyndham, Pryce and Lewis,' said a disembodied voice, once Ellie was back at work and had unearthed a number after a bit of judicious googling. Billy Kay's legal affairs were handled by a firm established in 1732, which had expanded into entertainment law over the last thirty years and subsequently opened offices in LA and New York, though Ellie hoped that the Clerkenwell branch would be able to help. 'If you know the extension of the person you wish to speak to, please dial it now. Otherwise leave your name and a short message.'

'This is Ellie Cohen. I need to speak to someone urgently. Very urgently indeed. Please call me back right away.' It was very hard for Ellie to leave a coherent message when all she wanted to do was burst into tears. As it was, she forgot to leave her number or direct her message specifically to whoever dealt with Billy Kay and had to ring again and leave another message, which sounded even more frantic and garbled than the first one.

Ellie sat rigid with terror at her desk all day, office door firmly shut so she'd have some privacy. It was impossible to settle to anything, even checking final drafts of important contracts that Vaughn needed a.s.a.p. He kept sending Piers to ask where they were, and every time she needed a wee Ellie had to gallop down the corridor like she was trying to break the landspeed record because it would be typical of the lawyer to call while she was in the loo.

At just after five Vaughn suddenly appeared in Ellie's office to demand an explanation for why she'd spent all day not doing anything that even remotely resembled her job.

'I've been waiting on a call,' Ellie said, and then her mobile rang and the number looked vaguely Central London-ish, so it had to be the lawyer and not, dear God no, another reporter. 'Um, I kind of need to take this.'

'I fail to see how I'm stopping you from answering your phone,' Vaughn snapped as he loomed over her desk. He did love to loom.

'It's a personal call,' Ellie said despairingly. 'Deeply personal. May I have some privacy?'

She didn't dare look at Vaughn's face, but picked up her phone and said a very cautious, very reticent 'Hello?' even as Vaughn strode towards the door muttering something under his breath that featured the phrase 'fire you'. That was the very least of her problems. Her biggest problem was sighing down the phone. 'Miss Cohen?' queried someone who managed to sound reproachful and censorious, as if he'd been the one waiting on her call. 'This is David Gold from Wyndham, Pryce and Lewis. Shall we pencil in a meeting? At your earliest convenience would be best.'

Ellie was alarmed and relieved all at once. Though the alarm that, yes, actually, bad times were a-coming quickly obliterated any relief that the lawyer was taking her seriously. 'Well, I can be with you in, say, half an hour?'

'Tomorrow morning will be fine,' David Gold backtracked, like the fact that her life was about to collapse in on her wasn't that urgent. 'Eight o'clock. My office.'

He didn't try to make it sound like a suggestion, and despite her fear Ellie curled her toes in irritation. Then she checked her calendar. 'I have a breakfast meeting at eight thirty in Piccadilly. Can we make it a bit later?'

'Surely you can rearrange your meeting.' Again, it didn't sound like a question, but Ellie couldn't. Not when she was meeting a really high-maintenance celebrity and the equally high-maintenance and exceedingly whiny artist who'd been commissioned to paint her portrait. It had taken weeks to find this mutually agreeable time slot.

'I absolutely can't,' she insisted. 'And I've been waiting all day for you to get back to me. All day! I don't think you appreciate how nightmarish this situation is.'

'Oh, it's hardly nightmarish.' He sounded positively breezy as if potential tabloid scandals were nothing to be scared about. 'Now, it would be much more convenient if you could come here . . .'

'I've already told you I can't, but . . .'

A sigh. 'I suppose I could come to you. Seven thirty? Where's your meeting?'

'The Wolseley,' Ellie replied waspishly; all this grandstanding about who was coming to whom and at what time felt like a power-play. 'I'll change my reservation.'

'Until tomorrow then.'

'So, do you think we have a case to sue them? I mean, they're clearly in the wrong, aren't they? You can get my box back and make sure that they—'

'Miss Cohen, this can all wait until tomorrow. To be honest, your message didn't make much sense. Neither of your messages did. You were somewhat hysterical.'

'Distressed. I was distressed.'

'Either way, we can discuss how to move forward when we meet tomorrow morning,' David Gold said smoothly. 'Have a good evening.'

He rang off, leaving Ellie even more discomfited than she had been before he'd called.

Chapter Eight

Normally Ellie loved having a breakfast meeting at the Wolseley, the former 1920s showroom of the Wolseley car company, once more restored to its former Byzantine glory. Every time Ellie was seated in the cavernous dining room with its immense marble pillars and arches, she felt as if she was on the set of a Busby Berkeley musical, and half expected to see a bevy of Ziegfeld Girls suddenly undulate down the sweeping staircase.

Not this Tuesday morning, though. It might have been airy and cool in the restaurant, but the tight armholes of Ellie's sleeveless white dress were getting damp and perspiration was beginning to dot her forehead.

With one eye on the entrance, she tried surreptitiously to blot her face with her Laura Mercier setting powder. And she might just as well dab a little more Secret Camouflage concealer under her eyes because two nights of imagining worst-case scenarios rather than sleeping had taken their toll.

'Hello?'

Of course, the lawyer would arrive in that exact moment when she'd yet to blend in the smear of concealer under each eye. Ellie reluctantly looked up at a familiar face and dropped her make-up bag. It was the man she'd met at Glastonbury! The man who'd made her tingle before they'd been so rudely interrupted. She could feel the tingles again; lifting up her hair follicles, slithering down her spine, racing all the way to her feet, then retracing their electric path back up again.

He was wearing an impeccably tailored grey suit, his tie an almost perfect match for his dark blue eyes, which were wide with surprise, and his curls had been ruthlessly tamed and submitted into a side parting. He seemed more buttoned-up than he had at Glastonbury and he was looking at Ellie in disbelief too.

Her own hair had been coaxed into a sleek, slick ponytail, her dress was tailored and form-fitting, and her only jewellery was the elegant platinum wristwatch that Sadie and Morry had bought her for her twenty-first birthday.

'Yes! Hello! Well, this is a surprise.' She smiled at him, but he didn't smile back, and stood there with a look of consternation, which suited him far less than the engaging grin she'd seen just over a week ago. 'I was so embarrassed about what happened at Glastonbury. I don't know what you must have thought of me.'

He swallowed. 'You? You're Velvet Cohen?'

Oh, no. 'Um, yes.'

None of Ellie's worst-case scenarios had prepared her for this. She watched in dismay as his face tightened. Then he looked down at the marble floor. It was like a door being slammed shut.

A second passed, then he was looking at her again and smiling. It showed off his even, white teeth and should have made Ellie feel more at ease but didn't.

'There wasn't time for introductions before, was there? I'm David Gold from Wyndham, Pryce and Lewis,' he said, and he held out his hand.

Ellie half stood up, went to shake his hand, realised her fingertips were smeared with make-up and abandoned her plans in favour of sitting back down and frantically patting the skin under her eyes with one hand as she tried to scoop up her cosmetics, which had spilled over the table.

'Sorry. For concealer, this stuff is really hard to conceal,' she mumbled, as a waiter pulled out the chair opposite so David Gold could sit down.

There was a stubborn streak that wouldn't cooperate. Ellie wiped it away with an impatient hand and steeled herself to glance across to see David Gold straighten his tie, then confirm that his cufflinks were in full working order. Ellie resisted the urge to check the concealer situation again and tucked her make-up bag away.

'This is such a weird coincidence,' she said, because she had to say something.

David Gold looked at Ellie – took his time about it too – then his eyes came to rest on her watch and his lips twisted. She was beginning to doubt that he was the same man she'd met. Maybe he had a twin, or a *doppelgänger*, because now he made a tiny moue of distaste, so fleeting that most other people wouldn't have noticed it. Ellie, however, was scrutinising his face for a sign, some small glimmer of that connection she'd felt at Glastonbury. She couldn't see one because he didn't appear to share her fond memories, though that was hardly surprising with the scene that Richey had caused. Ellie held her hands to her suddenly burning cheeks.

'Yes, it's very weird,' he agreed at last.

'You have to let me explain and apologise about what happened at Glastonbury,' Ellie said with a forced bright-ness just as a waiter approached their table. David Gold ordered a pot of tea. Ellie's stomach had been tied into several gnarly knots ever since his phone call the evening before, so she ordered only a cappuccino and sat back in her chair nervously to try again. 'Anyway, I was—'

'What happened at Glastonbury really isn't important right now. We've got a lot to get through.' As Ellie was processing that nugget of information, he gave her another smile that was kinder and seemed to have some substance to it. 'So to recap, a vengeful ex-boyfriend has documentary evidence proving your paternity and has sold his story.'

'Well, yes, but—'

'I'm really sorry that I haven't got happier news but the papers are going to run with the story on Sunday,' David Gold interrupted softly, as if he *was* genuinely sorry. 'Well, the *Sunday Chronicle* is. I'm afraid that the other papers will probably pick it up in their late editions.'

Ellie hadn't dared let herself hope that this mess could be salvaged, but it still came as a shock. Like when she stubbed her toe or banged her head on an open cupboard door, her eyes were watering and she found herself struggling to take in air, while David Gold folded his arms and looked at her from under his lashes. He was silent and still, as if he was waiting for Ellie to speak, but it was all she could do to breathe in and out. Talking wasn't going to be happening any time soon.

'Our objective should be damage limitation,' he said calmly. He looked down at his tea, which had just arrived, checked the knot on his tie yet again with long, elegant fingers and when he raised his head, his smile was a little wider, showing more teeth. Then he leaned towards Ellie and lowered his voice conspiratorially. The general effect was quite overwhelming. Purists might argue that the smile didn't quite reach his eyes but Ellie could feel herself being drawn into his gravitational pull. 'I appreciate that this might all seem very discombobulating but everything is going to be fine.'

'Is it?' she asked sceptically, because nothing seemed as if it was going to be fine. Unless . . . 'There's no way you can stop this? You can't make this all go away?'

'I have tried,' he said with a little shake of his head. 'I've had clients in similar situations so I know the ropes and I'm going to do everything I can to get you through this.' He took out his BlackBerry and peered at the screen. 'Does your mother know what's been going on?'

Ellie had momentarily allowed herself to feel buoyed up by David Gold's can-do attitude, but now she groaned and put her head in her hands. How was she going to break the news to Ari?

'You understand that it's vitally important that she doesn't talk to the press?' David Gold said firmly. 'Can you guarantee that?'

There was no need for him to act as if Ari was a loose-lipped loose cannon, when actually she'd never, ever spoken to the press. There had been times when no one could have blamed her for selling her story – for instance when Ellie's father was shifting millions of units and playing sell-out stadium tours and not paying maintenance despite the results of the DNA test he'd insisted on. 'I got the only thing I wanted from him, I don't want his money and I'm certainly not going to beg for it,' Ari would say, which was sweet and noble, but still, palimony would have been very welcome when she also refused to take money from Morry and Sadie, and the bailiffs were at the door, or Ellie needed new shoes and everyone else in her class was going to Brittany for a week to study the French in their natural habitat.

'My mother would never talk to the press,' Ellie said tightly. 'I'm offended you even think that she would.'

He put his hands up as if he was trying to ward off a swarm of angry wasps. 'I'm sure she wouldn't. I'm so sorry, I didn't mean to imply that, but what we all need to remember is that Olivia is the innocent victim in all this and, understandably, she's devastated.' He'd lowered his voice again as if he was letting Ellie in on a secret. 'That's why we have to work together to weather the coming storm.'

Ellie hadn't expected ever to see him again and never in several lifetimes could she have imagined that their connection would turn out to be more real than metaphysical; that he was her father's lawyer and he was being conciliatory and fairly considerate, which had to be a directive from her father. She wasn't on her own in this, although she was still about to be flung to the press. Her head was pounding with the effort to take it all in and try to ignore the painful prickling in her chest when he'd mentioned Olivia as if she was a close, personal friend of his and not just a glacially blonde woman in a newspaper photo.

'You'll be all right,' he told her softly. Ellie thought his voice might be the undoing of her. 'But you have to stay on message. Maintain a dignified silence. I'm sure you know the drill. Will you do that for us?'

Us? *Us?* Like she was on the same side as her father when there had always been an abyss between them. That simply didn't ring true for Ellie. 'I'm used to being more proactive.' Her voice was strained, as if all the air had been sucked out of her lungs. 'Maintaining a dignified silence sounds like a good idea but there has to be something more we can do.'

David Gold sucked in a breath. 'Miss Cohen . . . may I call you Velvet?'

'Nobody calls me Velvet. It's Ellie.'

'And you must call me David,' he urged her. He was being really nice – friendly, even. But at Glastonbury he'd been different. He'd grinned and joked and there'd been a sparkle in his eyes. Of course, he was in work mode now and, God, he was her father's lawyer so there was no way in hell that there could ever be anything between them, but Ellie wasn't sure she trusted David Gold's smiles. She actually shivered as if his ready smile was tempered with a cold, steely edge that froze everything in its path. 'So, Ellie, what did you mean when you said you wanted to deal with this proactively?'

'Well, I don't know,' she admitted. 'Couldn't we put out a statement that says . . . well . . . that we . . . that he . . .'

She faltered, then stopped altogether because much as

she preferred to be part of the solution rather than part of the problem, she had no brilliant plan. There was nothing to put in a statement that would pre-empt a tabloid story. Nothing to say about the non-existent relationship she had with her father that was going to give the *Sunday Chronicle*'s readers warm fuzzies over their tea and toast.

She slumped back in her seat. David Gold sipped his tea, then steepled his fingers. 'You have to trust that I know what's best for you,' he said smoothly, though Ellie rarely gave her trust to people she barely knew. 'So, I will continue to do what I can to smooth this over and you'll proceed with a say-nothing, do-nothing policy.'

'Do you even know how bad the story might be?' she demanded, pushing away her coffee because it would choke her. 'Can't we sue them?'

'On what grounds do you suggest we sue them? They have the DNA results, so we can't really sue them for slander.'

'But they were stolen,' Ellie reminded him, her voice rising perilously high so the two rapier-thin women on the next table, who had each spent the last half-hour picking their way around a pink grapefruit half, turned to stare at her. 'Every single scrap of so-called evidence they have was taken without my permission.'

'Well, it would be hard to prove that. Very hard.' He spread his hands wide, measured out another smile. 'Do you see what a tricky position we're in?'

'I'm just saying that there has to be something we can do,' Ellie said persistently. 'I don't want them printing lies about me or my mother.'

David Gold dipped his head in acknowledgement. 'No, neither do we.' He took a deep breath. 'It would really mean a lot to him if you were on board with this.'

Ellie stiffened. 'He said that?'

'I spoke to him last night. He's very . . . concerned about

116

you.' He was negotiating the words like a horse doing dressage. 'It's hard for him to reach out to you given the circumstances but he has your best interests at heart.'

Ellie had tried hard from a very early age not to entertain the idea that her dad might actually think about her, let alone care for her. Because it didn't matter how many gold stars she got at school or that she'd moved up a grade in gymnastics, he was never going to roll up on a Saturday morning and whisk her off for a matinée performance at Camden Odeon and a Happy Meal afterwards, like the absentee fathers of her friends.

Now as she sat there, under David Gold's pinstripe gaze, the walls that Ellie had put up were crumbling at the edges. For the first time, and using a suited, smiling emissary, her father was reaching out to her – but only because he wanted something. The resentment that she always tried to tamp down reared up and she would have loved to dash her father's hopes the way he'd dashed hers. Maybe, though, it was better to have him, and his undoubtedly expensive lawyer, on her side?

'OK,' Ellie said without much conviction. 'OK. Let's try it your way.'

'Good. I'm so glad we're all on the same page. Now, would it be possible for you to leave the country for a couple of weeks?' he asked, and Ellie was so blind-sided by the question that she found herself nodding. The nodding turned into a swift and violent shake of her head that almost gave her whiplash.

'No! No! That's impossible! I'm curating a really important exhibition, Emerging Scandinavian Artists,' she explained, because it would be nice if he reported back to her father that she was doing just fine without him. But then, as Ellie thought about the exhibition, which was less than a fortnight away and was in that fraught stage where half the pieces were in transit or languishing in Customs, and the catalogues still weren't back from the printers who'd totally screwed up the pagination on their first attempt, she realised that doing nothing might not work. 'My boss will be absolutely livid if my face gets splashed all over the papers . . . Look, could you not go to one of the broadsheets and get them to run something more sympathetic? Or why couldn't *he* grant the *Sunday Chronicle* an exclusive interview about his charity work or—'

'Absolutely not!' David Gold's smile slipped so all Ellie could see was the steel underneath. She flinched, and he must have realised that he was the one who'd gone off-message and also that there was only so much goodwill a girl could have to a deadbeat dad because he reached across the table, almost as if he was going to give her hand a comforting squeeze. Got as far as resting his hand on hers and, oh! That tug towards him, those tingles she'd felt at Glastonbury, increased, intensified so that Ellie expected to see blue sparks where skin met skin for that brief second before they both snatched their hands away.

Ellie folded her arms and stared stonily down at a splash of coffee on the tablecloth. No. No! No more what-might-have-beens. He was her father's lawyer, which meant he had a metaphoric ring fence, barbed wire and 'Danger! HazChem!' signs around him. On a very basic level, they might be sexually attracted to each other but not giving in to one's baser urges is what separates us from animals, Ellie told herself sternly.

David Gold had also put his hands to better use and was straightening his already ramrod straight tie again. He was also swallowing hard. 'I can only reiterate that in my considerable experience in this area, talking to the press is never a good idea,' he said, once he'd stopped swallowing. 'So, let's move forward, shall we?'

'Yes, but—'

'Good, then we're agreed.'

They weren't agreed as far as Ellie was concerned, and

there were still plenty of things that she wanted to say to David Gold. He still hadn't outlined his precise plan to get the *Sunday Chronicle* to possibly spike the story, but they were interrupted by a waiter who was ushering Ellie's next appointment to the table with much deference, as befitted an A-list WAG who was fake-tanned, had her platinum-blonde hair teased up into awe-inspiring gravity-defying splendour and, despite the fact she was five months pregnant, was poured into a bandage dress and teetering unsteadily in six-inch Christian Louboutins.

'Oh, Mandy, hi,' Ellie said weakly, as she stood up to greet Mandy Stretton, née McIntyre, WAG, spokesmodel, TV presenter, entrepreneur and owner of her own very profitable chain of express nail bars. She kissed Mandy in the vicinity of each cheek and tried to sound more enthusiastic. 'So great to see you! You look radiant. We were just finishing up here, weren't we?'

She turned to David Gold to perform an awkward intro-duction but he'd got up and was holding out his chair for Mandy to sit down, returning her smile with one of his own. This smile reached his eyes, made them crinkle up at the corners. It was much prettier than the smiles he'd directed at Ellie and made her pulse quicken.

Mandy wasn't immune either. She fluttered her eyelash extensions as he smiled down at her. 'I'm Mandy,' she said. 'I'm one of Ellie's clients. I was using another art dealer to find someone to paint my portrait while I'm preggers. Nude but classy, like that shot of Demi Moore on the cover of *Vanity Fair*, but he kept introducing me to painters who were, like, totes up themselves and wanted to do me all abstract with two noses or a transparent stomach . . .'

There was no point in trying to cut Mandy off once she started talking; Ellie would just have to wait it out and suffer a hundred agonies in the meantime.

'. . . Or else they'd get really snippy when I said that the background of the portrait had to be white. I can't re-decorate the lounge again, can I? Ellie totes got where I was coming from. So, are you having your portrait done too? You have excellent cheekbones. Not like my Daz,' she added fondly of her footballer husband, who might have scored a hat trick in the last England qualifier but was rather homely-looking.

'Oh, you're very kind but I don't think my cheekbones would stand up to that kind of scrutiny,' David said with a warmth that hadn't been in evidence earlier that morning. 'And I'm not very good at sitting still for long periods of time.'

Ellie realised Mandy was looking at her rather pointedly. 'Oh, sorry. Where are my manners?' She gestured jerkily at Mandy. 'Mandy, this is David Gold, he's um, a . . .'

'A business associate,' he interjected smoothly, taking Mandy's hand, and for one awful moment Ellie thought he was going to kiss it. He didn't, thank God. 'And of course, you don't need any introduction. Congratulations, by the way.'

Mandy giggled, then David Gold cracked a joke about lawyers taking a breakfast meeting with Satan that was actually quite funny and made Mandy giggle even harder. And it turned out one of his underlings represented one of Darren's team-mates, so he slipped Mandy a business card while Ellie sat there smiling tightly.

'I really must go,' he said at last as Mandy 'aw'ed her disappointment. He turned to Ellie. 'Please don't worry. I'll let you know if there are any new developments.'

Both women watched him walk away with a long-limbed stride. Ellie sighed in relief, then Mandy sighed too. 'There's just something about a man in a well-cut suit,' she said. 'He had a really firm handshake. Definitely a keeper, Ellie.'

'Definitely not my type,' Ellie stated flatly. 'Absolutely not.'

Mandy looked at her, aghast. 'But he's a lawyer! Whoever heard of a poor lawyer? OK, a lawyer isn't a Premier Division footballer but everyone has to start somewhere.'

Camden, London, 1986

It was only ever meant to be a short-lived affair in a summer-house in someone 's back garden.

When he wasn't in Camden with Ari, then Billy was in W11 with his wife. It made her feel sick with shame even to think about it, and it was good that she did think about it because Ari needed to remind herself what Billy Kay was really like.

When she was with him, even when he was inside her, he held back. Kept himself at a distance. His smile never reached his eyes. He always spoke lightly and playfully to her, but never deeply.

It made Ari try harder. Made her want Billy more. Made her long to be a warrior queen who could conquer his soul. Ari was sure that somehow she could say the right words, do the right thing, find a way to win his heart, because his wife bloody hadn't. Otherwise why would he be spending so much time with her?

Still, it wasn't wise to give Billy everything. He took and took and if Ari let him keep taking, there'd be nothing left of her, so she held herself back too. But Billy could sense every time that Ari tried to pull away from him. Every time. And he'd peel away her clothes, take down her hair and kiss her until she couldn't think straight.

He'd make love to her slowly and oh so sweetly, so differently from their usual frenzy and fury. Then he'd reach between them so he could press his thumb against her clit and stop.

'Tell me you love me,' he'd say, not even blinking as Ari scored her nails down his back in an effort to get him to keep moving because she was *so* close. 'Tell me, Ari!'

She'd shake her head and he'd thrust just hard enough to get her hopes up, then stop.

'Don't you love me, then?' he'd ask, his thumb teasing her clit briefly, and every time she'd fall apart and crumble.

'I do. I love you.' Ari would throw the words at him like they were stones, and she wanted to believe that they were just words she said so he'd start moving in her again and kiss her like he really meant it.

Sometimes 'I love you' was just a means to a beautiful end.

Chapter Nine

The funny thing was that when you were expecting the worst, sometimes the worst never materialised. When nothing happened, not even a tiny story tucked away on an inside page of the *Sunday Chronicle*, Ellie actually felt a little disappointed.

Probably disappointed wasn't the right word, but it was definitely an anticlimax after a week of worrying and angsting and having insomnia that not even an oxygen facial and huge amounts of Touche Veloutee could disguise.

After scouring all the Sunday papers and not finding a single mention of her name or the phrase 'secret lovechild', only a couple of pictures of her half-sisters stumbling out of a Mayfair nightclub after a few too many sherbets, Ellie knew the storm had passed.

She was camping out on their unofficial roof terrace, which could only be accessed by climbing out of the bathroom window and got rather whiffy with the scent of chargrilled meat when Theo had the restaurant's kitchen door open and the wind was blowing in the wrong direction. There'd been no wind, not even a stiff breeze, for weeks now and Ellie squinted up at the cloudless blue sky and decided to count her blessings, of which there were many.

For a start, she wasn't that Sunday's *cause célèbre*, and the silence from David Gold was deafening, so the story must have been killed. Maybe David Gold had used his charm and connections to call in some favours. Or maybe the editor of the *Sunday Chronicle* had decided that it was a non-story. After all, her father hadn't released any new material or organised any global charity concerts for the victims of child poverty lately. He wasn't exactly newsworthy, which meant that Ellie wasn't newsworthy either, which was good because she didn't have time to be newsworthy.

The Emerging Scandinavian Artists exhibition was now eight days away. The exhibits were mostly present and correct and all emerging Scandinavian artists had their travel itineraries, and their hotel bookings, confirmed. If the exhibition went well, then Ellie would earn a hefty commission. Maybe even enough that she could start flat-hunting soon.

Ellie stretched out her legs, which were tanned to a pale caramel colour and leaner, thanks to a week of being too stressed to eat more than trail mix and Greek yogurt, and gave a silent prayer of thanks because her life was pretty good.

Life would have been even better if she'd never had to warn her nearest (Vaughn) and her dearest (Ari and her grandparents) about her impending infamy.

'I have to tell you, Cohen, you're skating on very thin ice,' Vaughn had said after he'd listened to Ellie's ponderous explanation of the coming media apocalypse. 'If there are paparazzi camped outside and interfering with my business . . .' He'd tailed off with a meaningful look, his right eyebrow arched the way it always did when he was being a dick.

Breaking the news to her grandparents had been a cakewalk in comparison. There'd been a lot of recriminations about how it would never have happened if Ellie had been dating a nice Jewish boy, but they were completely down with the idea of maintaining a dignified silence, 'though if things get really bad, *bubbeleh*, then I'm sure the *Jewish Chronicle* would run a sympathetic piece'.

That had left only Ari, who'd said nothing, had barely blinked, while Ellie had filled her in on all the gory details. She'd poured herself a double measure of vodka, downed it in one, then smashed the shot glass she'd been drinking from. That was followed by two plates, and a shouty, sweary invective about the gutter press, the moral failings of anyone connected, however tenuously, with the Law Society, and Ellie's father's inability to man up.

'If he wanted to, he could stop this,' she'd raged, as Mrs Okeke from the flat above banged on her floor. 'But no! That would involve getting his hands dirty!' Ellie had been surprised that Ari had taken it as well as she had . . .

'What are you looking so chipper about?' said a voice, and Ellie turned to see Tess with her head stuck out of the bathroom window. Her friend glanced down at the newspapers. 'Oh shit! I was going to get up early and hold your hand while you went through them. Or is it not shit? Is that why you're smiling?'

'Bullet totally dodged,' Ellie said, holding up the *Sunday Chronicle* for Tess's inspection.

'Thank God,' Tess panted as she tried to manoeuvre herself through the sash window. It was a tricky procedure as the window only opened part-way and you had to fold your body in half while simultaneously trying to get both legs through the gap. 'Sod it! I can't do this when I'm wearing only a vest and a thong.'

'I'll come to you,' Ellie decided. 'I'm wearing bikini bottoms with full coverage.'

Ellie stood up and stretched, revelling in the heat of the sun and a distant but distinct wolf whistle from the four Australian guys across the road, who also had their own unofficial roof terrace.

'Does this mean you're going to start eating proper

meals again?' Tess asked. 'No one can survive on Greek yogurt and trail mix alone.'

'Too bloody right. I'm starving.' Ellie looked at her watch. It was just after eleven. 'If you start getting ready now, we could be having Sunday roast and cocktails at the York & Albany in just under an hour.'

Tess was already disappearing towards the bathroom before Ellie could get her legs through the gap in the window. 'Make it half an hour,' she threw over her shoulder. 'I'm starving too. I had sympathetic stress.'

Ellie sailed through the week on a wave of euphoria. She worked hard – the Scandinavian exhibition was the last big push before the art world's big hitters spent August in sunnier, beachier climes – but she was playing hard too.

She went to three exhibition pre-shows and after-show parties, attended a Jewish Cancer Care charity ball with Tanya, Emma and Laurel, schlepped all the way to New Cross for a Fuck Puppets gig and accepted an invite to Muffin's birthday drinks, which was at a chichi Chelsea bar full of braying posh people. Ellie didn't know what Muffin had been saying about her, but her friends kept telling Ellie that no one would ever guess she'd been 'to a state school with a load of poors. You don't look like a chav. You totes look like one of us.'

On Saturday night it was a relief to be back among her own people. Some of Ellie's old friends from Central St Martins were having a barbecue in the huge back garden of their shared house in Ealing and had hired the biggest paddling pool they could find in direct contravention of the hosepipe ban.

It was the perfect summer party. Ellie sat dangling her legs in the controversial paddling pool, drank far too many glasses of Pimm's and lemonade and got chatted up by a graphic designer who'd been in the year above her at college. Jacques was good-looking in a graphic designer-y way and listened attentively to what she had to say about the ratio of fruit to alcohol to lemonade in a perfect Pimm's cup. Ellie gave him her number and responded with determined enthusiasm to his suggestion that they meet up to go to an open-air screening of *Singing in the Rain*.

Now that everything was back to where it should be, Ellie could start searching for Mr Normal, and if normal meant hanging out with guys like Jacques and not utter lowlifes like Richey, or corporate, suity guys who smiled too much, then Ellie could see herself totally embracing normal.

'It's not like he's boring normal,' she told Lola and Tess as they caught the tube back to Camden where a friend of Tom's was hosting a special 'Girl From Ipanema'-themed night in a pub on the Chalk Farm Road. 'Like, he's called Jacques, not Jack. His mum's Swiss or something.'

'As long as he is normal,' Tess said. "I mean, he wants to take you to see a musical. Are you sure he's straight?'

'Don't be so homophobic.' Lola elbowed Tess sharply in the ribs. 'Going to see musicals isn't gay. It's ironic. Or is it post-ironic?'

'Maybe it's post-post-ironic and is back to being ironic again?' Ellie suggested, because she could never keep track of these things.

They argued about the difference between irony and post-irony all the way to Camden, then trooped up the escalators and down the High Street, grimly ignoring the hordes of beered-up men who'd apparently never seen three girls in short sundresses before.

Ellie was immensely relieved when they got to the pub on a road off Chalk Farm Road and she didn't have to listen to Tess and Lola argue about hipsters now they'd moved on from the difference between irony and post-irony.

She pulled open the door and took a step back as she was enveloped in a sticky, hot fug that smelled of stale beer and sweat. 'Yuck. Maybe it won't be so heaving upstairs. Let's go and find Ari.'

As Ellie reached the back of the pub, feet skidding over the wet floor, she bumped into Ari coming out of the back room where a cacophonous screech of guitars could be heard. She was with Tom, her face upturned as she said, 'Sometimes, I think there's been nothing truly new in music since 1968.'

'What about acid house?'

'That was a rip-off of sixties psychedelia with a Roland TB-303 Bass Line generator to give it the wobble sound. Like, the 13th Floor Elevators were—'

'Ari! Mum!'

Her mother beamed. 'Babycakes! Shall we go upstairs? This band are making my brain bleed.'

Upstairs Tom's friend Carl was playing a set heavy on the Tijuana Brass and there was room to dance.

They'd been there for about an hour when Tabitha arrived, though she didn't so much arrive as throw herself at Ellie. 'Sweetheart! My darling girl,' she cried and wrapped her arms around Ellie so tightly that she could hardly breathe. It wasn't usual behaviour from Tabitha, who reserved her occasional displays of affection for Tom and Aaron Barksdale, their Bedlington terrier. 'Oh, Ellie, I love you like you were my own and I have your back. Always.'

'Aw, I love you too.' Ellie hugged Tabitha in return. 'Are you very drunk, Tab?'

'No, you don't understand.' Tabitha shook her head. Usually she looked immaculate but her platinum blonde shampoo and set had wilted and her mascara was smudged like she'd been crying. 'I'm sorry to have to show you this.'

She thrust a newspaper at Ellie, which had become damp and pulpy from being clutched in Tabitha's sweaty grip. Ellie took it and as she unfurled it, the nagging doubts that had been at the back of her mind all week, like a mild toothache, returned. Then she was jolted so hard she almost fell off her heels.

On the front page of the *Sunday Chronicle* was a photo of herself taken three years earlier when she was a stone heavier (it was before she'd discovered superfood salads, five-day detoxes and toning trainers) on holiday in Ibiza. Ellie was posing in a red bikini, back arched, bum stuck out and holding aloft a strawberry daiquiri bigger than her head, and that wasn't even the worst thing.

Not even close.

The worst thing was the headline, writ large in 144 point Times Roman: **'SIR BILLY'S BASTARD DAUGHTER!'**

Chapter Ten

'Sweetie, what's the matter?' Ari asked sharply.

Ellie was incapable of speech. She shook her head and, as Ari's arms closed around her, she began to cry.

'Nothing is so bad that it's worth crying over,' Ari said. It was what she'd always told Ellie when she was crying over a skinned knee or panicking about her coursework. 'Everything can be fixed.'

'This can't be fixed,' Ellie sobbed, shoving the sodden newspaper at Ari. Tom had moved Ellie to a tiny anteroom behind the DJ booth, and sat her down on a flightcase. Tabitha had fetched a glass of water and Lola and Tess were watching anxiously, poised with wads of damp loo roll for when Ellie eventually stopped crying. 'I can't believe this. That headline . . . it's worse than anything I imagined.'

'I can't believe they'd use that word. Not on the front cover,' Ari said on an indrawn breath. 'That . . . that is low.'

'It's awful. I wondered . . . I thought if this did happen, I'd be able to deal with it, but I can't.' Ellie paused to take in several shuddering breaths. Every time she tried to stop crying, a fresh wave of tears burst forth. 'What are you doing?'

Ari was unfolding the soggy newspaper so Ellie was forced to look at the headline and the terrible, terrible picture, which had surely been lifted from her Facebook account. 'I have to see what other lies and bullshit they've come up with,' Ari snapped, trying to turn the damp pages. 'And it will be lies because . . . oh . . .'

Ari being angry was infinitely preferable to her going suddenly silent. A silent Ari was far more ominous. Ellie was in an agony of not knowing as Tess and Lola peered over Ari's shoulder and one look was all it took for Tess to burst into tears and Lola to turn even paler than normal and mutter, 'Oh God, shit just got real.'

Ellie hardly dared ask. 'What does it say about me? What?'

The three of them glanced at each other, then back at Ellie. 'You don't want to know,' Tess choked out. 'You really are better off not knowing.'

'But she has to know! She can't not know.' Lola looked at Ellie reproachfully. 'Why didn't you tell me that your real name was Velvet?'

'Because no one has called me Velvet since I was four.' Ellie held out a shaking hand. 'Give it to me.'

Ari started to pass over the paper, then abruptly retreated. 'No,' she said flatly. 'We're going home.'

'I have to see it, Mum.' Ellie made a swiping motion in the direction of the paper, as Ari side-stepped to avoid her. 'Give me the bloody paper!'

'You can look at it when we get home.' Ari was already stalking out of the tiny room. 'I know you're glaring at my back, but honestly, you'll thank me for this.'

Ari's flat was hot and stuffy and there weren't enough chairs for everyone, but Ellie was given the best seat in the house, an old barber's chair. Lola, Tess and Tabitha squeezed onto the pink Chesterfield, Ari perched on the arm and Tom hovered in the living-room doorway.

On the little occasional table in front of her, made from a repurposed Stooges album, was a mug of sweet tea, a tumbler filled almost to the brim with vodka and a packet of chocolate Hobnobs.

'Right, are you calm?' Ari asked.

'I'm perfectly calm,' Ellie managed to say, though her teeth were clenched so hard it felt as if she had lockjaw. 'Can I please have the paper?'

'OK, but we're all here for you if you—'

'Just give me the damn paper already!' Ellie reached forward and ripped a new, unsullied copy of the *Sunday Chronicle* out of Ari's arms.

She couldn't bear to look at the front cover again so she turned the page, and gasped.

'TRIPLE VELVET! MY 3-TIMES A NIGHT DRUG-FUELLED SEX SESSIONS WITH BILLY KAY'S SECRET LOVECHILD.'

It was so much worse than she could ever have believed possible.

She wasn't Ellie Cohen any more, but Velvet Underground, because that was the name on her birth certificate. First name: Velvet. Surname: Underground. In a fit of youthful rebellion and utter stupidity, Ari had changed her name by deed poll from Ariella Cohen to Ari Underground 'because it was the early eighties and I was obsessed with *White Light/White Heat* and it just seemed like a really punk rock thing to do and then I joined a band and I was in the *NME* and it stuck'.

Ellie wasn't an exhibition and sales manager at a prestigious Mayfair art gallery any more either, but

a star-struck gallery assistant making the tea for A-list clients like Mandy Stretton by day, but at night voluptuous Velvet, 26, turned into an insatiable sexpot who begged her boyfriend, music video director Richey Wallis, to make mad, passionate love to her.

'Velvet always wanted to have sex,' says Richey, his handsome face creased in a rueful grin. 'I'm a red-blooded bloke but even I couldn't keep up with her.'

As well as being obsessed with sex, Velvet, who was

raised by her benefit-claiming mother, Ari, on a notoriously rough council estate in Camden Town, London, was also obsessed with her famous father.

'It was all she could talk about. She had real daddy issues. Velvet loved to listen to her dad's music while we were in bed,' Richey remembers. 'She even used to perform a sexy striptease to his biggest hit, "It Felt Like A Kiss".

'I really loved Velvet but she was just using me for my music industry contacts. I took her to Glastonbury for our three-month anniversary but she abandoned me to blag her way backstage and chat up rap star Tone Jam. She thinks that by hooking up with people in the music biz, she'll get close to her dad.'

There was more. Much more. That she'd snorted lines of coke during one particularly tawdry sex session and begged Richey to invite a friend round for a threesome. The story was the perfect trifecta of sex, drugs and rock 'n' roll, except none of it was true.

Ari was portrayed as a hard-faced groupie-turned-single-mother who now lived in a luxurious Regent's Park flat paid for by taxpayers, and that Ellie's conception had been the result of 'a sordid encounter in a toilet in a grimy London club'. None of that was true, either.

But what if all those stories about the months in the summerhouse in the back garden of a playwright's house in Primrose Hill weren't true either? What if Ari and all her friends – Chester, Tom, Tabitha – had just invented that story to make Ellie feel better because nobody would ever amount to anything in life if they knew they'd been conceived in a toilet?

'It wasn't a one-off, was it?' she asked in a rusty voice. 'In a toilet?'

'No!' Ari, Tabitha and Tom snapped the word in unison. 'I swear! I swear on my life and Mum and Dad's lives,

134

and on my fucking Les Paul guitar, which I love almost as much as I love you, that there was no sex in a toilet ever,' Ari insisted, and Ellie had hardly ever seen her cry but her mother was perilously close to tears now. 'If you must know . . . well, I always thought, and the dates seemed to match up, that I got pregnant in Brighton, the first time we got together.' Ari swallowed hard and looked longingly at the vodka she'd poured out for Ellie. 'We were in a very nice flat in a square on the seafront. It was almost in Hove! You don't get much more respectable than Hove.'

Ellie subsided back in the barber's chair to read that

a source close to the Kay family said that Sir Billy has always been devoted to Olivia and his daughters. He regrets what happened with Ari Underground but he'd have to have been a saint to resist when Ari constantly threw herself at him. As far as he's concerned, it's all water under the bridge. He might have been a bad boy back in his younger days but Olivia is the only woman he's ever loved.

They'd reprinted the photo of Billy and Olivia from the cutting in her Dad box. The two of them looking at each other and smiling as if they were still madly in love after thirty years of marriage. By way of contrast, there was a picture of Ellie on the other side of the spread, captioned: 'She's a real wild child.' Or rather, it was a photograph of Ellie's bottom clad in ruffled panties as she was tipped over the shoulder of a burly rockabilly two weeks before at the Blitz-themed party she'd gone to in Shoreditch. God, they'd been following her round with their cameras for over a fortnight and she hadn't even noticed.

'What did I do to make Richey hate me so much?' Ellie asked. 'I dumped him and he deserved to be dumped, but why would he do this to me?'

'Anyone who knows you isn't going to believe a word of this,' Tabitha said, but she was wrong. There would be loads of people who'd be only too happy to believe every single lie captured for posterity by the *Sunday Chronicle*. Like her clients, who didn't know her that well because she tried to exude a cool professional demeanour around them, or Muffin, who not-so-secretly thought that she was poor white trash, or the surly barista who made her mid-morning flat white.

Then there were the people she didn't know, the countless faceless strangers reading about her antics and her so-called sex life, and looking at her breasts and her arse and judging her. Calling her a slut and a gold digger.

It was online too and once something was on the internet, it was there for ever. All these terrible lies would be instantly available whenever anyone entered Billy Kay's name into a search engine.

Ellie groped for the tumbler of vodka, picked it up with shaking fingers and gulped it down greedily like it was a glass of refreshing cold water. As soon as the vodka hit her stomach, it decided that it wanted out. She jackknifed off the chair, body-slammed into Tom, who was blocking her exit, and managed to get into Ari's minuscule bathroom and drop to her knees just in time.

She threw up and threw up and threw up. Each retch made her feel as if her ribcage was being turned inside out, and every time Ellie thought she was done another wave of nausea had her clutching the toilet seat even though there was nothing left inside her but bile, bitter and corrosive.

Then Ellie wasn't being sick any more but was still huddled over the toilet, crying and shaking until she felt a gentle hand on her back.

'Come on, my sweet girl,' Ari said softly as she coaxed Ellie upright. She pushed the damp strands of her daughter's hair back. 'Clean your teeth. You'll feel much better.'

It was going to take much, much more than a two-minute up and down and side to side with some Colgate to mend Ellie's broken soul, but it got the acid taste out of her mouth and she let Ari wipe her face with a piece of wet kitchen towel before she felt brave enough to go back into the lounge.

The others had beaten a tactful retreat, leaving mother and daughter alone. Ari tried to smile encouragingly as Ellie sat down in the barber's chair.

'It will all be fine, darling. This will all blow over.'

'No! No, it won't.' She was shouting and holding her hands out in front of her to push away Ari's platitudes. 'There is no way to make this better. Nothing is ever going to get better now. My life is ruined. My life is over.'

It sounded like such a melodramatic thing to say that for a moment Ellie wondered if she was overreacting. But if anything, she was underreacting because after tonight she was a joke. There was no way anyone would ever take her seriously as an ambitious junior art dealer now. Ellie was pretty much unemployable unless she wanted a career as a D-list celebrity who got paid to pose for pictures in her pants with her hands cupping her breasts. And every man she ever met from now on was going to think that she was a coke-addled nympho who'd give it up for some column inches or a backstage pass.

'Ellie. Honey. Babycakes, we'll sort this out,' Ari said desperately. 'It's not as bad as you think it is.'

'I can't even conceive how bad this is,' Ellie said, because she'd managed to think about how it would affect her job and the cruel joke that was her love life, but when she tried to delve deeper to analyse how she felt about her life being pulled apart and ripped wide open, and the fact that the one person who might have been able to stop it hadn't even bothered to lift a finger to help, to make a call, then Ellie got really scared, as if that part of her mind was strewn with land mines that would explode if she didn't watch her step.

She couldn't even tell Ari, because Ari would rant about Billy Kay and what a waste of space he was, and this wasn't about Ari and Billy. It was about Billy and Ellie – father and daughter – and that was something that she could never bear to think about.

Camden, London, 1986

It was nothing that Ari could put her finger on to hold it down and examine it at close range, but something important had changed between her and Billy.

Billy never mentioned Olivia and his kid and Ari certainly wasn't going to, but she thought that maybe he might have left them because he seemed to be living in the summerhouse permanently.

That didn't mean that Billy was in love with her – and Ari was trying so hard not to be in love with him – but maybe he was missing her when she wasn't around. If she was working at the Lizard Lounge, he'd call and ask her to come over when she was finished. 'Just to hang out,' he'd say. 'You don't even have to take your clothes off, though I love it when you do.'

Ari didn't always obey when she was summoned. But when she did make the trek down the Chalk Farm Road, Billy was never alone.

It wasn't like he had friends. Not like Ari had Tabitha and Tom, who were her sister and brother in a way that not even her real sisters and brothers were. Billy had an entourage of dead-eyed, cold-blooded satellites all orbiting around his sun. They looked down on Ari because she was competition and she looked tarty with her heavy make-up and spike heels, and because her parents had earned their money and their big house in Belsize Park rather than inheriting it.

They'd lounge around the playwright's garden on warm June nights and Ari would sit on a wall, smoke her Marlboro Lights and pretend that she wasn't bored shitless. The only people who spoke to her were Jimmy Vaughn, who was sweet when he wasn't wasted, though he was wasted all the time, and Georgina Pratt, who'd been a superfan of Billy's previous band but was too fat and ungainly to be a groupie.

And this was how Billy Kay reeled her in, because time alone with Billy was such a rare commodity, such a thing to be treasured, that when he did kick everyone out and only Ari was left, inevitably she'd go down on her knees for him.

Chapter Eleven

She was woken by the doorbell ringing. Or she might have been woken by the thumping on the door and the rapping at the window that accompanied the sounds of the bell, Ellie wasn't sure.

Her head felt twice as large as normal and her ribs and throat ached and for a moment she wondered how much she'd had to drink last night. It was a lovely moment. All she had to worry about was how bad her hangover was. Then she remembered why she'd really been sick and the events of last night came rushing back all at once in a horrible 3D cavalcade that didn't skimp on any of the details.

Now she remembered crying for so long and so hard that eventually Ari had forced her to take a sleeping tablet. Ellie had curled up on Ari's bed, still sobbing and hiccuping, and Ari had stroked her hair and held her until she'd fallen asleep.

Ellie kicked off the covers because she was sweaty and hot and lay there until the constant banging on the door and the ringing of the bell and the trilling of a mobile phone forced her to abandon her plan to spend the rest of her life holed up in Ari's bedroom.

Still wearing the bikini that she'd put on under her dress yesterday for the barbecue, Ellie staggered out into the hall and ran head first into Ari.

'What are you doing?' her mother hissed, shooing Ellie

back towards the bedroom with frantic flapping motions. 'Get back in there.'

'I need to pee and I need some water.' Ellie refused to budge an inch. 'Why are you whispering? Who's at the door?'

Ari rolled her eyes. 'Photographers, reporters and a couple of film crews.'

'Oh God.' Ellie leaned heavily against the wall. 'I really didn't think things could get any worse.'

'What can I tell you?' Ari shrugged. The banging started again and she was forced to raise her voice. 'They kept shoving notes through the door till I wadded up the letter box. The *Sun* is ahead with an offer of a hundred grand if you'll go topless.'

Ellie didn't need to think about it. 'Not even if they were offering a million.'

Ari patted her shoulder. 'That's my girl,' she said, over the cacophony of someone leaning on the doorbell. 'Sadie phoned. She says she and Morry love you and they don't believe a single word, but this is what happens when you date outside your faith. And all your aunties have been on the phone, pledging support and wanting to come round with crumb cake and flowers. All except your aunt Carol, who blames me for raising a child without a strong male role model.'

'Did she really say that?' Ellie asked, hurt throbbing in her voice, though Aunt Carol, Louis's mother, had never liked her.

'Well, yeah, but that's Carol for you,' Ari said. 'So what are we going to do, kid?'

Ellie shook her head. 'You know that usually, when something bad happens, I try and take some control of the situation so I don't feel completely helpless, but this . . . this is beyond anything I can control.'

Ari's smile was wan as she brushed her fingers down Ellie's cheek. 'Have a shower. At least you'll feel fresher.'

Half an hour later, Ellie was peed, showered and wearing the least outrageous outfit she could find in Ari's wardrobe: an old denim mini skirt and a faded Pixies T-shirt. The kitchen was out of bounds as the window looked out onto the walkway where most of the world's press were congregated and Ari had never got round to fixing her broken blind. Her mother had already had a very tense conversation with Alf from next door, both of them leaning out of their bedroom windows on the other side of the block, because he couldn't get out to go to William Hill and place a bet on the three thirty at Kemptown.

'Maybe I should just go home?' Ellie suggested, as she and Ari camped out in the living room and shared the last of the chocolate Hobnobs. 'I could put my head down and run for it.'

'You can't. Tess texted me while you were still asleep. It's even worse outside your place.' Ari shook her head. 'They might get bored in a bit. I hope so, we've only got enough milk left to share one mug of tea.'

They were sitting on the floor, curtains closed as, like the kitchen, the windows looked out onto the communal walkway. The assault on the front door had stopped, but occasionally someone would tap on the window and Ellie would jump and her stomach would lurch. Though it was yet another sweltering day and the flat was now hermetically sealed, she felt cold and clammy.

'I'm sorry about this, Mum.'

Ellie might have had a good eight hours' sleep thanks to a Percocet, but her mother had purple shadows under her eyes and, for once, looked every single one of her forty-eight years. She still had the energy to give Ellie her sternest look.

'You have nothing to be sorry about!' she reiterated. 'This is all my fault. I should never have introduced you to Richey.'

'You didn't force me to go out with him,' Ellie pointed out. 'That was my choice.'

Ari crawled across the living-room floor so she could put her arm round Ellie's shoulders. 'Look, I wish I could say that I was sorry that I ever met Billy Kay but I'm not, because without Billy, there wouldn't be you and I've kind of got used to having you around now . . .'

'Thanks. You're not so bad yourself.' It didn't even have a quarter of the snark of their usual tender exchanges but it was familiar ground on a day when nothing felt familiar. It was the two of them styling it out as they'd both done countless times before. 'And anyway, you can't help who you fall in love with, can you?'

'You really can't, even when you try extra hard to stop. I did love him back then, Ellie. As much as I was capable of loving anyone.' Ari hadn't spoken about back then in ages, and never with so much conviction. At any other time, Ellie would have pressed on Ari's weak spot and started asking questions but, right then, she didn't want to know; wasn't sure she could handle the truth. And as if she was embarrassed about revealing that much, Ari turned her head to stare at her hula girls above the mantelpiece. 'You will get through this, honey. I know it might seem like everything's gone to shit but you'll come back from this.'

Ellie knew that she should chime in on the chorus but she didn't have Ari's faith. They sat there in a silence punctuated only by the baying of the mob outside.

Ari nudged Ellie. 'They'll probably go once it starts getting dark.'

'That's hours from now!'

'Well, maybe I could—'

Ari was interrupted by Ellie's phone ringing. It had been silent up until now, as if her loved ones didn't quite know what to say to her and her not-so-loved ones had decided that twenty-four hours was industry standard before they called to offer insincere commiserations.

'Hello?' Ellie said without much enthusiasm.

'Hi. Sam Curtis here from the *Sunday Chronicle*,' oozed

the voice at the other end. 'How the devil are you?'

'Christ! You've got a real nerve calling me. How have you managed to not die of shame?' She pointed at the phone and pulled an agonised face at Ari, who widened her eyes, stiffened her spine and looked a lot like Porky, their late cat, whenever she'd spotted an insect. 'Have you any idea what you've done?'

'Look, Ellie, you're a big girl. You know how these things work,' Sam Curtis said, as if the complete destruction of her life was not that much of a deal. 'The public have a right to know the truth.'

'Excuse me? The truth? The truth in your story would only be visible under a microscope,' she growled at him. 'Seriously, how do you sleep at night?'

'Pretty well, thanks.' He chuckled. 'Now that we've got the social niceties out of the way, how would you feel about sitting down with me for a proper chat?'

Her anger rolled over Sam Curtis like he was coated in something non-stick. Maybe it would be a better idea to establish some kind of rapport.

'Let me think. Hmm, I'd rather open my veins with a razor in a warm bath,' Ellie said, and it was obvious she was joking so there was no need for Ari to try to snatch the phone away.

'Can I quote you on that?' Sam Curtis asked.

Oh, shit! 'No! Please don't quote me,' Ellie begged. 'Come on, have a heart.'

'It's time to get a clue, darling. The story's published; it's been picked up by all the other rags and here's what's going to happen. I take it that the charming Richey wasn't the first bloke you've had sex with, right?'

'What?' Ellie spluttered. 'How—'

'Yeah, yeah. How very dare me.' Ellie could tell he was getting a kick out of her anger and confusion, but still she couldn't hang up. Not until she knew how bad it was, even though it was currently very, very, very bad. It might even have upgraded to full-on catastrophic. 'Even as we're exchanging pleasantries, every guy you've ever shagged, even a few you haven't, are phoning up my colleagues on other papers to trade their stories of your fun sexy times for cold, hard cash. The going rate must be about ten grand right now. Probably more once your half-sisters, lovely Lara and Rose, put the boot in and do a photoshoot with their tits falling out of their dresses.'

'How do you even know this?'

'Because this is how it always plays out,' he told Ellie pityingly, as if he couldn't quite believe how naïve she was. 'Everyone has a part to play. How much is it going to take for you to start playing yours? I can tell you're not going to get your kit off so I won't waste time asking, but I could still go to twenty-five grand for an interview and photoshoot. Thirty if you show some skin. Nothing skeevy.'

'What's he said now?' Ari demanded. 'Why are you looking like that?'

She was looking like that – as if she'd suffered a swift and painful blow to her head – because thirty grand was a lot of money. It was a hell of a lot of money for one day's work and she wouldn't even have to suck up to some insufferable oligarch's wife or fill in Customs forms or deal with some uppity artist banging on about how she was stifling his creativity. It would be enough for a deposit on her very own place and put a sizeable dent into what remained of Ari's mortgage, and what the hell? She could even buy a Mulberry bag without asking friends and relatives for Selfridges vouchers for her birthday, Chanukah and Christmas presents.

And it was more – thirty grand more, to be precise – than she'd ever been given by Billy Kay, who'd never even stuck a fiver in a birthday card. Never given her a passing thought but had thrown her and Ari away like they meant nothing, like they weren't important. Ellie wondered just how important she'd become to Billy Kay if she shared that charming side of him with Sam Curtis's readers?

'So, Ellie, what do you reckon? I could have you in a car in half an hour, and what about we put you up in a fancy hotel until all the fuss has died down?'

Ellie was snapped back from her revenge fantasies into the present, where someone had started leaning on the doorbell again and Ari was talking on her mobile to Mrs Okeke from the flat above.

'Really sorry about this, Mary,' she was saying. 'No idea how long they're going to be there, but I hope it won't be all day because we're down to half a packet of rice cakes . . . No, not even the salt and vinegar ones, the regular ones . . .'

Thirty grand wasn't going to make Ellie feel better and it certainly wasn't going to make this go away. Besides, it was her story and she decided who she was going to share it with. God, she hadn't even told Tess until they'd known each other for seven years and had got drunk together at least six times. There was absolutely no way she would share her story with the *Chronicle* – not out of loyalty to Billy Kay but because she was better than that.

'No,' she said firmly. 'I'm not that kind of person.'

'Thirty-five grand. That's my final offer.'

'You don't get it,' Ellie said, and she was pleased that she sounded sure of herself now. Her whole life, everything she'd worked so hard to achieve, was slipping through her fingers but at least she still had her integrity. You couldn't put a price on integrity. 'My story's not for sale. I'm not for sale.'

'Everyone's for sale. Two more days of this and you'll be begging me for a little face time.' Sam Curtis managed to choke out a chuckle. 'You think this is bad? Honey, you don't know what bad really is.'

*

There were no photographers outside at five the next morning, just a mound of cigarette butts, crushed Styrofoam coffee cups and sandwich wrappers that Ellie had to step over when she opened Ari's front door.

Still, she held her breath as she reached the end of the walkway in case anyone was lurking in the stairwell, but it was empty and Ellie was able to step out onto the street and walk the five minutes to Delancey Street undetected.

The first thing Ellie did when she got back to her flat, which thankfully was not being blockaded by members of the fourth estate, was to start packing everything she might possibly need for the coming week. If Sam Curtis was right and Ellie's lame ducks went quacking to the papers, and Billy's celebutante daughters, Lara and Rose, fame-whored their way on to the front pages when usually they could only get a page-five lead, then Ellie could never go home again. Ari's place was out of bounds too. She might be able to stay with Sadie and Morry if they weren't besieged, or Chester, or even Chester's parents in Romford, but the commute would be a bitch and the practical solution was to book into a hotel.

Everything would be neat, organised and controlled in a hotel. Nothing would happen without Ellie's say-so, whether it was room service or turn-down.

Today she had to put her gameface on and pretend it was business as usual. She'd spent months working on the Emerging Scandinavian Artists exhibition and she wasn't going to let that suffer – not that Vaughn would regard her new notoriety as a good enough excuse for fucking up. Everyone else (but mostly Muffin) would be scrutinising everything Ellie said and did for an indication that she was falling apart. Whereas, her grandparents, Ari and Chester would expect Ellie to soldier on, and that was what she was going to do – until approximately ten thirty tonight. Then she could check into a hotel and simply be herself. She could cry. She could comfort-eat her way through all the chocolate and pretzels in the mini bar. She could even chew the carpet if that was what she needed to do to get through this, but she needed to keep it together for today. Just one day. She could manage that.

Ellie wrote a note to Tess and Lola to say that she'd see them at the exhibition that evening. Then, at six, she left the flat while the going was still good.

Anyone else with a wheeled suitcase, large holdall, small holdall, laptop bag, tote bag and handbag would have taken a taxi, but the heat wouldn't reach stifling for at least another two hours, she'd eaten most of a packet of chocolate Hobnobs the day before, and Ellie did all her best thinking during her morning walk through Regent's Park.

It was actually a relief to start panicking about all of the items on her gigantic to-do list and whether it had been such a good idea to ask the caterers to provide a pickled herring canapé. These were problems that had solutions as opposed to her other problems, and as Ellie fought hard to get into work mode, she did begin to feel a tiny bit better.

She forced herself to smile brightly at the baristas, who all nudged each other and whispered when she popped in to get her morning coffee. Then she went to the newsagent and had a perfectly pleasant conversation about the weather, just as she did every morning when she collected the newspapers on her way in.

See? You'll get through this, Ellie told herself, as she entered Thirlestone Mews. It's not going to kill you. It's going to make you stronger.

She had to hold that thought and throw herself and her luggage against the railings as she was almost mown down by a white van that came screeching round the corner; the driver slamming on the brakes just a fraction of a second in time.

Ellie gingerly rotated her shoulder then dusted down her pale blue poplin dress.

'You all right, love?' asked a voice from the driver's side window.

'I would be if you kept to the speed limit!' Ellie tried to attach her large holdall to her suitcase again – they'd become separated in the mêlée. 'You nearly ran me over!'

'Fuck me! It's her,' the driver said, and he didn't sound the least bit repentant, probably because he was jumping out of the van, a camera in his hand. The door slammed on the other side and another man hit the ground running. 'Velvet! Love! Just one picture.'

'Oh, no!' It was very hard to run over cobblestones with her heavy load in shoes with wobble-board technology built into their soles, especially when she was being pursued by a man who kept yelling, 'Can we go some-where quiet to talk?'

When she reached the gallery, Ellie was so spooked that she couldn't remember the door code. It took three attempts, with a camera shoved into her face and two men trying to physically bar her way as they offered her twenty thousand pounds for exclusive rights to her story.

Ellie didn't say a word, but her face got redder and redder as her sweaty fingers slid over the keypad. She didn't even dare swear under her breath and in the two minutes that it took to finally get the door open, more reporters and photographers appeared.

'Come on, Velvet. Crack a smile!'

'One picture! And if you show a bit of leg, we're golden here.'

'Have you spoken to Sir Billy? What did he say?'

'Any comment on what Lara and Rose said in the *Sun*?'

Ellie was pushed further and further back from the door because they were tugging at her dress, even pulling on her bag and suitcase as they shouted. Ellie could feel spittle on her face from a man who was pressed right up against her as he bellowed sweet nothings into her ear about how much his paper was prepared to pay for the rights to her innermost secrets.

It was a lot like being in a whirlwind: nowhere to hide or run, completely exposed to the elements, the click and whirr of cameras snapping at her and a sea of red faces all shouting at her as Ellie was pushed and jostled and shoved further and further away from the door.

In the end she had to fight her way through them to regain her ground. She used elbows and even kicked someone in the shin when he stuck a leg out to stop her.

At last she succeeded in covering the half-metre that placed her back in front of the door and got it open, even managed to get her many bags over the threshold, but shutting the door proved impossible as there were too many people intent on getting into the gallery with her. 'No comment! No comment,' she kept bleating, and with each 'no comment' she succeeded in closing the door another centimetre, until finally the last photographer had to remove the foot he had wedged in the doorway or lose it for ever.

'Oh God, oh God, oh God,' Ellie muttered under her breath. She did a complete circuit of the reception area, trailing her suitcase behind her. She was still holding her coffee cup and dimly recalled one of the press pack kindly offering to hold it for her while she tried to open the door. 'Oh fuck.'

Now they were ringing the buzzer and banging on the door as if Ellie might have changed her mind in the last two minutes and had decided that yes, she did want to sell her soul and the rights to some tasteful bikini shots to the highest bidder.

Suddenly all the items on Ellie's to-do list didn't seem that doable when she couldn't even let go of her suitcase handle. So much for only worrying about the things she could control.

Ellie prised her fingers free and rubbed the welts on her

palm as she wandered aimlessly through the gallery. There were three blank spaces on the wall waiting for emerging Scandinavian art to be hung, two bulbs missing from a light installation, and someone was arriving later this morning to assemble a Perspex sculpture, which was currently in pieces all over the floor, but how could Ellie think about emerging Scandinavian art at a time like this?

She walked back into the foyer, picked up the wad of newspapers and hunted in the reception desk drawers for the scissors. As she cut through the string that bound both tabloids and broadsheets together, Ellie felt as if she was picking at a scab that should have been left to heal but after yesterday's very nadir of badness, she had to know if the bad had increased exponentially overnight.

The huge picture of Billy Kay and his wife on the front page of the *Daily Mail* with the headline, BUSINESS AS USUAL FOR SIR BILLY didn't even hurt that much. Ellie turned to page five so she could read about how Billy and the Honourable Olivia were on holiday in Napa Valley, California and even

> the reappearance of an illegitimate daughter, the product of a misguided one-night stand with a groupie over twenty-five years ago, couldn't put a damper on Sir Billy and Lady Kay's vacation. The couple were all smiles as they lunched with friends at the French Laundry. A source close to Sir Billy said, 'It's common knowledge that Billy used to have a roving eye, but that's all ancient history. He and Olivia are such a solid unit.'

Ellie hated this revision of the past; that this supposed one-night stand was being sewn into Billy's history as if it were unassailable fact rather than complete fabrication, but it still didn't come close to the sordid lies Richey had spewed about their sex life. That was something, at least. Just call her Miss Glass Half-Full.

As she read on, Ellie started to feel a little less adrift. It wasn't just her. Billy Kay was being papped too. He was having cameras and microphones shoved in his face, and so was she. For once, they were in this together. They had something tangible in common, not just a few strands of DNA.

Ellie was realistic. There was no way she could be anything else. Billy Kay didn't think about her that much, if he thought about her at all, but she would bet all the money in her internet saver account that she was all he could think about right now. They'd be angry thoughts at first because an illegitimate daughter, especially one with such an allegedly colourful sex life, wasn't the right image for Sir Billy, godfather of cool, national treasure, silver fox, etc., etc. But then the thoughts might get kinder, warmer and more along the lines of, 'I can't believe she's twenty-six already,' and, 'She looks like Ari, but maybe she looks a little like me too, around the eyes.' There was even the very remote possibility that when he got home from Napa, he'd decide that it was about time that he got in touch with Ellie and she might even agree to meet him for a coffee.

She was getting way ahead of herself. Probably he'd just call her to make sure she was all right, Ellie thought, as she skimmed the newsprint and tried to find the bit where Billy talked about her. What a headspin! The first time that he talked about her, about their relationship, would be in a national newspaper:

. . . as Billy and Olivia left the restaurant after a long and leisurely lunch, they smiled for the photographers but refused to answer any questions about the secret addition to the Kay clan. 'I don't care to comment,' said Sir Billy.

'No comment' was one thing, especially as they were meant to be maintaining a dignified silence, but 'I don't care to comment' was callous and cruel. Like Ellie wasn't even worth the effort it would take to think up a suitable comment. Like Ellie was something he didn't want to think about. Like Ellie was nothing to him and would never be anything else.

She pushed the *Daily Mail* away with a shaking hand and was surprised by the angry prickle of tears. As long as she could remember, Ellie had never once cried over Billy Kay and she wasn't going to start now. She rubbed her eyes with an impatient hand, but it took several moments of swallowing hard, blowing her nose and getting up to splash her face with cold water before she felt like she'd banished the threat of angry tears and was able to reach for the *Sun*, though why she was continuing to torture herself like this, she didn't know.

'"SHE'S A GOLD-DIGGING LITTLE TRAMP!" LARA AND ROSE KAY OPEN UP ABOUT THEIR LONG-LOST HALF-SISTER.'

Eyes so wide it hurt, Ellie began to read the interview with Lara and Rose, who were 'devastated' about their new sister but not so devastated that they'd turned down the chance to be photographed in their bras and pants as they'd just been signed as spokesmodels for a lingerie brand.

'I don't care what she says,' sobbed Rose while comforted by older sis, Lara. 'That DNA test is completely fake and she's not our sister. She's just some horrible wannabe who's been hounding our family for years.'

'It makes me sick that this girl and her mother are trying to hurt my dad,' added Lara, the sexy model and singer who recently broke off her engagement to footballer Kai Houston after he cheated on her with glamour model Chanelle Scott. 'It's obvious that we're not related. She doesn't look anything like either of us and Sir Billy would never call a child of his something as tacky as Velvet.'

It was an impressive feat to move from dread to panic to woe-is-me, then to absolutely incandescent with rage in

154

the thirty seconds it took to read the first couple of paragraphs of the story. *Tacky?* She wasn't the one airing her personal business and appearing in her bra and pants in a newspaper.

Ellie ripped the newspaper in two, right across the photo of her two half-sisters' stupid, sad-eyed, trout-pouted photo. And again, and again, and again, until there was a pile of black-and-white confetti on the desk in front of her. She really wanted to throw it onto the floor and jump up and down on it, but contented herself with sweeping it into the wastepaper basket, then stomping up to her office to get away from the press pack outside. It was just as well there were railings between the gallery windows and the pavement, otherwise Ellie was sure that they'd have their faces and camera pressed up against the glass and leave greasy smears all over it.

She left her luggage in a neat little pile by her office door and, with a heavy heart, reached for her phone.

There'd been no point in trying to call him up until now, because she had only his office number. Of course, he had her mobile number and he could have called her at any time during the last week to warn her that a bomb was about to blow up in her face, but she'd heard zip from him. Now, according to the receptionist at Wyndham, Pryce and Lewis, David Gold didn't usually start work until eight thirty. Well, wasn't that just lovely for him?

David Gold finally called at five minutes to nine, as Ellie was racing back down the stairs to fish a document out of the printer in the back office because hers was out of toner. She also needed to do something with the switchboard, because all five lines were ringing at once, and it was unlikely that any of the calls were about emerging Scandinavian artists. Consequently, her blood was well and truly up and likely to stay there for quite some time.

'David Gold, here,' he said, when she answered her mobile. 'I got your messages.'

Ellie couldn't speak at first because speaking was very difficult when she was almost crying again, from sheer frustration this time, and thumping a printer that was refusing to print. 'Have you seen the papers?' She had to force the words out. 'I thought we were all maintaining a dignified silence, or did you not circulate the memo to those girls?'

'I understand that you're very upset and all I can do is offer my apologies. As far as I knew, there were no immediate plans to run the story . . .'

Ellie realised that she'd wanted him to be on the defensive, to get snippy with her so she'd have a worthwhile target for her rage, but it was hard to shout at someone who was purring platitudes at her. 'I didn't come down with the last rain shower, you know,' she said, quoting one of Sadie's favourite expressions. 'Those girls had enough foresight to get a spokesmodel gig and organise a photoshoot. That kind of synergy takes time and forward planning.'

'Obviously there's been a communication breakdown at our end. Honestly, I can't tell you how sorry I am.' David Gold's sincere voice wrapped round Ellie like a cashmere blanket, but she immediately shrugged it off because what he said and how he said it made no different to the awful things that had already been said by his clients *about her* in the papers. 'I'll endeavour to ensure that everyone's on message from hereon out. Heads will roll if necessary.'

'You said that you'd try to stop the *Sunday Chronicle* printing the story,' Ellie reminded him accusingly. 'When there was nothing printed last weekend, I thought it was going to be all right and now I've been labelled as some sex-addicted, Daddy-obsessed tart – which I'm not, by the way . . . I'm not any of those things – then to have all those quotes from friends of the Kay family saying that I was a result of a one-night stand and that my mum was some two-bit groupie . . . Have you any idea how I feel right now? Have you? Well, have you?'

She was ranting. She bit down on the inside of her cheeks so she'd shut up. There was a pause. Probably so David Gold could count to ten.

'Velvet—'

'Ellie! My name is Ellie!'

'Ellie, I can't even begin to imagine what you've gone through in the last twenty-four hours but we need to stay focused here . . .'

'This is hell.' Ellie was pleading with him now. 'My flat is surrounded, my mum's place is too, they're outside my office right now. The door keeps buzzing and banging, the phones are going mad and it needs to stop. Right now.'

'You're not going to like what I have to say, but I've had many clients who've found themselves in similar situations and I can assure you that these things, if left alone, die a natural death,' David Gold said, as though Ellie was talking about a mild head cold. 'It's not pleasant and I really wish there was some way that I could make it stop, but all we can do at this point is damage limitation. Now, it's absolutely imperative that you don't talk to the press.'

'It's not like I haven't had huge sums of money offered to me but I wouldn't do that because I value my integrity and my career, unlike . . .'

With a timing that verged on sublime, the front door opened a crack and a red-faced, pinched-looking Vaughn eased himself through the gap.

'I have to go now,' Ellie said to David Gold, who was still offering apologies like they'd been on special offer last time he went shopping. Those fifteen golden minutes they'd shared at Glastonbury were now a hazy memory – something that had happened in another lifetime.

'. . . so the best thing would be for you to come to our offices this afternoon so we can have a chat. Make sure we're all up to speed.'

'I can't go anywhere,' Ellie said quickly as Vaughn glared

157

malevolently at her. 'I'm under siege and tonight is the launch of the biggest exhibition I've ever curated.'

David Gold started to say something, but Vaughn reached across the reception desk, took the BlackBerry away from a gaping Ellie and turned it off. 'Do you want to know why I've let you stick around for as long as you have, Cohen?' he asked conversationally, as he perched on the edge of the reception desk. Not that he looked relaxed. He was so tight-lipped Ellie was amazed he could still form words. She also knew that Vaughn wasn't expecting an answer from her, because this was obviously just the opening salvo in a massive bollocking, and if she answered back the bollocking would spiral out of control, so she shrugged helplessly.

Vaughn folded his arms. 'The reason why you've lasted longer than most of your erstwhile colleagues is because you don't do drama. I don't like drama. I get enough drama at home. My wife could teach the RSC a few things about drama.'

Ellie sighed because she didn't need this. Not today. Not this morning. Not now. For someone who claimed that he didn't do drama, Vaughn was one of the biggest drama queens she knew.

'This is not acceptable.' Vaughn gestured at the front door. The letter box was open and someone was bellowing, 'The photos would be classy like, no nips or fluff,' through it. 'To have this circus outside *my* gallery, because of you . . .'

'I'm sorry, but it's not my—'

'No!' Vaughn cut right through her explanation with a clipped syllable and his hand slicing through the air. 'It's untenable. You're fired, effective immediately.'

Chapter Twelve

Ellie stared at him in disbelief.

He'd threatened to fire her many, many times before, but this didn't sound like a threat. It sounded like a fact.

'Vaughn, please,' Ellie tried to sound light-hearted as if it was a big joke. 'Way to kick a girl when she's down.'

'I'm not unsympathetic, but this is affecting *my* business,' Vaughn stated implacably, as if he wasn't going to have a change of heart after lunch like he usually did. 'Obviously, I'll give you a good reference but I need you packed up and out of here before the rest of the staff fight their way through the pack of vultures outside. That would be best. You know how I feel about fuss.'

He felt the same way about fuss as he did about drama. Ellie hadn't expected Vaughn to cut her much slack, but she'd expected a *little* slack. She knew that nothing was ever allowed to interfere with Vaughn's bottom line, but sacking her and wanting her off the premises immediately was cruel, unreasonable and simply not going to happen.

Vaughn thought Ellie's shocked silence was sullen acceptance. 'There must be some cardboard boxes in the packing room and you can leave by the fire escape. I'll even help you,' he added magnanimously, which was maybe the nicest thing he'd ever said to Ellie.

'No! I'm not going anywhere. You have no grounds to fire me,' Ellie said, hands on her hips. 'It's unfair dismissal.'

'I'll spare you the small print, but a cursory look at your contract should tell you that I can do what I want.'

'And a cursory look at my contract will tell you that I have a three-month notice period,' Ellie reminded him waspishly and his eyebrows rose, because he'd obviously expected her to go down without a fight. Well, she was sick to death of people thinking that they could do what they liked with everything she held precious. 'I've spent nearly a year working on the Emerging Scandinavian Artists exhibition and I am seeing it through to the end whether you like it or not.'

Vaughn didn't say anything. Ellie wondered whether she'd robbed him of the power of speech. Then he flared his nostrils. 'Inge or Alexandra can handle that.'

Ellie put her hands on her hips again. 'They absolutely can't! Do you really feel confident handing over responsibility of the exhibition to them? There are still a hundred and one very important things that need to be done, and this exhibition might be my baby but it's your reputation on the line too.'

She had Vaughn on the backfoot and they both knew it. The pupil had overtaken the master. Well, not really, but he bit his bottom lip and moved towards the stairs so he was out of range of the look of certain death that was on Ellie's face. 'Well, maybe Piers will have to step up then.'

Ellie didn't need to say anything. She found that a tiny inelegant snort said everything for her.

'Fine. You can work out one month's notice, I suppose,' he conceded, as if he were bestowing a huge favour. 'And why the hell are there a hundred and one important things to be done?'

'Because nobody RSVPs any more,' Ellie complained, following Vaughn up the stairs. She was back on track again. The work stuff, no matter how gnarly it was, could be handled. She could handle Vaughn too, which was good to know, and she was sure that in a few days he'd backtrack on her dismissal. Almost sure. 'You know what artists are like.'

'Sadly, yes.'

It felt reassuring to be back on familiar ground. This was what defined her; not the stories in the papers. 'I bet half the Scandis are MIA somewhere in Shoreditch and won't turn up at noon like we planned.'

'Get Alexandra on it. If need be, she can take a car to Shoreditch and physically round them up,' Vaughn decided, ushering Ellie into her own office. 'I wouldn't worry about the RSVPs, but get on to the caterers and tell them to double up the numbers, and order four . . . no, make it six, extra crates of champagne.'

Ellie tapped his instructions into her BlackBerry. 'Are you sure? It is pretty close to the end of the season. A lot of people have already gone away.'

Vaughn had one hand on the door handle but he turned to give Ellie a scornful look. 'It's just as well that you'll be leaving soon because I've obviously taught you nothing,' he said witheringly, though she was sure he was just trying to save face. 'Every single person on the guest list will turn up and everyone who calls today, who doesn't work for a national newspaper or a TV station, will be angling for an invite. Obviously, we're going to have a sell-out show. It's very early noughties, having a sell-out show.'

All members of staff were in by nine thirty, even Piers and Inge, which was 'an event we should mark on the calendar', remarked Madeleine Jones, Vaughn's personal assistant, who'd been drafted in for the day to help with the exhibition.

Madeleine and Inge manned the switchboard, replying with a terse 'no comment' to anyone who wasn't interested in purchasing works of art. Muffin, who was in a fury because both Vaughn and Madeleine insisted on calling her Alexandra, was tracking down four missing emerging Scandinavian artists with the aid of her iPhone, iPad and vast array of trust-fund hipster friends. Piers was charged with a variety of errands, most of them not that urgent, because he kept getting in everyone's way.

Just before lunch a vanload of policemen suddenly appeared and moved the gentlemen and ladies of the press back until they were gathered at the entrance to the mews and not at the gallery door. Everyone else, apart from Ellie, who didn't dare venture outside, went a circuitous route to access the outdoor world, which involved nipping across Vaughn's roof garden and going down the fire escape belonging to the eccentric architect from two doors down.

'Apparently Vaughn called the Mayor's office. I think they were at Eton together,' Muffin hissed when she and Ellie met briefly in the back office. 'The mews has been redesignated as a private road. They've even set up a little checkpoint and they're making people show ID before they're allowed to enter. It's like a police state.'

Generally Ellie disapproved of police states but in these circumstances she was very glad that Vaughn had probably donated an obscene sum of money to the mayoral campaign, which allowed him to use Her Majesty's constabulary for his own ends.

Exhibition days were always a white-knuckle ride, even when the gallery staff could enter and exit by their own front door, but by three o'clock that afternoon, everything was done. All the artists had been accounted for. Mariusz, the gallery handyman, and his team had finished nailing a contorted willow sculpture to the back wall of the gallery; assembled and hung a white Perspex bicycle from the ceiling; and fixed the halogen light in the downstairs loo, which always tripped the fuses when it blew out.

The guest list, which was twice as long as it had originally been, was signed off. Madeleine had thrown out a man from the *Daily Star* who'd pretended to be another Polish handyman, and for the first time in her life Inge had been on a coffee run.

Now, Vaughn had gathered all the staff in the gallery for a final walk-through before the caterers arrived. Theoretically, the exhibition was Ellie's responsibility so she should have done the final walk-through, but Vaughn always relished an opportunity to address his troops.

'If I discover that any of you have so much as breathed a word to anyone who could even loosely describe themselves as a journalist – well, I don't like to resort to cliché but the phrase "blacken your name" would cover this eventuality – I doubt you'd ever find new employment in any meaningful capacity. Not unless you harbour a desire to sell fast food.' He shuddered at the thought. 'Is that clear?'

Ellie felt Muffin, who was standing next to her, flinch and Piers had turned painfully red.

'What if you didn't know they were a journalist and you were only telling them that Ellie was a very nice girl and they should leave her alone?' he asked in a voice so panicked and high that it was practically a falsetto. 'I wasn't selling my story or anything, I was defending you, Ellie. I was doing a good thing, and anyway, they followed me all the way to the stationery shop and held the door open for me and it would have been rude to completely ignore them.'

Any minute now Piers was going to start huffing on his inhaler; he was already rooting around in his jacket pocket.

Vaughn shook his head. 'Fine. Piers gets special dispensation because he's a bloody idiot, but as for the rest of you . . .'

He tailed off meaningfully, and though Ellie had no intention of talking to the press, she still felt guilt prick at her, but not as much as Muffin, who muttered, 'Oh shit,' and stared resolutely down at her Marni polka-dot sandals. Ellie clenched her fists and breathed through her nose because wasn't it enough that Muffin had a ginormous trust fund and could afford £250 sandals? Had she dared to sell some choice snippets to the tabloids where she'd be quoted as 'a source close to voluptuous vixen Velvet'?

'You'd better not have,' she whispered at Muffin. She was determined to get through the day without crying or monumentally losing her shit, both of which could wait until she was safely tucked away in a hotel room, but her resolve was being severely tested. 'Or I will shut you down . . .'

'Don't go all Camden on me,' Muffin whispered back. 'It was only a pal who—'

'Why are you talking? Who gave you permission to talk?' Vaughn demanded. He was tetchy enough on a normal day but on the opening day of an exhibition when one of his staff was on the front page of every tabloid newspaper, his tetchiness was stratospheric. 'In circumstances like this, we close ranks. Never complain, never explain, right, Cohen?'

'I suppose,' Ellie muttered, though she didn't have the same ranks to close as the others. In her experience, the posh kids always stuck together. It was something to do with being carted off to boarding school before they were weaned, where they learned self-reliance, arrogance and bonds that were tightened by the old school tie. Still, as advice went, 'never complain, never explain' sounded more her style than 'maintaining a dignified silence', as if she were some doughty dowager duchess. 'It's all good,' she said crisply. 'None of us is going to say anything to the press that isn't about emerging Scandinavian artists, are we?'

There were murmurs of assent from the others, then Vaughn was distracted by the white Perspex bicycle, which was floating above their heads. 'Shouldn't that be more left of centre?'

They debated the positioning of the bicycle for ten increasingly heated minutes until they were interrupted by a furious buzz on the intercom followed by a hammering on the door.

'How did they get through the security cordon?' Piers cried indignantly, like he hadn't been blabbing to members of the press earlier, as he went to answer the door.

Ellie was more concerned with persuading Vaughn to leave the bicycle exactly where it was, but then she heard Piers give an excited little cry and someone gave an excited little cry in return, and Grace Vaughn appeared in the open doorway, laden down with garment bags.

For one fleeting moment, Ellie saw both husband and wife's faces light up before they resembled their usual expressions – a scowl and a pout respectively.

'Jesus Christ!' Grace exclaimed. 'It's harder to get into the mews than to get wait-listed for a fricking Birkin. I had to show my passport to a policeman!'

'Why were you trying to get into the mews when I thought you were busy organising the aftershow party?' Vaughn wanted to know. Ellie wanted to know that too. Grace did the aftershows; that was the deal. She had a knack for finding unusual venues, stuffing them full of models, artists, hipsters and magazine people, and blagging a whole load of free booze and a really good sound system.

'It's all under control,' Grace assured him airily. 'The caterers finally found someone who could supply moose meat for the sliders, though I still think that's kind of rank. Anyway, I bought you some shirt options and I got your Dries van Noten suit back from the dry-cleaners.' She looked around. 'I like that bicycle.'

'It's in the wrong place,' Vaughn said flatly.

'It looks all right to me,' Grace said, then she pouted a little harder. 'I'm half dead under the weight of all these bags. Could someone give me a hand?'

Piers rushed to oblige and Ellie decided that she could escape to her office. She had been booked in for a wash and blowdry and a spray tan this afternoon, but had cancelled both appointments.

This time last Friday, she could have gone anywhere she wanted, but now she couldn't pop out to get her hair done. Or go to EAT for a spicy chicken noodle salad, buy a pair of tights, pop in to see Louis with a pile of dry-cleaning; mundane everyday tasks that she'd always taken for granted. Now it was impossible simply to walk down the street without being trailed by a heaving mass of people all trying to take her picture and yelling deeply personal questions at her.

Ellie wandered over to the big picture window and was peering out to see what was happening in the mews when she heard a gentle knock on the door.

'There you are,' said Grace, ducking into Ellie's office without waiting to be invited in. 'So, how are you?'

'Well, I've had better Mondays,' Ellie said carefully, because Grace might be roughly the same age as her, and she might also be friends with Lola, but she was still Vaughn's wife and needed to be treated with caution.

They both smiled awkwardly at each other, because Grace also approached the gallery staff with a wariness that came from being Vaughn's much younger, much more shabbily dressed mistress before she'd become his wife. Ellie had been working for Vaughn for less than a year and had occasionally glimpsed a series of inter-changeable well-groomed blondes accompanying him to work events, then Grace had rocked up with her funny-coloured hair and her funny-coloured tights, and Vaughn had been smitten. Well, as smitten as Vaughn could be.

Grace was no longer out of her depth, even if she was

166

still smiling nervously at Ellie. She had the pampered, smooth look of the very rich, even if she did wear clothes that were better suited to street-style blogs than to being worn on a day-to-day basis. The funny-coloured hair was now a tousled honeyed blonde with a blunt-cut fringe that channelled Brigitte Bardot, and as Grace stepped nearer Ellie could see her thick, sooty lashes and the flawless skin that came from being relatively stress-free and able to afford the attentions of a top-class aesthetician.

'Look, Ellie, I just want you to know that I've shot those two girls, your half-sisters, or whatever you want to call them and they were total nightmares,' Grace suddenly blurted out. 'It's always the same when we do a shoot with people who are famous just for being famous, they have no talent so they over-compensate by being total divas.'

'Yeah, it just feels a bit weird to disc—'

'Kate Winslet made tea for everyone!' Grace informed her. 'You mustn't pay any attention to them, because one of them has had the worst boob lift I've ever seen and the other one tried to steal a Marc Jacobs jacket and a pair of Prada heels after the shoot. You're much, much better than them.'

It sounded like Ellie could hardly be any worse. She'd never stolen anything, not even pick 'n' mix from Woolies, not because it was wrong, but because she was too scared of being caught.

'I'm sure they can't be all bad,' she insisted weakly.

'Oh, they definitely are and you have much better legs than they do,' Grace said loyally. 'Vaughn pretends that we don't read the Sunday tabs but we do, and that picture of you being whirled over the head of that rockabilly guy was impressive. Are they that toned from those clompy fitness shoes you wear?'

'I think it's my genes. I mean, my mother's genes,' Ellie said, because Ari had amazing legs, as did her aunts, and even Sadie still had a perfect pair of pins, which age could not wither, though she lived in fear of varicose veins. 'I couldn't really speak for his genes.'

'Anyway, don't worry about Vaughn. I'm sure if he said he was going to sack you, it didn't mean anything. He threatens to divorce me at least once a week,' she added cheerfully. 'He'll sack Donut long before he sacks you.'

She could hardly tell Grace that she'd already agreed to work out a month's notice. Much as she would love to have Vaughn's wife fighting her corner, Ellie knew that nothing would be more likely to make Vaughn stick to his guns on the whole firing issue. She settled for a smile that showed a lot of teeth and not much conviction. 'You mean Muffin. She likes to be called Muffin.'

'Looks like a right donut to me,' Grace muttered, then she remembered that she was the guvnor's wife and had a certain standing to uphold. 'Anyway, I just came in to check that you were all right, and now I have an after-show party to organise so I'll see you later.' She waggled her fingers and was gone in a cloud of Diptyque's Philosykos.

Camden, London, 1986

'Billy Kay is never going to leave his wife for you because his parents have cut him off and she bankrolls him, he has a kid and, oh yeah, by the way, his music sucks.' Tabitha had volunteered to tell Ari what everybody else already knew. Now she folded her arms, which hoisted up her already impressive rack so she looked like a really cross Jayne Mansfield. 'Either you cut him off or we cut you off.'

'He's a bastard, I get it,' Ari said. 'But when I'm with him, even when I'm not with him but I'm thinking about him, he makes my heart ache, Tab. It literally *aches.*'

Tabitha scoffed because it was a stupid thing to say and generally Ari was far too cool to lose her cool over a guy. 'It's probably indigestion,' she said, and Ari figured that the easiest way to stop what was becoming a no-holds-barred infatuation with someone who treated her like his own personal sex toy was to simply stop.

It was as simple as that. Or it would have been if it had been with anyone else.

As soon as Ari stopped coming, Billy stopped calling. And the more he didn't call, the more distraught Ari became; gorging herself on the memory of every time he'd smiled at her, kissed her, backed her up against the wall and pushed her skirt up.

To get the Billy taste out of her mouth, Ari even went on a date with Chester. He was really sweet, insisted on paying for everything, even held doors open for her (and who did that these days?) but no matter what Chester was, he wasn't Billy, and when Ari wouldn't let him kiss her, Chester called her a bitch and stormed off. She really couldn't blame him. She was a bitch and Chester didn't deserve a bitch.

Billy, however, did deserve a bitch, and when he phoned, after three long, long, long weeks of missing him so much that she thought she might die from it, Ari stuffed loo roll into the toes of her pointiest fuck-me heels and set off for Primrose Hill.

When she got there, it was Billy who dropped to his knees. He looked sad, older than the last time she'd seen him. 'Don't ever go away again,' he said, his hands tight on her hips. 'I can't bear it. I need you, Ari.'

She shook her head. 'No you don't, Billy. You don't need anyone,' she said, but he was already pulling up her skirt, kissing her belly and either he didn't hear her or he didn't think it was worth the effort to deny the charge.

And then he was in her, all around her and this was what she'd come back for. His mouth on hers, his cock driving into her, fingers circling her clit because he loved to make her scream his name and then . . . he stopped.

Ari wasn't going to say it. She might not be able to stay away but she was done with Billy's bullshit, even when he looked at her with those soulful eyes.

'Do you promise you won't go away again?' he asked her, and she would never know how he had the self-control just to stop. 'You have to promise.'

She shook her head. 'No more promises, Billy.'

Stalemate. He narrowed his eyes and Ari set her face in firm, resolute lines, and all the time she could feel his dick hard inside her, the walls of her pussy fluttering around him and she thought that she might actually come without him. She tightened around him and Billy groaned.

'You really are a bitch, do you know that?'

'It's been mentioned a couple of times.' She was not going to think about Chester. Not right now. Ugh! And anyway, Billy's hands were in her hair, dislodging the pins that held her beehive together so he could tug her head back. It gave Ari an

170

edge that she didn't even know she craved and she squeezed him tight again.

'I love you,' he said, jaw clenched, like she'd forced the confession out of him, and in a way she kind of had. 'You're a bitch, but I love you. I wish I didn't but I do.'

Afterwards, when they'd rearranged their clothes and were sharing Ari's last cigarette, Billy nudged her with his arm. 'You're not ever going away again,' he said. It wasn't a question so there was no need to answer.

Chapter Thirteen

And then it was showtime . . .

By six thirty, though the invitations had said seven for seven thirty, the gallery was heaving with favoured clients, art lovers, critics and the one hundred or so other people who'd wangled their way on to the guest list at the eleventh hour.

Ellie was relegated to the back office-cum-packing room behind the reception desk after one of the girls manning the bar, set up at the end of the gallery, had been caught aiming her camera phone up Ellie's short, flouncy, blush-coloured dress as Ellie had been standing on a kickstep to adjust a mudguard on the floating bicycle.

'You'd better stay in here for the time being,' Vaughn had decided, and took hold of Ellie's arm to escort her personally to her little prison. At least he left the door ajar so she could talk to Piers and Inge, who were in charge of the guest list, while Muffin and Madeleine were on ushering duties.

It was hard to feel a warm glow of pride when you were banished, but Ellie gave it her best shot. There was no doubt the show was a hit. The guests had spilled out into the mews, where the press were still behind the police cordon, apart from one accredited photographer taking pictures for the party pages. Inge said she'd seen three members of a Norwegian rock group. Muffin had started a

172

rumour on Twitter that all of ABBA were coming and it was trending.

'Has anyone bought any art yet?' Ellie whispered at Inge.

'Two people from Tate Modern have been staring at the triptych for ten minutes.' Inge sighed. 'Everyone loves the floating bicycle. I love it too. I wonder how hard it would be to suspend a bicycle from my living-room ceiling.'

'You could probably get one of your boyfriends to do it,' Piers said. 'Although they look far too effete to be handy with hammers and hooky things.'

'You're far more effete than any other boy I know, Piers,' Inge said.

'Tristram is way, way more effete than I am. He wears a pocket square!'

'You've been seen in Hoxton with a monocle. Don't even think about denying it.'

While it was entertaining to listen to Piers and Inge have the most ridiculous argument it was possible for two people to have, there was a queue of people at the reception desk waiting to sign in and receive a catalogue lovingly put together by Ellie. She had to make do with hissing at the pair of them like an enraged swan.

'Less bickering, more queue-wrangling, please. You're probably keeping the Finnish Ambassador waiting,' she told them sternly, then could do nothing but seethe when Piers kicked the back office door shut and locked it.

It was ten minutes before Vaughn rescued her. 'Who locked the door?' he asked, but before Ellie could grass up Piers and maybe Inge, who'd been an accessory to the fact, Vaughn tugged her past her unrepentant colleagues (Piers even stuck his tongue out). 'We might as well let the dog see the rabbit, as it were.'

Ellie did feel a lot like a defenceless little bunny about to be thrown to the slavering hounds as Vaughn led her across the foyer and through the crowd of people. She stared down at her feet in her Terry de Havilland wedge sandals, which she saved only for best, as Vaughn led her to the middle of the room, right beneath the floating bicycle, which Ellie hoped was securely attached. She stared out at a sea of faces. The women in pretty, sherbet-hued summer dresses, the men in Savile Row shirtsleeves because the gallery was rammed and it was stiflingly hot, even with the front door and all the skylights open. There were a few defiantly underdressed artists and bloggers, and a girl wearing only a basque and tap pants, but generally the crowd were rich and understated.

Ellie tried to look both engrossed and entirely non-controversial as Vaughn welcomed the Finnish, Swedish and Danish Ambassadors (the Norwegian Ambassador was delayed in Aberdeen), the head of the Arts Council, the Minister for Culture and the lead actress from a hit Danish detective series, though her publicist hadn't returned any of Ellie's calls.

Then Vaughn talked about some of the pieces on display and what an exciting time it was in the Scandinavian art world. He mentioned the word 'zeitgeist' as he always did, then turned to Ellie.

'I'm sure Ms Cohen would like to say a few words almost as much as you'd like to hear from her,' he said smoothly, and Ellie wished she could glare at him and possibly kick his shins too. It was all very well never complaining or explaining, but it was quite another to parade her about to guarantee that the exhibition made more than just the art pages of tomorrow's newspapers.

She looked up, made eye contact with Madeleine, who smiled encouragingly, and took a deep breath. 'Wow! Well, I never knew there were so many people who shared my love for emerging Scandinavian art.' It was meant to be sassy and knowing, and the assembled guests chuckled, but Ellie's voice was so squeaky that she had great trouble getting to the end of the sentence. She turned a jerky ninety degrees and gestured at a spot in the middle distance. 'Enjoy the show. Please come and find one of the gallery staff if you need more information about any of the pieces on display. We're all happy to talk about the art.' It seemed important to qualify that. 'Only the art. Not about anything else.'

'Stop talking now,' Vaughn said quietly, through a pained smile. 'Otherwise I'm sending you to the back office again.'

For a long while, which probably lasted only a minute, though it felt like an hour, everyone stared at Ellie as she clung onto a glass of champagne and gazed unseeingly at a large canvas of the aurora borealis. Then she felt a hand on her shoulder and every muscle in her body seized up until she heard Tess say, 'Hey. Nice frock. Please introduce me to some fit Finns.'

Ellie turned her head and found that she could smile and say in her normal voice, 'The Finns, not to mention the rest of the Scandis, are sort of avoiding me.'

'Really?' Tess didn't bother to disguise her disappointment. 'I thought they were all quite open-minded?'

'They're not quite as open-minded as we all thought.' When all the emerging artists had assembled at the gallery earlier, they'd been very polite but there'd been a certain *froideur* in the air. 'You'll have to source your own Nordic totty.'

'If I must,' Tess sighed, but she was already pinning back her shoulders and shimmying a little to assess how her breasts looked in the deep blue Victoria Beckham trapeze top, which she'd snagged cheap at a sample sale, that she was wearing with tailored shorts and gladiator sandals.

'You look gorgeous,' Ellie told her. 'The Finns won't know where to put themselves.'

Tess was in the middle of telling Ellie in no uncertain terms just where the Finns could put themselves when a middle-aged man insinuated himself between the two of

175

them. 'Ellie, my darling, how are you?' he cried, throwing his arm around her shoulder and boxing Tess out of the way. 'Terrible business. Don't believe a word of it, of course, unless there's anything you want to tell your uncle George in the strictest confidence, eh?'

Ellie would have really liked to tell her 'uncle' George that he should have changed his shirt and reapplied his antiperspirant before he left the merchant bank where he worked but she forced another smile.

'Nothing to tell, George,' she said, tucking her arm into his and leading him away from Tess, who was surreptitiously wafting her hand under her nose. 'The truth is that I lead a very boring life.'

'I'm sure that's not the case,' George insisted. Even his scalp underneath the few wisps of hair he had left was a brilliant red. 'No smoke without fire, eh? Silent waters and all that, eh?'

'It's all hot air and bluster,' Ellie insisted, because surely George understood about hot air and bluster when they were the sum total of all his parts. 'Now, is there anything here that's caught your eye, apart from me, that is?'

A bit of lame flirting with George was all part of her job. For ten minutes Ellie put up with his arm round her shoulder, partial asphyxiation and a bit of light innuendo, as she persuaded him that the triptych by a Norwegian artist was a great investment, especially as one of his earlier pieces had been bought by the Getty Museum, and no, it wasn't a buy two, get the third painting for free kind of deal.

Once people could see that, a) Ellie wasn't suddenly going to revert to tabloid type, strip off her clothes and start humping light installations, and b) she was still a fully functioning display and exhibitions manager, they couldn't wait to come over. She was sure that she wasn't simply being paranoid: clients, acquaintances, even the cultural attaché from the Icelandic Embassy all seemed to think that she'd start over-sharing if they took her hand, tilted their heads and said, 'So, really, how are you doing?'

It was humiliating to have people staring at her, talking out of the corner of their mouths about her, and making it abundantly clear that she was among them, but not of them. It didn't matter how nicely she spoke, or how well she dressed, or even how shiny her hair was; these people gathered here to judge her were all cushioned by their wealth and their fame and their privilege, and Ellie had never had any of that. She'd only had Ari, but Ari had taught her well. And all of Ari's life lessons could be distilled down into eight succinct words: Never let the bastards get you down, babycakes.

So, if people wanted a piece of Ellie, then she wasn't going to waste the opportunity. By nine o'clock, when the private view was officially meant to have ended, she'd sold five paintings, one light installation and an origami sculpture, and had seven orders for floating Perspex bicycles. Everyone wanted a floating Perspex bicycle.

The crowd was thinning out and though several people were hovering and shooting Ellie longing looks as if they'd been waiting all night to talk to her, Madeleine, Vaughn and even Muffin were herding people out of the gallery.

Tess, and Lola, who'd come for only the last half-hour because she and Vaughn could barely tolerate each other, were standing under an open skylight to try to catch the breeze as they flirted with at least three emerging Scandinavian artists. Ellie could feel her fight face starting to slip. She hung back until Tess detached herself from the group and hurried over.

'It's all right,' she said to Ellie. 'Everything's cool. The Scandis don't hate you or think you're a skanky lady of ill-repute, they're just all really miffed about Pals and his floating bike getting centre stage.'

'Really?' Ellie asked. 'Are you just saying that to make me feel better?'

'I'm your best friend so I'm contractually obligated to say things to make you feel better, but not this particular time. Apparently, Pals will sell a floating bike in any colour to any fool who wants one. Let's not even talk about it because all those buff boys keep banging on about art, and Lola and I need to know what a Reidar Aulie is, because they keep going on about that too.'

'He was a famous Norwegian political painter best known for the work he produced during the Second World War,' Ellie said without even having to think about it because her knowledge of Scandinavian art was at its absolute peak. 'There's a mural of his in Oslo City Hall celebrating the history of the labour movement and actually—'

'Please, stop! I don't want to hear another word about art or Scandinavia or Perspex for the rest of the evening,' Tess begged. 'More importantly, Søren, sexy Danish sculptor with amazing green eyes and excellent muscle tone, has been wanting to talk to you all day. Said you'd promised to show him your double-jointed right elbow. I can't believe that you're *still* using that as a chat-up line.'

'It has never once failed me,' Ellie said gravely. She glanced over at the little group where Lola, who looked like she'd come straight from a burlesque revue, was holding court. Right on cue, Søren looked over, smiled and gestured at his right elbow. It wasn't enough incentive. 'I'm going to bail, Tess. It's been one hell of a day and I'm pretty much running on empty now.'

Tess looked at Ellie imploringly. 'Oh, come on! Let's go to the aftershow and drink free vodka and flirt with sexy artists. Did I mention the free vodka?'

It sounded like a plan, except . . . 'But what if there are photographers?' Ellie asked anxiously. 'It doesn't even need to be photographers. Everyone has a camera on their phone. Vaughn managed to keep the security watertight but Grace doesn't have that kind of sway.'

'Ellie, you can't live the rest of your life worrying about photographers and what the papers might say about you.'

'I think you'll find that I can. I mean, I don't know how not to at the moment.' Ellie shrugged and, once again, she was widening her eyes and staring at the ceiling to stave off the tears. Work had been a great distraction but now it was time to clock off. 'How long before everything goes back to normal?'

She got a hot, sticky hug from Tess by way of reply, then her friend said, 'I don't know when this is going to stop. But it's only going to ruin your life if you let it. Crap boyfriends aside, you're a strong woman, Ell. You will get through this.'

It was Tess, her best friend, and apart from artists and staff, everyone else had been removed from the gallery so Ellie could rest her head on Tess's shoulder. 'I will get through this, but not tonight. I can't deal with any more people.'

'Do you want to go home? Do you want me to come with you?' To her eternal credit, Tess managed not to sound too downhearted at the possibility of missing out on the free vodka.

Ellie straightened up and kissed Tess on the cheek. 'I wouldn't want to stand between you and a fit Finn. I'm . . . well, I'm going to check into a hotel for a few days so I'm hidden away from the press.'

'You'll do anything to get out of cleaning the bathroom,' said Lola, who'd come over to chivvy them along. 'What you need to do, Ellie, is get absolutely hammered. Then you'll feel so shit tomorrow, you won't care about the press.'

Ellie gave Lola some side-eye, not that it ever did any good. Lola was impervious to side-eye. She only responded to a raised voice, and if that failed, a good thump on her BCG scar. 'I can just see the front page of the *Sun* tomorrow with a photograph of me hurling into a wheelie bin.'

'Lightweight.' Lola gave her a swift up and down. 'Are you all right, Ellie? If you didn't want to be on your own, me and Tess could come with you. Order some room service, have our own little afterparty, right, Tess?'

Tess knew Ellie better than that. 'You're having an attack of the Greta Garbos, aren't you?'

Ellie nodded. 'Kind of am, with a little bit of Martha Stewart thrown into the mix.'

'Ell needs to be alone when she's stressed out,' Tess explained to Lola. 'She literally barricaded herself in her bedroom for three months when she was doing her finals and went ballistic if anyone so much as left a dirty teaspoon in the sink.'

'It's my way of dealing with stuff.'

Lola didn't look convinced. She also looked rather horrified at the thought that Ellie when under stress could be even more zero tolerance about clutter than she normally was. 'Well, if you're sure . . .'

'I am,' Ellie said firmly. 'But if either of you manage to sex up a Swede . . .'

'Or knob a Norwegian . . .'

'Or fuck a Finn, then I expect all the sordid details. Length, girth . . .' she started to clarify and then her blood turned to antifreeze in her veins as a smooth voice behind her said, 'Velvet? Could we go somewhere private to talk?'

Chapter Fourteen

Ellie really didn't want to turn round. For one fanciful moment she thought back to the boring Tuesday afternoons spent studying for her bat mitzvah and the story of the sacking of Sodom and Gomorrah, and how Lot's wife had been turned into a pillar of salt for looking round. Looking round really didn't have a lot going for it.

Even so, Ellie turned round. 'Oh, hello,' she said to David Gold with all the enthusiasm she could summon up, which wasn't that much. 'How did you manage to get past my boss? He's showing people out, not showing them in.'

That actually sounded rather rude, but apart from a lot of pretty assurances and big talk, he'd been precisely no help and now here he was turning up uninvited for a chat when Ellie wasn't sure how much longer she could hold it together.

'It would seem that my Law Society membership card has manifold uses,' David Gold said, and when he smiled at her it was an echo of the man she'd met at Glastonbury. He wasn't so buttoned up tonight. His red tie was loosened, top button of his shirt undone, suit jacket carried neatly in the crook of his arm, and his curly hair refused to be tamed by grooming products any longer. Ellie couldn't look at his face because when she did, and he was smiling one of those glib smiles that never made it to his deep blue eyes, it still made her synapses sing. 'Is there somewhere quieter we could go and talk?'

'Can't it wait until tomorrow?' Ellie asked. His eyes darted from her to Lola and Tess, then to the floating Perspex bicycle. If they could just postpone this chat until the morning, then Ellie would feel stronger, more able to deal with him and all the difficult, complicated feelings that he stirred up in her. Not just still being attracted to him, even though she should know much better, but also the difficult complicated feelings she had for Billy Kay, which David Gold made even more fraught. He was only one step removed from her father and he made Billy Kay become real rather than remaining just a shadowy totemic figure for all the bad stuff that had happened when she was growing up. 'I still have a few things to finish up here.'

'I know it's late, Velvet, but I'm afraid I really must speak to you with some urgency,' he said, head lowered so his breath ghosted against her ear. The phantom touch of the dispelled air from his mouth made Ellie feel heavy and weighted down, until Lola snorted in disbelief.

'Why are you calling her Velvet?' she demanded, staring at David Gold imperiously. He didn't flinch, even though Ellie had never seen Lola get fiercely protective before and it was very intimidating. 'And why aren't you listening when she tells you that now isn't a good time?'

Tess looked a little less intimidating. 'Aren't you going to introduce us, Ellie?' She was already holding out her hand to shake. 'I'm Tess, Ellie's best friend. We tell each other everything. How come she hasn't told me anything about you?'

It was a good question. During all the hand-wringing and pearl-clutching that Tess had gamely suffered through, not once had Ellie mentioned David Gold's name. She'd never even told her about the cute guy she'd met at Glastonbury because it had been so humiliating, and the bits that hadn't been humiliating she'd wanted to hoard for herself.

'I'm David Gold, Ellie's fa—'

'He's Billy Kay's lawyer,' Ellie interrupted. 'And this is Lola. Lola, David Gold.'

Lola didn't shake his proffered hand. 'So, Ells, what do *you* want to do?'

'You'd better go to the after party. I'll speak to you tomorrow,' she said to Tess, who nodded understandingly.

'OK, but if you change your mind, I don't mind keeping you company tonight.'

'Me too. We've got your back,' Lola said with another pointed look at David Gold, who looked faintly amused at Lola's Mama Bear routine. Then she and Tess hurried back to the Scandis.

'I'm sorry to turn up unannounced but I wouldn't be here if it wasn't important,' David Gold said in a low voice that made her blood surge, though Ellie couldn't tell if it was lust or fear about this important new development that simply couldn't wait. It took a second until she decided that she might be ready to look him in the eye, but before she could there was suddenly a woman right up in her face.

'You found her, then?' she barked at David Gold, in the rasping voice of someone who smoked at least thirty a day. 'Well, well! Let's have a proper look at you!'

Ellie took a step back. Then she took another step back because there was a lot to take in: a big-haired, buxom, forty-something blonde poured into a white jumpsuit, which shouldn't have worked but did. Probably because the woman had the most amazing cleavage, was dripping with gold jewellery and the overpowering scent of Dior's Poison, and obviously didn't give a fuck what anyone thought about her, when she obviously thought she was fabulous.

'Hello,' Ellie said. She didn't know who this woman was

or what she was doing with David Gold, but she was gazing at Ellie like she was a huge fruity cocktail and she wanted to slurp her right down. 'Sorry, you are . . . ?'

'I wondered when you'd show up,' David Gold said to the new arrival, and bent down to kiss her on each cheek. 'We were just going to find somewhere a little more conducive to a quiet conversation.'

'In a minute,' the woman said in a tone of voice that suggested that she was the one who was used to giving orders and having them followed to the letter. 'I just want to get a good look at little Velvet here.'

'It's Ellie,' he told her sternly, though Ellie was sure he was faking. 'She gets quite cross if anyone calls her Velvet.'

'Hello. I'm standing right here,' Ellie said and wished she hadn't as the woman took two steps in towering gold sandals that brought her back into Ellie's personal space bubble again. She was so close that Ellie could see where her fuchsia-pink lipstick was starting to bleed.

'I can't believe you're all grown up,' the woman told Ellie. 'I really don't know where all the time goes. So stupid of Ari and Billy to let this whole sorry business drag on for so long.'

'I beg your pardon,' Ellie said, forehead scrunching up in confusion because she didn't know this woman, but this woman seemed to have previous knowledge of Ari and Billy Kay. 'Have we met before?'

'Ah, Cohen! There you are!' Vaughn was striding towards them with a woman in tow. Ellie realised they were the last people in the gallery. 'I see Georgie found you, then,' he said to Ellie, who looked at him in bemusement. Vaughn knew her? Was she a client? 'Cohen, Georgie is Billy Kay's publicist. And Melanie's been looking for you.'

Melanie was a high-flying, over-achieving VP at Goldman Sachs, who Ellie had been carefully cultivating for months. Melanie got up at four thirty every morning so she could run ten miles, then have a blowdry before she was at her desk at six thirty, and had once told Ellie that if Margaret Thatcher had managed on four hours' sleep, so could she. She was the last person that Ellie wanted to deal with. Well, not *the* last person, but certainly one of them.

But Melanie, who was wearing a white Issa dress that Ellie had been lusting after hopelessly on Net-A-Porter, wasn't interested in talking to Ellie. 'David!' Her face lit up when she said his name. 'You do crop up in the strangest places.'

He smiled at her. It was somewhere between his Glastonbury smile and his lawyer smile. 'I'd hate people to think I was predictable.'

Then he put his arm round Melanie to pull her in for a kiss and his hand settled just a few crucial centimetres below Melanie's waist so that Ellie could tell that they knew each other intimately. Even if she hadn't been sure, then the kiss, a fleeting brush of lips against lips, would have clued her in.

So, that was the type of woman that he went for – and Melanie was a woman; no one would ever dare call her a girl. She was also made from the same mould as the woman he'd been with at Glastonbury. Another glossy, size-six female with a 'don't fuck with me' attitude, who looked like she never burped or picked her nails or ordered pudding.

Melanie brushed the front of David Gold's shirt with a proprietorial hand as if she was getting rid of an imaginary speck of dust. 'You said you were going to call me,' she reminded him in a playful tone with just the slightest edge.

'I know, I'm sorry. I've been so busy. Had to fly out to LA at a moment's notice,' he said, and Ellie filed that nugget of information away; wondered if LA meant

California, meant Napa Valley, where he'd had a council of war with Billy Kay. But now wasn't the time to pursue that when Vaughn was standing there like a beleaguered dad trying to get his children out of the house and into the car.

Melanie glanced over at him. 'David, do you know Vaughn?'

The two men sized each other up, then David smiled and held out his hand. 'Didn't we share an exasperated look at a UNICEF charity auction?'

At least Vaughn wasn't the type of person to fall for such easy charm. Except, he was smiling and shaking David's hand. 'When Larry was sitting next to his mistress as he bid on a pair of limited-edition Louboutins for his wife?'

They had a brief, perfectly cordial conversation about how hideous charity auctions were, Melanie and Georgie chiming in, and Ellie stood there on the edge of the group of the four glittering people who appeared to be at the very pinnacle of their careers, who effortlessly fitted in and were accepted wherever they went. Or maybe they were all riddled with neuroses and insecurities but were just much better at hiding them than Ellie was.

'I think you'll find this piece interesting,' Vaughn was saying as he led Melanie and, by default, David because she had a tight grip on his arm, over to the other end of the gallery, which left Ellie alone with Georgie.

'Shall we start again?' Georgie said with a wide smile. 'I'm Georgie Leigh, Billy's publicist. I'm not going to call him your father or anything crass like that, because he hasn't exactly excelled himself in that department.'

Ellie knew she should be on her guard but there was something too unguarded about Georgie. 'Hi,' she said, and she dithered for one second about whether to shake hands or air kiss, but Georgie was already pulling her in for a pillowy, highly scented hug, her hand rubbing a circle on Ellie's back. It felt oddly comforting.

'Do you know that the last time I saw you, you couldn't have been more than three months old?' Georgie asked before she'd even released Ellie. 'You were a babe in arms. Quite literally. I held you in my arms, though you'd just thrown up everywhere, but you were so beautiful I didn't even mind.'

'Oh? Ari's never mentioned you,' Ellie remarked in some surprise. 'Did you know Tom and Tabitha too?'

Georgie threw her hands up so the assortment of gold-studded bangles and bracelets on her tanned wrists jangled. 'It was so long ago, darling. I was more part of Billy's scene. Or I hung around on the sidelines, hoping desperately that he'd notice me,' she added wryly and Ellie knew what that felt like. Did she ever . . . ?

The relief of meeting someone from Billy Kay's camp that she could relate to, and who wasn't David Gold, was immeasurable. 'And now you're his publicist? I guess he did notice you after all.'

'Well, he let me do his press for free for a while and that seemed to go rather well. Hard for it not to when he'd released the best British album since *Rubber Soul*,' Georgie said, and for a fleeting second Ellie could see the fangirl that she used to be. 'Then other people wanted me to do their press and were prepared to pay for it and it's all worked out rather well.'

Ellie bit her lip. She was tired and it was hard to think clearly, but there was a tiny piece of information lurking just out of reach that she tried to grasp. 'Georgie Leigh . . . hmmm . . . Oh! Are you GL Communications?'

GL Communications was one of the best public relations companies in London, representing only a triple A list, high-end roster of clients including a Rolling Stone, two Oscar winners, Britain's most beloved TV chef, three thirty-something supermodels and at least five people who were described by the papers as national treasures. Ellie knew all this because the publicists at GL

Communications were a terrifying bunch who made her jump through many flaming hoops to get their clients on a guest list for an opening night. A firm assurance that they'd be happy to have their photo taken with the artist usually required a huge bunch of flowers from Jane Packer and first dibs on Ellie's firstborn.

'Guilty as charged,' Georgie said. 'Imagine you hearing about my little company.'

'It's hardly little,' Ellie demurred. 'You must be far too busy to have to be bothered with—'

There was another jangle-laden hand gesture. 'Don't you dare start apologising! I'm the one who should be apologising,' Georgie said emphatically. 'Nobody but me looks after Billy, but I've been in Mustique for the last two weeks at a spa retreat. I couldn't get any reception on my BlackBerry. Whoever heard of such a thing?'

'Happened to me when I was in the Cotswolds in April . . .'

'I don't know what my assistant was thinking. She should have arranged for a fucking carrier pigeon or flown out to get me when we first heard the *Sunday Chronicle* had been sniffing around. Has it been awful?'

All Ellie could do was nod. She knew that she should keep her own counsel until she'd spoken to Ari and got her take on Georgie Leigh, but Georgie had looked her right in the eye and hadn't tried to spin the situation and she seemed . . . simpatico. 'It's been hell,' Ellie told her. 'It keeps getting more hellish by the hour.'

'Has David been any help at all?'

The question threw Ellie and made her look uncertainly at the far end of the gallery where David Gold, Melanie and Vaughn were standing in front of a stark abstract painting. 'Well, it's been complicated . . .' she began uncertainly. 'I thought . . . he gave me the impression that he could make this go away and that the best thing I could do was to . . .'

'. . . Maintain a dignified silence,' Georgie finished for her. 'He's no PR. In fact, he's banned from my offices because no one does any work when he comes in; they're far too busy batting their eyelashes and asking if he wants a chai latte, but honestly, darling, I'm sure he did his best. After all, David's two top priorities are his career and Billy Kay. They're not mutually exclusive. The happier he keeps Billy, the more likely he is to make senior partner so I'm sure he did everything he could to get the story buried.'

'So, is Billy Kay not happy about the story? About his bastard daughter being splashed all over the front pages?' Ellie's time limit on not falling to pieces had half an hour left on the clock but she could already feel that white-hot rage lift its head and roar. 'Because I have to say that Lara and Rose Kay getting involved has just made the whole thing—'

'Darling, darling, I know, I *know*,' Georgie said, and she took hold of Ellie's hand and squeezed it tightly. It kind of hurt because Georgie was wearing almost as many gold rings as she was bracelets. 'Again, I take full responsibility. They're looked after by one of my girls who really should have known better and checked with me, but I was probably having a bloody hot-stone massage or something ridiculous when I should have been putting out these fires.'

'Well, it wasn't really your fault,' Ellie said, because actually if they were apportioning blame then this was still Richey's fault. There wouldn't have been a story if he hadn't told the *Sunday Chronicle* that there was one, and going further back than that, it was really her own fault for being such a naïve, trusting sap and being taken in by Richey's big brown eyes and cheeky grin. Well, she'd learned her lesson and learned it hard, Ellie thought, and her gaze came to rest on David Gold's back as he and Melanie walked towards the door.

Whatever it was that had been so very important that he just had to talk to her obviously wasn't as important as leaving with Melanie so they could have sex. Hopefully she'd still manage to get her four hours' sleep in.

I am being really bitchy, Ellie thought guiltily, which was a sure sign that she was overtired and overwrought and just generally over. 'It's been really nice to meet you,' she told Georgie and she meant it. 'But if there's still things we need to talk about can we do it tomorrow? Surely it will keep for a few hours?'

'Oh, darling, you look done in,' Georgie all but cooed, and she stroked her hand down Ellie's cheek, the way that Ari often did, which was a little disconcerting. 'Do you know that you still have the same peachy soft skin that you had when you were a baby? Anyway . . . I *have* to talk to you, but not here. My car's outside. We'll go somewhere, we'll have a little drinkie, get everything squared away and then my driver will give you a lift home. How does that sound?'

In other circumstances, on any other night, it would have sounded quite nice. But these were extraordinary circumstances. 'Look, Georgie—'

'The longer you prevaricate, the longer it will take,' Georgie said with a smile. The smile didn't disguise the fact that she refused to take no for an answer, which meant that what she wanted to talk about was going to be nothing Ellie wanted to hear. 'Get your bag and in five minutes, we'll be drinking ice-cold Martinis.'

It was easier to smile limply and walk in the direction of the stairs than argue the toss, but Ellie had no intention of discussing anything more with Georgie tonight. She almost cannoned into Vaughn, who was coming out of the packing room. 'Still here, Cohen?' He followed Ellie as she walked out of the gallery and began to climb the stairs. 'I think you'd better work off site for the foreseeable future, or for the rest of your notice period, whichever comes first.'

Ellie had been hoping that the success of tonight's launch meant that she and Vaughn could pretend her firing had never happened, but that wasn't Vaughn's style. Not when he could mess with her head. 'Give me five minutes before you set the alarm. I'm going over the roof and down the fire escape to avoid the paps. Getting tasered by the security company's fast-action response team is the last thing I need,' Ellie said lightly, despite the fact her heart felt like a lead weight.

'I'll email you tomorrow,' Vaughn said. 'Don't think you can slack off just because you're not actually sitting behind your desk.'

That made Ellie feel a little better, like she was still utterly indispensable. She carried that comforting thought with her, along with her luggage, as she almost broke her neck going down the narrow fire escape.

It descended to a tiny alley that ran behind the mews, which narrowed to a mere aperture that led out onto Albemarle Street. Ellie hoped that Georgie's car was parked somewhere else because the only thing she wanted to get into was a shower, then bed.

She'd call Georgie tomorrow morning and explain. Send her some flowers by way of an apology, Ellie decided as she dragged her suitcase along behind her, its wheels making a deathly racket on the cobblestones in the soft dark of the evening. She hoped it wasn't loud enough to alert anyone to her presence. Anyone in the employ of a major newspaper, that was.

Then her heart quickened as she saw a shadowy figure standing at the mouth of the alley. She wasn't sure if it was a photographer, or worse, because there were still worse things, like muggers and rapists. She was on first-name terms with panic and fear lately, but now a sense of menace crept over her like a cold fog drifting in from the sea.

Ellie took baby steps because she didn't want to seize up

in terror. She couldn't continue her planned route unless the person in front of her let her pass, but she couldn't retrace her steps either. He could easily catch up with her as she was wrestling her bags back up the metal stairs, and even if he didn't, Vaughn would have set the gallery alarm system by now, shutting her out.

She peered into the darkness, thought about trying to croak out an authoritative 'Who's there?' when the person stepped forward so Ellie could see his face in the dim light from the alley's one lamppost.

'So, this is where you've got to,' said David Gold. 'Let me take that from you.'

Her suitcase was standing next to her and then it wasn't, because he was wheeling it away. Ellie had a few choices, but in the end the easiest one was to follow him.

Camden, London, 1986

Everything was different this time. Billy wanted Ari and he didn't care who knew it. He even braved Tabitha's wrath to meet Ari from work with a bottle of wine and his guitar and walk her back to the playwright's house.

Though she was still trying hard not to love him, Ari loved watching Billy pick out chords on his custom-made Gibson acoustic guitar. When he worked out a sequence, Ari would improvise a melody line, snatches of words that might become lyrics, and Billy would smile. Like, he was actually taking pleasure in something.

Writing songs together was the key that finally unlocked Billy Kay's heart so Ari could see inside, and what she saw was a lost, lonely man who didn't know where he was going. 'You only get one chance to make it and I fucked it up,' he said one night as they sat in the garden with their guitars. 'It was the wrong time. I was in the wrong band. Had the wrong manager.'

'Maybe that wasn't your chance to make it,' Ari said. 'Maybe your chance is still there. It's not about timing, Billy. It's about the songs, isn't it? You can change someone's life with a song. You can change the world with a song.'

Billy smiled at her. He smiled all the time once you got to know him. 'You're not an idealist, are you, Ari? That's not very cool.'

'Yeah, but that post-punk nihilism thing is so tacky,' she drawled, as her fingers shaped a chord on her guitar, then another one and another one. 'What do you think of that? I like it. I like the sad chords.'

'You know you're going to make it, Ari, don't you?' Billy asked, reaching over to still her fingers on the fretboard. 'You're going to get everything you want from life.'

What Ari wanted was too large to be contained or put into words. She wanted everything, she wanted it right now, but she also wanted moments like this to last for ever. 'I'll settle for a headline slot at the Town & Country Club and a number-one album.' She held up her hand. 'A critically acclaimed number-one album.'

Billy shook his head. 'More. Bigger. Better. You're going to be a star, Ari. A legend.'

She laughed because so much naked ambition made her feel uncomfortable. 'I don't think legends pull pints in the Lizard Lounge on Monday and Tuesday nights.'

'Just you wait,' Billy said. 'You'll let me hitch my wagon to your star, won't you?'

It was always going to be easier to write 'I love you' in a song lyric than say the words out loud. Always. 'Wherever I'm going, you're coming too,' she said. 'Right?'

Billy nodded. Then he grinned. He looked fucking irresistible. 'Do you promise?'

These days it was hard to deny him anything. 'I promise.'

'It doesn't count unless you put your hand on your heart.'

Ari laughed. 'You're acting like a twelve-year-old,' she told him, and he pulled a face but she was doing it: putting her hand on her heart.

'Say that you need me, Ari.'

'OK, I need you,' she parroted back.

'No, like you mean it.' Billy's hand was suddenly on hers, covering her heart. 'Say that you need me, that you'll never leave me.'

When it came down to it, when you stripped away his studied nonchalance and swagger, Billy Kay was just as scared as everyone else. 'I love you, Billy,' Ari said, and it was the first

194

time she'd said it to him, first time she'd said it to anyone, and really meant it. 'I couldn't leave you. I'm not whole without you.'

He curved his fingers around her, so he had to be able to feel the thud of her heart tapping out the rhythm of her love. 'I love you too, Ari, and I promise that I will always be there for you. Even if we're apart, I'll still be yours.'

His need was terrifying. 'I'd never expect you to make a promise like that,' she said.

'I don't care. I'm still making it,' he said, and he leaned over to kiss her.

Chapter Fifteen

As Ellie started to follow David Gold out of the alley, he suddenly stopped. 'Georgie's waiting in the car. Where shall we go? I should be able to rustle up a private room at the Groucho.'

'I can't,' Ellie insisted. Her throat was scratchy and sore as though the tears weren't far off, but she was determined not to cry in front of him. 'I'm sorry. I just can't.'

'We're trying to help you.' He lowered his head as he lowered his voice and Ellie was suddenly aware of how they were boxed in, so close that she could feel the heat coming off his body. 'Why can't you understand that we're on your side?'

'I know that,' Ellie said, though so far all his good advice and warnings had amounted to this moment at five to eleven on a Monday night, when Ellie and a good quarter of her worldly possessions were trying to find a place to hide. 'But I'd rather you were on my side tomorrow and not right now.'

'Poor Ellie. You're having a very bad day, aren't you?' It was the first time he'd said her name without prompting. His voice was a soothing hum and he was looking her right in the eye so Ellie couldn't look away but tried to search for the truth in the shadows that danced across his face in the murky light. 'You say where you want to go and I'll take you there. But first I need ten minutes of your time.'

It wasn't worth getting in the car, though Georgie waved at her from where she was spread out on the back seat, as if she didn't harbour any ill will about Ellie trying to make a surreptitious run for it. She walked alongside David Gold, and even though her tote and laptop bag were digging into her aching shoulder, she forced herself to hold her head high, back so straight it would have delighted her old headmistress, and even managed to have a desultory conversation about when the weather might break.

It was a relief when they reached their destination: two narrow three-storey houses that had been converted into a small boutique hotel. Ellie surrendered her baggage to the care of a dapper, suited young man who opened the door for her.

'Lovely to see you again, Ms Cohen,' he murmured. 'Are you checking in for a client?'

'For myself,' Ellie said. Vaughn had set up a corporate account here for his Platinum Service clients because the hotel prided itself on discretion. They hadn't even kicked up a fuss when Vaughn had stashed a former YBA in a King suite while he persuaded him to go to rehab and the former YBA had taken a violent dislike to one of the arm-chairs and pissed all over it.

Ellie would not be pissing on any armchairs. She just wanted a room with a bed in it, an en suite with a deep tub where she could have a long soak and, if she could choke them down, a sandwich and a cup of tea.

She booked in, book-ended by her father's lawyer and her father's publicist, who both offered up their business credit cards, which Ellie refused as a matter of principle, then her bags were whisked away to her third-floor superior Queen room. She longed to go with them, but instead asked if they could use the small sitting room off the restaurant.

As soon as the door closed behind them, Georgie took

Ellie's arm and pulled her towards the sofa. 'We'll be much cosier like this,' she decreed, sitting down so Ellie had no choice but to sit too. 'I have to say, Ellie, again, this shouldn't have happened, but now that I'm back in London you don't need to worry. Every single editor of every single paper owes me at least one personal favour and David is a genius at crisis management. Aren't you, David?'

'I do try,' he said from where he was sitting in one of the bucket armchairs, legs crossed, arms folded, watching the pair of them with unconcealed fascination like they were an enthralling episode of *Casualty*.

He seemed very relaxed for someone who was meant to be managing a crisis, but there was a restlessness in the way his fingers drummed against the arm of the chair and the jiggling of his ankle, which made Ellie's nerves hum.

'So, what did you need to talk to me about?' she asked carefully.

'You're right. Let's just get this done.' Georgie unzipped her Gucci document case, pulled out a sheet of paper and thrust it at Ellie. 'Front page of tomorrow's *Sun*. Sorry to be the bearer of such bad news.'

Ellie smoothed out the A3 photocopy and read the headline: THE OTHER MEN OF SIR BILLY'S OTHER WOMAN.

There was a photo of Ari, an onstage shot, in a leopard-print catsuit, but caught at an odd angle so even to Ellie's forgiving eye she looked absolutely deranged. Then, of course, there were photos of the two most famous men 'fifty-year-old Ari has bedded': Billy Kay and 'Oscar winner and A-list Hollywood star, Tommy Wickham, who close friends say ageing rock chick Ari "stalked fanatically" even though he was involved with supermodel Caroline Knight'.

Of course the truth lay buried deep beneath the surface. Tommy had been a struggling actor whose biggest role had been in a mockney gangster film at the height of the whole Cool Britannia/Britpop thing. He'd hung round the edges of the Primrose Hill set where he'd met Ari because it was the mid-nineties and anyone who was vaguely hip and lived in the NW1 postal code was deemed an honorary member of the Primrose Hill set, even if they didn't exactly hang out with Kate Moss, Noel Gallagher and Jude Law on a nightly basis.

Despite Tommy not being Chester, his approval rating with Ellie had been high because he'd made Ari happy and would turn up on Saturday mornings in his clapped-out Ford Cortina to whisk them off on adventures to Brighton and Bath, or his parents' farm in Kent. It had been a proper, serious relationship until Tommy had asked Ari to marry him and she'd turned him down.

It was only after he'd gone to stay with friends in LA while he nursed his broken heart that his career had taken off and Caroline Knight, supermodel and a raging coke fiend, according to Ari, had started sniffing around.

In fact, none of the names in Ari's ex-directory held any surprises for Ellie. There was the guy she'd dated for three years when she was a teenager, who'd been in a punk band but was now a doctor; two guys she'd seen before Billy, who'd been in minor indie bands. One was now a Grammy-winning music producer and the other was a hip restaurateur. Another serious fixture had been a music journalist who was now married to an actress and had a successful career as a screenwriter; and finally a photographer who Ari had been seeing up until about a year ago.

This list of past lovers was nothing to be ashamed of as far as Ellie was concerned. Ari was attuned to recognising talent in other people even when they couldn't see it themselves, so Ellie wasn't surprised that her old boyfriends had all gone on to greatness; it just killed her that Ari was always the one that got left behind. But that aside, all she could think was, good on you, Mum, as she looked over at David Gold, then at Georgie, both of them staring at her intently as if they expected her to explode into a frenzy of tears and snot at any second.

'I hope these revelations about your mother aren't a shock,' Georgie said sympathetically. She treated Ellie to another hand squeeze. 'Rather a low blow, I thought.'

Considering what she'd been expecting, the front page of the *Sun* wasn't so bad. Ari would probably prefer not to have her sex life dished up on the nation's front pages, but Ellie knew that Ari would be able to deal with it. She'd probably get the cover made into a flyer for The Fuck Puppets' next gig. 'Well, they're not really revelations, are they? It's just a really inaccurate rehashing of the facts.'

David Gold raised his eyebrows in what looked like surprise and Georgie tightened her grip on Ellie's hand, until Ellie winced and pulled away because Georgie didn't know her own strength or that the bevelled edge of the ring on her third finger was very pointy. 'I'm sorry, my darling, that was the warm-up. What we wanted to talk about was this.' Georgie retrieved another photocopy from her document case. 'You see, I thought you'd promised that you wouldn't speak to the press.'

Oh God, now what? Ellie felt an ominous dread pressing down hard on her ribcage, which made it difficult to breathe. 'May I?' She held out a nerveless hand for a copy of the front page of tomorrow's *Daily Chronicle*. She could hardly bring herself to look at it, and when she did, she wished she hadn't.

BILLY'S KID DRIVEN TO THE EDGE
LONG LOST DAUGHTER ON 24 HOUR SUICIDE
WATCH
'I WANT TO OPEN MY VEINS WITH A RAZOR IN A
WARM BATH,' SOBS TRAGIC VELVET.

It was a fair cop. She should have hung up yesterday when Sam Curtis called, instead of yapping on so he could take her words out of context and splash them over the front page. There was also a picture of Ellie looking neither tear-soaked nor tragic, but very pissed off as she stood on the doorstep of the gallery. 'Well, I did say that, but I didn't say it like that,' she protested. 'It was a joke.'

'Ellie, I asked you to do one thing,' David Gold reminded her and Ellie wished that actually he'd stop calling her by her proper name if he was only going to say it to get her attention right before he pointed out how she'd fucked up. 'I told you not to talk to the papers. Not just because it would paint you in a very bad light—'

'You mean a worse light than the one I've already been painted in?' Ellie asked him and Georgie clucked and gave her arm a comforting squeeze.

'Yes, a much worse light,' he agreed. 'Because even if you think that you're telling your side of the story, they will twist everything you say to suit their own agenda. Even the most media-savvy people get burned by the press.'

'So true, and it's going to be very hard for David and me to look after you if you're going to go rogue, my darling,' Georgie said ever so gently. 'And just think what effect stories like this are going to have on your family, on your grandparents.'

That, at least, Ellie was spared. Morry and Sadie refused to have the *Chronicle* in the house, and she'd spoken to Sadie that afternoon about the best method for removing a vinaigrette stain from cotton so Sadie knew she wasn't thinking of topping herself. 'No one is going to believe that I'm contemplating ending it all,' Ellie said defensively. 'I mean, they papped me going to work. Who'd go to work if they were feeling suicidal? At the very least you'd ask for the morning off.'

'At the very least,' David Gold concurred, and when he

wasn't on a full charm offensive it was hard to tell when he was being sarcastic.

It was so late. They were all tired. Georgie had to be flagging if she'd flown in from Mustique, but it was impossible to know, what with the Botox and the fillers and the sheer force of her personality. Ellie wanted to give a silent cheer when David Gold stood up. They were obviously about to wrap things up and in another five minutes she'd be in her superior Queen room, shutting the door, peeling away each protective layer she'd wrapped herself in and . . . He walked as far as the sofa and sat down next to her, so that she was hemmed in on each side.

Despite the reassuring hum of the air conditioning, Ellie felt the first beads of sweat on her forehead as Georgie shifted position and Ellie found herself even closer to David Gold. Close enough that she had to tense her thigh muscles so her leg wouldn't touch his. She took a deep breath. 'I promise I will never knowingly talk to another reporter,' she insisted. 'I'm not going to even answer my phone unless I recognise the caller ID. I promise you that I'm not going to talk to anyone but – I don't mean to be rude, I really don't – you *have* to rein those girls in. You know, Lara and Rose. They shouldn't be saying anything to the press either.'

'I think we should talk about crisis management now,' David Gold murmured, as if she hadn't even spoken, as if her best efforts to convince them she could be trusted counted for nothing and they didn't appreciate Ellie trying to stick some of the blame on Billy Kay's more legitimate daughters.

Ellie didn't have the energy to do anything else but subside on the sofa with a tired sigh.

'Shall I take it from here, Georgie?'

'Please,' Georgie said, as if she too was emotionally drained, but at least crisis management sounded good. Or at least it was proactive.

'So, Ellie, forgive me for asking this but how many of your old boyfriends are likely to come crawling out of their corners with more stories about your, er, rather colourful sex life?'

'I beg your pardon!'

Ellie expected David Gold to crack his knuckles, but he didn't. Not when he could pull out his BlackBerry from an inner pocket and smile at her ruefully. She wanted to wipe the smile off his face with a Brillo pad. 'I'm aware that this is rather indelicate but it's best that I know exactly what we're dealing with. Nude pictures? Sex tapes? Threesomes? Bondage?'

'Oh my God!' Something in the back of her throat pinged with the strain. 'Please stop talking! And no, no, no, a world of no!'

'Darling, Billy asked us to help you and that's what we're here to do. I know it's embarrassing and I wish we didn't have to ask, but there'll be absolutely no judgement from us,' Georgie advised her kindly. She patted Ellie's knee again with a heavy hand. 'Right, David?'

'Absolutely no judgement,' he said in a carefully neutral voice. 'But we're all adults here. Everyone has done things they regret and we are on a clock, so while I understand that you need to make a few token outraged protests – I'd do exactly the same thing in your position – can we skip them, please?'

Ellie's mouth fell open and hung there for several, very unattractive seconds. It was bad enough . . . all of it, but to have him, David Gold, speculate on her sex life, to imagine all the things she might have done in the dark, in bed, with another man, was highly inappropriate and none of his bloody business. Especially as she refused to condense her relationships down just to mere sex, because they'd all meant so much more than that. Even Oscar, her friend with benefits, had been a close friend first; someone she'd laughed with and hung out with and looked out for, and the sex had come a close second to that.

And though it was the last thing she wanted to think about, Ellie wondered what David Gold had done that he'd regretted. Probably not that much. She was beginning to think that if you cut him, he'd bleed lawyer, so he probably made his lovers sign a legal disclaimer before he brought out the handcuffs or the video camera. Then Ellie went red as she thought about him directing the action with his usual honeyed tact. 'It would be terribly helpful if you could spread your legs a bit more, so I can see what your busy little fingers are getting up to . . .'

Ellie pressed her hands to her cheeks, which were so hot they physically hurt. This was all bad enough without developing an erotic fixation on her father's lawyer, who already seemed to think that she would stop at nothing to get her rocks off.

'Ellie? Please tell me there's no sex tape,' he probed gently, his thigh pressed against hers now because the sofa wasn't really big enough for three people to sit on. She could feel his touch searing a path along her thigh, which wasn't fair. She tried to ignore the burn, which echoed the painful blush on her face, because she didn't want to have a stupid, adolescent, uncontrollable crush on someone whose practised charm couldn't disguise his disdain for her. It was the pattern that Ellie always traced: falling for a man who would let her down and leave her broken up and blue.

Not any more.

She turned and glared at him, put everything she had into it. 'OK, I'm not a nun, but I'm not a tart either, thank you very much. Not that being a sexually active young woman is anything to be ashamed of but I haven't been as sexually active as the *Sunday Chronicle* says I have.' It was better to stop talking. Now. Ellie closed her mouth just as Georgie's phone rang with the melody of 'It Felt Like a

Kiss', Billy Kay's biggest hit. It seemed a little sad for his publicist to have it as her ringtone.

'Oh! I have to take this,' she said, hoisting herself up off the sofa. 'I'll be back in five. Don't do anything I wouldn't do!'

Ellie was going to do precisely nothing with David Gold, but now she had that tune in her head. 'It Felt Like A Kiss' was the song Billy Kay had written for Olivia, to beg her forgiveness after his affair, though Tabitha and Tom swore blind it was about Ari. Ellie didn't want to think about that and she didn't want to think about what it would feel like to kiss David Gold, but apparently she was, because once you'd imagined a man directing you in his own personal porn film, a kiss was positively vanilla. But then again, one kiss from someone could mean more than a two-year relationship with someone else. A kiss could change your life.

It was time to get away from him, or at least move from the sofa to the solitary safety of an armchair, but as Ellie started to stand up, David touched her arm and it was suddenly like she'd forgotten how to use any of her limbs.

It felt as if she'd never been touched before – as if all the pats and strokes and the thousands of other touches from other people didn't matter any more. *Oh God, please no. Not him. Not when he doesn't even like me. Not when I'm just a problem that he needs to make go away.*

Ellie wondered if David could feel it too because he leaned in close enough that she could almost taste him. Certainly if she moved a whisper closer and pouted her lips, they'd be kissing. Or she'd be kissing him because Ellie could guarantee that her kisses wouldn't be either welcome or returned. She was painfully aware of the prickle of her oversensitized skin and the gasping sound she was making as she struggled to remember how to breathe.

David didn't say anything, which was unnerving but also kind of hot, but then he moved a crucial, mood-killing three centimetres away from her. 'Now, where were we?' he said in a clear, calm voice as if Ellie was entirely alone in her fevered imaginings. 'I think you were saying something about being sexually active.'

'I can't keep repeating myself, but the *Sunday Chronicle* story was a tissue of lies and I was deeply mortified when I read it.' Ellie shut her eyes because she couldn't bear to look at him any longer. 'You met Richey at Glastonbury, didn't you?'

He nodded, or rather dipped his head down so slightly that it barely qualified as a nod. 'Yes, I did,' he said as if the memory wasn't one he cherished.

Ellie pressed her point. 'So, you probably formed a pretty accurate opinion of him, but until then, he'd been really sweet . . . Well, most of the time. The thing is . . . the thing is that I've always tried to see the best in people, whereas you seem determined to think the worst of me,' she finished reproachfully.

It was late and that smile that he wore like armour was beginning to chip. He ran a hand through his hair, the curls rushing up to meet his fingers. 'I don't think the worst of *you*. The nature of my job means that I have to think the worst of everyone until they prove otherwise. Cynical, I know, but that's how it is.'

It was a horrible way to look at the world and your fellow human beings, but it might have been the most honest thing he'd said to her so far. Now she could glimpse behind the mask of good cheer and bonhomie he'd constructed and she didn't like what she saw.

'It's not important what you think about me,' she said, and her voice barely wavered. 'I know what's true and what's not.'

'Good. Now we both understand each other's position, which is useful, I suppose.' He smiled at Ellie again; but this time it lacked even trace amounts of humour or warmth. 'Right, even if you don't want to give me a breakdown of your sexual activities I will still need names and contact details for all your exes.'

'Why would you need that?' Ellie asked.

'Oh, it's standard crisis management,' Georgie said from the doorway. 'It's best my office coordinates the press strategy and makes sure everyone's on the same page. Don't worry, your secrets are safe with me, Ellie.'

Georgie was definitely someone you wanted on your side, but seeing the best in people was what had got Ellie into this mess. She decided to double-check with Ari before she offered up her exes, just to be safe. 'That's ever so kind, Georgie, but it's all a lot to take in so I'm going to have a think and call you in the morning.'

'The quicker you give David those names, the quicker we can start kicking ass on your behalf.' Georgie treated Ellie to a dazzling smile. 'No offence, dear, but I don't want to read any more kiss-and-tells about your rather colourful sex life.'

'If I'd known this was going to happen, I'd have saved myself for my wedding night,' Ellie sighed. She knew she was being paranoid but she was sure that David Gold had just very softly snickered at the idea that she might be able to keep her legs closed. 'If I'm taking away one life lesson from this it's that the fewer people who know my business the better, so I'm not doing anything until I've slept on it.'

'You're being very obstructive,' David said *sotto voce*. 'Just how bad do you want this situation to get?'

It sounded like a threat, but trying to figure him out, what made him tick, if he really was on her team, was beyond Ellie. All of it could wait, because at this point she didn't care how bad it might get. It wouldn't matter if she were tucked away in the minimalist splendour of a superior Queen room cocooned in crisp white linen with the curtains closed and where nothing and no one could get at her. She stood up. David Gold stood up too.

Ellie started edging towards the door, half-steps at a time, David Gold on her trail. 'I'm getting the most terrific headache, I really need to go to bed, but again thanks for all your advice. I'm sure we'll speak soon.'

'Oh, we will. Have no doubt about it,' he said, then he reached in front of Ellie, arm grazing her side so she reared back in alarm and almost cannoned into Georgie, but he was only opening the door wide for her. 'Goodnight, I hope you sleep well,' he added as Ellie raced past him.

'I'll call you tomorrow,' Georgie called after her. 'We'll do lunch. It will be fun!'

Chapter Sixteen

Ellie had thought that as soon as she heard the reassuring soft click of the door to her hotel room shutting behind her, she'd burst into tears, but she stayed dry-eyed. She looked around cautiously.

All was soft and clean. Brilliant white and dove-grey accents. Everything was arranged in perfect order, from the pillows stacked up on the huge bed and the top cover folded invitingly down at an exact right angle. In the bathroom the bottles of toiletries were arranged in ruler-straight formation on the marble basin surround. It was ordered. It was calm. It was just what Ellie needed.

It was inconceivable that anything bad could happen to her in this room.

Ellie took off her sandals, feet sinking gratefully into deep, white carpet. She looked longingly at the bed, but as well as being bone weary, she was also grubby and hot. Messy and chaotic. After texting Ari to let her know where she was and whacking up the air conditioning, Ellie took a shower. The water sluiced away the dirt and grime that were the mementos of a dry, sticky day in the city heat.

She lowered her shower-capped head so the spray of water could pummel the back of her neck at the spot where all the tension was focused, and concentrated on breathing in and out very slowly and very deeply. By the time she was wrapping a pristine and plush towel around her, Ellie hadn't solved any of her immediate problems but she felt more like *herself* again.

As she went through the familiar, comforting rituals of bedtime from brushing her hair to hot-cloth cleansing to patting the delicate skin under her gritty red eyes with revitalising cream, she wasn't a figure of curiosity, a subject of speculation any more, or someone to be pitied or even a crisis to be managed, but *Ellie Cohen*.

But Ellie Cohen couldn't even face the thought of calling room service, though she hadn't eaten all day, and as she pulled back the covers so she could get into bed, she still had that sick feeling of dread spreading through her body in waves that started in the pit of her stomach. It was like the night before a big exam. Or when she'd just been dumped yet again. Or when there was some awful, snarly situation brewing at work that she needed to sort out.

Except, her dread was bigger than that. As she stared up at the ceiling, she wished that all she had to worry about were the kind of problems that had an expiry date. While her most pressing concern was hiding herself away from the press and cringing at the thought of tomorrow's papers, there were other demons lurking just out of reach, dancing at the back of her mind, where Ellie would prefer them to stay.

She found that if she concentrated on a tiny gap in the curtains that let in a shaft of light from the world outside, then it didn't matter that she hadn't cried, even though she really wanted to, or that she couldn't sleep, even though she really needed to. If she concentrated especially hard, then she needn't think at all.

Eventually the heat and the weight of the covers heaped around her forced Ellie from her vigil. She pulled back the quilt, turned over, plumped up the pillows and snatched five minutes of sleep here and there while she thought about Billy Kay. Rather, she thought about what Billy Kay must think about her. He'd spent a lifetime apart from her so he had no way of knowing that Ellie wasn't an amoral party girl constantly searching for the next thrill. It wasn't as if she could rely on David Gold to give her some good press, to tell Billy that when you took Richey out of the equation, everything in her life was running smoothly, whether it was her career trajectory or her credit rating or how she'd tamed the frizzy curls that he'd passed down to her, Ari's hair being poker straight.

But David Gold wouldn't pass any of that on, because David Gold didn't believe it was true. Apart from those fifteen minutes at Glastonbury when they'd been complete strangers who might have been perfect for each other, David Gold had every reason to believe that she was exactly like that girl in the newspapers who flashed her arse and fell apart at the first sign of trouble.

'I'm not going to fall apart.' Ellie said it out loud to the shadows in the furthest reaches of the room, so the words existed. 'And I don't care what he thinks about me. What *either* of them thinks about me.'

When there was a sharp rap on the door at six, it was a relief. Ellie had abandoned even the faintest hope of sleep and was watching one of the shopping channels where a camp man with an orange face was shilling a cubic zirconia jewellery set, so she was glad of an excuse to stagger off the bed, which had become her own personal purgatory.

Maybe if she'd slept better she might have paused, but it wasn't until the door was opened and she was momentarily blinded by the flashing light of a camera that Ellie stopped to consider who might be knocking her up this early as she stood there open-mouthed and squinty-eyed, in a skimpy cotton nightdress.

'Velvet! Want to give us a quote on your fragile mental state?'

'What the hell . . . ?'

'Lots of celebs stay at this hotel. Anyone in particular

you've got your eye on?' asked her early-morning caller, a leering middle-aged man with sweat patches under the arms of his straining white shirt, camera slung round his neck. Even though she was stupid from lack of sleep, Ellie instantly knew the spin he'd put on this. Any vaguely famous person that had stayed at the hotel in the last six months would be someone that she was having a torrid affair with. She was all set to spit out a denial when she remembered what had happened the last time.

Slamming the door was far more effective. Then, to the familiar accompaniment of a steady banging at the door, she phoned down to reception.

The night manager was extremely apologetic when he came up to Ellie's room. The reporter had booked into the Penthouse Suite, so wasn't trespassing and couldn't be ejected from the premises. He *had* promised to keep the noise down because other guests were starting to complain, but there was nothing the hotel could do if he wanted to camp outside Ellie's door for what was left of the night.

However, he could pretend there was a problem with the credit card the man had checked in with and while he was down at reception, Ellie, now back in the crumpled, flouncy dress she'd worn earlier, was led down the fire stairs to the manager's office, to stay, red-eyed and jaw-clenchingly awake, until she could come up with a plan B.

'This happens all the time,' Eamonn, the night manager, told Ellie helpfully as she tried hard not to rest her head on his desk. 'Celebrity signs in. An hour later, the press turn up. I don't know how they always find out.'

'Beats me.' Being diplomatic required more effort than Ellie possessed. 'Unless someone on your staff tipped them off.'

'Never!' Eamonn sounded appalled. 'Now, the Grillon down the road; they'd sell out their grandmothers for five quid and a fish supper. Apart from the people you came in with, who else knew you were here?'

Ellie couldn't imagine Ari passing her location on to the entertainment desk of the *Daily Mirror*, which left just David Gold and Georgie Leigh.

It was unthinkable that either of them had any hand in this, because they were taking their orders from Billy Kay, who'd sent them to help her in her hour of need. Not because his paternal instincts were kicking in but because he wanted her to keep her mouth shut so she could disappear back to her own obscure little life as quickly as possible. So, despite Eamonn's protestations, it was obvious someone at the hotel had tipped the papers off and she needed to find somewhere else to hunker down stat.

At eight o'clock, when Eamonn handed over to Mohamed, the day manager, Ellie decided it was a perfectly acceptable time to start ringing round to see if she could scrounge a place to crash. Her dreams of a minimalist, holistically healing white room had to be dialled back. It was clear that all hotels had a pet reporter on speed dial in case a celebrity OD'd in an en suite. Ellie could only stay in private residences belonging to people she absolutely trusted.

Lola and Tess were still under siege – 'though now that they know you're not here, it's a very civilised siege,' Tess explained when Ellie called her. 'Lola asked them to get us some milk last night when we forgot to buy any on the way home.'

She already knew that Ari was surrounded. Chester was in Benidorm. Sadie and Morry would have her to stay in a heartbeat but if word got out, then Ellie didn't want them besieged by a shoving, jostling mass of media mercenaries. They were too old and frail. Tabitha was on lockdown as she thought there were moths in her latest consignment of vintage dresses and Ellie was just wondering if she had the guts to ring Vaughn and beg for a room in his obscenely huge house, which was nestled behind a very convenient alarmed security gate, when the BlackBerry she was clutching in her sweaty hand rang.

It was David Gold. 'Good morning, Ellie. I take it that you didn't have the most peaceful of nights?' he asked without preamble.

Had he fitted her with some kind of tracking device last night? 'Well, no, I didn't, but how you—'

'Obviously it was too soon for the print edition but you're the lead story on the *Chronicle*'s website,' he explained as Ellie's fingers fumbled to type in the address. The page loaded before she had time to remember what she'd been wearing and mentally prepare herself. 'Shit, shit, shit.'

Her thin cotton nightdress had been no match for the glare of a camera flash and the *Chronicle* readers and, once again – oh God, no – David Gold could clearly see the dark outline of her nipples. At least she'd been wearing knickers. At least she'd been spared that final humiliation, not that it was much comfort. It used to be that if Ellie wanted someone to see her nipples, she let them come home with her.

'It could be worse.' His words weren't even a token comfort. 'And I hate to be the bearer of yet more bad news but the *Daily Mail* has a photo of you from yesterday and you're reaching up to touch that hanging bike and maybe you weren't aware that your dress—'

'Please don't say anything else. I get the picture.' Ellie's face once again hurt from the acid burn of mortification and she was swallowing hard to choke away the sobs that were rising up in her throat. Ari was a big fan of a fifties pin-up artist called Elvgren and his paintings of voluptuous women all caught in a state of accidental undress: skirts snagging on nails as they climbed over fences, frock hems caught between the teeth of playful puppies and an 'Ooops! You can see my panties!' expression of sheer coquetry on their faces. Nobody liked a girl who played coy. 'I can't take much more of this.'

Ellie hated to admit even to her friends, *even to Ari*, that there were things that she couldn't control, and telling David Gold this, when he was always so impeccably in control, was almost as humiliating as her press coverage. Why couldn't it have been Sadie who'd been her first phone call of the brand-new day?

'Do you need my help?' he asked baldly.

'I don't know,' Ellie stumbled. She'd never thought of herself as one of those girls who needed rescuing. Usually, she was able to rescue herself. 'What sort of help, exactly?'

'Why do I have to keep reminding you I have considerable experience in this field? I represent a number of clients from the entertainment industry who occasionally need extracting from similar predicaments,' he muttered darkly as if he spent a lot of time paying off hotel chambermaids and concerned parents whose underage daughters had been cavorting with . . . 'Is the hotel manager there? Put him on.'

Ellie looked at Mohamed, who'd just come back to his office and had spent the last thirty minutes fretting about the effects the events of last night would have on his hotel's reputation. 'Billy Kay's lawyer wants to speak to you.' She held out her BlackBerry, which he took reluctantly.

The conversation was brief. It was impossible to tell from Mohamed's nervous smile and his 'I see's and 'that's do-able's what David Gold was saying.

She found out half an hour later when a porter came to take her bags and Mohamed led her out through the kitchens to a loading bay where a huge trolley was waiting to be loaded on to a laundry van under David Gold's supervision.

He turned as Ellie and her entourage approached and

smiled. It wasn't a very comforting smile. She tensed already aching muscles.

'I'll give you a leg-up, shall I?' he asked, gesturing at the laundry trolley, and Ellie, who'd been expecting a non-descript people carrier with tinted windows, looked at him in dismay. And aghast. Also with sheer unadulterated horror. There was only so much she could handle in a twenty-four-hour period.

'But . . . but . . . is that dirty linen in there? Bed sheets that people have slept on and towels they've dried their hands on after they've been to the loo?'

'The housekeeping staff always put the less soiled linens on top,' Mohamed said, but Ellie knew he was lying, and anyway he'd used the word 'soiled' and things were either soiled or they weren't.

She wasn't being a princess, she really wasn't, but Ellie refused to go near the laundry hamper until several clean towels and sheets had been spread on top. She didn't care how bad it was for the environment to launder already laundered linen.

Then she climbed in, despite grave misgivings and the barely concealed smirk on David Gold's face. She was ceremonially covered up with yet another clean sheet, before the trolley was loaded onto the back of the van and the door slammed shut.

There was no reason not to shuck off her shrouds, but Ellie didn't know if the laundry service were in on the subterfuge so she stayed exactly where she was, trying to take only very, very shallow breaths so she didn't inhale the smell of other people's bottoms. I bet Angelina Jolie's never had to put up with this, she thought to herself as she tried to track where the van was going from the corners it was taking, but that proved impossible.

It was also impossible to know how long she was confined. It felt like an hour, but could have been five minutes before the van stopped and the doors opened.

'No, keep yourself covered,' she heard David Gold say as Ellie went to unveil herself. A hand delved into the trolley to haul her out; a tricky manoeuvre as she needed to keep one hand on her dress so she didn't flash her gusset to all and sundry, but especially him. 'Let me help.'

David wrapped his arm round her waist. Ellie was aware of his tightly corded muscles but it wasn't anything like that scene from *An Officer and a Gentleman* when Richard Gere sweeps Debra Winger up into his arms. He hauled her out like she was a sack of spuds. 'The car's just here,' he said. Then Ellie could smell leather, posh air freshener and an expensive car smell as she was pushed down in the well between front passenger seat and back seat.

David Gold got in on the other side as Ellie uncovered herself. She caught a glimpse of his annoyed expression before he flipped the sheet back over her. 'Stop that,' he snapped, all charm gone, then put his hand on her head to keep her down when the car pulled away and Ellie tried to sit on the seat. 'And stay there!'

'But hasn't the car got tinted windows? No one will be able to see me!'

'Maybe I don't want you to know where we're going.' While Ellie spluttered furiously, he continued, 'You might be our press leak.'

'Well, that's unbelievable—'

'Harry? Could we have the radio on? There's a strange squeaking sound coming from the back of the car.'

Ellie settled down with an aggrieved huff. He still had his hand on her covered head, like she was a bloody dog. She shook herself free and wondered if this was actually her crisis being managed or if she was cooperating with her own kidnapping. Maybe he was sick of lawyering and had decided to abduct Ellie and demand a ransom from Billy Kay, who'd never, ever pay up, even when Ellie had run out of fingers and toes to chop off and send to him in Jiffy bags.

'Ellie? Does Radio Four meet with your approval?'

Then again, if David Gold was kidnapping her, he probably wouldn't give her a choice of radio stations and with all these cloak-and-dagger machinations at least the press wouldn't be able to track her down.

They were twenty minutes into *Woman's Hour*, when David said, 'We're here,' as they were driven down a steep slope. The car stopped, Ellie heard the driver get out and she waited patiently, even though her knees were sore from kneeling on the rubber car mat and she still wasn't convinced of the cleanliness of the sheet.

Finally the door opened. 'Can I take this off now?' she asked, and at last David was pulling off the sheet.

He got out of the car as Ellie carefully eased herself from her cramped position. He stood there watching as she gingerly rotated her ankle, then reached down to rub her right calf, which was cramping.

'Sorry for all the subterfuge,' he said, as the car drove away. 'It's best if no one knows that you're here.'

Here was an underground parking garage but before she could ask exactly where she was, David Gold lifted up both her holdalls and grabbed her suitcase. 'Can you manage the rest?' he threw over his shoulder. Ellie picked up her laptop case, tote bag, handbag and a mysterious small cardboard box that Mohamed had given her as she left the hotel, and followed him to a lift.

'Shouldn't you be at work, then?' she asked stupidly, once they were on their way up to the fifteenth floor. He was wearing an exquisitely cut dark grey suit, crisp white shirt and dark blue tie. Though he must have got home late and been up early in order to read the papers and call her before eight thirty, he looked remarkably fresh-faced. No shadows under his blue eyes, no harsh lines around his mouth.

On the other hand, Ellie was painfully aware that she didn't have a scrap of make-up on, her eyes were piggy and swollen, and she was still wearing the creased and grubby dress from last night. She caught sight of her hair in the mirrors that lined the lift and wished she hadn't.

'You *are* work,' David Gold said. 'You're the first item on today's to-do list.'

He really seemed to take pleasure in reminding Ellie that she was a problem he was paid, handsomely no doubt, to deal with so Billy Kay didn't have to.

She was saved from having to respond by the lift doors opening. They stepped into a lobby, then walked along a corridor that curved around the building, glass brick tiles refracting the brilliant sunlight outside.

'This is nice,' Ellie said. There were window ledges filled with plants. It was light and airy, but snug and safe too. Probably not a hotel, but self-service apartments, she thought. They reached a door at the end of the corridor. David Gold opened the top and bottom locks and gestured her through. 'Very fancy.'

'Yes, that was the general idea,' he agreed. 'It's quite nice inside too.'

They were on a little dais, which led down to a open-plan living room, dominated by floor-to-ceiling windows. Over the buildings she could see a leafy expanse of green that stretched for miles. She'd never seen it from this high up before.

'Is that Hampstead Heath?'

David Gold didn't say anything at first. He busied himself parking her suitcase and setting down her holdalls, fussing until they were all neatly aligned, then turned to her with a shifty expression.

'How would you feel if I told you things only on a need-to-know basis?'

'Not very happy.' Ellie folded her arms. 'I need to know where I am. So will other people, like my grandparents and the gallery, and knowing where you are is a basic human need. It's why they invented GPS. I can get my phone out and go to Google Maps, but it would be a lot easier if you just tell me.'

His mouth pulled. No smile for her until she toed the party line. 'Very well, we're in Highgate.' He swallowed hard. 'Actually, we're in my flat.' He frowned. 'When I say that out loud, it sounds rather inappropriate, doesn't it?'

Camden, London, 1986

They'd been recording songs in the studio under the railway bridge for two weeks when one of the girlfriends of the band in the studio next door asked if she had a spare tampon and Ari couldn't remember the last time she'd needed a tampon.

She wasn't worried. She often skipped periods when she forgot to take her pill, then doubled up the dose to compensate. She'd also been missing periods because ever since that first encounter with Billy at the Black Horse months ago, Ari had been living on red wine, cigarettes and the edge of her nerves, and her cycle was always screwy when she was stressing about gigs or men and . . . No! Her sister Carol had been trying for a baby for four years. Four years! It was really, really hard to get pregnant and most likely she was anaemic and needed to eat more red meat. That was the most likely explanation.

Not that Ari was already five months pregnant, even though her stomach was as flat as it ever was. She felt like some stupid schoolgirl so in denial about her condition that even her parents didn't know she was up the duff until she went into labour after a hockey match.

Still, it was her body, her choice and Ari chose not to have it heavy with child. Didn't even think twice about it. When Patti Smith had had kids, she'd stopped making music and Ari thought she might die if she had to stop making music.

She wasn't even going to tell Billy because it would just fuck everything up when everything was so good. Then one night, a

221

few days after, she'd peed on a stick with disastrous results. Billy played her a song he'd been working on. It was good but she knew how to make it better, and after hours of plugging away Ari stumbled upon a chorus that sounded like nothing she'd heard before but was so catchy, she could have sworn she'd been humming the melody all her life, even as she riffed on The Crystals' 'He Hit Me': 'He touched me and it felt like a kiss.' She pulled a face as she scribbled down the lines in one of the Black n' Red Notebooks they were using to make notes on each song. 'Lyric needs work, doesn't it?'

Billy didn't answer at first. They were sitting side by side on a sagging sofa in the seedy studio that always smelled of damp, even on a hot September evening. Then he lifted her hand to his lips. 'You know something? The songs have never sounded like this before. You're my muse.'

It was the kind of crap that always made Ari snort in derision, but this time she burst into tears and when Billy held her and kissed her damp cheeks, she said it. 'I'm pregnant.'

'Is it mine?' he asked, without missing a beat.

'Of course it's yours,' she snapped back. 'Don't worry, there's no way I'm having it.' It was that simple. Ari pushed Billy's hand away when he splayed it across her belly. 'Don't,' she said. 'And don't go sentimental on me. It doesn't suit you.'

Chapter Seventeen

Ellie nodded. 'Inappropriate does seem to cover it.' Now that she knew exactly where she was, she couldn't step away from the front door because if she did, then she was committing to this crazy scheme. She'd never thought David Gold would do crazy. 'Is this just for today, while you sort something else out?'

'Really, when you've calmed down—'

'I'm not uncalm. I'm just . . . perturbed.'

'I can't imagine why,' he said a little sharply. 'You can't possibly think that this is some elaborate scheme to get you on your own so I can . . . what? What could you possibly think my ulterior motive might be for bringing you here?'

When he put it like that, like he was spitting out cherry stones, Ellie felt chastened and ashamed. It was as if he could read her mind: knew about her ridiculous crush on him and the dirtybadwrongporno fantasies that were beginning to blossom.

'It's just odd,' she said woodenly. She wasn't going to cry. She wasn't. But she'd had barely any sleep in the last two days and she was in David Gold's apartment with nowhere else to go, and if he kept barking at her, then she *would* weep. 'Please don't talk to me in that tone of voice,' she managed to add.

'I'm sorry,' he said, but he didn't sound it. 'Surely you understand that you need to be contained.'

'I'm not an airborne toxic virus,' Ellie protested, and when he stepped down into his huge living space, she stayed where she was. 'Mr Gold, when you said you were going to help, I didn't expect you were going to hold me hostage.'

'You're not a hostage,' he said, sitting down on a huge oatmeal-coloured modular sofa, so he could see the mulish expression on her face. 'You're a reluctant house-guest. A guestage, if you will. I think you can call me David now, don't you?'

Ellie didn't want to call him David as though they were first-name-term buddies. It was better to keep things on a professional footing. She also didn't want to stay in his flat where she'd have to remain on her best behaviour. Did he even have a spare room? And what if she bumped into him while she was wearing only a towel or something? Or he was in a towel? It was too unsettling. She'd never be able to relax, she thought as she took one tiny step that led her to the second stair down. 'This is really going above and beyond for the sake of your client, isn't it?'

'It really is,' he agreed smoothly, without even a hint of censure at said client.

'Did Billy Kay ask you to do this? Does he know I'm here? At this stage, it would be kind of polite for him to call me up, check that everything's OK, don't you think? Or is that entirely your remit? Making sure the bastard daughter is locked away in case she goes rogue again? You totally think I tipped off the tabloids about the hotel, don't you? Don't you? Why would I even do that? Why would you think that I'd want yet *another* picture of myself in yet *another* state of undress on the front pages? Do I look like any part of this is fun?'

She was nodding her head like a demented children's toy and her voice was climbing higher and higher to a pitch where she'd be able to shatter every single one of the floor-to-ceiling windows. Ellie was also aware that her legs didn't want to hold her up any longer. But mostly she was painfully aware of David Gold sitting there and looking at her as if she was a living, breathing encapsulation of everything that was wrong with the world.

Ellie sat down heavily on the steps staring at the living room, which was sleek and spotless, the walls a glossy white that didn't seem like paint, the wooden floorboards so smooth it was impossible to believe they'd started life as trees, and rested her elbows on her knees, her head in her hands.

'Velvet?'

'Can't you even get that right? It's Ellie!' It was almost a scream.

He stood up. For a second Ellie imagined that he'd stride over, slap her face and tell her to stop being hysterical. Lola would have, but he was walking away, only to return with a glass of water, which he handed to her, then sat down next to her.

'Drink that. You'll feel better.'

She was already gulping it down, her swallows deafening in the sound-proofed silence of his fancy fifteenth-floor flat. Not that Ellie cared any more. It was obvious what he thought of her and it wasn't anything good and there was no point trying to summon up the energy it would take to change his mind.

'Now, you need to stop firing an endless round of questions at me,' he continued, folding up his long bony legs. Tabitha had once told Ellie that she should never take a lover whose thighs were thinner than hers . . . 'Some of them are none of your concern. Some of them are extremely insulting to you, me and Billy Kay and some of them I'll try to answer when you're feeling calmer.'

Ellie swallowed again, even though she'd finished the glass of water. 'I've already told you that I am calm,' she said mutinously.

'No, you're not,' he said, and he put his hand on her

knee. It was wholly inappropriate touching but his hand was large, his skin cool, when she felt small and like she was burning up from some inner conflagration. His touch was comforting, anchoring, and Ellie needed to snap out of this. She didn't really know anything about David Gold, but he didn't smile nearly as much as he had at first, and that steely edge was showing more the longer she spent with him.

She looked around. There was a dining table at the furthest end of the living space and beyond that a kitchen. 'Have you got a spare room?'

'Let me show you,' he offered.

There was an archway through the kitchen, which led to an internal corridor off which was the master bedroom, the door firmly shut, a huge bathroom, a perfectly nice guest room, whose windows opened out on to a balcony that stretched the length of the flat, and a study.

'I absolutely can't stay here, even if you think that's only because I've got an urgent appointment with a tabloid hack,' Ellie said tightly, though after one glimpse of the double bed in the guest room with its fluffy white duvet and mound of pillows, she'd really wanted to hurl herself on it. 'Anyway, I couldn't impose.'

'If I minded the imposition you wouldn't be here,' David Gold said. He shut the door of the guest room. The tour ended back where they'd started: on the dais by the front door. 'Let's talk about this later. I need to get back to the office now.'

'I already told you, I'm not staying here. You said you've had clients who've been in this situation; I bet you didn't kidnap them. You must know a hotel I can go to where the staff won't tip anyone off,' Ellie argued, but her voice sounded as if it was coming from a long way away and she was leaning against the wall because her body wasn't doing a very good job of holding her upright.

'Please stop being so melodramatic. I'm asking you to

time for polka dots. Or another woman who was a more permanent fixture; some perfect size-six testament to all the qualities that Ellie would never possess.

Certainly a girlfriend couldn't have thought it was a good idea that the white glossy walls were actually cupboard doors, which slid back (after pushing and pulling had got her nowhere) to reveal a plasma TV and other audio visual accoutrements, CDs, which Ellie decided not to scrutinise because compared to Ari's collection of vinyl anyone else's music library was pitiful, books, mostly deathly dull law tomes and Scandi crime thrillers, and that was it.

This apartment belonged to a man who'd turned being urbane into an art form and used it to hide away anything that hinted at a personality. This apartment certainly didn't belong to the smiley, flirty guy she'd met a month ago but she had to forget about *him*. He was gone and he wasn't coming back. The man who was wearing his face was unfathomable like some deep, dark ocean, and Ellie was out of her depth and barely treading water.

The apartment also made Ellie rethink her plans for minimalist living because minimalist living was time-consuming and stressful. You had to tidy up after every minor task, from pouring yourself a glass of water to drying your hands on a towel after you'd washed your hands.

Even pulling out her laptop, iPad and assorted cables made Ellie feel that she was violating David Gold's hallowed living space. She set up shop on the dining-room table and logged into her work mail folder. It contained a huge bullet-pointed email from Vaughn of all the tasks he wanted her to action while she was off-site – from finalising contracts to working with his New York gallery on bringing the Emerging Scandinavian Artists exhibition to the mean streets of Chelsea. He also wanted her to start sourcing paintings on domestic life between the wars, the more obscure and female the artist the better, as he had a hunch that that might be the next big thing but 'to be on the safe side, find out if another series of *Downton Abbey* has been commissioned'. Ellie had thought she was too exhausted to bristle but she could feel her shoulders and her hackles rising.

Amid all the *Sturm und Drang*, she'd almost forgotten that he'd sacked her yesterday. It was a measure of how her neat, ordered life had descended into chaos that being fired didn't rate so highly, but now it was something to fixate on, brood over, wipe away the inevitable angry tears.

Vaughn hadn't even bothered to throw any small crumbs of praise in Ellie's direction for the success of last night's opening. She was still fired and he expected her to fit three months' worth of work into four weeks. The really annoying thing was that she'd tick off every item on his tasksheet and probably end up finding her own replacement, she realised with a despondent, resigned sigh. How she longed to have the private income and the balls to tell Vaughn what he could do with his month's notice and his gargantuan to-do list.

Of course there were follow-up emails from Piers, who wanted to know where she was so he could courier over contracts, the portable lightbox and case after case of tiny slides. Even Inge had stirred herself to email Ellie as 'all sorts of interesting things have arrived with your name on them and they won't fit on a bike. Might have to send a car. Where are you anyway? Still lots of paparazzi outside but would be lovely to see you at El Vino for lunch.'

Going to El Vino for lunch the day after an opening was a work tradition. They'd dose their hangovers with a couple of bottles of Pinot Grigio and perform a post-mortem on the launch party. Today they'd be gossiping without her.

Meanwhile, there was nothing Ellie could do on the work front until she'd persuaded David Gold to stop withholding his home address. The thought of ringing him filled her with dread. When she thought about him returning to the flat later on that evening, her heart started thudding so frantically that she had to place her hand flat against her breastbone and practise deep breathing. But while she was in a panicky place, she might just as well go with the feeling and, really, there was no putting it off any longer – she hadn't checked her non-work email since Friday evening.

There was the very real possibility that she might actually throw up all over David Gold's dining-room table when she saw that she had emails from a couple of her exes, her so-called lame ducks. Heart pounding all over again, fingers trembling, she read the two emails, expecting the very worst: that they'd sold intimate details of their time together and had had a last-minute pang of conscience, but though Andy (ex-gambler) cracked a very unfunny joke about how Ellie had never put out like that for him, he and Jimmy (former alcoholic) couldn't have been sweeter or more concerned about how she was holding up.

Ellie felt somewhat vindicated. Tess and Lola were wrong. She wasn't a bad judge of character if at least two of her exes were rallying around her. She wasn't some drunken party girl with morals as loose as her knicker elastic either. No, she was just your average, bog-standard twenty-something who'd had her heart broken as she searched for the one man who would never, ever break her heart. She still wasn't sure that she was going to pass on their contact details to David Gold, but if the tabloids managed to track Andy and Jimmy down, then Ellie was pretty sure (about eighty-seven per cent sure) that they'd never betray her, though she didn't feel that confident about some of the other blasts from her past.

David Gold rang as she was in the middle of a huge Facebook friend cull. She'd already Fort Knox-ed her privacy settings, though as most of her photo albums were already in the possession of the picture desks of most national newspapers it was too little, way, way too late. Now she was deleting any 'friends' she hadn't worked with or got drunk with in the last year, as well as any friends who felt the need to poke her or send her messages gleefully commiserating about her tabloid ordeal. Some guy that Tess had dated for all of three weeks when they were seventeen had asked if she'd pass a demo tape on to Billy Kay, and her second cousin, who'd gone hardcore Orthodox after visiting Israel in her gap year, wanted Ellie to know 'that your disgraceful behaviour just fans the flames of anti-Semitic hate', so Ellie was positively stabby with rage when she answered her phone.

'Hello!' she snapped, then realised it wasn't her God-bothering second cousin, Rivka, but David Gold. 'I'm sorry. I thought you were someone else.'

'It doesn't sound as if you followed my advice and had a nap,' he said obliquely. 'Apart from that, have you settled in?'

'I connected to the Wi-Fi without any problems and I'm a big fan of the ice-maker in your fridge,' she said, because in her experience it was best to start with the positives before you moved on to the more controversial items on the itinerary.

'Use bottled water in the ice-maker, not tap water.' He made a tiny noise that despite its minuteness still conveyed much irritation. 'Actually, leave it. I'll do it when I get home. What do you want to do about dinner tonight?'

It wasn't any of his business what Ellie was going to do about dinner that night because she would be out of his flat and out of his hair by then. 'Well, I already told you that I'm not staying with—'

'I could order something for tonight or . . . do you

cook?' he suggested, as though her protests weren't worth a moment of his attention.

'Hell, no!' He'd lured her to his flat under false pretences and now he wanted her to stay there under duress and chop, stir and apply heat to raw ingredients. She could only take so much. 'I can't cook. I only warm food up. Under supervision.'

'I see. I'll endeavour to make sure that you don't starve.'

'That's not really any of your concern as I'm going as soon as you get in. Though, I suppose if it came to it, I could survive for about a week on your cereal bars,' she joked, and he breathed in sharply as if he really thought she was going to scarf down all his precious, very dry-looking cereal bars. So much for his urbanity – one threat about the sparse contents of his kitchen cupboards and it was shot to pieces. 'So what time are you coming home?'

'About seven thirty,' he said, which was hours away and . . . 'If that's all, then I should be—'

'Don't go!' Ellie yelped. 'I need your address! Work have to send me important things today, and Ari and my grandmother like to know where I am at any—'

'Velvet, we agreed that we wouldn't tell anyone where you were,' he reminded her in a quiet voice that drip-drip-dripped down her spine. 'As a controlled experiment to see who, if anyone, was leaking your whereabouts to the press.'

'I can't believe you still think I've been alerting the media to my every last move,' Ellie said incredulously. 'I'm not going to tell everyone where I'll be, just the Gallery, who are under pain of death to keep schtum, and my mum and grandma, who I'd trust with my life because they're, you know, my mum and my grandma. And you know how you keep calling me Velvet as a way of cutting me down when you think I'm being a brat? It doesn't work. All it does is piss me off.'

It was infuriating the way he treated Ellie as if there was something distasteful and unlikeable about her. People, generally, liked Ellie and she worked hard to make them like her, but it was as if he could see right through her. Cut through all the effort and care she took to present herself to the world and saw what was underneath: a woman who was always a little lost, a little confused, straining for what was just beyond her grasp, no matter how much she managed to style it out and fool everyone else.

'I call you Velvet because it's your name—'

'No, it's really not—'

'And I'm afraid I can't give you an address. It's out of the question. Not yet. You need to give me time to formulate a strategy.'

'A what? You can't keep me here and . . .'

She was talking to dead air. David Gold had hung up on her. Ellie scraped back her chair, not caring that it might leave marks on the pristine wood floor, and skidded over to the front door, which resisted all her efforts to turn its handle.

He'd locked her in! Ellie hurled herself at the door, which was no practical help but she still continued to do it for another five minutes until she gave it up as a bad job. She couldn't even open the windows, and she imagined that as the afternoon sun became fiercer and brighter, it would bake her slowly from the inside out like a little doggie left in a car by a callous owner.

It would serve David Gold right when he finally came home to find Ellie dead from heat exhaustion, though actually it wouldn't be very pleasant for Ellie or her loved ones. It also didn't solve the problem of how she was meant to deal with the urgent items on Vaughn's bullet-pointed list if she didn't have a physical address for physical things to be sent to.

Ellie wasted precious time trying to pinpoint her exact

location with the aid of Google Maps on her iPad, streetmap.co.uk on her MacBook and the satnav app on her phone, but while her iPad had it narrowed down to the point where two streets converged near Highgate Village, her iPhone was convinced she was in Spalding, Lincolnshire, which was no help at all.

Then light dawned. She might not have an actual physical address but she knew someone who did.

At half past seven, as Ellie was sending the last of her speculative emails to a gallery in Leeds, she heard a key in the lock. She ignored the urge to run to the door to start berating David Gold before he could even set foot over the threshold and stayed where she was.

She even pretended she was engrossed in a very dry press release from the Arts Council as he came through the door. At least she thought it was David Gold, but his face was obscured by a huge bunch of flowers: wild roses, lilacs and lavender, all wrapped in brown paper and tied with a baby-blue ribbon. The strategy he'd been busy formulating obviously involved a major charm offensive, Ellie thought. She was determined to remain immune to it.

'How dare you give out my office address to all and sundry like it's your own personal mail box,' he thundered, so maybe she was wrong about his new strategy. He was also weighed down with several bags and the gallery's portable lightbox. 'I had to get a car home.'

That was what was bothering him? Really? 'Just add it to my bill.' Ellie could feel her brows knitting together in what she was sure was a murderous scowl. No one had ever made her feel murderous before.

'That's not the point,' he snapped, dumping the flowers down on the table, then slowly relinquishing his grip on the bags. 'I had my entire day disrupted signing for deliveries that apparently couldn't be signed for by my assistant. I was even called out of a meeting and I

235

always run home on a Tuesday. This is not acceptable.'

There was nothing Ellie could say because she was speechless. She kept opening her mouth but her brain wasn't capable of sending words down the pipe so she had to shut it again. By the time she finally managed to wheeze out an indignant, 'I'm sorry! Your day has been disrupted?' David Gold was already in the kitchen and tutting furiously by the time Ellie caught up with him.

'You've made a mess,' he cried and he did almost sound like he was crying as he pointed at the plastic tray that had once contained sushi. Ellie had washed it with hot soapy water and left it to drain on the draining board because she didn't know what the deal was *vis-à-vis* rubbish and recycling, and anyway, everyone knew that you didn't throw out stinky, fish receptacles without rinsing them first. She hadn't been raised by wolves. 'You can't leave things lying around.'

He was already stomping back into the living room and was now pointing at the bags that he'd dropped on the floor. 'You were the one who left them lying around,' Ellie reminded him tightly. 'And I hate to sound competitive but while you were having a bad day, I'm having a bad month. About ninety per cent of my life was in ruins last time I checked. Do you think I'm having any kind of fun?'

When Ellie quantified it like that, it made it seem worse: like the ten per cent that was AOK wasn't going to be enough to pull her through. She bowed her head, let her hair cover her face, because she could feel the weight of the world bearing heavily down on her and turned away because she didn't want to be this vulnerable in front of him. The tears surely couldn't be *that* far away now.

'Oh God, I can't do this,' he murmured, as if she were pushing him right to the edge and he didn't have the time or patience for it. As he brushed past her, not even able to hide his distaste as his jacket sleeve caught her arm, Ellie almost felt nostalgic for the smarmy smiles he'd used to give her. Mostly, though, she felt crushed as if another five per cent of her life had suddenly crumbled to ash. 'It's expecting too much of me.'

Ellie's voice returned at around the time she heard the door to the master bedroom slam shut so she had no other option but to stand outside and say heatedly, 'I don't want to do this either! I'm not going to speak to the press – as if – but I'm not staying here . . . Are you even listening to me?'

She wasn't sure if he was or he wasn't, but as she tentatively lifted a hand to knock, the door suddenly swung open and she nearly fell headfirst into David Gold's arms. She struggled away before there might be any touching, and of course she was blushing, but that wasn't important when David Gold was standing there in a white running vest and navy-blue shorts. Not short shorts, but still Ellie's eyes felt as if they were popping right out of their sockets. It had certainly taken her mind off the existential crisis that she'd spiralled into. It also explained why he had no form of sustenance in his flat apart from foul-tasting sports drinks and huge tubs of protein powder.

He was thin and probably could do with bulking up, but it was a lean, wiry thin. Like a greyhound with sleek muscles and a quiet strength. Ellie was standing there like a gormless idiot, drinking him in, until he physically shifted her out of his way, his hands on her arms, and for one unbelievable second Ellie was sure her feet left the floor.

'I'm going out for a run.'

For the second time that day, he walked out on her.

Chapter Eighteen

Ellie couldn't quite believe it, then, once again, she was hurling herself futilely at the door, which had locked behind him. It didn't miraculously open, even when she hammered on it with both fists until she realised that getting angry was simply making her feel worse.

She splashed cold water on her face and on her wrists, which Sadie swore was the most effective way of calming down. It did absolutely nothing to lower Ellie's blood pressure so she phoned Ari. Ari always knew the right thing to say.

'Sweetie? Tried to call but your phone was switched off,' Ari told her. Ellie had tried to call her too, but *her* phone had been switched off. 'Saw the photos on the *Chronicle* website. They are the most unbelievable scum. Are you all right?'

'No, I've been much, much, much better.'

'What's up? Well, apart from—'

'It's not that. Well, it's mostly that,' Ellie admitted, though the argument she'd just had with David Gold – if you could really call it an argument when he kept absenting himself each time she raised her voice – was painfully fresh in her mind. 'Have you ever met someone and maybe you didn't even like them, because they were a total and utter tool, but still felt attracted to them?'

'Yeah, but only when I was younger and I thought

that love had to be doomed and desperate and involve china-smashing rows at three in the morning or it didn't mean anything,' Ari said drily, which wasn't very encouraging.

'But have you ever been with someone and even though you've never kissed them, when they stand close or look at you in a certain way, it feels like a kiss?'

'Ellie, do you really think this is the best time to launch into another relationship?'

'I'm not.' That was the truth, after all. 'I . . . I'm just very confused. Have you though, Mum? Have you had those kinds of feelings?'

'Yes, and nothing good ever comes of them.' Ari sort of chuckled but only sort of. 'Well, maybe one good thing.'

'So what do I do?' Ellie asked desperately. 'Because I don't want to feel this way about this person.'

'Well . . . hang on! Where are you and who's this person treating you like shit?'

'They're not.' Though he wasn't treating her well. 'Just someone. You don't know them.'

'But I know you, Ellie, and I know when you're lying to me.'

'I'm not lying!'

'You're being evasive so you don't technically have to lie. Where are you and who are you with?'

Sometimes Ellie hated that she and Ari told each other everything. What she wouldn't give for some benign neglect. 'You'll get mad if I tell you and I can't deal with you being mad at me right now.'

There was silence as Ari processed this. 'You know I don't normally lay down the law because that's not my style. I'm a cool mum . . .'

'You are. You're the coolest.'

'. . . But I'm telling you now to get out. Run. Don't look back. Men like that will hurt you, darling, and I can't bear the thought of you suffering from that kind of hurt.'

239

Ellie couldn't leave because she was locked in someone's flat and as she wondered how she could possibly say that out loud to her mother, she knew that Ari was right. She needed to get the hell away from David Gold.

'I will,' she said, and she really meant it. 'But, you know, sometimes I am going to get hurt, Mum. It's just the way the world is.'

'You do not get hurt. Not on my watch,' Ari insisted grimly, but Ellie knew there wasn't much Ari could do about vindictive ex-boyfriends or morally ambiguous lawyers.

'I do love you, Mum,' was what she said instead. Then, desperate to change the subject: 'Anyway, enough about me. How are you holding up?'

'Oh, me? Don't worry about me.' There was the faint sound of displaced air as Ari made her patented 'pffft' noise, which didn't really work over the phone. 'Except I'm pissed off with Chester and he's pissed off with me.'

'Why would you be pissed off with Chester?' Ellie asked in surprise, because Chester wasn't even in the country. Every year, without fail, Chester went to Spain for a Northern Soul week with a gang of his oldest friends. 'I thought he was still in Benidorm. Or he was when I spoke to him earlier.'

'He is, and I told him to stay there when he wanted to come rushing back,' Ari told her tartly. 'He got really snippy, but all I said was that we didn't need him.'

'Well, to say that you don't need him does sound a little callous,' Ellie said, because she'd had much the same conversation with Chester, but when she'd told him not to rush back it was because his week in Benidorm was sacrosanct, no matter how much Ellie did need him.

'But we don't *need* him. I love Chester, you know I do, but you and me, we can manage fine, just the two of us,'

Ari insisted. 'That's the way it's always been. That's the way it's going to stay.'

'I know we can, but I don't see you turning down Tabitha's offers of help . . .'

'Oh! Talking of Tab, she says you can sleep in her spare room, as soon as she's got the moth infestation under control.'

'I think I'll pass,' Ellie said quickly, before Ari could derail the conversation, because it was going in a direction that she didn't like. 'So why is it all right for Tabitha to be there for us, but not Chester?'

'Because Chester, God love him, is a man and you can never, ever rely on a man, babes. They'll always let you down. It's in their DNA.'

'Well, Grandpa's never let me down,' Ellie pointed out, as she always did when they started down this well-worn path, but Ari just sniffed. Usually Ellie backed off, but this time she ploughed forward into the tangled undergrowth. 'Is this what happened with Billy Kay? Is this why he left and never wanted anything to do with us, because you said that we didn't need him?'

'What?'

'Obviously I don't know the exact circumstances but this no-contact thing of his . . . maybe it wouldn't have been so drastic and absolute if you'd, I don't know, left a window open for him. A metaphorical window.' This wasn't what Ellie wanted to say or how she'd wanted to say it, and from Ari's silence ticking away like an un-exploded bomb at the other end of the line, she wished she'd left well alone.

'So, are you saying that it's my fault that Billy Kay didn't send you birthday cards or call you up for a chat? Or are you implying that he *did* send you birthday cards and I lay in wait for the postman to intercept them so—'

'No! Of course I'm not saying that! What I'm saying is that I thought I'd accepted the fact that Billy Kay wanted nothing to do with me a long time ago and that I'd made my peace with it, but now that I've been outed as his secret daughter I realise that I'm not actually at peace with it. Not at all.'

Ari sighed as if all the fight was draining out of her. 'Look, babycakes, we've been through this before. What is the point of dredging it up all over again?'

They'd never been through it before. Not really. Ellie knew that now wasn't the time, but one day when this was all over – and Ellie hoped that day would come very soon – she was going to sit down with Ari and find out what had really happened with Billy Kay. The affair. The break-up. All the painful, gory details, apart from the sex stuff, which she absolutely did not need to know about.

She wasn't going to let Ari fob her off with, 'It's too painful to talk about,' or, 'You'll never understand because you're too smart to let someone snatch your heart away.' She couldn't get by on the crumbs she'd been fed by Tabitha and Tom, and even Sadie when she'd had one glass of semi-sweet white wine too many. Ellie was a big girl now and she could deal with the ugly truth. But on reflection, she probably couldn't deal with the ugly truth right now.

'Sorry, Mum. I'm tired and cranky. I didn't mean to take it out on you.'

'Right back at you, honey. We will get through this. What do I always say? When life gives you lemons, you slice the lemons and make a gin and tonic.'

Ellie wouldn't have said no to a gin and tonic administered by rapid drip, but while she had Ari on the phone, she needed advice that wasn't cocktail-related. 'By the way, I need to ask you something and when you answer, don't exaggerate for dramatic effect, OK?'

'I don't exaggerate for dramatic effect. I feel things deeply. It's what creative people do.'

'Yeah, yeah, whatever.' Ellie looked up at the halogen

spotlights in the ceiling for inspiration. She really didn't want to keep bringing up Ari's past but this was something she couldn't put off. 'Do you know a Georgie Leigh? I think she used to be called Georgina Pratt?'

There was silence and for a moment Ellie thought they'd been cut off until Ari made a strange, indecipherable bitten-off sound. 'She is fucking evil incarnate,' she said in a voice that was flatter than Holland. 'Why?'

Ellie tried to hit the highlights, but she hadn't got any further than Georgie turning up with David Gold last night before Ari was butting in with: 'You do not have anything to do with her. You do not speak to her. You don't believe a single word that comes out of that cesspool that she calls a mouth, do you hear me?'

Ari was shouting, but she didn't sound angry so much as scared and rattled, as if someone had shaken her hard enough to loosen her internal organs.

'But maybe she's changed? It's been a long time, Mum. She was really nice. Very understanding. Very sympathetic,' Ellie said. 'I'm sorry if I've upset you, but—'

'I'm not upset. I'm worried about you. Georgina Pratt is not good people. She's very, very bad people.'

'It's just that she's Billy's publicist so I do need to talk to her, I suppose.'

'I don't see why,' Ari argued. 'She used to be absolutely toxic. I can't believe that she's changed that much, and as for that lawyer—'

'You've never even met him!'

'There's no such thing as a nice lawyer. Everyone knows that. That expensive lawyer and Georgina Pratt are there to do what Billy wants. I'm sorry, baby, but I don't see you factoring that highly on the list of Billy's priorities. All he cares about is himself so it's a pretty fucking short list.'

Ellie was always going to take Ari's side. Always. Even if it turned out that Ari had murdered Georgie's family in cold blood, then framed Georgie for the crime, Ellie would find some extenuating circumstances and plead Ari's case. So, really, it didn't matter whether Georgie had changed her ways, if she was Ari's enemy, then she was Ellie's enemy too, not to be trusted with Ellie's exes or anything else belonging to Ellie. And the same went for David Gold.

It simpled things up. If they were on Billy Kay's team then, according to Ari, they couldn't be on Ellie's team too. But if she was being honest with herself and not still clinging to silly childish dreams, Ellie had always known that Billy Kay wasn't going to come through for her. 'You're right, Mum. Between the two of us, we manage just fine, don't we?'

'Damn right we do. Now promise me you'll get the hell out of Dodge.'

Getting the hell out had to wait until David Gold returned. In the meantime Ellie had had five missed calls from Tess since she'd been on the phone to Ari.

'What's going on?' Tess demanded, as soon as she answered the phone. 'I got your message saying that all personal effects and correspondence had to be sent to the hot, intense lawyer's office. Where are you actually staying?'

'He's not hot,' Ellie cried, because talking to Ari had made it clear she needed to kill this crush, stat. 'He's very, very cold and, Tess, I'm locked in his bloody flat!'

'Really? Are you? How kinky! So, you're staying with a Jewish lawyer of good prospects and marriageable age who owns his own home,' Tess practically chortled. 'Isn't that a full house in Jewish bachelor bingo?'

Ellie felt as if she'd run the gamut of every dark, draining emotion in existence during her call to Ari – she wasn't mentally prepared to now be mercilessly teased. 'Shut up! It's not at all funny! I'm not staying with him. I was brought here under false pretences and now I'm being held hostage . . .'

There was a noise in the background and Ellie heard

Tess say, 'It's Ellie. She's all shacked up with the cute lawyer from last night. Shall I put her on speakerphone?'

There was a click, then the disembodied static of being on speakerphone and Lola saying gleefully, 'You're hooking up with that David guy? Haven't we talked about getting involved with dudes that we haven't vetted first? Bet you any money that he's another lame duck. Come on, what's wrong with him?'

'What's wrong with him? What's bloody right with him?' When he wasn't there, infecting her brain with his pheromones, it was easy not to want him. 'He's controlling, his charm is just a front, he *hates* me and he's got really severe OCD.'

'Now I researched a segment on OCD and actually it's not just about being super tidy; they have rituals and a prescient sense of doom,' Tess explained earnestly.

'For fuck's sake, who even cares?' Lola demanded. Ellie had to agree with her.

'You know how you take the piss because I always remember to buy milk just before we run out and you say that's my secret superpower? Well, he has a barely started two-litre bottle of milk *and a* spare one!'

'Oh my God, what kind of freak is he?' Lola exclaimed, and then both of them giggled and it wasn't even the least bit funny.

'He's locked me in and he keeps slamming doors in my face and he told me off for washing out my sushi container and leaving it on the draining board, and I just can't take any more.' Ellie's voice was climbing up the upper register again and she'd been on the verge of tears so often in the last few days that her throat ached and her eyes itched from trying to keep them at bay. 'He only wants me here because he thinks I've been running my mouth off to every newspaper in town, but at the same time he doesn't want me here. It's awful.'

'Ellie, we were only teasing,' Tess said gently, and then

Ellie heard Lola stage whisper: 'Christ, she's cracking up. I'm amazed that she's lasted this long.'

'I'm on speakerphone, I can hear every word you're saying,' Ellie sniffed, then there was another sniff and . . . 'I just want to come home.'

Tess and Lola were much better at managing crises than some other people that Ellie could mention. As it was late Tuesday evening and the press scrum outside their flat had whittled down to a paltry two photographers and one guy with a video camera, they cooked up a convoluted scheme whereby once she managed to escape, though they were foggy on the details, Ellie would be driven up to the restaurant's back door, where an extendable ladder would be placed so she could enter their flat via their unofficial roof terrace.

Also, 'You should wash and blowdry your hair, Ellie,' Tess added. 'You always feel better once you've done that.'

By the time she put the phone down, Ellie was calmer. Once she'd filled them in on David Gold's many character flaws, which was a good form of aversion therapy, Tess and Lola had been suitably disparaging, because that's what friends did.

'He's gone for a run?' Lola had spat incredulously just before they'd said their goodbyes. 'It's like a hundred degrees.'

'It would serve him right if he dropped down dead from heatstroke,' Tess had said, then paused and told Ellie in a serious voice to give it another hour and if David Gold hadn't returned then she was to call the police and the fire brigade to rescue her, and possibly the ambulance service because they needed to know there was a dead lawyer somewhere on or around Hampstead Heath.

David Gold wasn't dead, though, because not half an hour later Ellie heard his key in the lock again. This time she was ready. She was standing by the front door with most of her bags packed and the bouquet of flowers, sent by Mandy Stretton née McIntyre, who'd scrawled on the card, 'Keep your pecker up, sweetie,' cradled in her arms.

As the door opened and he stood there, red-faced, coated in a fine sheen of sweat and with a wary expression on his face, Ellie charged at him, dragging her suitcase behind her. 'I'm going,' she said unnecessarily, and he had to duck out of her way because, so help her God, she would have mown him down and possibly kneed him in the groin if he'd tried to impede her progress. 'Sorry, I've had to leave some of my stuff behind. I'll get someone to pick it up tomorrow.'

Then she was beetling down the corridor towards the lift. Not beetling very fast because she was loaded up like a pack mule so it was easy enough for him to catch up with her. 'Velvet . . . Ellie. Where are you going?'

'Well, I'm hardly going to tell you!' She still didn't exactly know where she was going. Her first priority was to get in the lift. Without David Gold. 'I have options and even if I have to go back to my own flat and be pushed and shoved and have vile questions shouted at me by a pack of rude, ill-mannered reporters then it still has to be better than being locked up in your apartment.'

It would probably be better if she focused on getting into the lift rather than coming to a halt so she could give David Gold a telling-off. He was a few metres away from her but she could still feel the waves of heat coming off him – it was like standing downwind from a blast furnace. He was panting slightly, his hair wet with perspiration, the curls kicking in again, and it was no wonder that he was so lanky when he went running for hours in the middle of a heatwave.

'You're not thinking clearly,' he said a little breathlessly.

'You don't know me. You don't know how I think,' Ellie argued. She took a firm grip on her suitcase handle and carried on towards the lift. Then she stopped and turned

247

because David Gold was following her. 'Look, just go away.' She made a shooing motion with the hand that was clutching the flowers and her laptop case. 'Go and have one of your electrolyte drinks before you die from dehydration.'

'You have absolutely no idea of where you're going, do you?' he said, catching Ellie up and walking alongside her. 'I promise you that if you turn up at your flat, you're going to be besieged again.'

'Then I could call my grandfather and he could come and pick me up, and I could lie on the back seat of his Volvo with a rug over me so I couldn't be spotted by any photographers,' Ellie explained. 'Or I could go and stay with Tess's parents.' That was low down on her list of options as Tess's parents had moved out of London to Hertfordshire or Herefordshire, or some other place that was in the countryside.

They were at the lift. David Gold pressed the button so he couldn't be that dismayed that she was escaping. Ellie turned to him. He was dripping sweat onto the parquet flooring, which was disgusting. She assiduously avoided any activities that might cause her to sweat. 'Look, the only reason you brought me here was because you think I'm in cahoots with the press.'

He shrugged. 'It's a logical assumption.'

'No, it's not! It's an insulting assumption, especially when the other reason you want to keep me under surveillance is so you can pump me for my exes' contact details so Georgie Leigh can use them for her own evil ends. Anyway, for all I know, *you* might be the one who's in cahoots with the press.'

For once it was his face that flushed darker, and for a few seconds he stared down at his trainers. When he raised his head Ellie could see that she'd hit on some kind of truth. 'We don't know each other very well, do we?' he said as if he wasn't talking about this argument, but about them, about two unsure, distrustful people thrown together.

'We don't,' Ellie agreed, as the lift finally arrived with a triumphant ping. It was the perfect moment to ask him if he was still the same man she'd met in the middle of a field on a hot Sunday afternoon, but she couldn't bring herself to. 'So, did you leak my location to the press, last night?'

He shook his head. 'No, I didn't. Did you tip off anyone?'

It was Ellie's turn to shake her head. She made sure to look him right in the eye. 'Then it had to have been Georgie.'

The lift doors suddenly began to close and Ellie threw herself at them, but David got there first, stepping into the lift to hold the button to keep the doors open.

'You don't know that it was Georgie for certain,' he said, but Ellie did. She was sure of it.

'My exes: why did you need to know about them? Who asked you to get the lowdown on them? What were you going to do with the information?'

'Usually in these situations, I contact all parties involved and slap them with a pre-emptive gagging order and a lot of nasty legal threats. It's largely nothing more than grandstanding. Not that they know that,' he finished with a wry smile.

Ellie made sure her gaze was steady and true. 'So, that's what you were going to do, was it?'

'It's what *I* was going to do. I can't speak for anyone else.'

She rubbed the back of her hand over her tired eyes. 'None of this is fair.'

He made one of those fleeting gestures towards her that he always thought better of just before he touched her. 'I'm sorry. I haven't really appreciated how difficult this must be for you,' he said very, very gently.

Don't be nice. It will break me, she thought, and she was able to lift her shoulders half an inch and pull a face to convey that message.

He very deliberately pulled her suitcase away. 'You're not going anywhere tonight,' he decided, and just as deliberately he took her wrist and though his hand was hot and sweaty, Ellie still shivered and she still followed him out of the lift and back down the corridor to his flat.

Camden, London, 1986

Ari was booked into the clinic – she wished she wasn't as far gone as she was, but she couldn't change that. It was Billy who was having trouble dealing with it.

'It's our baby,' he murmured on the night before the termination was due, his curly head resting on her belly. Ari was too bloated with indigestion to push him away.

'It's not a baby,' she told him for the hundredth time, the word making her lips curl. 'It's just a parasite squatting in my uterus. We agreed, Billy.'

'We did. Anyway I've already got one and that hasn't worked out so well.' He changed position, so he was spooned in behind her. 'I had this idea before Lara was born that I'd try to be a good father, but I've never been much of a father or a husband or any of the other things that people expected me to be.'

'I've never expected anything from you,' Ari reminded him because if she didn't expect anything from him, then he'd never disappoint her.

'I know you didn't, but everything's different with you, Ari,' Billy said, cupping her chin so she had to turn her head to look at him. 'Just think. It's my genes, your genes. It's our legacy just as much as the songs are, and the songs might never get heard, but this . . .' His hand curved over the bulge that had started to make its presence felt and meant that Ari couldn't get into her tightest dresses any more. 'We made this. Our love made this.'

'We weren't in love when your sperm found a way to my egg.' She knocked his hand away. 'For fuck's sake, I thought I was

251

the one who was meant to be a slave to my hormones. I'm *not* keeping it!'

'I'm not asking you to. We're going somewhere and a kid would slow us down, but you could have it, couldn't you?' He shrugged, tried to make a joke out of it. 'We could probably get Georgina to look after it if we paid her in chocolate.'

'She would. She'd love that. It would be the ultimate Billy Kay fan artefact,' Ari said sourly, but when Billy's hand covered her stomach again, she rested her hand on top of his and she thought of the baby. A little boy with Billy's dark eyes and sweet smile. Not his nose, though. Her nose. And, hopefully, a sweeter temper than both his parents.

Chapter Nineteen

Ellie perched on the edge of David Gold's vast sectional sofa upholstered in a nubby oatmeal, while he was in the shower, and sipped very carefully from a mug of camomile tea. She dreaded what his reaction might be if she spilled any on his taupe upholstery.

There was the soft sound of footsteps and she looked up to see him coming through the archway into the kitchen. He opened the fridge and pulled out one of his sports drinks.

'Isn't it too hot to go running?' Ellie asked. It was more to fill the silence than anything else, but she was curious to know why any sane person would want to hare around the Heath during what the weather forecasters were calling the worst drought in nearly forty years. 'It can't be good for you in this heat.'

'You sound like my mother,' he said with a grin as he walked into the living room. He was wearing jeans and a dark blue T-shirt, his feet bare, and her mind was reeling, shifting, adjusting its position on him yet again, because he wasn't wearing a suit and, for once, his smile didn't seem to have an agenda. 'I'm running a marathon in Hawaii in September so I need to train when it's hot. Don't look at me like that. Lots of people run marathons.'

They did, he was right. But to go all the way to the other side of the world to run over twenty-six miles was excessive. 'It's not your first marathon, then?'

He shook his head. 'Eleventh. No, twelfth. It becomes addictive after a while.'

'Really? 'Cause I did a sponsored five-k run for charity and after that I swore that I would never go faster than a slow jog ever again,' Ellie said with a shudder. There had been pulled muscles and cramp and lots and lots of sweat.

'So you don't get an exercise high? Pity.' He slid back one of the glossy white cupboard doors to reveal the TV and reached up to one of the high shelves. 'These unlock the windows.' He held up a small bunch of keys for Ellie's inspection. 'There's a shameful amount of M&S ready meals in the freezer, and I'm sorry that I snapped at you when I got in from work but it's been a very stressful two days. Though I'm sure your two days have been much more stressful.'

'More like four days,' Ellie amended with a weak smile, because his apology had been very gracious and it would be churlish to ignore it. 'And I shouldn't have given out your address but I needed my work stuff.' She was getting that throbbing note to her voice again, like the tears weren't far off. Even more than washing and blowdrying her hair, Ellie was sure that if she could just cry it out, she'd feel a whole lot better. 'I did need those things – well, I didn't need the flowers – but I can't sit around and do nothing. I have to keep busy or I'll just . . . well, I don't know what I'll do. At least I still have a job, just, and it's about all that's keeping me together at the moment.'

David slid back one of the windows. It was still hot, but there was the faintest, gossamer hint of a breeze. 'What do you mean by you *just* have a job?'

Ellie sighed. 'I got fired yesterday. Vaughn, my boss, he hates fusses and dramas, and he has a lot of top-drawer artists and clients who also hate fuss and drama.' She rested her elbows on her knees and cupped her chin in her hands. 'He's always threatening to fire me and the rest of the staff, but usually he relents by lunchtime so I'm waiting to see if being sacked sticks or if he'll change his mind.'

David Gold was heading for the other end of the sofa now and that meant that he was looking at her. Ellie shook her head so her hair was covering her face and would hopefully obscure any stray tears that might have the audacity to leak out of her eyes. 'You're handling this very well,' he said softly.

'I'm not. I'm really not.' If she were handling this well, then she wouldn't be on the verge of tears at least once every hour. 'I'm trying to act like it's business as normal, but my normal has completely disappeared.'

'Most people in your position would have taken to their beds by now, so the fact that you're even trying to get on with work is admirable,' David Gold assured her. It was just as well that there was a huge expanse of sofa between them because Ellie suspected if he were close enough to pat her hand in a comforting fashion, it would be her downfall. 'This won't last for ever.'

Ellie managed to shrug. 'Everything has changed now. There are seven, maybe eight people in the world who really know me and love me unconditionally. Then there's everyone else who's read all the stories in the papers and are now judging me and finding me completely wanting.'

Once the paparazzi had packed up their cameras and recorders and moved on to their next victim, Ellie would still be at the mercy of the general public, who were cruel and unforgiving. Men in white vans would bellow rude things about her sexual availability out of their windows, old women would glare at her in shops and mutter stuff under their breath and, even without being a tabloid sensation, she always dreaded having to walk past a gang of teenage girls or rude boys. Now . . . well, now, she might just as well walk the streets of London with the words 'kick me' stamped on her arse.

'I will get through this,' she said, and it wasn't even for

his benefit but as a vow to herself that she wasn't going to fall apart. She was better than that. Ari had brought her up to be stronger than that. 'It's just going to take some time.'

'Ellie? I really think you should stay here for tonight. But if you don't want to, then I'll drive you wherever you want to go.'

David Gold had changed. He was being kind, as if he had no ulterior motive, but was genuinely concerned about her emotional and physical wellbeing. Besides, the thought of having to take her chances on the mean streets of London made Ellie's stomach hurt and she clasped her hands firmly together so they wouldn't shake.

It was funny, really: up here, high in the sky, looking down at the world, Ellie felt safe. Or safer. 'It is getting rather late,' she said carefully, and he ever so slightly ducked his head in one of those almost imperceptible nods, like he was answering a question she didn't have the guts to ask.

'Stay here for the night, sleep on it and decide what you want to do in the morning?' he suggested. Ellie wanted to sigh and sink back on the sofa in relief, but it wasn't the kind of sofa you could sink back on; he didn't even have any cushions and she didn't know what was up with *that*. Still, this new understanding between them, the hauteur that had disappeared once he'd changed out of his suit and tie, made Ellie relax her guard, although . . .

'Withholding your address was not at all cool,' she told him as sharply as she could. 'It was weird and serial killer-y. It might be a good idea if nobody knows my actual geographic location, but that's my call, not yours.'

This time the nod was more decisive. 'I'm happy to give you the address but as your *ipso facto* legal advisor, I would counsel you not to pass it to anyone else.' He held up his hand as Ellie opened her mouth to dispute that. 'I'm sure your friends and family wouldn't divulge your whereabouts to the press, but addresses get written down on pieces of paper, which get dropped and left lying around or typed into phones, which get hacked.'

'Well, OK, I suppose that's a fair point.'

'I'll tell you the address and it's up to you what you do with it, if you decided that you wanted to stay indefinitely.' He wasn't even looking at her, but staring down at his toes. The thought of other people's bare feet, especially men's bare feet, always made Ellie feel bilious – she'd even forced ex-boyfriends with particularly hideous feet to keep their socks on – but David Gold had quite nice feet. They were thin and narrow, like the rest of him, and there was no hair sprouting on his toes and his nails were neatly clipped. Now she was staring at his feet too, couldn't tear her eyes away.

If she still got tingles when he was in a suit and doing his snake-oil salesman patter, then being around when he was doing casual with a grin would be the undoing of her. Not in a getting naked way either. 'I couldn't impose,' she said.

'I already told you that you wouldn't be. Most nights I only come home to sleep.'

If his flat was nothing more than a very expensive crash pad, then surely there was no harm in staying for a day or so? 'Do you really think that if the press don't know where I am, they'll stop printing stories about me?' she asked hopefully.

'Well, at least there won't be any *new* stories, and as an added bonus I'll give you a keycard so you can use the residents' gym.'

Ellie didn't do gyms. They were generally full of sweaty people making grunting sounds. 'That's very nice of you but—'

'There's also a swimming pool. In summer, they open up the skylights,' David Gold said casually, like he wasn't that bothered about the skylights.

Ellie did do swimming pools, though. She'd even packed a couple of bikinis just in case. 'Well, if it's not too much trouble I'll stay for tonight, then see how it goes.'

They were still staring at his feet. He wriggled his toes. 'Do you like Thai food?' he asked suddenly. 'It's just it's late and what with my run and our little spat . . .'

'I do like Thai food, and now you mention it, I am quite hungry,' Ellie admitted. 'Pad Thai?'

'Pad Thai,' he agreed.

Come Thursday evening, Ellie was still in residence. She suspected that she'd outstayed her welcome but David was never around to serve her with an eviction notice and, besides, she didn't really want to go.

In hiding on the fifteenth floor of a luxury flat development, where no one was able to lurk with camera waiting to steal a piece of her for posterity, she'd settled into a nice, comfortable routine. In the mornings she'd sleep in to a very decadent quarter to eight, then as the sound of the front door closing penetrated her subconscious, she'd get out of the very comfortable bed in David's spare room, the mattress firm but with just enough give, and open the patio doors so she could breakfast on the balcony.

Ellie spent most of the day camped out there, slathered in suncream and peering over her laptop at the lush green acres of Hampstead Heath in the near distance. The BBC and the Met Office kept promising rain but the rain never came, and though Ellie knew this was global warming and global warming was generally a very bad thing, her tan was coming along beautifully. Her limbs were now the exact same colour as Brûlée, which was the fake tan shade that she normally had to work up to. She'd stay outside until noon, then the fierce midday sun would force her inside and she'd set up shop on the dining-room table.

Spending so much time solo wasn't easy. As well as questioning her commitment to a minimalist lifestyle,

Ellie was also questioning her ability to eventually live on her own. At home, if Tess or Lola weren't around, Ellie often went downstairs to the restaurant to sit at the bar and drink a glass of wine with Theo. At work, even though she huffed at the constant interruptions, someone, usually Piers, was always coming into her office to look things up in her reference books or borrow her stapler, but mostly for a chat.

Now Ellie worked to the accompaniment of property shows. In the afternoon she switched to programmes about people finding tatty bits of junk in their lofts to sell at auction, which was a bit more work-orientated. When Ellie found herself shouting things like 'Any fool can see that's not Ming dynasty,' or, 'You haven't checked for an artist's mark, you bow-tied buffoon,' it was time to down tools.

She'd change into a bikini, pull on the thick towelling robe that David had lent her and take the lift to the residents' gym on the top floor. Ellie usually had the pool to herself so she could spend an hour alternating breast-stroke for ten lengths and front crawl for ten lengths with her head held at an odd angle because she feared the damage that chlorinated water could wreak on her hair.

Then she returned to the flat for a shower and was back on the balcony with her laptop to soak up the late after-noon sun, even though air-drying made her hair go wavy. At seven, she'd have dinner, then do some more work, Skype her loved ones or catch up on the last season of *Mad Men*. Just before ten, Ellie would do a thorough sweep of the apartment. Cups and plates went in the dishwasher, not the draining board, and she now knew what was rubbish and what was recyclable, and discarded things as appropriate.

At any time between ten thirty and eleven, David would arrive home. Ellie wasn't sure if that was usual; if he had client dinners or a Wednesday night poker game, or if he was out every night flirting with a succession of sleek, effortlessly elegant, go-getting thirty-something women at some hip pop-up restaurant or other, but she stuck around long enough to say goodnight, before retreating to the guest room.

All in all, staying in David's flat wasn't the ordeal that Ellie thought it might be, but she'd never been so mind-numbingly, climb-the-walls bored in her life. She got why he was avoiding her, and being on her own for hour upon hour was better, *safer*, than being around him. Not when she still didn't trust him not to be working some elaborate double-bluff on Billy Kay's behalf. Nor did she want to be one of those sad women who panted after a man in the face of zero encouragement, especially when the man in question was out of bounds. Boredom was preferable to making a complete fool of herself or being caught as she came out of the bathroom with a towel precariously wrapped round her like something out of a *Benny Hill* sketch.

But at twenty to eight on Thursday evening, Ellie was sick to death of her own company, and of Skype-ing Sadie, who was somewhat aggrieved there were no photographers outside her house any more. On Tuesday, when Morry wasn't at home to park Sadie's car on the drive, as he'd been doing for the last forty years, a lovely young man from a picture agency had done it for her.

'You shouldn't have let him in your car, Grandma,' Ellie said wearily. 'They're not doing it to be nice but to plant a tracking device or something. I bet you let them in to use the loo, didn't you?'

'I never let them in the house,' Sadie insisted. 'They've gone now anyway, so do you think you might come for Friday night dinner tomorrow? And where are you staying? Ariella wouldn't say.'

That's because Ariella didn't know and wasn't very happy about it.

Sadie peered out of the computer monitor at her as if she was scanning what she could see of her granddaughter's location for clues. 'I told you already, I'm laying low until all the fuss has died down.'

It seemed as if all the fuss *was* dying down. Ari had lost her press tail, Tess and Lola said that the scrum outside their flat was down to one news agency stringer and two Japanese Billy Kay superfans who'd flown all the way from Tokyo.

David had been right. Once Ellie had been removed from the sights of the telephoto lenses, the rollercoaster started slowing down, and she thought that it might stop altogether soon. It probably was time to think about leaving her fifteenth-floor idyll and going back to the real world.

The real world had never seemed more exciting, more inviting, more thrilling. Then Ellie heard someone at the front door and experienced a good three seconds of sheer panic. It was far too early for David to come home.

'I have to go now, Grandma,' she said quickly. 'I don't think I can make it to Friday night dinner, but it's not my turn this week anyway.'

'I know, *bubbeleh*, but we're worried about you,' Sadie said, and then because she was Ellie's grandma and she was in her eighties and wasn't exactly down with computers, she pursed her lips and leaned in close.

'I'm fine, *bubba*, and I miss you too,' Ellie said, and she inched forward and kissed her laptop screen, because it made Sadie happy even if it did make Ellie feel like she was six, especially when she saw David walk out onto the terrace, through the French windows in his bedroom. 'I'll speak to you tomorrow.'

Ellie closed her laptop and waved feebly at him. He was in his running gear and must have run home from work with his suit and shoes and work documents in a specially designed backpack. Apparently running home from work

261

was a thing and there were products to enable this bizarre behaviour. He was sipping an energy drink as he slowly stretched out his hamstrings. 'Oh! I wasn't expecting you home so soon. Um, good run?'

'I had to swerve to avoid a cyclist and almost fell off the towpath into the Regent's Canal, but apart from that it was quite uneventful,' he said, and he raised his eyebrows and smiled at her.

He's much too thin, Ellie thought. He works too hard. He runs too hard. 'I'll get dinner together while you're in the shower,' she said, because that was the one useful thing she could do to remedy the strain on his face that was apparent when he wasn't smiling. Then she paused, because she was doing it again.

As soon as she spent any time with a man in a non-work setting, she tried to fix him. David Gold didn't need fixing. He wasn't a lame duck. He was a finished product. He owned his own home. He had a good job with prospects. In her vast and varied experience, lame ducks didn't have prospects.

He was saying something now about the contents of the fridge. On the Tuesday evening, while waiting for their Thai meal to be delivered, they'd awkwardly compiled an Ocado order together.

'I could make a salad with tomatoes and feta cheese and we've got lots of chicken left,' Ellie said, and she wished she didn't sound quite like the little wife anxious to have dinner ready for the precise moment that her man wanted it on the table. 'I mean, unless you had other plans for tonight.'

David raised his eyebrows again, but didn't smile this time. 'Ordinarily, I'd be happy to take you out for dinner, but you are meant to be in hiding.'

'Not me, you,' Ellie pointed at him, so he'd be clear about her intentions. 'If you wanted to see your girlfriend. Or invite her over. I'm happy to stay in my room.'

He walked along the terrace so he could put his drink down on her table then folded his arms as he stared down at her. 'It wouldn't be fair to send you to your room for the *entire* evening.'

'But you'll probably see her on the weekend, right?' *Just let it go, Ellie.* It was no business of hers when he did and didn't see his women. Or maybe it was just one woman. One special, exclusive woman.

'Are you trying to get rid of me, Ellie? Do you have plans to sneak someone in as soon as I'm off the premises?' he asked in a tone that she hadn't heard before, which was a delicious mix of stern and teasing.

Ellie was proud that she wasn't so far gone that she'd forgotten how to roll her eyes. 'I just don't want to cramp your style, that's all,' she said as she stood up, because the sooner she removed herself from this conversation and his stern, playful tone the better. 'You will tell me if I am, won't you?'

'You'll be the first to know,' he agreed. 'So, dinner in half an hour, then?'

After dinner, and after Ellie let David load the dishwasher because he had a system and it was best to let him get on with it, they decamped to the huge sofa with a bottle of wine and two glasses.

It would be odd not to chat while they were sharing a sofa and a bottle of wine, and Ellie had had no one to talk to face to face in real time for days. Also, she needed to discuss her reintroduction to the wider world.

'So, according to my friends, there's only one freelancer and two Japanese girls outside my flat now,' she told David as he poured out two glasses of Sancerre rosé. 'It should be safe to go home, so I'll be packed and ready to leave by the time you get back from work tomorrow.'

He handed her one of the glasses. 'Are you sure?'

Ellie nodded firmly. 'I can't stay here much longer. During the week is one thing, but the weekend is different. You must have plans, people you want to see.'

The windows were open and Ellie let her eyes drift significantly towards the vista and the wider world outside, but David's eyes were fixed firmly on her. In fact, for one fleeting second, Ellie was sure they were fixed on her legs. She was wearing the denim skirt she'd liberated from Ari's wardrobe with an old Smiths T-shirt. If she'd been in her own home among her own people, Ellie wouldn't have given her outfit a second thought, but she was sitting on David's couch and suddenly she was aware of how much leg she was showing. She tried surreptitiously to tug at the hem of her skirt, and he turned his head to stare at a spot on the floor, so he *had* definitely been looking. Maybe he thought the skirt was a come-hither gesture and that the press stories of her alleged nymphomania were true and she was planning on jumping him before the night was through. That she'd only been pretending to be a nice girl and . . .

'I don't mind having you here.' David cleared his throat and Ellie realised that she'd been staring at the same spot on the living-room floor too. 'You're very easy to live with,' he added, and he sounded quite surprised by it, though if he'd been around more and Ellie wasn't tidying up as she went along and resisting the urge to sprawl with her bare feet on the upholstery he might not think she was such a perfect house guest. 'Why don't we wait and see what's in the Sunday papers? Could you bear to be cooped up for that long?'

Ellie hadn't expected to feel so relieved. 'Well, if you're sure.' Her shoulders slumped. 'What if there are all sorts of fresh revelations in Sunday's papers?'

'We'll cross that bridge on Sunday.' He shifted position on the sofa, which brought him closer to her. Not close enough to touch; he always behaved as if there were a fifty-centimetre exclusion zone around Ellie at all times, but as if he longed to sprawl on his sofa too. 'What do you normally get up to on the weekend?'

On the weekend, there was Reformer Pilates with a Groupon discount and farmers' markets, and sometimes leaving London to poke round antique fairs, but there was also partying, clubbing and drinking. A lot of drinking. Then a lot of nursing a hangover with brunch and the Sunday papers. Which didn't make Ellie anything like the Velvet of tabloid fame, but she still flushed guiltily, sat up straighter and noticed that David was looking at her again. Not because they were having a conversation and it was polite to make eye contact. It was more than that. Ellie was painfully aware of everything she did from wriggling to get more comfortable to touching her hair, and when she licked her lips, which had suddenly become very dry, he licked his lips too so Ellie wasn't really paying any attention to what he was saying.

Then David wasn't looking at her so much as waiting patiently for her to respond to what he'd just said. 'Oh, you know. Shopping and going out,' she said vaguely, which made her sound rather inane. 'What about you? What do you do when, you know, you're not running round the Heath?'

It was only polite that she asked, but she was also curious to know the answer, to know what he did when he was dressed down and kicking back. Who he did it with. 'Well, I—' he said, and then his BlackBerry, which was on the coffee table in front of him, began to ring. Ellie glanced at it, glared at it, in fact, for daring to interrupt, and saw the name flashing up on the screen.

David must have seen it too because he snatched up the phone and was on his feet in one fast, fluid movement. 'I need to get this,' he said sharply, and walked away but not before Ellie heard him say, 'Hi, Billy. What can I do for you?'

She sat there, staring down at her hands as if they belonged to someone else, then was startled out of her funk by the sound of David's bedroom door closing behind him. Ellie was standing in front of it before she knew what she was doing, not even sure how she'd got there. She wanted to press herself against the door, briefly wondered if that old trick with a wall and a glass was an effective means of eavesdropping, and then she stopped, realised what she was thinking of doing and was appalled. It was the shock she needed to walk back to the living room and sit down again.

It was impossible to get her head round the fact that a few metres away David Gold was speaking to her father. It was that simple for him. Never mind that it was past ten thirty on a Thursday night, David was probably on-call 24/7 to sort out his A-list client's legal emergencies. Billy Kay thought nothing of ringing him because it was really simple to make a fucking phone call. Took two swipes on a smartphone. But Billy Kay had never, ever bothered to make the effort to take two measly swipes at a touch-screen and call her up. Even now.

No matter what had happened between him and Ari, Ellie was his daughter. His flesh and blood. She looked down at her hands again, watched them flex in frustration and wondered what would happen if she stormed into David's bedroom, snatched the phone out of his hand and said—

'Sorry about that.'

Ellie jumped. Nearly screamed, because she was that overwrought, as if her skin had been stripped off and all her nerves were on the outside.

'Where were we?'

She looked at David in disbelief. 'That was Billy Kay,' she informed him, like he didn't already know. 'You were just talking to him.'

'I was, and now I'm talking to you,' he said calmly, as if her distress wasn't a palpable thing in the room with them. Ellie was sure it was. He was holding his BlackBerry and it was all Ellie could see.

'I can't even process this,' she said. 'He's my biological father, and obviously I can't remember ever meeting him, I've never spoken to him, but you . . . you can just pick up your phone and call him whenever you want.'

'Hardly. But I'm his lawyer; it's not exactly a nine-to-five job. Issues come up,' he told her stiffly. The tension, which had hung heavy in the air before, had changed density, become thicker.

'It just struck me, that's all. It's not like the papers have said. I'm not obsessed with him.' Her voice was getting shrill and the best remedy would be simply to shut up, but she'd started this and now she had to finish it. 'But did he ask after me? What did he say about me?'

The steel shutter came down again. 'This is not something I'm prepared to discuss with you.'

Ellie was tempted to argue the point. It occurred to her that this was the perfect opportunity to learn a little bit more about Billy Kay. The real Billy Kay, not Billy Kay the rock legend and elder statesman of cool. David Gold knew, better than anyone else she'd met, what he was really like. How he took his tea. Where he liked to go for lunch. How he looked when he said Ellie's name. It wasn't fair that David was holding out on her.

'I used to try not to think about him at all so he just became background noise but now I can't get him out of my head.' She gestured at his phone. 'You think nothing of getting a call from him but for a long time that was all I ever wanted.'

'I don't want to hear this, Ellie,' David said, and he turned away from her.

Ellie was at his side so quickly that it made both of them blink. Then she made a wild grab for his BlackBerry, horrified that she was doing it but unable to stop. 'Give it to me!'

She was all hands as he tried to fend her off and keep a firm grip on his phone, and Ellie thought that maybe she called him a bastard, then he managed to turn her round so he could wrap an immobilising arm round her waist, trap her flailing arms. She instantly quietened, but he still growled, 'Just stop it,' in her ear.

His body was hard against her back and his hold tightened when she tried to free her arms. 'Let me go.' It was a croaky whisper. 'I'm sorry. Let go of me now.'

He didn't, but Ellie could feel him take several shuddering breaths. Then: 'If I gave you his number, what would you even say to him?'

Was he considering it? Ellie opened her mouth, took in some air, then shut it. 'I don't know.'

'What do you mean, you don't know?' he asked, no taunt in his voice, more curiosity. 'He's your father. However much you think or don't think about him, you must have imagined what you'd say to him if you had the chance.'

Of course she had. She'd thought about it a lot so this should have been a no-brainer, but it was as if a mist had descended, wispy clouds fogging her brain. She tried hard, but all her fantasies about Billy Kay mostly consisted of Ellie being in the same place at the same time as him and looking fabulous.

Even as a small child, she'd imagined a white party dress with clouds of tulle, black patent shoes so shiny she could see her reflection in them, hair tamed, nails clean. And now she was older, the picture was still the same, minus the clouds of tulle and the black patent shoes. She wanted Billy to see what he'd missed; that she'd turned out fine without him; that she was the kind of person anyone would want in their life. But she never spoke to him, never got that far, because she always got scared that even in her fantasy he'd reject her.

'That's not any of your business,' she said. 'I'm not going to make any more lunges for your phone – I don't know what came over me – so please, get off me.'

268

As soon as David released her, Ellie wished she were back in his arms. Despite the sultry heat of the night, she shivered.

'Will you please respect that I'm bound by attorney–client privilege?' It was a plea, as if she was goading him beyond all endurance. Ellie felt that she'd reached her endurance point long, long ago and was running only on fumes at this point.

'Aren't I your client too?' she asked a little belligerently.

David's chin tilted again, as though he'd recognised the challenge in her voice and was prepared to meet it. 'As I doubt very much whether you could afford my hourly rate, not to mention the conflict of interest, no, you're not my client.' Ellie didn't know how he did it, how he could go from a man caught between a rock and a hard place to the reincarnation of Robespierre just by flaring his nostrils and adding ice chips to his voice. 'It just so happens that at this moment in time, your best interests coincide with the best interests of my client.'

'Well, I'm sorry that the best interests of your client mean that you have to suffer my continued presence,' Ellie flung at him, as she marched back to the sofa. She picked up laptop and glass of wine, and wished that she had time to refill her glass but that would have ruined a good exit. 'I'll leave you in peace.'

'You're behaving like a surly teenager. I'm not sending you to your room.'

Ellie longed to spit out a very surly 'Whatever' as she'd never done during her adolescence because teenage rebellion was wasted on Ari, who'd always laughed whenever Ellie had tried out a hissy fit for size. 'I'm going of my own free will. I have lots of important things I need to do,' she added grandly. 'Goodnight.'

Chapter Twenty

Ellie woke with a start when she heard the front door close. She'd been dreaming that she was on stage singing a duet with Billy Kay, but she didn't know the words, then Lara and Rose had snatched the microphone away from her. At some point during the night, she'd kicked the quilt to the bottom of the bed, now she starfished her body and tried to ignore the sweat gathering in the hollow of her throat, behind her knees, hair clinging to her damp neck.

It was hard to concentrate when it felt as if her brain had been replaced with a wad of cotton wool. She kept replaying last night's scene over and over again. She felt sick with shame as she remembered the way she'd tried to snatch David's phone away from him; how he'd had to fight her off. Then she'd remember how he held her against his chest, arm tight around her, forearm pressed to her breasts, though that had barely registered at the time. This morning it was all Ellie could think about.

It was as if she no longer knew who she was, but vacillated between Ellie Cohen and Velvet Underground, and the person who was there to witness her identity crisis, to see her behave in a way that she never had before, was David. If only he'd known her before, even before Glastonbury, then he'd know she was acting out of character.

Or maybe this was who Ellie was supposed to be. When she was stripped of all that made her look good – nice

Jewish extended family, fancy job, expensive hair products – what was left didn't measure up. Maybe what was left had always been substandard, shopsoiled and tarnished before the tabloids ever got hold of her. Certainly that was what David must think of her after seeing her in action last night. Ellie wished she could be defiant and uncompromising, that she didn't care what he thought, but she did.

Then she had to wonder why she did and why she was so attracted to him. Last night on the sofa, before Billy Kay had called, her whole body had been attuned to his presence, had strained towards him.

Finally, she thought about Billy Kay and how he was still absenting himself from her life. Ellie waited for the familiar hurt to flare up, but when it did it was a new hurt as she replayed that heart-ripping moment when his name flashed up on David's phone, and then she remembered the shocked look on David's face when she'd launched herself at him to retrieve said phone and she was back at the beginning of her shame spiral.

No wonder it took half an hour to write a five-line email to Vaughn updating him on her progress with what she insisted on calling the *Desperate Housewives* exhibition, even though he'd told her not to.

In the end, because she wasn't really working, Ellie broke with routine and swam before lunch. Instead of counting lengths, she found herself counting all the ways that Billy Kay had let her down during her lifetime. She redoubled her efforts to count lengths, but realised she was totting up all the times that David had looked at her with what she liked to think was a dark intent. It was possible, she thought then, that being confined to quarters was driving her to the brink of her sanity.

When she came back from her swim and it was impossible to feel any worse than she currently did, Ellie decided it was time to assess the damage. So far, she'd avoided the newspaper websites and gossip blogs because every time she thought about checking them out, her stomach dipped and swayed as though she was top deck on turbulent seas, but it was Friday and she was going to be out of David's flat by end of business today, no matter what. Though it *would* make it harder to leave if one of her exes had over-shared, or Lara and Rose had given another exclusive interview about how Ellie had ruined their lives. Then the paps would be back like a bad case of nits.

There *was* a big story in the *Daily Mail* about how single mothers like Ari and children brought up on state hand-outs and reality TV like Ellie were the root cause of all the evils in modern society. The *Daily Mirror* had a photo of Richey out on the town with two girls – one had made it to judges' houses on *The X Factor* and the other was apparently a model. Richey was wearing a tight white vest, which showed off his muscles and tribal tattoos, a baker boy cap and a grin that now looked more cheesy than cheeky. Ellie wondered what she'd ever seen in him apart from the muscles, until she was distracted by the *Chronicle*'s headline: 'BILLY'S BELLES – HOW DO THEY MEASURE UP?'

There were full-length photographs of Ellie, Lara and Rose and the journalist had thoughtfully marked their corresponding body parts out of ten. Lara had the best smile, breasts and feet, Rose was ahead on nose, lips and waist, but Ellie had the best eyes, hair, bum and legs, which was demeaning to all three of them, but also oddly validating, not that Ellie would admit that to a living soul. There was even a little sidebar on her beloved toning shoes: 'The £70 sneakers that give Velvet her va-va-voom!'

None of that was as bad as Ellie had feared. But the stuff on the gossip sites was much, much worse. The upskirt photo taken at the gallery had made it on to TMZ. The

Billy Kay fan forum discussion boards weren't mincing their words either, which was a shame because the words they were using were 'slag' and 'whore' and 'tart'. Someone who had to have known her in real life was regaling the readers of Holy Moly! with the story of the time that Ellie had nearly broken her ex Oscar's penis.

The only way to deal with the contents of the Pandora's box that she'd just opened was to not deal with it; to try to pretend that the horrible people who had nothing better to do than spout poisonous remarks behind the anonymity of a fake name were talking about someone else. To hold herself very still and practise taking deep breaths until she stopped shaking and the goose bumps had flattened out. It kind of worked. She was even able to force down a couple of pieces of fruit for her lunch and reopen her work folder, though all she did was stare at her to-do list for twenty minutes without actually to-doing anything.

It was after Ellie had come back from an unprecedented second swim that she accepted what she couldn't change: her work ethic was gone for the week. It was Friday afternoon and she'd earned the right to sit on the balcony, sip a glass of the Sancerre rosé from the night before and paint her toenails.

After applying a top coat of creamy pale pink polish, Ellie found herself back on her laptop. This time, her hands, acting independently of her brain, were typing David's name into Google so she could do some digging. Ellie was surprised she'd held out so long.

There was a lot to dig. She discovered that he'd been back in the UK for only a few months. He'd spent five years in the States, setting up an entertainment division for Wyndham, Pryce and Lewis in their New York and Los Angeles offices. 'For a law firm that used to pride itself on traditional values and a very nineteenth-century notion that a gentleman's word was his bond, the dynamic David

Gold, made junior partner when he was twenty-eight, is determined to drag his colleagues into the twenty-first century,' claimed one profile from the *American Law Review*. There was a picture of David sitting at a desk, the New York skyline visible from the window behind. He was smiling faintly, showing just a flash of even, white teeth to dispel the myth that all British people had blackened pegs in their mouths, and looked like he could handle anything the legal profession threw at him.

The more she read about him, from the double first from Cambridge to the rumours about him and the startingly beautiful, Oscar-nominated indie actress he represented, to his sub-four-hours marathon average, the more Ellie knew David was out of her reach. Well, that and the fact that he had his fingers in all of Billy Kay's pies.

After twenty-six years of pep talks from strong women like Ari and Sadie and Tabitha, nothing had ever felt beyond Ellie's reach. If she'd wanted something, then she planned and worked and went miles out of her way to get it. But now Ellie was full of doubt and uncertainty, and David was number three on a list of New York's Legal Hotties. Besides, whether or not she was able to get him wasn't the issue when she was meant to be getting as far away from him and all the painful emotions he roused in her as soon as possible.

Her time would be much better spent looking for a bolt-hole – maybe a little self-catering cottage in Cornwall, if there were any left unoccupied in late July – and she might be able to book a bed on the sleeper train from Paddington to Truro tonight, Ellie thought.

Then she heard the front door open. Her stomach did the turbulent seas shimmy again because it wasn't even four and David wasn't due home for at least another three and a half hours. She hadn't had time to practise being personable yet aloof like she'd planned. Ellie wriggled her shoulders, looked up and screamed when she saw a woman staring at her from the doorway of the guest bedroom. 'Bloody hell! Who are you?'

The woman had flailed when Ellie had screamed so she couldn't work for a tabloid because their employees were made of tougher stuff. Then she took a couple of steps forward so Ellie could see her face and Ellie's heart started thudding all over again. She was pretty sure it was the woman who'd been with David at Glastonbury. Pretty sure, but not one hundred per cent certain.

She also looked a bit like Melanie from Goldman Sachs. David obviously had a type.

'I'm Jessica,' the woman said. She was tall, tanned, slender and dressed in a sleeveless white blouse, beautifully cut skinny black trousers and heels, her glossy brown hair twisted into a topknot. The overall effect was cool and elegant and not altogether friendly.

Painfully aware that she was sporting a fetching pair of neon-orange toe separators and damp hair, Ellie got to her feet and shook the hand Jessica was proffering. 'Um, hi. Er, how did you get in?'

'I live across the hall. I've got a spare set of keys,' Jessica informed her in precise Home Counties tones that made Ellie stiffen. The other woman held up a keychain. 'I kept an eye on the place when David was in the States.'

It still didn't explain what she was doing in David's apartment.

'I'm Ellie. David's letting me stay here for a few days,' Ellie said, twisting anxious hands behind her back. Her own accent had climbed a few notches, the way it did when she felt intimidated. 'So, was there something I could help you with?'

Jessica shook her head. Her hair was more blonde than brunette when it caught the light. She wasn't the woman Ellie had briefly met at Glastonbury. It was also clear that Jessica knew who she was, because she folded her arms and pursed her lips as Ellie slunk past her. She didn't want Jessica standing in the guest room, because *she* was the guest so that made it *her* room, and Jessica might be David Gold's current girlfriend, or his overly friendly neighbour with benefits, or even his stalker, but she was invading Ellie's private space. She also didn't want Jessica to keep staring at her underwear hanging on the clothes dryer on the balcony because she'd done a wash that morning.

'Don't worry, I know where everything is,' Jessica said as she caught up with Ellie, overtook her and strode confidently towards the kitchen. 'I just got back from Brussels and the Waitrose delivery isn't due until six. I'm all out of herbal tea.'

She reached up to the cupboard to get down the tin of camomile teabags into which Ellie had made major inroads. Then she turned round and fixed Ellie with a gimlet look that no doubt struck fear into the nameless bureaucrats of Brussels.

'Some of the residents wondered who was going in and out of David's apartment when he wasn't there,' she said, though Ellie suspected that one person might have mentioned it and Jessica had hotfooted it over. She was certainly running a proprietorial hand over the granite worktops, which was fine with Ellie. Jessica could run a proprietorial hand over anything of David's that she wanted to, and Ellie was only gritting her teeth, nails digging into her palm, because hostility was coming off Jessica in waves, like she'd doused herself in it in Duty Free. 'No need to ask what you're doing here. It's obvious now. David is clearing up another one of Billy's messes.'

Billy? Messes? As in messes in the plural, like they were a regular occurrence. Ellie wasn't confident that she could speak and what came out of her mouth was more a grunt than anything else. 'Billy?'

'You know perfectly well who I mean by Billy,' Jessica told her kindly. She looked round the kitchen, and if she put the kettle on so she could drink her camomile tea here, instead of in her own flat, then Ellie was going right now. She'd even leave her luggage behind if she had to. 'David and I had dinner with him a couple of times in New York. Charming man.'

Jessica's romantic status with regards to David Gold was still indeterminate but one thing was certain, she was a bitch. A month ago, it would have been a point of principle with Ellie to believe that there was no such thing as a bitch, just someone who she hadn't got on side yet, but that was then. Now Ellie didn't want to get Jessica on side. She wanted to smack her. Hard. Repeatedly.

'Right, you've got your teabags or whatever it was you came for, so you can go now,' Ellie said brusquely.

Ellie's unparalleled brusqueness was wasted on Jessica. 'Do you parade around half naked like that in front of David?'

Ellie wasn't half naked. She was wearing a Breton top and shorts, cuffed Whistles shorts, not bootie shorts or short shorts or jeans that she'd cut off so you could see her arse cheeks. It was on the tip of her tongue to say something placating about the heat, maybe offer Jessica a cold drink, because it was awful to be on the receiving end of such passive aggression and not do anything about it. But Jessica didn't get to come into Ellie's so-called safe house and speak about Billy Kay like that. Like, going for dinner with him was a delightful thing that happened to people who weren't Ellie.

Worse, the extent to which David's life, and not just his career, was entwined with Billy Kay's hadn't been apparent until Jessica had rubbed it in her face, so Ellie wasn't going to play nice. 'You need to go,' she said, her face settling into an unfamiliar arrangement that she was sure resembled Ari's best 'bitch, please' expression. 'As you're so at home here, I'm sure you know the quickest way out.'

Jessica didn't even wrinkle her perfect, retroussé nose, but held the tin of teabags in front of her like it was a protective nosegay and Ellie had a bad case of plague.

She was almost at the front door and Ellie was holding her breath, when Jessica turned. 'You know, dear, I wouldn't read anything into this,' she said sweetly, sweeping out her arm to encompass both Ellie, and David's open-plan living space. 'When it comes to his career, David is very single-minded. Well, not just his career . . .' She trailed off with a suggestive smile about as subtle as breeze block, so Ellie could be in no doubt of exactly when David had shown Jessica how single-minded he could be in pursuit of his goals.

Ellie forced her features into blankness. Grim blankness. 'I don't know what you mean.'

'I'll spell it out for you, shall I?' Jessica asked sweetly. 'Billy Kay is David's biggest client. When David poached Billy Kay from his old law firm, he made junior partner. Now he's determined to make senior partner by the time he's thirty-five. That's in three months' time and this . . . you . . . it's simply to keep Billy happy. Keeping him happy really mounts up the billable hours for David.'

'Yeah, well, I know that David didn't ask me to stay here out of the goodness of his heart,' Ellie blustered. 'I needed somewhere off the radar in a hurry. He provided one. End of.'

Jessica nodded her head. She was vile. If all her insinuations were true then Ellie had to wonder what the hell David saw in her – well, when he wasn't being single-minded in pursuit of his goals with Melanie and the woman from Glastonbury and a whole host of other women who looked like they'd rolled off some Duchess of Cambridge-approved assembly line. '. . . as long as we understand each other,' Jessica was saying. 'Even if *he* can ignore all those stories in the paper about you, little gallery girls aren't his style. Not really going to further his cause on the partnership fast track.'

It was the worst insult yet. Ellie was *not* a gallery girl. She was a display and exhibitions manager. She was Vaughn's protégée. She was almost an art dealer in her own right. Gallery girls were privately funded, pretty girls who worked in galleries until they got married. They had no ambition, other than plighting their troth to a man with a bigger trust fund than theirs, preferably a friend of Prince Harry.

Muffin was a gallery girl. Two-thirds of the posh girls had been gallery girls, but Ellie had worked bloody hard to get where she was, even if where she was was currently working out a month's notice. She might not have gone to Oxford or Harvard Business School like Jessica probably had but she was not some career dilettante.

'Do you know something?' Ellie heard herself say, and she couldn't understand why the words she was thinking were coming out of her mouth unchecked. 'If David hasn't made a commitment to you after years of being neighbours and New York dinner buddies, then he's never going to. Not when he's fucking a whole bunch of other women who all look like you and dress like you, probably so none of you will clash with his suits.'

Jessica's lips drew back in a snarl. 'You utter—'

'I mean, even someone like me with my disastrous track record when it comes to relationships can tell that he is *never* going to put a ring on it, Jessica, so if I were you I'd just jog on. It's the dignified thing to do.'

It was the meanest, bitchiest, most spiteful thing that Ellie had ever said to anyone. She wasn't even sure that Jessica had deserved it, or if she was simply the most convenient target for all the hurt and ugliness that had been brewing inside Ellie all week.

The door slammed shut behind Jessica and she stood there, hands clenched into fists, panting like she'd just run one of David's marathons. Then she marched back to her bedroom, poured herself a glass of wine and downed it in one, like the party girl that everyone thought she was.

She had to get out of here. She wasn't going to be used solely to advance David's career and be tucked out of sight because it kept Billy Kay sweet. What made Billy Kay happy was nothing to do with her.

Camden, London, 1986

In the end, she let Billy talk her round, and Ari's sister Carol was desperate to take the baby, so really Ari was doing what her father would call a *mitzvah*, a good thing. She was a bloody saint, especially when she managed not to lose her temper on the day that Carol and Sadie came to visit her in the summer-house. Sadie sat on the one good chair and told Ari she was a disgrace and that if anybody they knew found out she was pregnant, she'd die of shame.

Billy came in just as Carol gave Ari the number of a lawyer who specialised in private adoptions and fudging the details.

'This is the best way to play it,' he said to Ari, though she still wasn't convinced.

Sadie looked him up and down and sideways, then sniffed. 'I suppose you've told Ariella that your wife doesn't understand you.'

Billy steadily met her gaze. 'Other way round. I don't understand my wife, I never did.'

Ari's bump got bigger and bigger so she couldn't even see her feet any more. Carol came to Camden every week to buy her bags of groceries and bottles of pre-natal vitamins, and to beg Ari to stop wearing stilettos.

Carol also booked doctor's appointments and scans and pre-natal classes that Ari never attended because she and Billy were in a mad sprint to get the songs finished.

It felt like the songs would never be finished, because there was always another hook in her head, a perfect chorus that

281

wouldn't leave her alone. Ari had to give birth to the songs before she could give birth to anything else.

Billy worried about her, especially when she could barely squeeze her bulk past the mixing desk and she got thrown out of the Saturday Girls for constantly being late for rehearsals and being hugely pregnant. But worrying didn't come naturally to Billy. 'You look like crap,' he'd say. 'Go home and go to bed and I'll be back later.'

The summerhouse in November was Arctic, even with a Calor Gas heater. Ari would get into bed but it was hard to write songs on her guitar when she was buried under a mound of blankets, towels and old coats. Instead, she'd end up stroking her bump and because there weren't any witnesses, she could finally say her silent sorries to the kid that would never be hers.

Chapter Twenty-one

Ellie was still planning her escape half an hour later.

She'd emailed her old college friends Esme and Sue, who lived in Paris, about the availability of their sofa bed, removed her freshly laundered underwear from the clothes dryer, but had got sidetracked by *Deal or No Deal* on her way to the kitchen to put the dirty wineglass in the dishwasher.

'No deal, you utter numpty,' she railed. 'Not when you've still got the two hundred and fifty thousand and you just found the penny. For fuck's sake, what is wrong with you?'

'People ask me that all the time,' said an amused voice, and David walked through the front door.

Ellie was horrified. 'You're not meant to be home for ages,' she reminded him in an accusatory voice, because for the second day running he'd caught her off guard. She was still parading around in shorts, it was obvious she'd been drinking, and she hadn't even removed her toe separators. It wasn't the image she wanted to project, not after last night. Especially when he'd probably had Jessica on the phone spitting fury and demanding he leave work right away to come home and evict her. He looked very chipper for a man on that kind of mission.

'Sometimes I finish early on a Friday night and no, before you ask, I have a big training run tomorrow morning so I got the tube home.' He held up an M&S carrier bag. 'I bought you supplies for the evening.'

'That's very kind of you.' He seemed in such a good mood that Ellie didn't want to ruin it by continuing last night's tiff. Instead, she'd have to ruin it when she mentioned Jessica's visit, because he was going to find out sooner or later. Probably sooner. Still, it was best not to hit him with the highlights as soon as he got home. 'Supplies just for me?'

'I'm going out,' he said, passing the bag to her as he relieved her of the wineglass. 'You'll be all right on your own, won't you?'

Ellie could use his absence to make a speedy getaway.

'I have a ton of stuff to do,' Ellie said, and rather than watch him take out everything she'd put in the dishwasher and rearrange it according to his arcane, ergonomic system she gazed out of the window. If he was going out, then she could call Chester so he could give her a lift to somewhere that wasn't here. 'Do you think you'll be gone long?'

'Depends,' David said. He looked rather discomfited and Ellie instantly understood why. He was obviously seeing one of his glossy, go-getting women. Which was fine. Good luck to him. And good luck to whichever woman it was tonight, because she was always going to play second string to his career. Unless he was seeing Jessica, in which case, Ellie wished her only bad things.

'Right. So, you're seeing a girlfriend, are you? That's good, because . . .' She needed to strike pre-emptively and tell him that Jessica had popped round, in case he had a hot date with her, but the words stuck in Ellie's throat. How could she even begin to explain what had happened? 'I'd hate to think that I'm, well, you know, getting in the way.'

'I don't know why you're suddenly so fixated on my love life,' David said, looking at her curiously. 'I'm going out for dinner.'

Ellie nodded. 'That's nice. Where are you going? Somewhere romantic?'

'I'm going round to my parents' for dinner, on my own. I'm not sure that counts as romantic. In fact, it would be quite disturbing if it did,' he drawled. Ellie no longer had to torment herself with thoughts of Jessica and David together. Now she could imagine David being fussed and clucked over by his mother as she nagged him about his unmarried, childless state.

She even grinned. 'Will there be chicken soup, even though the temperature is in the low nineties, and will you not be allowed to move on to the main course until you've finished every last drop in your bowl?'

David grinned back at her, entirely without guile. 'You've met my mother, then?'

'I haven't, but I have a grandmother who always makes a major thing about Friday night dinner.' Ellie let out a breath big enough to ruffle her hair. 'I have to spend the week leading up to it on a juice detox so I'll have room for the huge amount of food she shovels down me.'

Now, instead of doing a runner to someplace as yet unknown, Ellie wished she were on her way to Belsize Park. It was far, far too hot for chicken soup and it wasn't even her night, but she wanted to sit around Sadie and Morry's big table with her family, the people who loved her and accepted her. Well, apart from Aunt Carol, but Ari always said that that was nothing to do with Ellie and everything to do with Aunt Carol being a sour-faced cow since birth.

If David went soon, instead of calling Chester Ellie would call Morry. He'd come and pick her up and she could speed-eat her way through four courses, and if there really weren't any photographers around, then she might just as well stay with her grandparents. So, really, she had to tell him that she was going and just . . . go.

'You don't look very happy. Is a pizza and a bottle of wine not going to cut it?' David asked, and for a man who'd spent the day being dynamic and thrusting and doing shady things on behalf of his celebrity clients, *and* had a sweaty commute home, he seemed very smiley and relaxed. Like he'd put all the horrors of the week behind him and was ready to have some fun, in which case her vacating the premises would improve his mood even more.

'It's not that,' she began. 'It's just . . . I have to . . . I've decided I can't stay here any more. In fact, I've already started packing.'

His smile disappeared and he stilled, which made Ellie tense up, because it was the stillness of a big animal just before it pounced. 'Oh,' he said, eyebrows raised. 'I thought we talked about this last night and we agreed—'

'We did,' she interrupted. 'But now I feel that it's . . . it's inappropriate for me to continue staying here.'

'Inappropriate?' David carefully enunciated each syllable as if the word was unfamiliar. 'Have you just stumbled out of the pages of a Jane Austen novel?'

'No! And yes, it is inappropriate me staying here with you. People will talk. They'll speculate, and I'm fed up with people speculating about me.' She was getting a little strident as she worked up to her confession.

'If no one knows you're here, then how can they speculate about you being here?' He was always able to cut though Ellie's bluff with an incisive question that showed it up for the bullshit it was.

'Well, I go swimming every day. I see your neighbours, and then—'

'We had an agreement, Ellie, that you'd stay here until Sunday. I don't see what's changed since we discussed it last night.'

A lot had happened. Billy Kay had phoned. They'd fought. Jessica had popped in on a mission that redefined the words 'flimsy excuse' and Ellie had fought with her too. And even fighting with David and knowing that he preferred women like Jessica hadn't stopped that physical pull towards him. That was another reason why she had to go, but none of that was easy to explain when he was standing in front of her.

'It's not just that. I'm going crazy being stuck indoors for days on end,' Ellie improvised, though every word was true. 'Sitting out on the balcony isn't doing it for me, and the hum of your air conditioning system is driving me bonkers and did you know that your fridge makes this weird noise like there's an angry cow trapped inside it?'

Ellie hadn't realised her cabin fever was so far advanced. 'I always wondered where that noise was coming from,' David murmured. He looked at Ellie. Then down at her feet, which were still sporting toe separators, because she was an idiot. Ridiculous. Making a mess of his ordered life.

'Well, I suppose you can come with me if you want. My mother always makes enough food to feed the entire street.' He stared at her with narrowed eyes.

'That wasn't what I meant,' Ellie protested. 'I wasn't angling for an invite. I'm going. I'm really going.'

'You can just as easily go after dinner,' David pointed out. 'I was planning to walk across the Heath to their place. If you wore shades and, I don't know, a hat, I doubt anyone would give you a second look.'

That was enough to dent Ellie's ego and force her to get a bloody grip. 'I couldn't,' she said automatically, because she wanted to be gone before he spoke to Jessica, and after what Jessica had told *her*, Ellie trusted him even less. What kind of man dragged his parents into his ruthless power-plays? Though a walk on the Heath and chicken soup did sound like her dream Friday night.

'I'm going to have a shower,' David said casually. 'If you do change your mind, I'm leaving in half an hour.'

Forty-five minutes later, Ellie was on the Heath and clutching a huge bunch of gerbera daisies she'd insisted on buying from the flower stall on the corner of David's road, because you didn't turn up for dinner at someone's house empty-handed, especially when they hadn't even invited you.

Ellie had forgotten how dry and stiff the heat was. Now it wrapped around her, brushed against her bare legs and pricked her arms as they walked the gravel path that led past Kenwood House, came out briefly onto Spaniards Road, then walked across Sandy Heath to the Heath Extension. The rich green space she'd seen from her fifteenth-floor eyrie wasn't rich or green. The grass had been bleached and withered by the sun and the footpaths that stayed muddy for weeks during rain-sodden winters were now scorched earth. Ellie wobbled over huge cracks in her Swedish Hasbeens sandals, the most suitable, meet-the-parents footwear she'd packed. When the paths became even more roughly hewn and featured hillocks and sudden drops, David took her hand to guide her to more level ground.

It wasn't proper handholding; it was medicinal hand-holding so Ellie didn't go arse over tit, but it still made her heart beat a little bit faster. She wouldn't have needed to hold his hand at all but Ellie had forgotten that it was that strange hinterland between Friday afternoon and Friday evening that she called the Friday dump. Everyone realised they had an hour to clear their desks and their in-trays and cross all those items off the to-do lists that they'd written on Monday morning, and her phone wouldn't stop ringing.

So instead of telling David about Jessica's visit – she'd even rehearsed her first line: 'Your friend Jessica popped round, I'm afraid we kind of got off on the wrong foot' – she gave Vaughn an update on exporting Emerging Scandinavian Artists to New York. Then Piers called because he'd lost an invoice. Then her opposite number in New York phoned to bitch about one of the Scandinavian artists who was now pretending that he hadn't told everyone that he'd make them a floating Perspex bicycle to order in any size or colour. Finally, as they were leaving the Heath for tarmac so hot and sticky that Ellie had to prise the sole of her sandal off it every time she took a step, she had Lola moaning about Tess.

Without Ellie there as a buffer between Lola's brattiness and Tess's bossiness, they were currently engaged in psychological warfare over *Come Dine With Me*.

'. . . there's only two per cent of space left on the TiVo because she records episodes she's already seen. I deleted four repeats so there was room for a BBC4 documentary about outsider art and she went mad and then she had a go at me for buying non-quilted loo roll,' Lola ranted.

They were walking along the road that skirted the Heath, passing huge double-fronted Arts and Crafts houses. Then David stopped at a pretty white house with leaded windows, a creeper plant trailing lazily around the front door, and a huge oak tree in the front garden. He gestured at her phone.

'I'm sorry,' Ellie mouthed and turned her attention back to Lola, who was now venting about Tess's heinous crime of asking her to listen to her music on headphones after eleven.

'She has the radio on so loud in the morning that it wakes me up. Why can't she listen to that on fucking headphones?'

'Sweetie, we've all had a stressful week – I read that more murders are committed at ninety-two degrees than any other temperature,' Ellie said soothingly.

'Do I have your permission to kill her, then?'

'No! No killing. Can't you please try to get on? Go to Saino's, get some wine and Kettle Chips, then tell her that everyone in Britain has seen that episode of *Come Dine With Me* where the woman falls asleep and her guests have to cook the dinner themselves, like, five times.'

Lola gurgled. 'That was a classic!'

'See, there you go. You can bond over that.' Ellie glanced at David who made a winding it up motion with his hand. 'You catch way more flies with honey than you do with vinegar.'

'If you're not off the phone in ten seconds, I'm leaving you out here,' David said, as he unlatched the garden gate. 'I'll tell my mother that you'd rather spend the evening playing Pollyanna than eating her chicken soup.'

Ellie scowled at David's back as he strode up the path.

'. . . only reason I agreed to move in was because you were living there and you're cool and Tess isn't. She's so vanilla.'

'Don't you think I've got enough to deal with right now without you giving me crap about Tess?' Ellie suddenly snapped. 'I don't fucking need it. OK?'

Lola didn't say anything. Ellie suspected she might have shocked her into silence for the first time in her life. She hurried over to David, who was waiting for her on the doorstep.

Not that Lola could stay speechless for long. 'Christ, what crawled up your arse?'

'Got to go now,' Ellie chirped. 'Love you, mean it!'

It was the mock-ironic way they always said goodbye, but it earned Ellie another pointed look from David as he rang the doorbell at the precise second it swung open to reveal a plump, smiling woman with silvered dark brown hair swept up in a messy bun, and eyes the exact same shade of blue as his.

'I thought I heard your voice,' she said. Then she saw Ellie standing on the doorstep. The smile was gone in an instant. 'Or voices. You didn't say you were bringing someone for dinner. I hope there'll be enough to go round.'

'You know there'll be plenty to go round, even if I brought twenty people with me,' David said mildly. Ellie was all set to retreat, to step back onto the path, but his

290

hand was suddenly at the small of her back to push her steadily and inexorably towards the woman who'd given birth to him and who was staring at her in horror like she'd just taken a dump on her hollyhocks.

'It's very nice to meet you,' Ellie said as she proffered the gerbera daisies at the older woman, and for someone who was all about crisis management and clinical assessments of other people's characters, David had really underestimated his mother's reaction to having an extra mouth to feed. 'Sorry to turn up unannounced.'

His hand was still on her. Long fingers splayed against the base of her spine, she could feel the heat of his skin through the cotton of the blue and white striped wrap dress she'd changed into. It didn't feel at all comforting, quite the opposite, especially when he gave her a none too gentle prod and she had no choice but to walk through the front door, and his mother had no choice but to stand back so Ellie could enter.

'It's Velvet, isn't it?' she asked in a tight voice, reluctantly taking the flowers from Ellie. 'Welcome to our home.'

Chapter Twenty-two

Ellie bit the inner skin of her bottom lip hard so she could focus on that familiar pain as David steered her through the wood-panelled hall with its beautiful black-and-white tiled floor into a huge living room-cum-dining room that stretched from the front of the house to the open French windows at the back. The walls were lined with floor-to-ceiling shelves full of books, framed prints and photos, little ornaments, tchotchkes and objets d'art: a tiny painted elephant, a vase made from a buckled, twisted piece of green glass, a set of netsukes. Ordinarily, Ellie would have liked to linger by the shelves and explore their contents, get to know about the people who lived here as she asked about the provenance of each treasure, but tonight she just wanted to choke down one bowl of soup and get the hell out.

At the French windows, the room extended into an L-shape and round the corner was an open-plan farmhouse-style kitchen with a scrubbed pine dresser full of mismatched plates and cups: blue and white Delftware, vintage gold-rimmed china be-sprigged with flowers, and a scrubbed pine table, one end obscured by piles of news-papers and magazines. There was even a scrubbed pine worktop, and copper-bottomed pans hanging from a rack above the range. The smell of a fragrant, aromatic, roasting chicken was the smell Ellie always associated with Friday night dinner, with coming home, but not this Friday night.

'Your son's brought someone round,' David's mother said in the same tight voice to a tall, thin man with a keen, clever face, these characteristics emphasised by tortoise-shell-rimmed glasses and a head of thick, luxuriant white hair, who had suddenly emerged from behind a door Ellie had thought was a cupboard. 'This is Velvet.'

'Ignore her,' David said, and Ellie wasn't sure if he was talking to her or his father. 'This is Ellie, who's been staying with me for the last few days, and you shouldn't believe *everything* you read in the papers. Anyway, I thought you didn't read those kinds of papers.'

'I'll only have *The Times* and the *Guardian* in the house, but judging by the browser history on your mother's computer someone refreshes the *Daily Mail* on an hourly basis,' he said, seizing Ellie's hand and shaking it enthusiastically. 'I'm Ludovic. Awful family name. Call me Ludo. This is Ruth.'

Ruth Gold was not amused about the *Daily Mail* reference. 'I thought you were going to change before dinner,' she said sharply to her husband.

He glanced down at his frayed chinos and grey cotton shirt, its breast pocket flapping forlornly. 'But it's only David.'

'David and Velvet,' Ruth Gold corrected him.

'It's Ellie. Nobody calls me Velvet,' Ellie reminded her very softly. 'Sorry again for turning up like this.' She didn't even dare look at David because she was sure that if she did her eyes would promise him unimaginable agony. He must have known his mother didn't want her family Friday night disrupted by one of the most notorious women in the country. 'Look, I could just . . . I'll go . . .' She was already backing away, but didn't get very far, because David was standing behind her, and his hands came to rest on her shoulders. This time his touch did feel comforting.

'Don't be ridiculous,' he said, and he must have

signalled something to his mother, because Ruth Gold wrinkled her nose, then sighed.

'Of course, you'll stay for dinner,' she said stiffly. 'I wouldn't dream of asking you to leave.'

Ellie didn't want to stay. She wanted to be with people who liked her, who'd be kind to her, but they were in short supply today. She had no choice but to stay put and offer to help lay the table. Her offer was rebuffed very jovially by Ludo so she perched awkwardly on a stool, clutching a Campari and soda, as Ludo and Ruth bustled about the kitchen and David slouched against the worktop next to her. Ellie couldn't even imagine why he'd wanted her to come to his parents' house for dinner or why she'd let herself be talked into it.

'I'm only going to stay for an hour,' she whispered to him just as Ruth announced that dinner was ready, and Ellie didn't think he'd heard her.

Although Ruth had spent most of the day standing over a hot stove in a hot kitchen on a hot day skimming the fat off a slow-simmering chicken soup, Ludo had staged an intervention at four thirty that afternoon, and insisted that the world wouldn't end if they had a cold Friday night dinner.

'I'm so sorry,' Ruth said to Ellie for the fifth time, as the four of them sat having dinner on the patio, which looked out over their rambling back garden. Two huge garden umbrellas were angled to keep the glare of a sun yet to set off the weather-beaten wooden table. 'Are you sure you don't mind having poached salmon? Because I have chicken. It would be no trouble to make you up a plate.'

'This is lovely,' Ellie insisted for the fifth time, and in other circumstances, she might have smiled and mentioned that Sadie would have been equally mortified if a stranger had rocked up for Friday night dinner only to find that chicken wasn't on the menu, but she was sure that Ruth Gold would find some way to take offence if she did. In the big scheme of things, it really didn't matter that she'd met two people today who didn't like her. Not everyone had to like her and Ellie could see now that her entire life had been spent wanting people to like her, and going all out to make it happen. There was no point in wasting her energy any further, because now everyone she met would already have a negative opinion about her and there was no smile in her repertoire or crisp white dress in the world that would change their mind. But she was a guest in Ruth's house, and Ruth was David's mother, and Ludo was charming and the dinner *was* lovely. There was a whole poached salmon, home-made potato salad, crusty baguettes, and Ludo had persuaded her and Ruth to have another Campari and soda.

It was hard to reconcile Ruth and Ludo, who were so voluble that they invariably talked over each other, as David's parents. There was no shade or shadows to them. Ludo happily told Ellie that the two of them had met at university forty years ago when they were doing post-graduate work and were both engaged to other people, and had been together ever since. Ludo was a Professor of Ethics at University College London and Ruth was a Professor of Modern and Gender History at Birkbeck.

They were very impressive as parents went, but they didn't talk about lofty academic topics or tell embarrassing anecdotes about what David was like as a child, for which Ellie was hugely grateful. Not just because she didn't want to think about a younger, cuter, possibly verging on adorable, version of him, but also because she couldn't think of anything more likely to send him into a silent, seething, stiff-backed fury. Instead, Ellie was content to observe, rather than join in. She sat and smiled and nodded a lot as the three of them talked about the new installation at the Serpentine Gallery, daytime TV (Ludo was a big fan of *Pointless*) and the chances of another week of punishingly hot weather.

Was this what it would have been like if Billy and Ari had stayed together and the three of them had been a family? Somehow, Ellie doubted it. Dinner table talk would probably have been much more rock 'n' roll-orientated.

'It's worse than 1976,' Ruth sighed as she fanned her red face with a napkin, then lightly touched Ellie's arm as if she might be thawing towards her a teensy little bit. 'You're very quiet. Is everything all right? Would you like some more salmon?'

'I couldn't eat anything else,' Ellie said, and then, because old habits died hard and Ruth did seem really nice when she wasn't being disapproving: 'This dill mayonnaise is amazing. Did you make it yourself?'

Ruth's smile was a fraction wider than it had been. 'I did. Would you like the recipe?'

'She really wouldn't,' David replied with a wicked grin. 'Not if it involves anything more complicated than chopping or stirring.'

'I can heat things up too,' Ellie said. 'And assemble. I'm very good at assembling pre-cooked items.'

'You don't cook?' Ludo and Ruth asked in unison and also in some consternation.

'No. My mum said it was far more important that I could play a musical instrument than make rough puff pastry or debone a duck,' Ellie explained. 'I've tried to learn but I don't think my brain is wired in the right way.'

'You're exactly the same,' Ludo said to his son. 'Remember when I tried to teach you how to make an omelette? What could be simpler than that?'

'Lots of things,' David said, with a smile. He was leaning forward, elbows propped on the table, a bottle of fancy imported lager resting against one tanned cheek and Ellie could understand why Ruth, and even Ludo, would occasionally shoot him a brief, proud look as if to confirm that yes, we did raise this fine, upstanding man. This might be what he was really like with people who weren't simply items on his to-do list. 'String theory. What the Hadron Collider actually does. The plot of *Inception*. Far too many variables in cooking an omelette.'

'It's impossible to tell if the pan is too hot, not hot enough or just the right temperature,' Ellie added feelingly. 'And whenever I try to crack an egg, I end up with more shell than yolk and whatever the white stuff is called.'

'Albumen,' Ruth said, and she patted Ellie's hand again. 'I use ready-made mayonnaise so I'll email you the rest of the recipe if you give me your address before you go.'

Ellie agreed that she would, and it seemed that they were done with the salmon and the salad, and though apple strudel had been mentioned she couldn't force down another mouthful.

Ruth was already gathering empty plates. As Ellie stood up to help her Ludo turned to David. 'I would ask if you read my piece in the *Law Review* about how a moral imperative is still relevant in today's society but it would only lead to an argument, so would you like to come and see the foundations I've marked out for my new office shed?'

There was obviously back story there. Ellie had noticed that, apart from the few surreptitious proud looks, there hadn't even been a hug and a kiss when he walked through the door. Ellie could never remember a time when she hadn't been greeted by hugs and kisses from Ari or Sadie.

Still, it wasn't her place to ask, and once it was just her and Ruth in the kitchen loading the dishwasher, the conversation became strained again. 'How long will you be staying at David's, do you think?' Ruth queried after a long silence.

'Really not that long,' Ellie assured her. 'I might go and

stay with friends in Paris but I'll probably end up at my grandparents' tonight.'

'Oh! Are they local?'

'Belsize Park.' Ellie gingerly slotted mayonnaise-encrusted utensils into the cutlery drawer. 'So it's only a short drive from Highgate.'

'If you don't mind me asking, what do your grandparents think about this mess you've got yourself into?' Ruth asked, and Ellie did mind her asking but there didn't seem a polite way to say that. She contented herself with frowning at Ruth's back as the other woman abandoned the clearing-up entirely in favour of making another batch of Campari and sodas.

'Well, they think I'd never have got into this mess if I only dated nice Jewish boys, but they love me quite a lot so they've been really good about it.' It popped out before she could pop it back in. Ellie actually put a hand to her mouth in horror as Ruth looked her up and down, expression thoughtful. Ellie wondered if she'd just confirmed Ruth's worst fears; that she had her talons firmly embedded in her son, which was not even remotely what she meant. Yes, he was Jewish, but he wasn't *that* nice and he already had several girlfriends.

'Your surname is Cohen, isn't it?' she repeated. 'Belsize Park.' She looked at Ellie again, standing in her kitchen in her nice Banana Republic dress that didn't show too much skin, with her shiny straight hair and subtly polished toenails, and frowned. 'I'm sure there are at least fifty Cohens in Belsize Park but you're not related to Sadie and Morry, are you?'

'They're my grandparents!'

Ruth Gold's smile was as sunny as the late evening sun that spilled through the windows and gave the kitchen a golden glow. 'Your grandmother is a remarkable woman. Remarkable,' Ruth exclaimed enthusiastically. 'And your grandfather is a darling. Oh! Both of them do so much for charity. They were on our table at a quiz night in aid of Darfur and I think one of Sadie's other daughters, Carol, is married to . . . either Ludo's second cousin or is it his first cousin once removed?' She held out her arms. 'Ellie! I don't know what you must think of me. Obviously one doesn't like to believe everything one reads in the papers but it's so easy to get caught up in it. And knowing you're related to *that* man. Can you forgive me?'

Ellie flapped one hand. 'Don't even mention it. How were you meant to react when I turned up like that?'

It was something else that Ruth and Sadie had in common: the inability to mention Billy Kay by his given name, which was . . . interesting.

Ten minutes later, they were nose to nose on the sofa, and now that Ruth had got over her initial suspicions and Ellie had decided that actually, yes, she did care what Ruth thought about her, they were getting on just fine. Ari was the best mother in the world, hands down, no contest, but Ruth Gold wasn't too shabby herself. She had a challenging career, a beautiful house, had raised a family, collected interesting things like netsukes and first editions of children's ghost stories, and was a firm believer that everyone should have a creative outlet.

'I cross-stitch, and crochet very badly, and Ludo has become obsessed with gardening. What do you do?'

Ellie pulled a face. 'I'm not sure I have a creative outlet. Most of the artists I work with tell me off for *stifling* their creativity in the name of commerce.'

'They sound horribly self-indulgent,' Ruth decided. She swirled the ice cubes round in her glass. 'Anyway, you work in a creative field so it's not so important. I wish David wasn't so career-focused. Do you know that last year, in the middle of the Yom Kippur service, he had his phone on vibrate and left synagogue to take a work call? I was mortified.'

This was not a conversation that Ellie could have any

part of. 'He has his marathon running,' she said a little desperately.

Ruth didn't say anything, but the ice swirling became a little more manic. 'Well,' she said, then paused. 'Well, I'm sorry, but someone who runs that many marathons is running away from something. He is not happy, Ellie.'

'He seems very good at his job,' Ellie said as brightly as she could. She'd sworn she was going to stay for only an hour and she should have stuck to her original plan. 'About to become senior partner, from what I hear.'

Ruth made a face like she'd ordered lobster and been presented with fish fingers instead. 'He'd be furious if he knew that I'd said this to you . . .'

'He's your son, it's only natural that you worry about him . . .'

'. . . bad enough before he went to the States. He's meant to practise law, not find loopholes so his clients can get away with murder. Not literally. Well, maybe literally, for all I know,' Ruth said, smashing the hell out of the last of her ice. 'What is going on with the two of you? Or is this all some Machiavellian scheme involving *that* man and—'

'Look, please, Ruth . . .' Ellie held up her hands in protest. 'I couldn't step out of my front door without finding myself in the middle of a baying mob of paparazzi, and yes, moving me into his spare room was entirely for Billy Kay's benefit, but at least David has given me a few days' peace and I'm grateful to him for that.'

'I just want him to be happy. Are you sure there's nothing between the two of you?'

There was, but it was one-sided and ill-advised and not something Ellie was going to discuss with David's mother. 'I'm sure he's not *un*happy,' she demurred. 'And he's very successful, and I don't think he's short of female company. Not that I—'

'Oh, is he?' Ruth asked sharply. 'Well, he certainly hasn't introduced any of them to me.'

'Not even Jessica who lives across the hall?' Ellie prompted, though she should have left well alone.

'Jessica? Who's Jessica?' Ruth demanded with a pointed look so, for a moment, her friendly expression was replaced with something more forbidding – Ellie could see who David had picked up that little trick from. 'The last time David introduced us to any of his girlfriends was when he was fifteen and seeing Daniella Rabin from next door.'

'I must have got my information wrong, then.' It was strange and unsettling that David kept all the different bits of his life separate rather than overlapping. He wanted to be all these different things to different people, but by doing that surely he had to lose something of himself? None of this was any of her business, no matter how much she longed to pry into the dark corners of his life. Ellie looked around frantically for a new topic. 'So, does your daughter live near here?'

It was the perfect diversion. Sophie Gold (she'd refused to take her husband's name, much to the horror of her in-laws) lived in Finchley with Justin and their two children. Ruth couldn't wait to show Ellie photos of her grandsons on her iPad.

'I think Sophie and Justin are probably done on the baby front,' Ruth explained as Ellie made cooing noises because it was impossible not to coo at pictures of a three-year-old and a one-year-old with heart-shaped faces, big brown eyes and dark curly hair dressed as bumblebees for Halloween. 'Sophie wants to concentrate on her career now. She has her own web design firm. You two would really get on. When all this silly business with the papers has died down, you must come for dinner again.'

'I'd like that,' Ellie said, and she would, though she was sure that David would probably like it a lot less. 'And I'd really like to pick your brains about some research I'm doing. Any leads you could give me on female art groups in working-class communities or women's organisations between the wars?'

'How interesting! One of my colleagues might be able to help you,' Ruth said eagerly as her husband and son came in from the garden.

'We should probably go,' David said and if Ellie had thought that there was a tiny little bit of tension earlier, now she was sure that if she held out a hand she'd feel it hard and sharp against her fingertips.

'Oh, must you?' Ruth cried, taking hold of Ellie's hand. 'I've hardly had time to get to know this gorgeous girl.'

'Well, if this gorgeous girl wants to walk home across the Heath while it's still light, you'll have to postpone getting to know each other,' David said flatly. His expression was so bland, it was beige.

'You have to promise to bring Ellie again.'

'Or Ellie could come by herself?' Ludo suggested with a smile. 'If you're too busy greasing the wheels of a soulless, shallow industry.'

'If you're so bothered about the lapsed morals of the legal profession, maybe you should practise law again instead of writing incomprehensible pieces about the—'

'Boys!' Ruth struggled to her feet. 'It's been a lovely evening. Don't spoil it.'

It was already spoiled, but Ruth was determined to put a brave face on it and Ellie didn't want to leave on such a sour note so she smiled and nodded and talked in a cheery voice that sounded very fake to her own ears. When they left, David was handed a cool bag packed with the unserved chicken dinner and Ellie was presented with a warm, tinfoil parcel of apple strudel.

Before the door had even shut behind them, Ellie heard Ludo say enthusiastically, 'What a cracking girl. If she could only cook, then she'd be perfect for him.'

Camden, London, 1986

Then one night Billy went AWOL. Fine. Artistes didn't always come home in time for dinner. But he wasn't at the studio and he didn't turn up for three whole days.

When he did he was tired and unshaven. There was a scratch mark down one cheek. Ari suspected that if he took off his shirt, he'd have scratches down his back too.

'Where have you been? Who the fuck have you been with? You've been with *her*, haven't you?' Ari spat at him before he could even get through the door. She could never bring herself to say Olivia's name. Billy didn't have that problem.

'Of course I've been with Olivia,' he shouted. 'The kid, Lara, she was sick.'

'So? Are you a doctor? What use could you possibly have been?' Ari shouted back at him, hormones and fear and resentment making her Medusa-mad.

'She's my daughter,' he insisted furiously. 'What the fuck did you want me to do?'

'You left me! You left me on my own in this freezing shithole. You got me in this mess,' she gestured down at her swollen stomach, 'now you have to stay with me!'

Billy looked at Ari like he didn't even know her any more, though she was still wearing five inch fuck-me heels and a huge beehive despite Carol's fears that the Elnett fumes would hurt the baby. He looked repulsed at what she'd become.

'Fuck this and fuck you!' he said. The door wouldn't slam

303

properly because the wood was damp and warped, but it was still one hell of an exit.

A week went by and Ari knew he was never coming home again.

She winkled the address out of Jimmy Vaughn for the price of a wrap of speed but didn't have the guts to ring on the bell. So she spent long hours standing in the cold in Powis Square, then retreated to the warm fug of the pub on the corner.

There was another person hot on Billy's trail too. More often than not Ari would see Georgina Pratt sitting with her nose pressed to the window as she nursed a vodka and Coke. Ari actually felt sorry for the kid, sorry enough to waddle over and give Georgina the benefit of her five extra years of experience in dealing with men.

'Listen, sweetheart,' she said kindly. 'Go find a real boy and stop mooning after Billy. He's not worth it.'

'He is.' Georgina rounded on Ari, her pudding face contorted into an ugly scowl. 'He is worth it and he loves Olivia, not you. They're perfect for each other.'

Ari pointed at the bun in her oven. 'Not that perfect for each other, are they?'

'They are, and you're just an ugly tart who's ruined everything,' Georgina said. Then she stood up and, defying all laws of man and God, threw her drink in the face of the woman who was eight months pregnant.

Chapter Twenty-three

Ellie didn't hear what Ruth thought about this, but she looked over at David, who treated her to a chilly smile. 'Sorry to drag you away, but if we'd stayed any longer, I think they'd have started making plans to adopt you.'

'They were really nice,' Ellie said, as he held the gate open for her. 'Considering I turned up uninvited, they made me feel very welcome.'

'Duly noted, Pollyanna.'

'How do you even know about *Pollyanna*?'

'Younger sister,' he said obliquely. 'I used to charge her fifty pence a time to read her a bedtime story.'

'When I hear stories like that, I'm glad I'm an only child,' Ellie told him as they crossed over the road and walked through the gap in the hedge that led back onto the Heath extension. Then she remembered that technically she wasn't an only child; technically, she had two half-sisters.

Ellie risked a glance sideways at her father's lawyer, sure he was going to spend the walk back to Highgate being cold and distant, but instead he smiled at her. He was stuck halfway between the Inns of Court and Glastonbury tonight. It was very unsettling. 'Well, despite the financial advantages, there were lots of times that I wished I was an only child too. Particularly during the Care Bear years.'

'Ari would never let me have Care Bears or Barbies or even a Polly Pocket,' Ellie said, and as they came to the first dip in the path, which involved scrambling down a small but steep slope, he was already holding out his hand to help her.

'Was that because she was a single parent? You notice I didn't say anything about being on benefits,' he added drily.

'Except you just have, and not having those things was nothing to do with lack of funds and more to do with Ari being terrified that I'd be one of those girls who was obsessed with everything pink and princessy.'

'Did her cunning masterplan work?' David gave her an appraising look. 'I've yet to see you wear anything pink, but you have filled my bathroom with what seems like an excessive amount of hair products.'

Ellie was in the middle of telling David that Sadie would buy her whatever toys her pink, princess-loving heart desired as long as she did well in her weekly spelling tests and would keep them hidden at her house away from Ari's disapproval, when she was interrupted by his phone ringing.

'I should probably get this,' he said, looking at his phone, but he said it without much enthusiasm, as if he'd much rather listen to the denouement of her story, in which Ari had discovered a contraband Barbie bangle in her weekend case and had gone on an hour's rant that contained words like 'body fascism' and 'third-wave feminism', then made Ellie write out fifty times, 'Barbie is a toxic plastic tool of a patriarchal culture.'

'Hello. How are you?' he asked tonelessly.

It wasn't dark yet but dusk was settling in, softening the light and lengthening the shadows. The heat was becoming more humid and it was so quiet and still on the Heath that Ellie could hear the high-pitched, garbled voice of David's caller.

She took a step away when he said, 'You could have just called me at work, Jess, if you were worried I had squatters in my flat.'

The ice in his voice cut through the humidity. Ellie trembled.

The tinny voice on the phone sounded more hectoring now and Ellie dreaded to think what it might be saying. She also couldn't bear to look at David's face for clues on how the conversation was proceeding. There was a wooden bench a few metres away, so she wasn't in earshot, though she could imagine only too well what Jessica was saying to him.

David was pacing up and down as he talked, long legs covering the same well-worn path again and again. Ellie had to stop looking at him, stealing glances that he didn't even know she was taking. Like she was trying to commit the shape and size and measure of him to memory. It was silly when she still wasn't sure that she even liked him that much, and he was certainly going to like her even less once he'd finished talking to Jessica.

Now was definitely the time to start planning her speedy getaway again. The Universe obviously agreed with her because when she checked her phone, there was an email from her friend Esme in Paris.

Sweetness!

So good to hear from you. Of course the offer of our sofabed still stands, except you need to know a few things.

1. In Paris it has rained for seven days straight.
2. On Monday, it will be 1 August. Paris decamps to the country and the coast for the whole of August so everywhere that's fabulous will be shut.
3. Sue and I are going to St Tropez to stay with friends on Monday. You're welcome to come along too. Said friends live in a freaking chateau. They're bound to have a spare room.
4. Or you can apartment-sit. Would be totes totes totes

lovely to see you before we go or can leave keys avec concierge who is staying in Paris because she's très, très, très old et boring.

5. Also! So many straight men I can set you up with either in Paris or St Trop.

Holla once you've booked your tickets.

Love you, mean it,
Esme

David was still pacing with phone clamped to his ear. From the set of his shoulders and the speed of his strides, it didn't appear that he was anywhere close to ending his chat with Jessica.

That made it easier to act decisively. Ellie called Madeleine Jones, who sorted out all the gallery travel requirements, and if she minded being called so late on a Friday evening she didn't mention it. She simply agreed to Ellie's request for a seat on the next available Eurostar heading to Paris 'even if it's first thing tomorrow morning. In fact, first thing tomorrow morning would be great', and promised to email her the ticket details.

Ellie didn't have the guts to call Vaughn. Also, Grace took a very dim view of work-related phone calls after eight p.m. so she emailed him with a *fait accompli*.

David was *still* on the phone and dusk was quickly becoming dark. Then he looked straight at her. 'Ellie?' He was off the phone before she even realised the call was over, and marching towards her.

She stood up and brushed down the skirt of her dress nervously. 'Everything all right, then?'

'No, everything is not all right.' He was standing in front of her now and even the faltering light and the long shadows couldn't disguise the tight, angry lines of his face. 'Were you going to tell me that Jess came over?' His voice was tight and angry to match.

308

'Well, of course I was! I did try when you first came home.'

'You didn't try very hard.'

'There never seemed to be a right moment.' Ellie risked looking up at David, but got as far as his chin, before she averted her gaze down to a scrubby patch of withered grass. 'Look, she came round. She didn't like me; I didn't like her. And she shouldn't have just come barging in like that. It was an invasion of my privacy. It was an invasion of *your* privacy.' That sounded all wrong, like she was on the defensive, on the attack: all things that would prolong an argument. 'She insinuated . . . no, she *said* some really offensive things to me and ordinarily I'd have just let it go, but even I have my limits.' David hadn't moved. Half a step nearer and technically he'd be right up in her face. Ellie needed to do better. 'She was really hostile.'

'Oh, she speaks very highly of you too,' he said, his breathing slightly ragged. 'Said you gave her some very useful relationship advice.'

'Yeah, well, I'm sure she didn't tell you—'

'Just drop the act, Ellie!' He took that half-step nearer and Ellie couldn't take a half-step back because the bench was in the way. 'That nice-girl routine is wearing paper thin now. That's how you ingratiated yourself with my mother, wasn't it? God knows what you said to her!'

She didn't recognise herself in the bitter words that he was flinging at her. 'I don't ingratiate myself. Before this all started, this business in the papers, people liked me! They would open up to me. I have one of those faces. I'm a people person.' She flung up her hands but really she wanted to grab his shirtfront and shake some sense into him.

'You're not a people person, you're a people pleaser. There's a huge difference.' Ellie flinched, eyes blinking, air in short supply when he cupped her chin, turned her face up to catch what was left of the light, *touched her*. 'I know who you really are behind that sweet smile,' he told her simply, as if everything she showed the world was a façade that he needed to rip down. 'You have that wide-eyed ingénue act almost note-perfect, but it is just an act, isn't it, Ellie? I saw you last night after Billy phoned. Inside you're as dark and fucked up as the rest of us.'

'No I'm not!' It was one of the worst things he could have said. 'Just because you've seen me during the most *awful*, extraordinary days of my life doesn't mean you know the real me!' Ellie wrenched herself out of his grasp, nearly giving herself whiplash in the process. Her hands were clenched into fists, which she used to beat him back, because he was still far too close. 'Get away from me!'

He stepped back, held up his hands to ward off any more blows. 'Everyone's got an angle. Even you. Especially you.'

'My angle? My angle is that I've always been stupid enough to believe that people are fundamentally good,' Ellie spat. 'And as for you . . . You . . .'

'What about me?' David asked. He didn't sound angry any more, but expectant.

'If anyone hides behind a smile, it's you,' she flung at him. 'Yeah, you can be really smooth and persuasive, but underneath you're calculating and as cold as the grave.' There was so much more to be said on the subject, and Ellie couldn't sort out the mass of words ricocheting around in her head, so she settled for snatching up the apple strudel still warm in its tinfoil shroud and throwing it at him. 'I'll give you darkness, you sanctimonious fucker!'

She stumbled away, as fast as she could in her unsuitable footwear, veering off the gravel to follow an overgrown footpath that plunged her deep into the heart of the Heath, where overhanging trees made strange shapes in the gloom and the undergrowth brushed against her legs. She'd have been terrified if the anger hadn't seized hold of her and refused to let go.

After ten minutes or so, Ellie started to calm down, pulse slowing, footsteps faltering. She came to a halt and tried to get her bearings. Her bearings proved elusive. She was lost, but it was impossible to retrace her steps when her steps hadn't followed any recognisable pattern and had just been about getting as far away from David Gold as possible.

Now she could hear her own erratic breaths, the thud of her frantic heart. There were other sounds. Nature sounds. Things skittering through the bushes. Though it was too hot for a breeze, there was *rustling*, and she was a city kid, born and bred, who didn't do nature. Nature was far more scary than being on your own on Dalston High Street at three in the morning.

With fumbling fingers, Ellie managed to find her iPhone, go to Google Maps and pray she had enough of a 3G signal to navigate her way out of this mess. She was peering at the screen, willing the page to load, when a hand gripped her shoulder. Her heart spasmed painfully and she honest-to-goodness screamed until a voice said, 'Thank God, you're wearing white. I'd never have found you otherwise. Somehow I didn't think you'd answer your phone.'

Ellie shook off David's hand. The anger was back and she had to fight against it; curling her toes, tensing every muscle, forcing herself to take deep breaths before she trusted herself to turn round.

He was standing there, adjusting the strap of the cool bag, and was that a smile? Did he think that he could say horrible, hurtful things to her and then it wouldn't matter because he'd rescued her from a terrifying, lonely night on the Heath?

She wanted to *kill* him. 'I'm sorry,' she managed to say, though she wasn't remotely sorry, but she couldn't bear to feel this unhinged for even a second longer. 'If it's any consolation, I've never called anyone a fucker before.'

'Not really, no.' He shook his head. 'You got angry, Ellie. Why can't you just stay with it? Own it. Just stop pretending to be so bloody perfect because you're not. No one is.'

Ellie could feel her face begin to droop, to fold, her eyes start smarting, and before she could even tell herself not to cry, she'd burst into tears that were long overdue. It had been one hell of a week and she needed to cry it out. But to be crying because David had the wrong idea about her was pathetic.

She didn't want the tears to turn into a big, ugly cry, but all she could do was hang her head as her shoulders shook and, God no, she was flapping her hands in front of her face.

Why did girls do that? Why was she doing that?

'Ellie? There's no need to cry,' David said more sharply than was necessary, when he was responsible for a lot of the tears that she was currently shedding.

She turned her back on him and wished that he had enough tact and consideration to hide behind a tree until she'd got the tears reined in. Instead, he just stood there, looking at her. 'Please go away!' she said in between sobs. 'Give me some privacy.'

But he didn't give her privacy. She felt his hand on her shoulder again, trying to turn her round to face him. She batted him away with a flailing arm.

'For God's sake, Ellie. Tears aren't going to make me feel sorry for you,' he said, because he was fucking relentless.

'I thought you wanted me to show an honest emotion,' she spluttered. 'Well, I'm crying. I'm owning my crying. Why isn't that good enough for you?'

'Don't do this to me,' David said softly, so softly that she wouldn't have heard him if he hadn't been close enough that he could suddenly wrap his arms around her.

Ellie's first instinct was to panic and struggle free. Her second instinct was to stiffen and go completely still so the message penetrated his incredibly dense brain that his touch was unwelcome and unwanted, but then he smoothed back her hair from her hot, damp face and he pressed his lips to her equally hot and damp forehead so fleetingly that Ellie thought that she'd imagined it.

Then David did it again. But it wasn't fleeting. It was his lips firm against her forehead and her third instinct was to melt against him, limbs as pliable as warm dough, because he was touching her, properly, deliberately, for the first time since Glastonbury, right at that moment when she needed the comfort of someone else's touch, even if that someone despised her.

The tears slowed to a crawl and Ellie was sniffing, ready to retreat, but David hugged her a little tighter and shushed her and kept his hand smoothing through her hair like a mantra as he pressed more kisses to her forehead and the bridge of her nose and her eyelids when she obligingly closed her eyes. When he reached her mouth she was already tilting her face up, raising herself on tiptoes so nothing could go wrong before it had even started.

It no longer felt like a kiss just to be near him. It *was* a kiss. Ellie couldn't tell if David got to her lips first, or if she was already straining towards his mouth. All she knew was that her arms were round his neck, fingers raking through his hair and their mouths were locked together in a fierce clumsy kiss. There was a clash of teeth, then he turned his head ever so slightly and she shifted ten degrees in the other direction and then everything aligned; planets, time, space and their mouths on each other, and Ellie started to cry all over again from the sheer relief that she was kissing and being kissed by David Gold.

They were kissing and she was crying, and her nose was running and her mascara must have streaked down her cheeks, but it was still perfect. A moment that she'd thought about so many times but her dreams didn't compare to the feeling of David's hands framing her face like she was utterly precious, even as she could feel his tongue in her mouth, his hard cock nudging between them.

She didn't know how much longer she could have carried on without his kisses.

Then the cool bag, which had managed to stay on David's shoulder throughout all the excitement, slipped and banged against Ellie's hip on its descent and the spell was broken.

They weren't kissing any more, but standing a respectable metre apart.

It was dark and hard to see his face so Ellie wasn't sure what he was thinking. She was tempted to get in there first, to say that it was a terrible mistake and she hadn't been in her right state of mind all week, and that it could never happen again, when he cleared his throat. Ellie waited for David to spit out some legal disclaimer and refute any pleas of culpability that she might make.

'I've thought about nothing else but kissing you ever since Glastonbury. Even after I found out who you really were.' Ellie felt that same, blessed sweet relief again. He'd felt the same way, could sense that fierce pull tugging them closer and closer to each other. Then relief gave way to cold, grim reality, because of who she was, Billy Kay's daughter, and who he was, Billy Kay's right-hand man. 'It's why I've tried so hard to keep my distance. This complicates everything.'

Ellie was already fishing in her handbag for a tissue to wipe the snot and smeared make-up from her face. 'I know,' she agreed, because David was right. A kiss was all it could ever be and it should never have gone as far as that. 'This is stupid. Things are already too complicated.'

'It just so happens that I'm good at dealing with complicated,' he said. Ellie wasn't sure what he meant, although they were in an obscure corner of the Heath and a lot of his immediate problems could be solved by burying her in a shallow grave to be discovered by a dog walker weeks from now. 'Complicated is actually more straightforward than crisis management.'

'Oh, so now I'm something to be dealt with, rather than managed, am I?' Ellie said in a hurt voice, as she finished scrubbing at her face. Her skin felt tight and sore, and her lips were stinging from his kisses.

'I'm not arguing about this. Not when we're in the middle of the Heath in darkness, not far away from an area popular with the local dogging community,' he said in an amused voice, though Ellie couldn't imagine what was funny about *that*. She also didn't know why he was taking her hand and she was letting him, curling her fingers around his, squeezing so he squeezed back. She was also trying really hard not to peer and squint into the undergrowth, which was still rustling, in case some local pervert was hiding and had been getting his rocks off watching them kiss. That was *not* how she wanted to remember their kiss.

'Let's go,' she said, with a shudder. 'I'm sure there's something in the bushes.'

Ellie thought that as soon as David had led them out of the woods and they could see Kenwood House in the distance like a lodestar to guide them back to the right path, he'd drop her hand.

He never did. He held her hand, even once they were walking along Hampstead Lane. Was still holding her hand, his thumb absent-mindedly stroking her knuckles as they entered his building, waited for the lift, travelled up to the fifteenth floor.

They stopped holding hands only when they were through his front door. Like the first kiss, there was an unspoken agreement about what was going to happen next.

Chapter Twenty-four

For one all-too-brief-moment Ellie was pressed against the door, David's body holding her there as he teased her with the promise of a kiss, until the teasing and the waiting became unbearable. Then they were half-falling down the three steps into the living room, staggering across the floor, mouths still locked together.

David fell backwards onto the sofa, Ellie on top of him, kissing him fiercely as his hands fisted in her hair. He even let her pin his arms above his head, watching her with heavy-lidded eyes as she tightened her hands around his wrists to see if he'd try to break free. He didn't, but he sighed. Not a sad sigh, but a sigh that was full of longing and wonder, or so it seemed to Ellie as she licked a path along his ridiculously sharp cheekbones.

'I've been wanting to do that since the first time I saw you,' she said. She hardly recognized her voice, it was so breathy. 'There have been so many times over the last few weeks when I didn't think you were the same man I'd met at Glastonbury. I was beginning to think that it had never happened. That I just imagined it.'

That should have cast a shadow over the two of them, because all the bad times that had happened since were a direct consequence of the five minutes after that first meeting, and when David strained against the bonds she'd made from her fingers, Ellie let him go.

His hands settled on her hips. 'I can assure you that us

meeting at Glastonbury wasn't just a dream you had. Unless I dreamed it too,' he said. Ellie waited for him to elaborate, dreading that he might mention Richey, but he just smiled, eyes darkening. 'So, was there anything else you wanted to do to me?'

Ellie showed him. For a man who was still so much of a mystery, there were things about him that were unambiguous. He wanted her. That was obvious from the desperate rise and fall of his chest when she slowly unbuttoned his shirt, the insistent promise of his cock against her belly, even through his jeans, and the way he beckoned her closer with one finger so he could whisper in her ear: 'Shall I show you what I wanted to do to you?'

Ellie let him roll them over. She gazed up at him as he straddled her and slowly unpicked the knot that kept her wrap dress wrapped. She'd never thought that untying a bow could feel like torture, but it did when his eyes never left her face and his plump bottom lip was caught between his teeth as he parted the edges of her dress like he was opening a present that he'd waited months to arrive.

David wasn't looking at her face any more but at her breasts; it was too hot to wear a bra, not that Ellie had much to lift and separate. She wished her breasts were lush and voluptuous but David made a throaty, approving sound, then swooped down to take one tightly budded nipple in his mouth, to soothe the ache with his tongue while his thumb rubbed and teased the other breast and Ellie lifted towards his hungry, voracious mouth, hands firm on the back of his neck so he knew not to stop.

No one had ever made Ellie sob in sheer frustration before. She tugged David's shirt off, then wriggled her hands between them to unbutton his jeans and pushed them down with her legs and even her feet, gasping when he twisted on top of her as he kicked them off, cock right *there* for one glorious second. Then they were skin to skin. Almost skin to skin.

David's hand trailed between her breasts, traced each rib, followed the curve of her belly and the jut of her hip-bones until he reached the white lace of her briefs. When Ellie looked up at him from under her lashes, she knew what he was asking, just from the arch of one eyebrow and the hesitant quirk of his mouth.

'I'm keeping them on,' she said, because she didn't have another option.

'I could make you come without taking them off,' he told her without any bravado. 'If you wanted.'

She did want. That was the problem. Or it was one of the problems. 'I'm not going to be another one of your women,' she reminded him, just in case he'd forgotten Jessica, or Melanie from Goldman Sachs, or the girl from Glastonbury and goodness knows how many others.

'Ah, and it becomes complicated again,' David said, and Ellie was so sick and tired of complicated. 'That's an issue you don't need to worry about.'

He was retreating, still on top of her, but his mind was somewhere far away. To that place where he had other women he could have sex with who didn't come with so much baggage.

Ellie folded her arms to cover her breasts. David was levering himself off her in an instant. She grabbed the two sides of her dress and yanked them together, then gave all her attention to trying to find the tiny hole in the side seam so she could poke the right tie through it.

By the time she'd succeeded, David was back in his jeans and shirt, and rooting through the fridge to emerge with a bottle of white wine. 'I think we need to talk,' he said to her. In Ellie's experience those six words never led to anything good, but she nodded and struggled to sit up and swing her legs round so she was no longer sprawled in gay abandon across the sectional sofa.

He sat right next to her, close enough that his thigh was pressed against her, and when Ellie took a glass of wine from him he ran a finger across her knuckles. She should probably have jerked her hand away for appearance's sake; instead she hung her head so she could see the spot on the little toe of her right foot that she'd missed with the nail polish earlier.

'Ellie, let's not lapse into an embarrassed silence. We were both consenting adults who kissed. It was very good, very enjoyable kissing. There's no reason to look quite so devastated.'

'I have every reason to,' she said, 'until I know whether you're seeing anyone else. I don't ever want to be the sort of girl who kisses other girls' partners. It's the worst thing a woman could do.'

'Not the worst thing,' David mused. 'Surely murder or even theft would be—'

'Well, it is theft, isn't it?' It was also rule one of the girl code. Chicks before dicks every time. You never body-shamed another woman and let her know she'd gained or lost a few pounds and you never – repeat, NEVER – let another woman leave the ladies with her skirt tucked into her knickers. But mostly, you never put the moves on another woman's man, and if you did, then you deserved the long, lonely death that was coming to you. 'Are you involved with someone else, because Jessica seemed to think you two belonged together. And what about Melanie?'

'People don't belong to people. They're not possessions,' David said heatedly.

'Are you really going to argue about semantics? Really?'

'I've known Jess for a long, long time. We were involved for a short while, now we're not.' Ellie could feel his eyes on her but she resolutely stared at that one imperfect spot of her pedicure. 'I'm thirty-four. I've been sexually active for quite some time and I don't have the inclination for a long-term relationship right now, so there are a couple of women I see casually. Non-exclusively.'

Ellie couldn't help the tiny, inelegant sound she made as David spelled out in no uncertain terms why she'd be a fool to take this any further. Not just for all the reasons that she'd already gone through in her head again and again, but because she didn't want to become just another woman he saw on a casual, non-exclusive basis. If she was having sex with someone, then she wanted it to mean something and she wanted to mean something to the person she was having sex with.

'We shouldn't have kissed,' she said, and she folded her arms and tried to look prim and proper as David sat back and folded *his* arms, though his eyes were glinting as if he wasn't really seeing Ellie sitting next to him but remembering what she looked like under her clothes. 'I suppose, at least, we got it out of our systems but you have to admit, it was a really bad idea.'

'It was probably one of the worst ideas I've ever had,' he agreed, and Ellie didn't know how he had the stones to say such crushing things in a calm voice without even a flicker of remorse. 'Except I've been thinking about kissing you all week. Why do you think I kept away? I actually spent Wednesday evening camped out in Pizza Express with my laptop, for God's sake.'

Her stupid, foolish heart, which should have known better, perked up. 'But this still shouldn't have happened and it's not going to happen again,' she said. It sounded like she really meant it. 'I'll see you in the morning.'

She'd never meant to stay another night in David's flat but there she was, in his bathroom, cleaning her teeth and doing her final email check before bedtime.

Madeleine Jones had come through for her, as she invariably did. There was a seat booked for Ellie on the 15.45 Eurostar leaving from St Pancras tomorrow.

It was absolutely for the best, Ellie thought as she perched on the edge of the bathtub to wait for her serum to settle. Just because you had feelings for someone didn't

320

mean you had to act on them. Sometimes you had to exercise a little self-control.

With her face slathered in night cream and her mind made up, she opened the bathroom door to find David standing there.

'It's all yours,' she wanted to say. Or, 'I'll be out of your hair by tomorrow afternoon,' but she said nothing. David didn't say anything either.

Then Ellie's wash bag landed on the floor with a thud because all her arms wanted to do was to hold him and they were kissing again, without rhyme or reason, but simply because they couldn't *not*.

They kept kissing as they moved along the corridor until David awkwardly nudged open his bedroom door with his foot. It was unknown territory, because she wasn't a snooper, but as she was gently draped on top of a pristine white duvet, Ellie opened her eyes wide enough to take in a spartan room and another set of those glossy cupboard doors that looked like walls, behind which, no doubt, all of David's suits and shirts, even his socks and ties, were arranged in serried ranks.

When she thought about that side of him, how he hid away anything that might reveal too much, Ellie wondered what she was doing here. Then David was lying next to her on the bed with her, not holding her or kissing her, but gazing at her in the lamplight like she was a work of art.

'You are beautiful, though, Ellie,' he said, like that was a huge problem, and anyway she wasn't. On a good day she was pretty but right now she could sense that her Origins night cream was still sitting on the surface of her skin and her hair was scraped back and she was frowning. 'If we simply kiss for a few more minutes, then what's the harm in that?'

'No harm at all,' she concurred, reaching out for him.

But these weren't just kisses. They were kisses that

made her fall apart a little. They were kisses that were fierce but sincere. Kisses like they'd never get enough of each other, of the taste and the graze of teeth on bottom lip or a tongue dipping lazily in and out of a mouth.

These kisses were a line that should never have been crossed, so when David's fingers found the tie on her wrap dress again, Ellie rested her hand on top of his.

'No,' she said unequivocally. 'We are keeping our clothes on. *All* our clothes on.'

He smiled against her mouth, though Ellie didn't think there was anything much to smile about. 'Noted,' he murmured, and his hand settled on the dip of her waist and he kissed her with his eyes open as if he couldn't bear not to look at her.

His eyelids fluttered and his kisses got slower, then his limbs slackened because it was late and they'd both had a lot to drink and a lot to argue, and he was falling asleep on her.

Ellie shifted so she was lying on her back and David curled himself around her, arm across her belly, anchoring her to the here and now. By rights, she should have been sleepy too, except it was too hot, because it was always too hot now – even having a sheet over her felt like a fourteen-tog duvet – and she was still wearing her clothes, and though David hardly had an ounce of fat on him, he was heavy slumped against her.

She lay there for a while. The room grew stuffier because if you left the windows open then you were feasted on by every mosquito in Western Europe, according to David, which was why he shut all the windows every night.

It was impossible to sleep when the air conditioning made a high-pitched whistling sound, and David kept nuzzling against her neck. Ellie hoped he didn't want to snuggle and she really hoped he didn't snore, and then she realised why she was too wound up to sleep.

'I don't manipulate people.' Her voice sounded deafening in the still of the room. 'And I'm not a people pleaser. I'm just . . . I try to be *nice.*'

There was no reaction. She should have brought this up much earlier, probably between coming home and snogging on the sofa, but at the time she'd been much more preoccupied with snogging on the sofa.

'You want to do this now?' David struggled to prop himself up on one elbow.

'Generally, in my experience, if you're nice and friendly to people, they're nice and friendly back,' Ellie said, because no, this could not wait until tomorrow. 'How is that manipulation?'

'Are you nice and friendly even to people you don't like?' David asked idly, but his questions were never idle, they were calculated, always.

'There's something likeable about everybody,' Ellie insisted. People put up walls to hide their vulnerability, because they were afraid of rejection or because they didn't want anyone to know they were shy, but they were just walls and walls could be knocked down with a genuine smile and enquiry about their general wellbeing. If that failed, Ellie would find something, anything, noteworthy about the person who was giving her a hard time, whether it was their charity work, latest art acquisition or new handbag.

It was always validating when people called the gallery and asked for the 'friendly girl' rather than the 'posh girl with the attitude' or 'the posh girl who was too busy gazing into space to take any notice of me when I wanted to buy some art'.

'Everyone has at least one redeeming quality,' she clarified. 'Yes, I try to find that redeeming quality so I can establish some rapport with them, but that doesn't mean I'm manipulative.'

David sighed as if he knew that he wouldn't be going to

sleep any time soon. 'I didn't use those exact words,' he said calmly. 'And I'm sorry to break it to you, Ellie, but there are plenty of people who do not possess one solitary redeeming quality, and if you tell me that Hitler was a vegetarian and that he loved children, I *will* open the window but only so I can dangle you off the balcony.'

'I'm just saying that it was a very unfair accusation.' Arguing with a lawyer who had a string of letters after his name to prove just how good a lawyer he was should have been daunting, but after tonight David seemed a lot less daunting. Anyway, she had right on her side. 'No one goes through life scowling and being rude, and still expects people to like them. Only the very rich or the very famous.'

'The rich and famous are my stock in trade, and I've yet to meet anyone from either camp who wasn't avaricious, amoral and/or utterly lacking in anything approaching a conscience.' He said it without heat or outrage, but as if he was discussing a very dull book he'd just read. 'They may seem wide-eyed the first time they arrive in my office with a contract that their record company or their agent wants them to sign, but as soon as they're halfway to their first million, they'd sell out their mothers for a bigger slice of the pie.'

'That's not true. I've met plenty of rich and famous people and yes, OK, they can be demanding, but they can also be very nice.'

'Ellie! How can you be so naïve?' David sounded less bored now and more exasperated. 'Nice is just an angle.'

'No it's not!' Ellie was about to venture that they should probably agree to disagree because she didn't want a prolonged argument, when David sat up. 'I don't want to shatter your dreams,' he said, then proceeded to do exactly that.

Without once breaking lawyer–client privilege, he painted a world where there were no such things as scruples or decent, honest folk. Everyone had a price. Whether it was the movie star who grudgingly agreed to pay off his girlfriend after he'd beaten her up so badly she needed reconstructive surgery. Or the tween pop idol who made his entourage sign a non-disclosure agreement so they wouldn't tell the press he was banging his forty-year-old female manager. Or the much-loved but much-closeted A-lister who dated a selection of beautiful, leggy Z-listers, who were each under contract – a contract that was terminated two weeks after his annual appearance on the red carpet at the Oscars.

And finally, there was a lawyer who would draft these contracts and non-disclosure agreements and, representing the best interests of his clients, would draw up verbose sub-clauses, addenda and codicils, which ensured that the wide-eyed hopefuls that tripped into his office would barely make a penny even if their songs or their screenplays touched the hearts of millions. He was witness to all the schemes and machinations of the great and the good to ensure that they stayed great and good and he did nothing to stop it.

'On the contrary, I facilitate it,' David told her. He was sitting on the edge of the bed now, his shoulders so hunched that Ellie longed to knead and smooth until all his tension melted away, but she didn't think he'd let her. 'So, please don't tell me that people are pure and good and righteous because it's simply not true.'

If David believed that, then Ellie wondered if he still believed that she'd been complicit in her own downfall; that she and Richey had split the thirty pieces of silver between them. Or that this was her revenge on a father who'd never once expressed an interest in her. It didn't even matter what her supposed angle was. What was important was that David believed that she had one.

After everything that had happened tonight, if he still thought she was on the make, that she wanted to cash in on her notoriety, then Ellie knew that they could keep arguing about this until the sun came up and the sun went down again, but there was no point. It was all entirely hopeless.

'You should get some sleep if you want to get up at dawn o'clock to do some hideous training run,' she said softly, and she caught him by one bony wrist so she could tug him to lie back down next to her. 'Come on, think some nice, happy thoughts to get you snoring again.'

'I told you that I don't have happy thoughts and I certainly don't snore,' he said a little huffily. 'I have excellent peak respiratory flow. People with excellent peak respiratory flow don't snore.'

Maybe he was joking. Ellie couldn't tell. She lay next to him in the dark, staring at his clean, precise profile, and again she longed to rub the furrow in his forehead with her fingertips and smooth it away, but she didn't. She just kept hold of his wrist and measured out the beat of his pulse until it was slow and steady and he was asleep.

Ellie knew that she wasn't going to sleep. Not tonight. Because this was going to be the only night she spent with David Gold and she wanted to stay awake to see what his face looked like when he was dreaming and to prove or disprove the snoring theory, and if by some miracle he got cold and shivered in his sleep, she'd be there to put her arms round him.

She was going to let herself have this one night and then it would be over. Her other lovers – the lame ducks, the fixer-uppers, the men who needed mending and putting back together – were never going to be the sort of men that Ellie couldn't live without.

But David didn't need mending. He didn't have habits that needed breaking or a problem that could be solved by a couple of nights of chatting it out and persuading him to seek the help of a trained professional.

David was a finished product. He could make his way

through the world and navigate life without any help from Ellie. His cynicism was deeply engrained and invisible to the naked eye, like a glass wall, so that every time Ellie tried to get close to him, she'd end up smashing her face against it.

Worse than that, she'd revert to type. She'd try to fix what couldn't be fixed and it would break her heart that he could never truly be happy. And how could you really love someone who didn't know how to get happy?

London, Camden, 1986

Billy came back to her on Christmas Eve. He didn't come crawling back on his knees to beg forgiveness but he had roses, champagne, his custom-built Collings acoustic guitar ineptly wrapped in Christmas paper and a hangdog look on his face.

'I love you, Ari. I love you better than anyone else,' he said. 'You said you loved me too. Have you changed your mind?'

Ari would never know how you could love someone with everything that you were, but not like them very much. 'Next time you leave, I won't have you back,' she told him, but she let Billy wrap her up in a blanket and take her into the house, where in deference to her condition and because it was December, the playwright and the playwright's crazy Japanese girlfriend, who'd once accused Ari of stealing her Christian Lacroix coat (like that would ever, ever happen), had agreed to let them have a centrally heated room on the third floor with an en-suite bathroom.

They lay in bed together, not sleeping, but holding each other, and on Christmas Day Billy cooked them beans on toast, which they washed down with the champagne, and instead of giving him a present, Ari gave him ten pence so he could phone his daughter and wish her a happy Christmas.

Ari suspected that Olivia had thrown him out for good, but she didn't care because Billy was there and he was all hers now, refusing to leave her side. He wouldn't stop telling her that he loved her and saying stuff like, 'My life didn't really begin until you were in it, Ari.'

It was like how they used to be or, if she was being honest with herself, how Ari always wanted them to be, but they never were.

Billy's parents had finally cut him off, but they borrowed two hundred pounds from Carol for three more days of studio time and finished the backing vocals on the last track on the last day of the year.

'I feel sad,' Ari said to Billy as they walked home to Primrose Hill through the backstreets, away from the distant sounds of New Year's Eve parties. 'Like nothing good is ever going to happen again.'

'Only good things are going to happen,' Billy promised. 'You're going places and I'll be there with you every step of the way.' Then he kissed her under the glow of a streetlight. The taste of him made Ari forget that there was something important she had to do before she could get on with her destiny.

Hours later she woke up with a dirty grey pain clamping its teeth around her stomach.

Chapter Twenty-five

When Ellie woke up she was on her own without even a David-shaped indentation on the duvet next to her, BUT there was a note on the pillow.

> Ellie,
> Didn't want to wake you. Have to do 20km this morning with my running club. Hope you slept well. Back at 11-ish – we'll talk then.
> David

It was ten. Usually Ellie only ever slept in that late on a Sunday, and only when she'd had a skinful the night before. As she showered, dressed, listlessly packed her bags and tried to force down a cup of coffee and a toasted bagel, she certainly felt as sick and weary as she did when she was hungover.

Then she checked her email and was reminded that she was going to Paris, which, according to legend and popular culture, always had the cure for whatever ailed you. Somehow she doubted it. Paris wasn't *that* amazing, which was something she and Vaughn agreed on.

> Cohen
> No one stays in Paris in August, apart from idiotic tourists and surly Parisians who don't have the funds to leave Paris for an entire month.

You also have a very idiosyncratic idea of what working your notice out entails. Still, if you're set on this course, there are a few jobs I need you to do.

See attachment.

Vaughn

The attachment was another bullet-pointed list of items, which made Ellie's head swim. When she got back from Paris and was feeling more like herself, she was going to have it out with Vaughn about her notice, the withdrawal thereof.

After last night, Ellie never wanted to have it out with anyone ever again, but some things couldn't be left unsaid. Once she'd made the bed and attacked all surfaces in the spare room with a damp cloth so it looked as pristine as it had on the day she'd arrived, she tore out a page from her Smythson desk diary, which Vaughn always bought each of the staff as a Christmas present, and chewed ruminatively on the end of a pen. After ten minutes of staring at the blank page, she wrote,

Dear David,
Thank you so much for putting me up and putting up with me this last week.
  I think we both realise that after last night I can't stay here any longer. This situation between us is unworkable.
  Even if we rewound back to Glastonbury, and this time there was no Richey, no other women you see casually, no Billy Kay, do you think we'd have managed more than a couple of dates? I don't, because we both see the world in such a different way. You're so fixated on figuring out what my angle is that you can't see who I really am.
  You've witnessed the very best and worst of me,

because I'm living in extraordinary times, but you
have to believe me when I tell you that the ordinary,
everyday me is not that bad. I'm not a saint – hardly!
– but I try to do the right thing. That should count for
something but it doesn't with you.

I'm going to Paris. It's a work trip but also, if I need
to lay low for a little while, then it might as well be in
Paris.

If you need to talk to me about anything relating to
Billy Kay, you have my number. There's not much
point in talking about anything else.

I am sorry. I wish things could work out differently.
I wish we were different.

Thanks again.

Ellie

It would certainly never make the ranks of the Hundred
Greatest Love Letters Of All Time, but it was the best that
Ellie could do, especially when it was almost eleven and she
didn't want still to be kicking around when David came
back.

Ellie left the flat, even peeping round corners and slowly
prising open doors as if she were on a stake-out, but there
was no sign of David, no paparazzi, and after a short down-
hill walk she was on the 134 bus to Camden.

Camden was heaving with tourists, and teenagers in
heavy combat boots and heavy combat jackets, despite the
heat. Ellie kept to the back roads, until she reached the little
alley off Castlehaven Road and the rehearsal studios where
whatever band Ari was currently in rehearsed at noon
every Saturday, without fail.

There was no point going home before she went to Paris.
She had everything she needed, including clean clothes,
and though she was desperate to see Tess, it had been six
days since she'd last seen Ari, and Ellie really needed to see
Ari.

It wasn't until she turned the corner that Ellie realised that she really needed to see Chester too, because there he was, sitting on the wall outside the studio, looking reassuringly Chester-like in white Fred Perry and pork pie hat as he alternated bites of a bacon butty with sips from a Styrofoam cup of tea.

He looked up at the same moment that Ellie abandoned suitcase, holdall and smaller holdall in the middle of the courtyard so she could get to him quicker.

'Princess!' he exclaimed, holding his arms out wide so Ellie could hurl herself into them. 'How are you?'

'I've missed you,' Ellie told him. Then Chester was hugging her like only Chester could. He put everything into his hugs so the recipient was never in any doubt of the sincerity of the hug. 'Did you have a nice time in Benidorm?'

He had. Ellie sat on the wall next to him as he talked about lazing on the beach by day and listening to Northern Soul by night. 'If it had been up to me I'd have come home as soon as I read all the stuff in the papers but . . .' he tailed off uncertainly.

'I know you and Mum had a bit of an argy-bargy.' Ellie sighed. Chester put up with quite a lot from Ari, and the Northern Soul week in Benidorm was his annual break from putting up with quite a lot from Ari. If Ari had just told Chester that, instead of making such a big deal about not needing him, there would have been no fight, but Ari never did anything easy. 'Look, you called me every day and there was nothing much you could have done and it was fine. I've been fine. I'm not saying it's been easy but Billy's lawyer's been very . . . helpful,' she added stiffly.

'Are you sure?' Chester scrutinised Ellie's face. 'Some of that stuff in the papers was way out of line, even for them. If I ever track down that Richey, he can forget about having working kneecaps.'

'You mustn't!' Ellie was genuinely horrified. 'A week in Benidorm is one thing, but being sent down for God knows how long is something else completely. Promise me you'll leave him alone.'

'If that's what you want.' Chester gestured at her luggage. 'You going home?'

'No. I'm going to Paris.'

'Really? Because I spoke to my mum and dad and they said you're welcome to stay at theirs,' Chester said, tugging at the collar of his shirt.

'I'm going to Paris for work. Not because of the stuff in the papers,' Ellie lied, because she couldn't tell Chester about David. Besides, there was nothing to tell. It was over before it had even begun. 'It's really kind of Ron and Julie, but Paris does have the edge over Romford. Just a slight one.'

Chester grinned at that as Ari emerged from the studio clutching a bottle of water. Her hair was tucked up in a Rosie the Riveter-style headscarf and she was wearing a vest, cut-off jeans and a malevolent scowl, which disappeared as soon as she saw her daughter.

'Babycakes!' she said joyfully, hoisting herself up on the wall next to Ellie and putting an arm round her. 'I was just wondering if you were still cloistered or if there was any chance of a sighting of my favourite daughter.'

'I can't. Going on a work trip to Paris. I'm staying at Esme and Sue's,' Ellie added, and she didn't have to say any more because for Ari's last two birthdays, they'd gone to Paris and stayed with Esme and Sue. Ellie was hoping it might become a birthday tradition.

'I thought Paris was dead in August. Won't all the shops be closed?'

Ellie hadn't really believed that anyone with sense and money left the greater Paris area until September the first, but maybe it was true. 'Do you think?' She shook her head. 'There's an M&S on the Champs-Elysées. That won't be closed.'

'Of course everywhere will be open apart from a few

poncey restaurants that you wouldn't want to go to anyway,' Chester declared stoutly.

'Do you have to go to Paris right this very minute?' Ari asked as if Chester hadn't even spoken. 'Why don't you go on Monday and stay round mine this weekend? I swear I'm living paparazzi-free these days.'

'I can't. My Eurostar ticket isn't flexible and, God, I have to get out of London,' Ellie insisted, as if Ari was about to snatch her non-flexible Eurostar ticket from her. 'After everything that's happened, I need some space to get my head straight and think about what I'm going to do next.'

'OK, honeychild, it was just an idea,' Ari said, lifting up her shades so she could fix Ellie with a look. 'Everything all right? Well, apart from the obvious, which really isn't that obvious any more. I knew all the press attention would die down. And I hope that you told Georgina Pratt where she could go with her PR bullshit.'

'Georgina Pratt?' Chester stroked his chin. 'Where do I know that name from?'

'I'll tell you later,' Ari said shortly. 'It's not important right now.' She turned back to Ellie. 'Anyways, where have you been staying for the last week?'

'Didn't you say something about—'

'Not now, Chester,' Ari snapped, cutting right through what he was about to say. She seemed ratty and rattled, which wasn't a surprise. Like Ellie, she must have been thinking about Billy Kay a lot but, unlike Ellie, Ari must have had to confront her most gruesome demons and wonder if she could have done things differently. Ultimately, it had been Billy's decision to stay away, not to provide any emotional or financial support, but maybe if Ari had been more . . . 'I've hardly seen Ellie at all and now you're gatecrashing what little time I do have with her.'

'Mum!' Ellie glared at Ari. 'I'm happy to see you both. Don't ruin it by arguing.'

Ari and Chester shared a sideways look that wasn't the

fondly exasperated sideways look of old friends that Ellie had seen countless times before. This was an entirely new look that was angry yet resigned. As if they were both fed up with the predictability of their relationship.

'Just because Mummy and Daddy fight, princess, doesn't mean we love you any less,' Chester said.

'You're not Ellie's father, Chester,' Ari said so coldly that Ellie gasped. Then she reached round Ellie to remove his hand from her daughter's grasp. 'Never have been, never will.'

'More's the pity,' Chester said and the way he sounded went beyond anger or resignation.

Ellie had heard enough. She jumped down from the wall. 'I don't want to hear this,' she told them, hands on her hips. They'd sort it out, they always did, but she didn't want to be around them until they were friends again. 'I'm going to say goodbye now.'

'Sweetie, don't be like that,' Ari pouted. 'Being cross doesn't suit you.'

'That we can agree on,' Chester conceded. 'Turn the frown upside down.'

Chester's eyebrows shot up and Ari stared at her curiously as Ellie tried to find the smile that always came so easily to her. It felt more like a terrifying grimace, but how was she meant to look carefree when she had the weight of many cares pressing down on her?

'I really do have to go,' she said heavily.

'I'll give you a lift,' Chester said, as he fished his van keys out of his pocket, because no matter what Ari said, Chester was the closest thing she'd ever had to a dad, and dads didn't let their daughters get on a hot, stinky, crowded tube with the amount of luggage that Ellie had. 'Let me take the suitcase and the holdalls.'

Ari nudged her. 'Am I allowed a hug and kiss before you disappear?'

Ellie was hugging and kissing her before the question had

even been asked. And then they were done. Or Ellie thought they were, but Ari wouldn't disengage, which was odd because Ari was usually quite a perfunctory hugger. 'Come on, Mum, you have to cut the cord some time. I have a train to catch.'

Ari cupped Ellie's face in her hands and stared at her intently as if she'd expected the last week to have fundamentally changed the way her daughter looked. 'I've missed you so much, kiddo. It's been six whole days.'

'I missed you too, Mum.' Ellie squeezed Ari extra tight, then finally managed to free herself. 'Are you all right? I know this must be hard for you too, but it's not like you to be such a cling-on. You're not about to tell me that you're ill, are you?' Her eyes widened. 'Oh my God! Are you ill?'

'No! Apart from dying of heatstroke.' Ari put her hands on Ellie's shoulders and gave her a little push. 'Go on, then. Bugger off to Paris. See if I care. Just bring me back some nice biscuits in one of those cool art-deco tins. And I'm still missing a couple of Françoise Hardy albums. I'll email you a list.'

Ellie clicked her heels and saluted. '*Jawohl.*'

'Shouldn't that be *d'accord*?' Ari smiled. 'Oh! So you never told me who was making you so unhappy or who you've been staying with all week. I hope they're not one and the same because that sounds like a recipe for heartache.' Ari had a good line in penetrating stares and it was all Ellie could do not to squirm. 'Anything you want to tell me, darling daughter of mine?'

Ellie was saved by Chester leaning on the horn and sticking his head out of the van window to shout, 'Get a bloody move on, Ellie! If you miss the train, I'm not driving you all the way to Paris.'

There was time only to give a disgruntled Ari one last hug, then Chester actually revved up the van as if he was planning to drive off and she had no choice but to run after him.

Chapter Twenty-six

It always amazed Ellie that she could get on a train in London and arrive in Paris. Not Bath or Leeds but a city in another country where they spoke a different language. As she looked out of the window of the taxi that was taking her to Le Marais, the old Jewish quarter now beloved of hipsters, fashionistas and artists with trust funds, the wide avenues, elegant Hausmann buildings, even the street signs painted on deep blue plaques edged in green, looked exotic and exciting.

Originally, Ellie hadn't been excited about coming to Paris. As the train had plunged into the Channel Tunnel and hurtled out of it into countryside that didn't look like the rolling green fields of England any more, she had felt her spirits sink lower and lower. It was all very well running away to Paris to escape her many problems but they'd still be waiting for her when she got back.

It certainly hadn't helped that she'd been compelled to buy every single celebrity magazine that the newsagents at St Pancras had to offer and had spent an hour poring over pap pictures of herself and reading a detailed break-down of her beauty regimen. (Her hairdresser had revealed that Ellie 'would rather risk cancer than go without a Brazilian straightening treatment on her luscious long locks', which now meant she'd have to find a new hairdresser.) Lara and Rose had welcomed the readers of *OK!* into their 'beautiful Notting Hill penthouse', and even though they were still devastated about having a newly minted half-sister, they were also super-excited about launching their own rock-chick-inspired footwear range with an online retailer.

When she hadn't been reading things that made her stomach roil, Ellie kept checking her phone for an email or a text from David. Each time she'd felt the bitter pang of disappointment because of course he hadn't been in contact; she'd made it perfectly clear in her letter that what they had was over before it even left the starting blocks.

But now Ellie was clinging to the edge of the seat as her morose taxi driver took a corner much too fast and nearly knocked a girl off her *bicyclette*, and what did it matter if she was running away? She was in Paris. She was in a city full of patisseries and the delicious cheese that was so smelly you were forbidden to carry it on public transport, and carafes of really deep, dark red wine that gave you filthy hangovers, and the restaurant on Place d'Italie that did a Thai *pot au feu*, and the sparkling lights that lit up the banks of the Seine at night, and . . .

By the time Ellie was hauling her luggage up the stairs of the narrow apartment building on Place du Marché Sainte-Catherine, she wasn't even cursing the fact that there was no lift, because who cared? She was in Paris!

As she reached the third-floor landing, the door opposite the stairwell burst open, and two shrieking voices greeted her. 'Ellie Cohen!! About bloody time!'

'My taxi driver took the scenic route.' With the last bit of strength left in her arms Ellie hauled her suitcase up the final stair and set it down. 'I swear to God, that thing just gets heavier and heavier.'

Sue grinned at her. 'Still haven't learned to travel light then?'

'Travelling light is for people who don't know how to accessorise,' Esme said. She grabbed the holdall, which was still attached to Ellie's shoulder, and yanked them both through the apartment door. 'You've brought the sunshine from London. Oh, Ellie! It's so good to see you!'

Ellie always felt positively Amazonian next to Esme and Sue, who were tiny, tiny women. Esme was a streak of lightning with a mop of messy platinum blonde curls and fragile birdlike limbs. She worked for one of the couture houses as something called an artist without a portfolio, and was impulsive, seventeen different kinds of funny and couldn't be trusted with money, iPhones or secrets.

During the year the three of them, and Tess, had lived together in London, Esme had popped out for milk and phoned twelve hours later to let them know that 'I seem to be in New York,' been arrested twice, slept with an A-list movie star and had to be rescued by the fire brigade when she'd climbed on the roof to rescue next door's cat and had got stuck between two chimneys. It had been the most exhausting year of Ellie's life, but in weekend doses, Esme was delightful.

Sue, who worked at Sotheby's Paris office, would have got more credit for having a wild side a mile long if she hadn't been best friends with Esme. The difference was that Sue always managed to extricate herself from whatever scrapes she'd got into. Like the time she'd been accused of card-counting at a rinky-dink Park Lane casino but had protested her innocence very calmly and convincingly by claiming that she'd failed her Maths GCSE. She'd also dated a bona fide prince, though Sue insisted that 'he wasn't a prince, just a minor Belgian royal', and was dark-haired, dark-eyed, terribly amused all the time and had a casual, easy elegance that Ellie knew she'd never be able to emulate no matter how many white dresses she bought.

Sue was looking terribly amused now, and chic in a strappy little black dress, as Ellie told them about her traumatic taxi ride. Esme was wearing a beautiful, nude-coloured flapper frock encrusted with thousands of tiny sparkling beads, and a pair of cheap flipflops. Ellie felt decidedly *de trop* in her cuffed shorts and a Breton top which was crumpled from the journey and besides, you couldn't really do Breton tops in France. It was culturally insensitive.

'So, shall I jump in the shower, then slip into something—'

'No time for that,' Esme cried. 'We're meeting friends for pre-dinner drinks in ten minutes in Bastille. You'll love them. They'll love you. It'll be much mutual loving.'

Ellie tugged at her top, which was clinging to her because, despite the rain she'd been promised, Paris was as hot and humid as London. 'I need to change.'

'You don't. You look adorable,' Sue said, picking up Ellie's Mulberry bag and draping it back over Ellie's shoulder. 'A Breton top in Paris. It's so witty.'

'Beyond witty,' Esme echoed. 'Tell us all your news over dinner. Never mind being the scourge of the tabloids, girls only run away to Paris to escape men.'

'You invited me!' Ellie reminded her as she was pushed out of the door.

'Yes, but you could have said no. It can't be the man in the papers. Nobody who wears tight white vests and has a tribal armband tattoo is capable of breaking a girl's heart,' Sue said, as she locked the apartment because Esme wasn't trusted with her own set of keys. 'Who was he?'

'No one,' Ellie insisted. 'My heart is very resilient. It doesn't break that often.'

'One aperitif and two glasses of red wine and you'll be telling us everything,' Sue said and Esme agreed, but Ellie begged to differ. Maintaining a dignified silence had become a way of life by now.

Sixteen hours later, Ellie longed for swift and sudden death because death would be preferable to having to live when the inside of her head had been colonised by a troupe of tiny people jumping up and down in hob-nailed boots while beating sticks against her temporal lobes. They also had a bunch of mates who were hanging out in her stomach like it was their own private rave tent.

'Oh God,' she muttered out loud. 'I must have had a dodgy *moule* last night.'

'You didn't have any *moules*,' Sue said gently, as she removed the soggy ice pack on Ellie's forehead and replaced it with a freshly frozen one.

'Stop talking about *moules*,' Ellie groaned. It wasn't a rogue mussel that was responsible for her current malaise. It was a quiet Saturday night with Sue and Esme and their lunatic friends, which had started with Kir Royales in a little bar in Bastille, then a three-course meal at Swann et Vincent with white wine and dessert wine. By then, Ellie had been feeling a little wobbly – she'd had to request a bread basket instead of pudding to mop up some of the alcohol – but she'd still jumped in a taxi to Montmartre to sit outside a café and have coffee and brandy before climbing twisty uphill streets, only to descend down some rickety stairs to a cellar where she'd drunk ice-cold beer and danced to really bad dubstep with a specialist in Egyptian Antiquities from Venezuela, and then . . . Ellie couldn't remember getting back to Le Marais. All she remembered was waking up an hour ago on Esme and Sue's sofa with a bucket on her chest. It was an empty bucket but Ellie wasn't sure how much longer it would remain that way.

'Are you sure you don't want to come to St Tropez?' Esme asked again. Ellie had never noticed before how shrill her voice was. 'There's room on the private plane we're getting from Orly. Honestly, Ellie, once you've flown on a private plane, it ruins you for non-private planes. You have to experience it once in your life.'

'Can't go. Stay here,' Ellie whispered. 'Stay here and die.'

'Please don't,' Sue said, and after an hour of clattering about and banging things and talking at the very top of their vocal registers, they were off on their holidays, leaving Ellie a catatonic lump on their art-deco Jules Leleu sofa. Eventually she managed to stagger to the Monoprix to buy Evian, Diet Coke and ready-salted crisps, which were all she could choke down when her hangover was this evil.

Once she was sufficiently rehydrated, Ellie shifted location to Sue's bed, where she slept until eight the next morning, woken only by the cafés in the square below opening their awnings and putting out tables and chairs, because it was a complete myth that Paris ground to a halt during August.

Paris in August was perfect. Esme's favourite cheese shop was *fermé* but the café where she liked to have her morning *tartines à la confiture d'abricot* (Parisian cafés hadn't really embraced muesli) and black coffee was open, as were the Jewish bakeries on Rue Saint-Antoine. She bought structured white dresses and drapey blouson tops at Sandro, Zadig et Voltaire and Maje, and canvas tennis shoes at Bensimon, but Ellie wasn't in Paris simply to shop. Or lounge on the sand at one of the Paris Plages, the artificial beaches set up each summer along the Seine. No, shopping and sunbathing were morning activities, then after a leisurely lunch, Ellie would start work.

Work involved trying to track down pieces by an obscure Surrealist painter by pretending she was interested in pieces by another obscure Surrealist, because Vaughn didn't want anyone else on the trail. He also wanted Ellie to sniff out any new trends and artists and get a general sense of what was happening on the street. Vaughn was always obsessed with what was happening on the street.

So, armed with her company credit card, Ellie spent her evenings meeting up with artists, sculptors, painters,

343

filmmakers and people who did stuff with lights and fibre optics and holograms, who all thought that art dealers and the employees of art dealers were in league with the devil unless these employees had company credit cards and were happy to get their round in.

Ellie could allow herself to breathe out because, finally, there was real distance between her and her scandal. She could even make Billy Kay fade back into the background, because no one in Paris was obsessed with celebrities in the same way that people in Britain were unless it was Carla Bruni or a member of the House of Grimaldi. Her Parisian acquaintances simply shrugged when the subject arose and talked about how bourgeois celebrity culture was. They'd only have been impressed if Ellie's long-lost father turned out to be Serge Gainsbourg, or Johnny Hallyday, at a pinch.

There was never any shortage of interesting and interested men in Paris either. So unlike British men, who were useless at picking up signals or wouldn't admit they fancied you until after they'd actually kissed you. Men who claimed to have wanted you since the very first moment that they saw you, but still suspected you of being an avaricious schemer. Also men who already had girlfriends. Ellie had had quite enough of men like that.

But she wasn't interested in any of the men who showed signs of being interested in her, despite the fact that she was sure she was wearing her heartbreak on her sleeve. Maybe heartbreak was exaggerating her fragile emotional state but Ellie's heart had definitely been damaged. Before, she'd always suffered at the end of a relationship from the knowledge that she hadn't been good enough, that it had all gone wrong *again*.

Now, she was grieving a relationship that had never happened, which was pathetic. In mourning simply for a few kisses and a night spent holding someone who'd been asleep. People always said that it was better to regret something you had done, rather than something you hadn't done, but imagining what she and David could have had was torture, and Ellie was sure that she bore its scars. So when men offered to buy her a drink, or asked her to dance or lingered too long as they kissed her on each cheek at the end of an evening, Ellie shied away.

That was why, on Friday morning, she decided not to meet up with Stéphane, who owned a small gallery in Belleville and had offered to show her around. Stéphane had smouldering dark eyes, a sultry pouty mouth and a lock of black hair that fell across his forehead and made a girl yearn to push it back and let her hand rest against his skin. Oh, no, Ellie wasn't going there, but making her own way with the aid of a guide book and her own lousy sense of direction.

Belleville, where Edith Piaf was born, in the north-west of the city, was a shabby, eclectic neighbourhood with a large Asian community and a bustling Chinatown, and was as close as Ellie would ever get to the Montmartre of the 1920s, when Montmartre had been home to a colony of artists drinking absinthe and pastis in dark cafés and having torrid affairs with each other.

The cheap rent and abandoned warehouses and factories of Belleville had brought the artists in the 1980s and they were still there, although they weren't drinking absinthe in dark cafés but eating pho in the amazing Vietnamese restaurant where Ellie had lunch, elbow to elbow with elegant French hipsters and little old ladies with a firm grip on their bulging baskets from a successful morning's marketing.

After lunch, Ellie went exploring. It was almost five when she discovered a little alley between two buildings and, curious, slipped down it to find herself in a huge walled garden bordered by the backs of buildings, most of them derelict, apart from a big industrial space with its doors wide open in the summer heat. What she saw in that space made her inch forward, eyes wide, mouth open.

It was a forest of trees. Spectral, otherworldly trees bowed to the ground under the weight of their branches and drooping leaves. Trees shaped not by some divine hand but by a man and woman who were busy mixing up huge amounts of papier-mâché.

Inge, when she could stir herself, insisted that good art made you *feel*, and Ellie had always nodded and agreed, but it was only now, on a sticky hot Friday afternoon in a working-class area of Paris, that she finally got it. She was getting tingles, not dissimilar to the tingles she'd got when she'd walked right into David's arms all those weeks ago. Looking at this enchanted forest of paper trees made her appreciate the fragility and futility of nature, how it celebrated life and death and made her feel humble and a bit teary, but also made her want to jump up and down and clap her hands in delight, because, really? This must have been how Brian Epstein felt when he first heard The Beatles.

She managed to convey some of this to Claude and Marie, the artists, who sat her down, made her some mint tea and showed her a time-lapse film they'd shot of a tree's year-long cycle. The barren, bare branches of winter, the first tiny buds appearing, the froth of pink and white spring blossom. Then the lush, redolent glory of green leaves and how they lost their vigour in the dog days of August, turning gold and orange as autumn settled in, then becoming desiccated wisps that floated gently to the ground.

Ellie longed to call Vaughn, but she didn't. She simply gave her card to Claude and Marie and begged them to keep on making paper trees and not to seek any other representation, and of course they could totally stay with her when they came to London for the Frieze Art Fair in October but she'd be in touch way before then.

It was a relief to feel excited and happy. It was even a relief that when the excitement and happiness fizzled out, instead of being sad again, Ellie seethed about the injustice of her imminent unemployment. She still didn't think she had an angle but she certainly had no compunction about keeping Claude and Marie under wraps until Vaughn played his hand.

Ellie wandered out onto the Rue de Belleville. She'd planned on grabbing a table and a cold glass of *citron pressé* outside Aux Folies, but there was a fetid scent in the air and she decided to return to her flat. Every artist she met told her that Paris had been anaesthetised and sanitised and had lost its heart and soul, but at least it didn't smell like a *pissoir*. Her phone rang just as she was about to descend into the Metro to catch line 11 back to Le Marais.

It was an English number familiar enough that she fumbled to slide the lock on her phone to take the call.

'Miss Cohen?' It was odd that her hopes could both rise and fall at the sound of his voice. She couldn't believe that David'd gone back to that 'Miss Cohen' crap even after he'd kissed her, mouthed her breasts, had his hands full of her. He couldn't make it any more obvious that she was back in the box marked 'strictly business'.

'Is there something I can help you with?' Ellie asked as tersely as she could.

'I have some documents you need to sign,' he said, like his brusque tone completely trumped her terseness. 'I'm sending an overnight courier on a wait-and-return. Address, please?'

'What documents? What could I possibly need to sign?'

'Standard documents,' he insisted. 'You were meant to sign them when you turned eighteen. I need to get all these loose ends tied up.'

He was also clear that he wanted nothing more to do with her. Ellie felt another little piece of her heart chip away but, God help her, she wanted to keep him talking a little bit longer because even his most clipped chat about contracts was still him talking to her.

'What's so important it needs an overnight courier?' she asked sulkily.

He launched into an explanation so dense with legal terms it could have been Pig Latin or him making up words as he went along. It was impossible to follow, especially when she was buffeted by the Friday rush-hour crowd and a busker to the left of her was belting out 'La Vie en Rose' on a mouth organ.

'What's the address?' David asked when he came to the end of his long, legal spiel. 'And please make sure you're in at eight tonight to sign the documents.'

'Don't they have to be witnessed? I'm not sure I want a courier to witness my signature and I should have time to read them over. Anyway, eight is only a couple of hours away. Is he already *en route*? You might have given me some warning. I could be in St Tropez for all you know!'

'Well, you're patently not,' David snapped impatiently. 'For goodness' sake, Ellie, just give me your bloody address!'

Ellie gave him her bloody address, then hung up. She was tempted not to be waiting obediently back at the flat at eight – she had had vague plans to meet up with some friends of Esme and Sue's for Cuban food – but after talking to David, she wasn't up to going out. People would expect her to be friendly and engaging, albeit in halting GCSE-grade French, and the effort might kill her.

She'd stay in and wait for the courier, but she bought two bottles of wine on the way home. She could light some candles and open all the windows to let in the breeze and the sound of people carousing in the street below.

By seven thirty, Ellie had tidied up, drunk one glass of wine, eaten three olives and decided that as soon as the courier had been and gone, she was going out. If she stayed in all she'd do was brood and replay every word of their phone call, then rewind the night they'd spent together, though she hadn't spent such a chaste night with a member of the opposite sex since she was seventeen. By then, she'd have probably got through both bottles of wine, and she'd be drunk and melancholy and desperate enough to do something really stupid like phone David Gold and beg him to love her because she was kind of in love with him.

Ellie prowled around the flat. Originally an atelier, it was a huge triple-height space so she got dizzy just looking up at the ornate ceiling mouldings. A mezzanine floor had been added to one half of the room, though it still felt light and airy, which was where the two bedrooms and the black-and-white art-deco-tiled bathroom were situated. It was a beautiful apartment but Ellie felt hemmed in and she needed to do something that would make her feel better, make her not feel like *this*, even though the last words Esme had said to her before she left on Sunday morning was, 'Help yourself to anything, but even think about borrowing any of our clothes or accessories and we'll kill you.'

Sue had even followed it up with a text message, ostensibly to remind her that Madame Lelong, the concierge who lived in the basement flat, came up to clean on Monday and Thursday afternoons, but really to warn Ellie that she'd *'hunt you down like a dog if I hear you've been seen with my Chanel 2.55 bag'*.

Though she planned to own a Chanel 2.55 bag one day, Ellie wanted nothing to do with Sue's handbags or her chic black, fitted clothes, because Sue was ridiculously small. So was Esme, but at least she had outfit options, and it wasn't as if Ellie was going to borrow any of them, she just wanted to try them on.

Esme possessed two wardrobes built into recesses, five clothes rails, and the broom cupboard in the hall, which had been customised with cubbyholes each large enough

349

for a shoe box. Stuck to each shoe box was a Polaroid of the pretty, pretty, pretty shoes inside. It was a crying shame that Esme wore a size two and Ellie had size-seven clodhopper feet.

Very carefully Ellie rifled through the rails, unzipping garment bags to gawk at silk and satin and charmeuse and taffeta and chiffon and knits so fine they might have been made from cobwebs rather than wool. There was nothing that was going to fit and most of it was beaded or sparkling; no wonder Esme had found a job where she could wear a ballgown to a Monday meeting if she wanted.

It wasn't until she was head first in the second wardrobe that Ellie found the dull gold trapeze dress. Made from a soft slubby silk, it was sleeveless and had myriad knife-edge pleats cascading down from a mandarin-collar neckline. It took Ellie many long, tense minutes to ease the dress over her head, arms raised like a champion diver so she could work them through the armholes, then much gentle tugging before finally she was wearing one of Esme's dresses. It was probably knee-length on Esme but swirled about Ellie's thighs so if she bent over even a little she flashed her knickers.

Not that Ellie dared bend over or make any sudden movements, because, within scant seconds she realised she'd made a terrible mistake. The collar of the dress was choking her (how could Esme's *neck* be thinner than hers?), the armholes pinched her skin and the flimsy, delicate material was stretched perilously tight across her shoulders. Which made it the perfect time for two short, sharp buzzes on the intercom. Walking slowly like she had a big book balanced on her head, Ellie managed to get down the mezzanine stairs to press the intercom.

'Courier? I'm on the third floor.'

It was not an ideal situation. Ellie didn't want some motorbiking desperado in the flat while she was fashion-incapacitated and showing far too much leg. She'd send him away until she'd begged Madame Lelong to come upstairs and extricate her from a dress that probably cost more than three months' salary *and* commission.

Ellie heard someone come up the stairs, then a knock on the door, and even reaching up to open it put a terrible strain on the dress.

But that was nothing compared to the terrible strain on her heart because standing there in a crumpled suit and carrying two M&S carrier bags was David Gold.

Camden, London, 1987

'You're going to be all right, Ari,' Billy said calmly.

He helped her get dressed, buttoned her into her leopard-print faux-fur coat and led her out into a world covered in snow to catch the number 24 bus to the Royal Free Hospital.

The pain was constant and all Ari could do was sway on the spot as she was asked questions she couldn't answer because she'd never kept any appointments or taken any tests, and someone really needed to call Carol.

'I will,' Billy said. Ari wanted to beg him to stay because he was a calm, still presence in the corner of the room as she was hooked up to machines. She couldn't do this alone; suffer pain that started deep in her spine and ripped through her in never-ending waves. 'And I need a cigarette. I'll be back in ten minutes, baby.'

Billy didn't come back in ten minutes. He wasn't back in two hours, and Ari stopped caring because she couldn't think about Billy any more. All she could think about was how stupid, how dumb she'd been to only think about the baby in the most abstract way and to imagine childbirth as something you screamed your way through while your partner mopped your face. It wasn't like that all.

Labour was a silent battle between her and her body. Ari curled up in a ball and for the first time she could sense the baby as an insistent pull, a compelling voice in her head. 'You'll be OK. I'll be here soon. Everything's going to be all right.'

Then she was being told to push, but her body wanted to do that anyway and it took for ever, then no time at all until someone said, 'It's a girl. Congratulations! You have a daughter!' A squalling, bloodied red scrap of flesh and bones was held up for Ari's inspection.

It had lots of dark, curly hair. The midwife said that was why Ari had had indigestion for months – nothing to do with Billy breaking her heart on a weekly basis. And for what? So she could birth his daughter, who looked like a furious little monkey: fists clenched, chicken legs pistoning, wet mouth open wide on a scream.

Carol should be here. This was Carol's moment, not hers, and where the fuck was Billy? They whisked the baby away, still screeching, then it was back, and before Ari could tell them she wasn't interested, no thank you, not today, she'd made alternative arrangements, a nurse dumped the baby on her chest.

It was terrifying. Ari didn't want to touch this thing, this angry thing that she'd made, and then it shut its mouth and stared at her and she felt it.

'Oh God, nobody told me,' she whispered, and cradled her perfect daughter to her.

Before this moment nothing in Ari's life had been real, but this tiny beautiful girl was real.

It wasn't possible that Ari deserved such a prize – and then she remembered that she wasn't allowed to keep her.

Chapter Twenty-seven

Ellie wondered if the dress was cutting off the flow of blood to her brain and David was actually a hallucination because he was smiling at her like he was pleased to see her.

If she'd been able to, Ellie would have raised an arm and pinched him to see if he was real but she settled for a hoarse, 'Why aren't you in London?'

His smile became more conspiratorial. 'I left London just after lunch. Technically, I suppose I bunked off. I've never bunked off anything in my life.'

Ellie would have done anything to smile back at him but she was too shocked and she was slowly being garrotted, and smiling might cause her neck to expand even further. 'Yeah, but what are you *doing* here?'

David's smile dimmed a little. 'I told you I needed your signature.'

'You said that there was an overnight courier coming.'

'Yes, but I didn't say exactly who the courier would be.'

It was too much to hope that he'd come here to see her, but why else would he be standing on a landing of an apartment building in the fourth *arrondissement*? It was time to call his bluff. 'So, what exactly do you want me to sign?'

'Well,' David said, and he stared down at the tips of his immaculately polished black brogues. 'Well, I've given this a lot of thought.'

'I don't know why there was anything to think about,' Ellie said, and she still refused to let herself believe. 'You said you needed my signature. On what?'

'OK . . .' He took a deep breath and shut his eyes. 'I did think about opening my shirt and pointing in the general direction of my heart and saying, "On this," but I decided that it wasn't really my style. Far too cheesy.'

Ellie would have liked to fold her arms but it was impossible in her current predicament. She settled for looking unamused, even though on the inside she was doing a series of air punches. 'Beyond cheesy,' she confirmed. 'I would have just gone with a simple, "I'm here because I really missed you."' She forced herself to look David right in the eye, which wasn't hard when he was watching her cautiously like she might be about to slug him. 'Because, God knows, I've tried not to, but I've missed you.'

'I have missed you,' he said. 'I've even spoken to Melanie and the woman you met at Glastonbury, whose name is Karen, and told them that I'm not in the market for a friend with benefits right now.'

'Are you still Billy Kay's lawyer?' Ellie asked hopefully, but David shook his head.

'I am but I came to Paris on the spur of the moment. I *hate* doing things on the spur of the moment,' he said plaintively. 'That has to count for something.'

'Oh, it does, it really does,' Ellie assured him. She should have felt relieved, ecstatic even, but she still couldn't believe he was here, that this was happening, and also the collar of the dress was still choking her. 'Why don't you come in?'

'I'd much rather kiss you,' he said. He carefully put his M&S bags down on the floor and stepped forward with a resolute glint in his eye.

Then he was holding her face in his hands, gazing at her more tenderly than he'd ever done before, and he kissed her. It was a whisper-soft, gentle kiss for no more than five seconds, until Ellie sighed, and his tongue drove into her mouth, and he was pulling her towards him and—

'No! Don't touch me!' Ellie shrieked, slapping his hands away, which was really hard when she had to keep her own arms pinned to her sides.

David looked utterly confused. 'But I thought you wanted me to touch you,' he said waspishly, because Ellie was being the poster girl for mixed signals.

'I do!' she protested, especially when he licked his lower lip and everything south of her navel turned liquid. 'I want it more than anything.'

'Is this about me representing your father because—'

'Don't say that! Not right now,' Ellie hissed. 'I'm trapped! Trapped in a couture dress!'

'What the hell are you talking about?' His eyes travelled over her and stayed locked at the spot, mid-thigh, where the hem ended. 'Why don't you just take the dress off? I could help, if you liked?'

As plans went it got Ellie's vote, but things were never that simple. She explained her predicament to him as he put away the contents of one of the M&S bags, which contained everything for a Friday night dinner from ready-cooked chicken to apple strudel, why her size-eight-to-ten body was stuck in a size-four dress.

By the time she finished, with a detailed description of the terrible revenge that Esme would exact, they were in Esme's room. Apart from the clothes there wasn't much in it except the ornate bed, which rose up out of an ormolu frame and was canopied with acres of gold and white tulle. It had been constructed as the centrepiece for a runway show, then deconstructed so it could be reconstructed in Esme's bedroom.

David stared at it in repulsed fascination, then shifted his attention back to Ellie, who was sure she was turning blue. 'I need your help!' she all but wailed. 'It's getting hard to breathe.'

'You need to stop panicking for a start,' he said sharply, because he wasn't a man who'd go soft simply because he was soft on a girl. 'Let's deal with this logically.'

Dealing with things logically meant that David frisked her in his search for a concealed zip, hands resting in places for so long and so caressingly that it almost counted as foreplay, though he didn't even crack a smile. But there were no concealed zips and his next two suggestions, to cut her out of the dress or lube her way with washing-up liquid, were non-starters.

'How did you manage to get it over your head in the first place?' David asked. 'Or get your arms through the armholes?'

'With great difficulty and very, very slowly.'

'I don't understand it. You're tiny,' he said, and he had to be a little bit in love with her to think that because it was colossally untrue. 'Your head doesn't look abnormally large either.'

Ellie scowled. 'My head is perfectly in proportion, thank you very much.'

'Hmm.' David sat gingerly down on the edge of the bed as if he suspected it might suddenly swallow him up. 'We could use gravity. Could you stand on your head if I got you a cushion and helped prop you up?'

'It's definitely worth a try,' she agreed, but Esme's gold satin cushions were too slippery for Ellie's head to get purchase on, and her movements were so impeded that she had to lie flat on her back while David grabbed her legs and tried to hoist her up one hundred and eighty degrees, and by then she was giggling too hard to cooperate. Mostly from embarrassment when her ivory lace briefs came into sight but also because the more she giggled, the more annoyed David got, which just made her giggle even more.

'This is never going to work,' David said in disgust, after

the tenth attempt to pull her legs flush with the wall. 'You might try to take this seriously.'

'I am,' Ellie snorted from where she was leaning up against the wall. She blew out a few times to try to get herself under control. 'I think you're on to something with the gravity thing, but maybe we don't need quite so much gravity.'

'You might have a point,' David said and he peered over the half-wall off the mezzanine to the floor below. 'OK. I have an idea.'

Ten minutes later, Ellie was in a modified Downward Dog pose on a Paul Follot-designed art-deco coffee table (fortunately it was a very sturdy coffee table), a silk scarf tied over her hair, the dress over her head so she was flashing her goodies, not that she cared about that any more, as David slowly worked the collar over her fat head, while she coached him.

'Little tugs, little tugs, little tugs,' she exhorted. It was a lot like delivering a baby. 'Gently, gently. Stop! Stop! My ears!'

He carefully tucked her ears under the scarf. 'Take a few deep breaths and let's go again.'

'All right! Let's do this!'

They did it. Lots and lots and lots of little tugs, then the collar eased over the widest part of Ellie's head. She tensed her arms as David worked the dress down them, the silk scraping her skin because she didn't have upper arms the width of a cotton bud like Esme. Once he'd reached her elbows, Ellie took over. She kneeled back on her haunches to free herself from her prison of gold silk, knife-edged pleats. She didn't even care that she was in her bra and pants.

David was on his knees in front of her, when he suddenly collapsed backwards and lay on the floor in the foetal position. 'Oh God!'

'What? What's the matter?' She was at his side in an

instant, fingers closing round his wrist to check his pulse because all their exertions might have brought on a cardiac episode. Well, that and the marathon training in intense summer heat. 'Your pulse feels fine. Do you have a pain in your chest?'

'Stop!' David wheezed. He didn't sound at all well, then his arm suddenly shot out and pulled her on top of him and Ellie realised that he was laughing. Or she hoped he was laughing because tears were streaming down his face and now that she was sprawled across him, she could feel him shaking. 'I have never had to work so hard to get a girl undressed.' His choked laughter eased to a chuckle. 'I had a whole seduction routine planned.'

'Really?' Ellie couldn't hide her disappointment. 'We could pretend the last half-hour never happened. You could go out into the hall and we could start over.'

'We could,' David agreed, a hand reaching up to slip her bra strap off her shoulder. 'But that wouldn't be a very effective use of our time.'

It was just one small, almost inconsequential gesture. Baring her shoulder, even though she was already on top of him and starting to squirm a little because she could feel his hard-on pressing urgently against her belly even through the fine-weight wool of his suit trousers, felt as shocking as if he'd just stripped her naked on the concourse of the Gare du Nord.

The light, teasing mood had abruptly shifted to something darker, more charged, and it frightened Ellie a little. Maybe it was too soon for this. David hadn't even been here an hour and already they were horizontal and she was in her underwear and he hadn't even loosened his tie. 'But we haven't even said hello to each other,' she reminded him, playing for time because a few short hours ago she was convinced they'd never see each other again and now here they were. 'It wouldn't take long to say hello.'

'Hello. That's enough talking,' David said shortly, and when she opened her mouth to protest at his unnecessarily harsh tone, he rolled them over and quietened her with a kiss.

She'd been here before: weighted down by David's body, wrists held because he liked to be in control, but as soon as Ellie struggled, his hands fell away. Then she could put her hands on him again, because they belonged there, and the feel of his closely cropped hair rubbing against her palm, the muscles that bunched under her hand as she stroked his back, felt familiar and safe. At the same time he felt shocking and new, especially the faint scrape of his stubble against her face as they kissed, the wet clash of their tongues, his leg worming its way between her thighs so she had something hard to wriggle against.

With his hands free, David was able to slip down the other bra strap and Ellie could have stopped touching him long enough to reach around and undo the clasp, but she never wanted to stop touching him, and when he pushed up the cups of her bra it wasn't a good look, but Ellie didn't much care.

'You see, if we went with your plan and rewound to saying hello, you'd probably be making me a cup of tea right about now, when all I want to do is this . . .' David lowered his head and sucked one hard, aching nipple into his mouth. Ellie had to bite back a gasp so she wouldn't distract him from his endeavours. 'And you wouldn't be getting wet. You are wet, aren't you, Ellie?'

Oh God, it was always the quiet ones. And if she hadn't been wet, just hearing his voice all dark and treacly asking her if she was would have taken care of it.

Ellie stared up at David. It was the best he'd ever looked. A hectic glitter in his eyes, a flush on his cheeks and a half-smile tugging up the corners of his mouth. Ellie had often seen him looking so self-assured that it seemed like arrogance and was intensely annoying, but right now, in this context, it took her breath away.

Maybe that's why she sounded so husky when she said, 'And you're getting hard.' To prove her point all she had to do was to twist a little and she could feel him against her inner thigh. 'It can't be comfortable.'

'I've been hard ever since we flipped your dress over your head, because I have to agree with the papers, your arse is truly incomparable, and yes, I'm feeling a little . . . *constricted*,' he admitted. 'Could you help me with that?'

'I could,' Ellie agreed, though it was a little odd that he'd studied the tabloid pictures of her bottom and formed an opinion about it. She thought about David checking her out when she'd been his guestage, surreptitiously, so she never knew. It should have been creepy, but actually the thought was quite hot. Him sitting on his uncomfortable sofa with his best poker face on but maybe licking his lips and his eyes darkening as she was putting something away in the fridge. He was licking his bottom lip now as she reached between them to fumble with the button on his trousers. It seemed like for ever until she was able to slide her hand into his shorts.

He felt so good, big and hard, and Ellie was aching for the want of him. She looked down the small space between their two bodies just to get a glimpse of her fingers wrapped round his cock, to see and imagine what it would feel like pressing into her or against her tongue, as she tasted him. Oh, the things they could do . . .

David was looking down too and when she finally tore her eyes away, he lowered his head and kissed her. Ellie could feel his dick quicken in her grip and she was kissing him back just as hungrily until she pulled free.

'You need to take your clothes off,' she gasped indignantly. She wanted to ping away his shirt buttons with busy hands but couldn't bear to let go of his cock. She also suspected he hadn't brought a change of clothes so she could hardly rip the shirt he was wearing to

361

shreds. 'You've still got your tie on! It's ridiculous!'

'Sorry,' David murmured, stealing another kiss, then nuzzling her neck. 'You're going to have to let go if you want me to get undressed.'

'I know. I am,' Ellie said, making no move to do anything of the sort until David prised away her fingers one by one from his cock. Then he took away his hardness and his heat so she wanted to cry from the loss, but it was only so he could sit up and toe off his shoes, not even undoing the laces, which must have been a first, and yanking off his socks before he attacked his tie with the same vigour. He did carefully unbutton his shirt, which made Ellie smile as she worked the clasp on her bra, pulled it off and wished her breasts would burst forth in sensual abandon.

Not that David seemed to mind – he gave both Ellie and her breasts an appreciative glance – but as she hooked her fingers into the waistband of her briefs, he shook his head. 'Leave something for me to take off,' he said, as he kicked off his trousers, then coaxed Ellie back into his arms.

She was already rubbing up against him, tugging on his bite-able bottom lip with her teeth as his hands slid down to cup her arse, and then they were rolling this way and that on the hard wooden floor. It was undignified, and Elle winced when she banged her elbow, but they came to a gentle stop underneath the Philippe Starck table. David wedged his thigh between hers and he lowered his head to draw heavily on her breast with his diabolical mouth, one hand teasing and tugging at her other nipple. Ellie thought she might come just from that.

'I'm not usually this easy,' Ellie heard herself suddenly announce. She didn't even know why she was saying it because normally she was all about owning her sexuality, never apologising for it, but she couldn't bear to think that David might still think there was some tiny semblance of truth to the stories he must have read as he was admiring how her arse looked in a bikini.

He looked up from her breasts, which were damp and swollen from his attentions. 'Really?' He quirked an eyebrow upwards. 'I am.'

'I bet you're not,' she said with a giggle.

'Well, only very occasionally, but mostly I wanted to make you smile.' He rubbed his mouth against hers. 'You were looking a little lost. Is this too much?'

'No, no . . .'

'Because I didn't come here for this . . . well, I hoped . . .' He kissed her; an almost chaste peck on the lips if his tongue hadn't darted out for a quick foray, then he was actually putting some distance between them. Ellie pouted as he rolled onto his side and propped himself up on one elbow so they weren't skin to skin any more. 'I was going to woo you. Would you rather be wooed?'

'Not right now, no!' She'd never heard herself sound so desperate. 'You can woo me later. Wooing is not what I need at this precise moment.'

'Do you need this?' David was already tugging at her briefs, shifting slightly so he could rest his hand, heavy and warm, between her legs. 'It feels like you need this.'

'That's exactly what I need,' Ellie confirmed, tilting her hips in an invitation that he couldn't miss.

'I have a theory that if I touch you like this, all the muscles in your thighs will begin to quiver,' he drawled, circling her clit with the tip of his finger, and Ellie arched even closer towards him.

'Don't tease,' she gasped as his finger speeded up. 'Nobody likes a tease.'

'I want you to like me lots and lots,' David said, then he slowly pushed two fingers into the soaked heat of her pussy and smiled when Ellie moaned. 'Or I want you to beg, I can't decide which.'

Even when he was being playful there was an edge to him. Ellie liked both the playfulness and the edge, they tempered each other, but right then she could have done without either of them.

'I'm not begging,' she hissed mutinously, clamping down hard on his fingers when he tried to drag them away. She was going to cry if he didn't get inside her. 'Why should I beg you to fuck me, when you want it as much as I do?'

It was his turn to moan and whimper because she had her hand clasped round the warm, thick length of his cock again and wasn't planning to let go any time soon.

'I'm in charge here,' David insisted, but maybe that would have been more convincing if he wasn't gritting his teeth as Ellie stroked her palm against the wet head of his cock. 'Just ask me nicely and I'll fuck you.'

'We don't have to fuck,' Ellie told him sweetly. She was only able to tease him because his fingers weren't deep in her pussy any more but trailing up and down her leg. Then he sucked them into his mouth and hummed in approval.

'You taste delicious,' he said. Two could play at that game.

'Oh, don't you want to go all the way, then?' Ellie asked, eyes widening in faux surprise. 'OK, if you prefer, there's this little thing that I do with my tongue . . .'

David didn't say anything, but his nostrils flared and his jaw tensed, and Ellie was suddenly flat on her back again. 'Condom?' he ground out as though talking was causing him all kinds of pain.

'It's all right, I'm on the pill,' Ellie said, and then neither of them said anything because he was shoving her legs up round her ears and sinking into her like he was coming home. It was too much. Too soon. Neither of them was ready for this.

Then Ellie felt something deep inside her heart unfurl and she was pulsing around the hard length of his cock.

David flung his head back. 'God, you are the most

impossible woman,' he rasped, and he began to move. Went from still to fast and hard and deep in one pounding stroke and Ellie squeezed him tighter with her legs, her arms, her everything, screwed her eyes shut and took a leap, let herself freefall, because it felt new, but very right; the feeling of David on her, inside her, all around her.

Chapter Twenty-eight

Mad, brain-scrambling lust was one thing, but once it was over, wooden floors weren't very comfortable to lie on, no matter how much Ellie wanted to savour the afterglow.

Besides, she knew how the rest of the scene would play out. She'd be unable to make eye contact and David would do that thing where he shut down all facial expressions and pared his conversation to only clipped monosyllables. She moved away from him because the floor was hard and his chest was too bony to make a good pillow, and also now that the passion wasn't clouding her brain they both smelled kind of ripe. Slowly she managed to stagger to her feet.

David looked up at her from his recumbent position. She should have been mortified because she was naked, legs clamped together, and from where he was on the floor every lump and bump, freckle and mole was visible, but he didn't look as if he found the sight of her repulsive. On the contrary, his eyes rested briefly on all Ellie's main attractions, then travelled up to her face, which was rosy red, and he smiled like it was all good and as if, hard wooden floors notwithstanding, there was nowhere on earth he'd rather be.

His slow, lazy smile made Ellie get over her post-coital nerves and she was able to casually say, 'I'm going to have a shower.'

'Is it big enough for two?' David asked. When Ellie said

it was and that, unlike a lot of showers in Paris, it had superior water pressure, he asked if he could join her.

It wasn't the kind of shower you could have sex in. There was nothing to grab onto and the floor wasn't grippy, but they could kiss and lather each other up and Ellie could point out, rather drily given the circumstances, that her breasts probably needed a lot less attention from the bar of soap than other parts of her.

David snaked his hand between her legs. 'Like this intriguing place?'

Ellie wasn't ready to go again so she twisted out of his grasp, warned him not to touch her hair with his hands because she didn't know what effect almond soap would have on her straightening treatment, and sank to her knees.

David was hard as soon as Ellie dragged one soap-slicked finger along the big vein that ran down the underside of his cock and she was happy to alleviate his agony, because she was nice like that. She placed one sweet kiss on the head of his dick before she took him into her mouth.

She thought about drawing it out, teasing him as payback for the heinous way he'd behaved earlier, but he'd already started to moan and the grooved floor of the shower cubicle was agony on her knees. There *was* a thing that she did with her tongue but now she settled for hollowing out her cheeks and rewarding the way he said her name so desperately by cupping his balls.

He tasted clean, a little soapy. Then Ellie tasted *him*, salty and slightly bitter in her mouth, and she knew all his secrets but still wanted to know more. David's hands fisted in her hair when she sucked him deep and it was hardly the time to tell him to cut it out, not when he was coming in her mouth with a startled cry.

Later, much later, Ellie dumped the ready-cooked chicken, a roughly sliced baguette and some cherry tomatoes on a huge platter and they sat cross-legged on the rug in the living room and ate dinner with their fingers. Then David kissed the red marks on her shins left from kneeling too long in the shower.

And later than that, as Ellie was standing at the kitchen sink doing the dishes and wondering when she was going to wake up because this had to be a dream, she heard David come up behind her, then he was the one dropping to his knees. 'Don't turn round,' he said in that growly voice that thrilled and scared her in equal measure. She yelped when he pushed up the skirt of her pale grey maxi dress. 'And for God's sake, don't break one of those glasses.'

The glasses were probably commissioned especially from Lalique so Ellie tried to keep very still as David's hands firmly parted her thighs and his mouth licked across her clit. She just had time to place the glasses very gently on the draining rack, then she was gripping the side of the sink and grinding against his mouth as he sucked hard on her clit while his fingers twisted deliciously inside her. Suddenly she was coming, almost falling over from the ferocity of it, only the hard bite of his hands on her hips keeping her safe.

It was too hot to sleep in each other's arms but they slept side by side in Esme's ridiculous bed, and every time Ellie stirred during the night, David seemed to sense the exact moment she was teetering on the brink of wakefulness and worry, and he'd open his eyes, mutter, 'Please go back to sleep,' and she did.

Saturday morning there was sleepy sex on the fluffy angora wool rug on Esme's bedroom floor because they both agreed it was morally reprehensible to have sex in one of their hostesses' beds. Then they left the apartment to get breakfast in the café downstairs before they headed out to the flea market at Porte de Clignancourt, though

David was sure they'd be closed 'because it's August and everything in Paris is closed in August. Apart from the tourist traps.'

'You're a tourist,' Ellie reminded him. They were pressed tight together on a crowded Metro, but she didn't mind. David smelled much nicer than the man on the other side of her, who'd evidently bathed in bouillabaisse.

She didn't even mind that David was dressed in his suit trousers, work shoes and a brand-new navy-blue T-shirt, which he'd bought during a trolley dash round M&S before he caught the Eurostar. He was looking slightly fashion challenged, but how could she mind, when he smiled and kissed her forehead and said, 'I'm not a tourist. I didn't come to Paris to see the sights. I came to Paris to see you.'

As they explored the stalls of the Marché Vernaison and the smaller Marché Antica, ate *crêpes* for lunch, then headed back to Le Marais so they could laze on the grass at Place des Vosges, David's head in her lap, Ellie felt as if she was having an out-of-body experience. Or that she was watching an actress who looked like her, talked like her and walked like her starring in the movie of her life.

Ever since she'd been a flat-chested, frizzy-haired teenager Ellie had always dreamed about a time when she was older and chicer and had a lover who took her to Paris; having a lover was so much more sophisticated than having a boyfriend. She'd spend French lessons imagining Paris with her lover by her side and how they'd walk hand in hand along tiny cobbled streets and sit outside cafés whose names would be written on their awnings in big art nouveau fonts and they'd eat a lot of cheese and drink red wine and have sex like people did in French films where it would be all intense and their bodies would make strange shapes and they'd stare at each other without speaking for long, long moments.

The future was now. She was living her teenage dreams. Well, the essence of her teenage dreams because she still didn't have boobs. She was in Paris with her lover. David Gold was her lover, which was unbelievable. But he was there, by her side, *holding her hand* and swinging her arm as they slowly walked to Chez Omar late on Saturday evening, to see if they could get a table for dinner.

It was perfect. But they couldn't stay in Paris for ever or preserve the weekend under glass so they were trapped in the moment without real life being able to intrude. Real life was snapping at their heels and in real life David was Billy Kay's lawyer and she was Billy Kay's daughter, and there was no fudging those two facts.

Above all, he was still a man who could break her heart.

Ellie didn't want to ruin their golden Paris hours by thinking about what could go wrong, and anyway, listening to David trying to order couscous in perfect French but without even the slightest attempt to try a French accent was distraction enough. 'The dead languages are much easier,' he told her after the waiter had gone. 'Latin and Ancient Greek don't require much in the way of an accent.'

There was still so much that they didn't know about each other, Ellie thought, but David had his hand on her knee under the table, tracing figures of eight on her skin with his fingertip, and that was all she needed to know.

They drank red wine and ate couscous with lamb and root vegetables in a rustic broth. The large family at the next table kept shooting them indulgent glances when Ellie stroked the back of David's neck or he stole a lingering kiss, because they were in the city of lovers, and everyone loved lovers. Except when Ellie was single, and then she found lovers indulging in PDAs really quite annoying.

'You realise that one of us is going to have to learn how to cook,' David suddenly said, when the waiter had removed their main courses largely untouched because it was too hot to eat anything that came in a rustic broth. 'One person without any culinary skills is OK, but two people who can't cook suggests that we're—'

'Slatterns?' Ellie suggested, and she tried not to think about what he was really saying. That he thought they'd be together long enough that neither of them being able to cook would become an issue.

'I don't think a man can be a slattern. I was going to say a couple who can't cook suggests that we're lazy, profligate and don't eat nutritionally balanced meals.'

'Oh, I think you can eat nutritionally balanced meals even if you can't cook,' Ellie argued, because Ari had been excellent at chopping up celery and carrots that were going cheap from Inverness Street market at the end of the day and serving them for dinner with pitta bread and hummus.

'I'm just saying, we're going to have to add a couple of basic meals to our non-existent cooking repertoires,' David said earnestly like he really meant it. 'How about I learn to roast a chicken and you do something vegetable-based in case we have some vegetarians round for dinner?'

'A stir-fry? That can't be hard. I just put vegetables in a pan and stir and fry.'

David kissed her on the nose, much to the delight of the older women at the next table, who actually clucked at them. 'It will be your signature dish. Shall we order some mint tea and a box of the little pastries to take back with us?'

He smiled as Ellie ordered in stilted French that would have had Madame Westcott, her arch nemesis from her GCSE days, shrieking '*Mon Dieu*'. 'I think you mixed up a couple of your tenses,' he told her when by some miracle the mint tea turned up as requested. 'But you've definitely mastered the Parisian shoulder shrug.'

It was then that Ellie decided not to worry. Or it might have been when they got back to the apartment and they were trying to fuck standing up, Ellie pressed against the wall in the one blind spot in the living room that couldn't be seen from the huge picture windows front and back. It wasn't as easy or as hot as it was in theory or in the movies. Ellie kept knocking her head and David's cock kept slipping out and bumping against her clit, which wasn't entirely unpleasant. In the end, David turned them round and slid down, until his back was against the wall, his legs bent and Ellie could brace herself against his thighs and ride him to a furious and messy finish.

'Next time,' he said against her mouth, while his dick was still half hard and he shuddered each time the walls of her pussy fluttered against him, 'next time we come to Paris we're staying somewhere that has beds we can actually fuck in.'

'I'll hold you to that,' Ellie agreed breathlessly. 'Going to mark it on my calendar.'

'It's also the first item on my to-do list when we get back to London. I'm going to have you on my Tempur mattress.' David leered at her ever so slightly. 'In fact, it's all I can think of, because this position is really uncomfortable and don't think it's not nice to have you sitting on my cock because it is, but I'm running a marathon in a month and I don't want to slip a disc.'

Ellie released him in an immodest scramble but later, as they brushed their teeth in the adjoining basins in the art-deco bathroom, she suddenly hoped that this was one of those rare instances when things just fell into place, no matter how complicated they were.

David even said as they tried to get to sleep with two foot of bed between them, 'Next time we're in Paris, it should be winter. We'll find a hotel without central heating so we're forced to huddle together for warmth. It will be romantic.'

'Didn't think you were a snuggler,' Ellie said, lifting up one of her legs to bat away the bead of sweat that was tickling her.

'I'm not. Only in special circumstances.'

She had to put it into words: her optimism about them, about their future, but also her doubt, because if you got too cocky, too convinced that everything was going your way, then inevitably it would all go horribly wrong. 'You keep saying things like that, then I'm going to think that you're too good to be true,' she said lightly. 'Don't they say that things that are too good to be true usually are?'

David didn't say anything at first but then he rolled over so he could see the anxious expression on her face even in the dim light. 'Don't, Ellie,' he said softly. 'Let's not worry until there's actually something to worry about.'

'But—'

'But nothing. If you start looking for problems, you're guaranteed to find some.'

Which was all very well . . . 'Yes, but . . .'

'Please stop it,' David begged. 'I've had more sex in the last twenty-four hours than I've had in months, and if you don't let me sleep then I'll be too exhausted to fuck you on the kitchen worktop, which was what I had planned for tomorrow morning. It must be the only horizontal surface in this flat which isn't an antique.'

Ellie had to smile. 'Imported Italian marble, apparently. Remind me to give it a quick wipe down with a damp cloth before and after, though, will you?'

David chuckled just like he knew she would, and then he was reaching out to pull her to him, so they were spooning, sweaty skin to sweaty skin. 'Go to sleep, Ellie. Even when you're not talking, I can hear your brain whirring because you're worrying about all the things you think you should be worried about.'

Ellie wasn't worrying any more. Or, at least, she was going to try not to. She took a few calming breaths and wriggled in his arms. 'It's far too hot to snuggle,' she complained, but her eyes were already closing and it was easy enough to match the beats of her heart to his and let the rhythm soothe her to sleep.

Camden, London, 1987

Billy turned up late the next afternoon. Didn't say where he'd been and Ari didn't ask.

He sat there, dressed all in black, pale and inviolate with a mocking smile as he took in the flowers and the squash bottles, the other mothers flushed and red-eyed, proud-faced fathers holding their progeny. Then he looked at his woman, but Ari only had eyes for her daughter.

Her heart had never loved until now . . .

'You look different. Younger. Not sure I like it,' Billy commented, which was fair enough as he'd never seen her without make-up before, but he should have been saying other things. Ari didn't know how he could glance at the baby and not fall in love hard and in an instant.

'You know, Billy, this is one of those times when you can drop the studied cool,' Ari drawled, and when she held the baby out to him, like an offering, he stroked her cheek with a careless finger.

'Is she meant to be that hairy?' He took her from Ari and cradled her in the crook of his arm, didn't even need to be told to support her head, and Ari was hopeful all over again. 'We'll call her Velvet,' he decided.

'That's not a proper name,' she said because, oh God, she'd already turned into Sadie.

'Velvet Underground,' Billy insisted, shushing the baby when she started to fret. 'Let her have a cool name for a few days at least.'

Because soon she'd be Carol and Sidney's, and they'd call her something boring and safe like Laura or Samantha or Alison.

Carol turned up almost as soon as Billy left with a vague plan that he might possibly come back later to take her home.

'Give her to me,' Carol demanded before she'd taken off her coat or put down her handbag or John Lewis bags stuffed full of frilly pink clothes. 'Give her to me now!'

Ari wanted to cry because it physically hurt when she handed Velvet over. She didn't trust Carol not to steal her away there and then, but Ari hadn't signed any of the forms that the solicitor had sent her, or been interviewed by a social worker, and so Carol had to give her back, though she did it with a bad grace and a deep sigh as Ari settled Velvet back in her arms and kissed the top of her precious head while the baby rooted for her nipple.

Chapter Twenty-nine

When Ellie woke up, they were unsnuggled again but David was curled up on his side, one arm outstretched as if he'd been reaching towards her as he slept.

Sleep softened his face, as if someone had airbrushed him overnight. Her eyes drifted down to the easy rise and fall of his chest – she could have counted his ribs if she'd wanted to – and came to rest on his cock, which was also asleep. Ellie knew that she could wake it up, wake David up, with the barest of kisses, her lips ghosting over the length of him, and by the time she reached the head of his dick, he'd be half hard and wide awake.

It was a lovely thought but she decided to let him sleep. If he was still snoring ever, ever so gently after she was showered and dressed, she'd go out and get flaky French pastries for breakfast, because he was meant to be carb-loading, and she didn't want to share him with Paris this morning.

He *was* still asleep when she tiptoed back into the bedroom to pick an outfit, but was now sprawled over Ellie's side of the bed, face buried in her pillow, like he'd missed her. Ellie was still smiling as she gathered up keys, then hunted for her beloved Mulberry bag, which had been unceremoniously thrown across the atelier last night when David had taken it out of her hands as soon as she walked through the door so he could have his way with her. Good times.

She found her bag when it started making a ringing noise. Her phone, which had been blissfully silent for most of the weekend, was now flashing Tess's number. With a guilty start, Ellie realised it had been days since they'd last spoken.

'I'm a bad friend, I should have called,' she said by way of greeting.

'Oh, I should have called you too,' Tess demurred. 'But things have been crazy at work. Are you all right?'

'Never better. Honestly, you will not believe what I've been up to.' Ellie angled a glance upwards. The half-wall of the mezzanine level didn't have any sound-blocking qualities. It was probably best that she lowered her voice. 'Not even what. Who. And no, he's not a lame duck. He's like an anti-lame duck.'

'We'll see,' Tess muttered. 'I'm not going to lie, I'm jealous. My sex life is going almost as badly as my career. Ha! That's a joke. What career?'

Ellie winced in sympathy. 'What's been going on? Tell me everything.'

The freelance contract that Tess had been told would become permanent now looked as if it wasn't going to be renewed, as there were three freelance researchers on the show and only enough money in the new budget for one of them.

'Zach sucks up to the producers like crazy and I try to suck up to them too, but why should I treat them to ice cream when they earn way more than I do? And Emily is boffing the head cameraman and I'm not boffing anyone, either in work or out of work,' Tess finished mournfully. 'It's been months since I had any action.'

'Oh, poor you. That sucks,' Ellie said, as she frantically tried to think of some positives to the situation. 'But, hey, you've got two years' experience now on a prime-time show and you don't know for sure your contract won't be renewed. You might pull off something amazing like booking Madonna or—'

'I wish. I'd even settle for Vanessa Feltz.'

'As soon as I get back to London, you and me are going out for some hardcore drinking and some serious catching up,' Ellie said. 'We'll find you a man too. Everything will feel bet—'

'Shit! God, Ellie, I'm so sorry . . .'

'Don't be silly. There's nothing to be sorry about. What are friends for?'

'No, what I mean is I'm not phoning for a moan. I'm phoning because the shit's hit the fan. Again. It's half eight on a Sunday morning in England, I wouldn't even be up, let alone calling, if there wasn't a bloody good reason.'

Ellie had forgotten what it felt like: the fear. The icy chill that settled on her skin and raised an army of goose pimples in its wake, that churning in her belly as though her internal organs were all tangled up. She even had that rusty taste at the back of her throat. She really hadn't missed it. 'What's happened now?' she asked.

Tess sighed. 'It would just be easier to . . . Are you near a computer?' Ellie was already moving towards her laptop on the dining table. 'I think you should sit down, then go to the *Sunday Chronicle* site. I'll stay on the line.'

With shaking fingers Ellie booted up her MacBook and as she waited she wondered which one of her exes had sold his story.

Then she heard a sound from upstairs and the clamminess and the churning in her guts were nothing compared to the feeling that she might actually throw up or faint. With one hand she double clicked on her Google Chrome icon and the other hand gripped the edge of the table hard enough to hurt so she had something to focus on that wasn't a front-page story on how she was fucking her father's lawyer. Except they couldn't say that in a newspaper. No, they'd probably go with '*Ooh là là!*' or, oh God, '*Voulez-vous coucher avec moi, ce soir?*' with a photo of them kissing on the street, because they had done that a lot – a hell of a lot – and she could barely get her fingers to type in the *Chronicle*'s URL.

'You still there, Ellie?' Tess asked. 'Where are you up to?'

She was still waiting for the page to load and then she was . . . 'Oh God . . . fuck my life . . .What the *fuck*, Tess? I mean, like, what the actual fuck . . . ?'

'I've never heard you swear so much in one go,' Tess said worriedly, but Ellie was all out of expletives. She was all out of words. Full stop.

WORLD EXCLUSIVE!
BILLY THE KID (YES, THERE'S ANOTHER ONE!)
THE DADDY OF COOL'S SECRET SON

Billy Kay had a son hidden away. A nineteen-year-old called Charlie. It was there that any similarity to Ellie and her secret lovechild status ended. Because, in all the pictures of Charlie, from tiny baby to tousle-haired, sulky-faced present day, he was photographed with the man who had never once acknowledged Ellie as his own.

Billy had a relationship with his illegitimate son, had bonded with him, sent him to Eton, taken him to see Arsenal, had him and his mum, a former model, over for a sodding family Christmas dinner *chez* Kay.

So, what did that make Ellie? Chopped fucking liver?

Cherubic-faced Charlie is a physics genius in his second year at Cambridge where his fellow boffins have no idea that his father is one of the most famous men in the country. Turning his back on a life of sex, drugs and rock 'n' roll, unlike his recently discovered half-sister Velvet, Charlie prefers string theory to guitar strings and loves quiet nights in with his equally brainiac girlfriend, Kim, who's studying Maths. He's a son that any father could be proud of.

'Charlie's mum, Miranda, and Billy fell madly in love at a time when he and Olivia were having problems,' a close family friend confided to the *Chronicle*. 'Obviously Olivia was devastated at the time, but she understands better than anyone just what a passionate man Billy is. It's to Olivia's credit that Miranda and Charlie have always been treated as part of the Kay family. It's a completely different set of circumstances compared to his illegitimate daughter, Velvet, who was the result of a tawdry one-night stand.'

Ellie was sure her heart had just irrevocably splintered. What was wrong with her? Why did Billy love Charlie and not her? Why was Charlie in his life when she'd been all but expunged from his history?

It was obvious why.

'I have to go,' she said to Tess.

'Are you all right?' Then Tess 'tsk'ed herself. 'Of course you're not. Are you going to stay in Paris?'

'Don't know. Look, I really have to go. I'll call you,' Ellie said, and she didn't wait to hear what Tess thought about that because she'd already hung up.

Ellie's eyes were drawn to the galleried bedroom because the man up there had known all along she had a half-brother knocking about. She'd deal with him later.

'Oh, hi, babycakes,' Ari said when she answered her phone on the first ring, like she was already up and waiting for Ellie to call and that was why she sounded so wary. 'So, have you seen—'

'Yes! I've seen it. Did you know about this Charlie?' Ellie could hardly say his name, this boy, this stranger who shared some of her DNA. She couldn't believe that on some level she'd never sensed his existence; felt as if something nameless and intangible was missing from her life. In fact, it was even hard to believe that he was real and not a figment of a newspaper editor's imagination.

'Of course I didn't, Ellie! How could I?' Ari demanded. 'You know that I haven't spoken to Billy Kay in—'

'He's my father! Why can't you ever call him that?' If forcing the words out wasn't such an effort then Ellie thought her voice might be louder, that she'd rouse the man upstairs, but all she could hear was Ari's ragged breathing. 'He's not just Billy Kay; he's my dad. This is all your fault!'

'What the hell are you talking about, Ellie?'

'He'd have been in my life if you hadn't driven him away!' Ellie bit out. 'You might not have needed him but did you ever stop to think that I might have needed him? Might have wanted to have a relationship with him? What did you do to make him stay away? You must have done something!'

Ari gasped as if she was in pain. 'You're not being fair, Ellie. You weren't there. You don't know what went on . . .'

'Because you would never tell me! I have a right to know!' She'd never spoken to Ari like this, so belligerently, so *J'accuse*. Couldn't even remember them ever having a fight. They bickered and niggled at each other sometimes, but now Ellie was so angry with her mother that it was all she could do to keep a tight grip on the phone and not hurl it across the room. 'He kept that other woman, Miranda, around. He has a relationship with his son . . .'

'You obviously didn't finish reading the piece because that other woman lives in a fucking granny flat in Billy and Olivia's house. Is that what you expected me to do? To let us be the support act? To be happy that you were always going to be second best?'

'But you don't know that. You don't know what my relationship with him would have been like because you made sure that he left and he never came back,' Ellie hissed, hand cupped round her mouth. 'Was being part of a family not punk rock enough for you? Or were you just angry that he went back to his wife?'

'Now, you're just being fucking ridiculous,' Ari snapped. 'You don't get to know everything, Ellie. It's not just your story, it's my story too and some parts of it are mine and mine alone.'

'You are so selfish,' Ellie told her. 'You deprived me of my dad and made this big deal about how we didn't need anybody because we had each other. You always made out that being poor was some kind of noble exercise in self-reliance when actually it was the fucking pits.'

All the little half-thoughts that Ellie had always shied away from because they were so ugly were spewing out of her mouth unchecked. Even as she heard her voice saying these terrible things, made more terrible because they were a version of the truth, she was scared that she and Ari wouldn't come back from this.

'Oh, so you'd rather I'd have run to Morry and Sadie every five minutes like some spoiled little princess?'

'No, I'd have rather that you called up my dad and said you were sorry and hey, guess what? I'm not as independent as I thought I was and my little girl needs her father—'

'Stop calling him your dad! It takes more than supplying some sperm to turn a man into a father and—'

'You don't know what he'd have been like as a father because you never gave him that chance, did you?'

'Now, just you listen to me, you little—'

Ellie hung up on Ari; pressed the red button and terminated the call, because there was no right way to end the conversation after she'd finished dumping on her mother's head twenty-six years of bitterness and resentment that she'd hardly let herself feel, let alone ever articulated to another living soul.

Her heart was racing, her shaking hands were mottled underneath her tan, and part of Ellie wanted to call Ari back and say sorry but part of her wasn't sorry at all. Even now, Ari was still holding out on her. If she'd been blameless, if it had all been Billy Kay's fault, then Ari would have had no qualms about telling Ellie. But the fact that she never had meant that Ari had to be partly responsible for Billy not letting the door hit him in the arse on his way out of their lives.

Ellie took deep but ragged breaths. When she could feel her heart-rate slowing down to a more normal rhythm, she thought again about calling Ari. Though maybe this was the lull between storms and more terrible accusations would burst forth. They hadn't even touched on the subject of Chester, or why Ari had never sued Billy for even the minimum palimony that she was owed by law. No, she couldn't risk it. Not yet, Ellie decided as she heard a light tread on the stairs.

David was wearing boxer shorts and a sleepy smile, which disappeared as soon as he caught sight of the expression on Ellie's face.

'What's the matter?' he asked sharply.

How could he not know? How could he have carried on sleeping while Ellie's world had broken into pieces? She angled her laptop so David could see the headline.

'Oh, for fuck's sake!' he snapped. 'How did this happen?'

Then he was standing behind her, fingers on the trackpad of her MacBook, yet somehow wasn't touching her, even though he was all around her. Ellie could feel the tension coming off him as he kept scrolling down, reading faster than she would have thought possible.

He stepped back from the laptop, from her, and when Ellie turned round in her chair, David had his arms folded, face grim. She was sure her face was grimmer.

'So, it just slipped your mind that I had a half-brother.' She didn't want to be angry with Ari any more. There was someone who deserved her anger far more. 'You didn't think it was worth mentioning?'

'Do you really expect me to believe that you didn't know anything about this?' David demanded.

Ellie stood up so she could face him then wished she hadn't because he looked as cold and frozen as the sea in winter. 'How was I meant to know? It's not like Billy Kay told me during one of the weekly phone calls that we never had!'

'I'm sorry.' He sounded approximately ten per cent less stiff. 'I don't know how this story even got into the papers.'

'Is that it?' Ellie asked incredulously. 'A half-brother suddenly emerges fully formed in the pages of the *Chronicle* and that's all you have to say?'

'What do you want me to say?' David asked as he walked away from her to unplug his phone from its charger on the kitchen island. 'Really, tell me! What can I possibly say to make you feel better? Whichever way you look at it, it's a mess.'

That wasn't good enough. Not when Ellie had a hundred questions that she needed answers to, but all that she could hear in her head was white noise. 'I can't believe this. That you . . . you knew . . .'

Then the static was replaced with a ringing sound from both their phones. 'I'm not ignoring you, but I absolutely need to take this,' David said, and he turned away from her again to march back up the stairs, leaving Ellie to take a call from Sadie, who spent half an hour trying to find some kind of silver lining.

'This Charlie, it doesn't sound like you'd have anything in common with him,' she pointed out. 'And could you imagine having to live in that man's spare room?'

Ellie couldn't, even if the spare room was a wing of Billy Kay's huge Georgian country house in Sussex. She was also forced to agree with Sadie that the arrangement seemed fantastical. 'This other woman and his wife, are they both having relations with him? Do they have a rota? How on earth would that work?'

'I don't know, Grandma. I'd really rather not think about it.' Ellie stared hard at her laptop. 'Do you think this Charlie looks a little bit like me? Round the eyes?

'At least the press don't know where you are, *bubbeleh*,' Sadie said finally. 'Yes, we have a few people hanging around outside, but there's nothing you can do about it. You have a nice holiday. Don't you worry about us.'

Catholics had nothing on Jewish grandmothers when it came to piling on the guilt. Ellie would once have loved to relocate to Paris permanently but she had a feeling, as she heard David move about upstairs, that Paris had been ruined for evermore. Besides, Sadie's best friend, Bernice Keonig, was happy for Ellie to stay in her guest bedroom.

Staying in David's guest room certainly wasn't an option. Ellie was already heartsick for the thirty-six hours they'd just spent together when it had all been so simple. No boundaries to define. No need for Serious Talks.

That was all over now, she thought sadly as she heard David's voice drift over the half-wall. It was hard not to hear him, when he was almost but not quite shouting, 'Billy, how many more times can we go through this? Miranda and Charlie did sign non-disclosure agreements, but it's beyond my powers to make absolutely everyone they come into contact with sign one too. I can't legally bar Charlie and all his friends from having Facebook accounts either.'

There was a horrible sensation creeping over Ellie's scalp as David gave a short, humourless bark of laughter. 'We always knew this was going to be a possibility. The *Chronicle* told us they had this story weeks ago. I'm sorry our plan B strategy didn't work, but that was initially Georgina's remit, not mine.'

Ellie was standing in the middle of the living room, hands on her hips, her face peering up so when David looked down, it was obvious she had been hanging onto his every word. He didn't even have the decency to look away when he said, 'I know precisely where she is and I will deal with her. And yes, I'm sure Charlie is very upset that his privacy has been compromised, but by the time he's back at Cambridge this will all have died down.'

He'd hardly had time to hang up before Ellie was scrambling up the stairs, almost falling down them again, in her haste to get right up in his face, so close that she could have pursed her lips and kissed him if she'd wanted to, which she absolutely did not. 'This whole thing has been a set-up, hasn't it?' She prodded him in the chest with her index finger, until he slowly and deliberately pushed her hand down, which should have made Ellie even angrier. Instead it made her want to cry. 'Did you and Georgina put Richey up to it just to protect your precious Charlie?'

'Of course we didn't,' David said immediately because she was asking the wrong question. 'However, it was fortuitous timing and as far as the *Chronicle* were concerned, you were the bigger splash. That's all I can tell you.'

That, right there, was the reason why Shakespeare had written the line, 'The first thing we do, let's kill all the lawyers.'

'None of this was a surprise, was it? Not even when I first contacted you about Richey stealing my papers.' Ellie took a step backwards because she couldn't bear to be so close to him. 'I was just the . . . what did you call it? Your plan B strategy? You let Billy Kay throw me under the bus!'

David stood there in his boxer shorts and managed to affect the same kind of ease as if he'd been wearing one of his grey suits and a starched, impossibly white shirt. He even gave her one of his Wyndham, Pryce and Lewis tight smiles. 'I'm very sorry, Ellie, but I can't discuss my clients with you.'

'You *bastard*,' she managed to say, and she was shaking uncontrollably again, unable to even clasp her hands together, as if she'd lost control of all of her motor neurone functions. 'You've been playing me the whole time? Keeping me tucked away in your flat . . . This weekend, it hasn't meant anything to you, has it?'

'Ellie.' David's face, his voice, softened and he tried to take her hand but she cowered away from him. 'How can you think that?'

'Because I'm always wrong when it comes to men. I actually thought you were different.' Ellie looked up at the ornate architrave above her because she couldn't look at him any more. 'God, you're just like all the rest, aren't you?'

'I've tried to do the right thing by you.'

'You wouldn't know what the right thing was if it was delivered to your door gift-wrapped!' David was still far too close for comfort. Close enough that Ellie could smell his sleep-warm body and just the faintest hint of citrus from his aftershave, and she didn't understand how she could still want him even now. 'Did Billy Kay ask you to "deal" with me? Are you billing him by the hour for shagging the daughter he never wanted?'

'Don't talk about yourself like that,' David snapped and he took hold of her icy-cold hands before Ellie had time to cringe away from him again. 'Don't talk about us like that.'

'Like there was even an us!' Ellie insisted. If she got through this dry-eyed it would be a miracle. 'Not while you're his lawyer.'

'I've worked years to get where I am and I'm not giving that up, Ellie, no matter what I might feel for you.' He sounded affronted at the mere suggestion.

'How can you feel anything for me when all you've done is lie to me?'

'I haven't lied to you. I simply didn't tell you

about things that would have impinged on client confidentiality.'

Ellie struggled in his grasp but not too hard because she didn't want to act like a girl in a really bad horror film and, God help her, this could be the last time he ever touched her. 'You can't work for my father—'

'A warning before you go any further; I don't respond well to threats or ultimatums.'

Ellie glared at David so hard she was sure she'd detached a cornea. 'Him or me,' she said, and she wished she wasn't saying it because she already knew that their fun sexy times couldn't begin to measure up to finally making senior partner, which would obviously be his reward for managing this crisis, for managing her.

'The reason that I'm so good at my job is because I compartmentalise. There's work, then there's my private life, and in an ideal world there'd be clear blue water between them.' He smiled ruefully as Ellie looked at him stony-faced because there was no way she was making this easy for him. 'Unfortunately, it's not an ideal world but in another two days this will be over, I give you my word, and then there is no reason why we can't continue to see each other.' David frowned when Ellie's hands slackened and he had to loosen his grip.

'I don't want a relationship like that,' Ellie said dully. 'I don't want a man who's going to compartmentalise his feelings for me. I am worth more than that.'

'No one's saying that you aren't—'

'You are. You're saying that you'd never take me to some fancy partners' dinner at your firm and you'd never have a picture of me on your desk or, like, if you were standing around the water cooler with your lawyer mates, you wouldn't say, "Oh, me and my girlfriend, Ellie, are going away on a mini-break this weekend," would you? I'd be hidden away; your dirty little secret, because you wouldn't want anyone to know that you were involved with a client's daughter. Especially when you'd been colluding with that client and his press representative to drag that daughter's name through the mud.'

David's eyes flickered, then he averted his gaze. 'I haven't colluded. I may have been party to collusion but lawyer–client privilege prevents me from—'

'Oh, fuck you and your lawyer–client privilege!' It was exactly what Ellie needed to hear to break free from the inertia. Standing there and trying to reason with him was useless. It was like trying to argue with one of his thick, boring legal books with the really long-winded titles and teeny tiny type. 'Unlike you, I can't compartmentalise the way I feel and I'd never want to.'

'Believe me, that's painfully evident,' David said, and his transformation back to sneering, supercilious legal eagle was complete. 'Having a temper tantrum won't get us anywhere. Let's sit down and talk about how we're going to move forward like calm, rational adults.'

'I don't feel very calm and rational right now,' Ellie ground out, searching around the room with wild eyes. 'You want to compartmentalise? Well, compartmentalise this!' She snatched up his brogues and threw them over the low wall where they hit something on the floor below, which crashed with the sound of breaking glass. Ellie didn't even dare look to assess the damage.

Still David didn't lose his temper. 'That doesn't even make sense,' he told Ellie, who didn't lose her temper either, not ever, except she'd been losing her temper a lot over the last week and always because of David Gold.

'You want sense, then I'll give you sense. I want you to get the fuck out of here right now because I never want to see you again.'

Chapter Thirty

There was no horde of snapping, snarling photographers waiting at St Pancras, just Chester standing at the ticket barriers, with a smile that lit up his whole face as he saw Ellie suddenly emerge from the far side of the platform. She was trying to be incognito, which was hard when you had as much luggage as she did.

'Hello, princess,' he said, and wrapped Ellie up in a very gentle bear hug, like he thought she might break if he was too enthusiastic.

Ellie thought she might break too. She was still trying to process the half-brother adored by the same half-family that had never even bothered to send her a birthday card. The hour she'd spent crying in the train toilet hadn't helped either. Or banished the memory of David following her instructions, stuffing his things into an M&S carrier bag and getting the fuck out of the apartment. He hadn't said a word but his lips were compressed into such a tight thin line that Ellie didn't think he was physically capable of speaking.

But when she'd stood by the door so she could slam it shut after he'd gone, he tried to touch her face. 'This is ridiculous, Ellie. I know you've had a terrible shock this morning but don't you think you're overly melodramatic?'

'No, I think my melodrama is perfectly justified in this case,' she'd told him and he'd had the nerve to smile as if she'd just cracked a joke.

'I'm not going to say goodbye because this isn't over,' he'd said, and Ellie didn't know if he was talking personally or professionally, and that was always going to be the issue for them. Not their biggest issue, which was that David was a hard-hearted, cold-blooded bastard, but a problem nevertheless.

Now Chester relieved Ellie of her heaviest bags as they walked to where he'd parked. Then he kept up a stream of idle chatter, mostly about the weather and how it had been the longest gap between rainfalls since records began, as they edged out into the late Sunday afternoon traffic.

Chester didn't stop talking until they joined a long queue of cars waiting for the lights to turn green by Chalk Farm tube station.

'So, shall I put on the radio or shall we hook up your iPod?' he enquired cheerfully, but Ellie wasn't so immersed in her own unhappiness that she couldn't hear the strain in his voice or see it in the deep grooves at the side of his mouth.

'Have you and Mum made up yet?'

'No,' Chester said flatly.

'We had a dreadful row this morning,' Ellie admitted, and it was hard to know what she should be prioritising in terms of grief when she was currently spoiled for choice. 'I said some vile things to her and I know I should apologise but the thing is that I'm still angry with her. Secretly, I've been angry with her about Billy Kay for years, and I just let it fester and then it all came pouring out.'

'Oh, Ellie.' Chester sighed. 'You and Ari will be all right.'

'I hope so.' Ellie wasn't sure. She and Ari had always made it through the hard times, but then it had always been Ellie and Ari against the world and not Ellie and Ari pitted against each other. Billy Kay's shadowy presence spoiled everything. Everything that had happened was because . . .

'I've met someone!' Chester suddenly burst out like the words couldn't be contained any longer. 'A woman.'

If he'd wanted to pull the plug on Ellie's pity party, then he'd certainly succeeded. 'What? Since when? Were you in Benidorm with a woman?' Ellie didn't mean to sound quite so accusatory but she hadn't thought that Chester was like that; that he had those kinds of feelings towards women who weren't Ari.

'Not exactly. I was in Benidorm with a bunch of mates and one of them is a girl called Claire. Well, she's not a girl. She's thirty-eight.' Chester glanced over at her. Ellie tried not to look quite so devastated at the thought that Chester's world didn't revolve around Ari ... and her. 'I've known her for years. And, yeah, there's always been something flirty between us, but the thing is, Ell, I always thought that eventually me and Ari would end up together. I mean, we were together, weren't we? Apart from the whole . . .'

Ellie was grateful that Chester didn't actually spell it out. 'You were like an old married couple,' she said. 'Everyone thought so.'

Apparently, after Ari had told Chester to stay in Benidorm and he'd been moping about the beach and the dancefloor, Claire had decided to deliver some much-needed home truths, then kiss Chester into the middle of the next week.

'It's not all about Claire,' Chester explained haltingly, but he looked dazed and happy at the memory of her kiss. 'She's a lovely girl but we've only been on two proper dates. But she's right: it's time I faced up to the fact that despite everything I've done for your mum – that I'd do anything for her – she's never going to love me like she loved Billy Kay. No matter how much she tries to deny it, she still loves him, and on some level she reckons they'll be together again one day. And I just can't put up with it any longer. You don't know what he's like, Ell. I'm not even going to tell you 'cause he is your dad, after all, but he treated Ari like shit and all this time she's been waiting for him to come back to her.'

'Well, I think it's more like she never got over him because he broke her heart.' Ellie wasn't absolutely sure about that because Ari had always withheld on the topic. But now Ellie wondered if it had simply been too painful for Ari to talk about Billy Kay. Generally, the amount that someone could hurt you was governed by how much you'd loved them. Or thought you might grow to love them, if you'd had a chance to be with them for longer than one weekend in Paris.

'I'm done, Ellie,' Chester said with a note of finality. 'I've wasted more than half my life loving a woman who's always going to be in love with someone else. This summer has brought it all back. I'm nearly fifty and I've left it too late to have a family of my own, to have kids . . .'

The world didn't revolve around Ellie; it carried on spinning regardless of her wishes, but she couldn't bear the agony of losing someone else. 'Oh, Chester! Please . . . I know I'm meant to be strong and independent, but I can't do without you.' She reached for the tissue box stashed under the dashboard and blew her nose, then Chester's hand was covering her hand, snotty tissue and all.

'You'll never have to manage without me, Ellie,' Chester said, squeezing her fingers so tight that she wanted to protest that he was hurting her. 'I know my timing's lousy, but I didn't want you finding out from anyone else.'

'But do you promise me that whatever happens, even if you and Ari never speak again, you and me are still rock solid?'

'For ever and always, princess.' If Chester cried, then Ellie would too. He swallowed manfully instead. 'It would destroy me if I lost you. End of.'

It wasn't quite end of as far as Ellie was concerned. Some things had to be spelled out very clearly. 'Look, I'll admit that I used to think about what it would be like to have some kind of relationship with Billy Kay, but I always wanted *you* to be my dad. Not a faux dad but my proper dad. You do know that, don't you, Chester? Like, if I ever get married, you are so walking me down the aisle, OK?'

Chester sniffed and they sat there in silence for a few long moments, both of them struggling to keep the tears at bay. Ellie was still biting down hard on her bottom lip when Chester breathed out, then gripped the steering wheel and stared straight ahead. 'I don't think you get walked down the aisle at a Jewish wedding, but yeah, I'd like that.'

'But I'm not getting married right away,' Ellie reminded him. 'Maybe not ever, because apart from you and Grandpa, and Tom, most men are horrible, conflicted scumbags.'

'Are we talking about Richey or have you got a new ex-boyfriend that you want me to have a word with?' Chester nudged her. He suddenly looked a lot happier, as if Ellie's chequered relationship history was a cause for celebration, a safer subject to talk about. 'Well, do you?'

Ellie still wasn't sure that the threat of tears had passed but she nudged him back. Hard. 'Weren't you saying something about putting the radio on?'

The house of Sadie's best friend, Bernice Koenig, was at the other end of Hampstead Garden Suburb from where David's parents lived and looked just as Arts and Craftsy from the outside. Inside it was chintz as far as the eye could see. Anything that wasn't chintz was gold-plated.

As well as loving a bit of glitz, Bernice loved Sadie's progeny as if they were her own, because 'me and my Larry, God rest his soul, were never blessed with children'.

She gathered both Ellie and Chester to her bosom, then led them into the dining room, where a buffet had been laid out, and through the open patio doors into the garden where a lot of familiar-looking people were congregated.

Bernice hadn't known the correct social etiquette for having a tabloid star to stay, even when she'd changed that tabloid star's nappies back in the day, so she'd thrown a party. Filling their plates and perched on garden furniture were Ellie's grandparents, aunts and uncles, various cousins and assorted children of cousins. Tess and Lola were on their way over and Chester was exhorted to stay and 'eat something! It's not healthy for someone to be so thin.' Bernice, who was five foot ten in her stockinged feet and built like a fishing rod, thought anyone under fifteen stone needed fattening up.

After the horrors and revelations that the day had heaped upon Ellie, it was soothing to sit in Bernice's back garden surrounded by her real family. Even Aunt Carol, who'd never been her greatest fan, got pinch-faced with annoyance as she brandished a copy of the *Mail on Sunday*, which had run an opinion piece dubbing Ellie the poster girl of what they called the FBAs, which stood for Fame By Association or 'the desperate wannabes who aren't famous for being famous but famous for knowing someone who's famous'.

'Do you have to read the whole thing out?' Ellie asked as she nibbled on a smoked salmon and cream cheese bagel, but there was no stopping Auntie Carol, who had Ellie cornered on a sun lounger so there was no escape.

'They've quoted some so-called psychologist who says your pathological need for attention is because you never had a paternal signifier,' Carol read out with just a smidgen of sadistic glee. 'Grandpa has always been there for you, hasn't he?'

'He has.' Ellie nodded. 'Always.'

'Sometimes to the exclusion of his other grandchildren,

but I suppose they do all have fathers . . . fathers that are married to their mothers.'

It was kind of comforting that Auntie Carol had reverted to type and was being her usual undermining, bitchy self, but Ellie still gave a grateful yelp as she saw Tess and Lola come through the patio doors, each clutching a laden paper plate and a glass of orange squash.

There were a few moments of awkward plate and glass redeployment, then Lola opened her arms wide and drawled, 'Come on, ladies, let's hug it out,' and five minutes later, the three of them were sharing a sun lounger, which sagged dangerously under their combined weight, and combing the rest of the Sunday papers, even though assorted aunts, uncles, grandparents, honorary grandparents and Chester all assured Ellie that she was better off not knowing.

The girl portrayed in the papers would forever be a girl clutching an alcoholic beverage and showing too much skin. She was Billy Kay's bastard daughter, as if that was all anyone needed to know about Ellie, when a few weeks ago, that was the one thing no one had known about her.

'It's so unfair,' Ellie sighed. 'Everyone gets to stick the knife in me. Even Billy Kay. He might not have spoken to the press but whenever they say "a source close to Sir Billy", it's obvious it came from his publicist. Mum tried to warn me about her and it turned out she was right and she *was* double-crossing me the whole time. They all were.'

Tess looked up from the *Sunday Mirror*'s charming photo essay called 'Like Mother, Like Daughter', which charted key fashion moments when Ari and Ellie had worn vaguely similar outfits. Ari in a leopard-print coat at a Pulp gig fifteen years ago, Ellie at a charity auction last winter in aid of the World Wildlife Fund wearing a little black dress and a pair of leopard-print pumps from Office. Ari with her hair swept up in a quiffed ponytail; the bloody photo of Ellie being flung over the head of a quiffed

Rockabilly, and to round things off a picture each of the honourable Olivia and Miranda, the erstwhile model, both looking refined and elegant.

'Are you still maintaining a dignified silence?' Tess asked. 'I'm not angling to get you on TV, by the way. I'm just enquiring as a concerned friend.'

'I know that,' Ellie assured her, though she was already stiffening in suspicion because it was hard to trust anyone any more. 'I don't know how I'm meant to be reacting. Jesus wept, when is this going to be over?

'Let's face it, Ellie, this is never going to be over. Not now your new baby bro has rocked up,' Lola announced, putting down the *Sun on Sunday*, which had an obviously photoshopped picture of Charlie bookended by Lara and Rose on its front cover and an exclusive interview with the sisters. 'And not while these two trolls are guaranteed column inches so they can bang on about how you've given them an attack of the sads. As for Billy Kay – I bet you any money that in less than a month he'll be releasing a new record and doing a tour. I bet you fifty quid!'

'You are *so* cynical,' Tess told her.

'I can't help it. I was born cynical,' Lola said, and Tess rolled her eyes but it was good-natured eye-rolling so they'd obviously made up since falling out over *Come Dine With Me*. 'Look, Ellie, you need to be proactive about this shit. Make it happen, instead of having it happen to you.'

'But the tabloids will twist everything I say,' Ellie protested, not that she had any intention of talking to them, though maybe she did need to do something to take control of her public image. But what?

'Maybe an interview with a broadsheet?' Tess suggested. 'Call one of your mates on the arts desks and pitch a piece about emerging Scandinavian artists, but really it would be about how you're not the chavvy tart that the tabs say you are.'

'Or what about YouTube, like that bird from that TV talent show whose ex posted that video online of her noshing him off . . .'

'Lola, don't use the word "nosh" in that context when there are elderly Jewish people about.'

Lola grinned at Ellie. 'Whatevs. One minute everyone hates that girl for sending home that lady who worked in Sainsbury's and having really bad fashion sense, and the next, she's become a feminist icon. And she got to put her point across without it being spun by anyone else.'

Tess looked as if she was in a thousand agonies. 'I'm not saying anything,' she said with a pious air. 'Not even that I'm a freelance researcher for a TV show that goes out live every morning to five million people and has two really lovely presenters who were voted "the people we'd most like to have a coffee with" by Mumsnet. I'm not saying that.'

'Except you totally have just said that,' Ellie pointed out. An idea was forming in her head. 'So, if it goes out live that means I can't be edited, right? I get to say exactly what I want to say. Hypothetically speaking. I'm just curious.'

'Well, within reason. No swears. Nothing libellous and you don't get question approval before the show.' Tess wrinkled her nose. 'If you did choose to go on, then it has to be your decision. I'm not pressurising you in any way.'

'But you do know that they're not renewing all the researchers' contracts and Tess is too bossy to suck up to anyone and she's not knobbing a cameraman, so she needs a bit of leverage,' Lola said. 'And she is your best mate, apart from me, and it would be helpful if she could pay, like, her share of the rent.'

They both looked at Ellie pleadingly. She stared down at the bagel that she'd barely made a dent in. Maintaining a dignified silence hadn't made the media circus pack up its tents and move on to the next town. Meanwhile, everyone else, from Billy Kay's other daughters to leader writers for the tabs, got to weigh in with an opinion on Ellie, even though they had no idea who she really was.

Even Ellie had lost sight of who she really was, or who she tried to be, but she knew what she didn't want to be. For as long as she could remember, taped to Ari's bathroom mirror, then transferred to her own bathroom mirror was a Nora Ephron quote: 'Be the heroine of your own life, not the victim.'

She'd been playing the victim too much these last few weeks; being rescued, when she was more than capable of rescuing herself. It was time to write her own script.

'The presenters of *On The Sofa* – they're not at all controversial. It will just be a nice chat, right?' Ellie widened her eyes and tilted her head. '"Oh Ellie, we'd love to know about the real you, rather than all these dreadful stories in the papers. How have you been holding up?"'

'Right, right.' Tess was nodding so frantically that Ellie thought her neck might snap. 'Jeff and Angie do what they're told. He's obsessed with the camera getting his left side and Angie is sweet but as dumb as a bucket of mud.'

'If I do it, it has to be tomorrow. Is that a problem?' Ellie asked. The oily aftertaste of the smoked salmon was making her feel sick, or maybe it was the prospect of going on national television. It might be the only way that Ellie could have her own unedited right to reply, but that didn't make the prospect any less terrifying. She had to have at least three vodka shots before she could think about doing karaoke and occasionally the *On The Sofa* studio audience could get quite chippy. 'If I don't do it right away I know I'll lose my nerve.'

Tess knitted both brows and hands together imploringly. 'So, are you saying that you're going to do this?'

Ellie took a deep breath. She even thought about putting her head between her knees so she didn't faint. Instead she took a sip of lukewarm, oversweet orange squash. 'Yes. Yes,' she repeated, her voice getting firmer. 'But it has to be tomorrow and I don't want them using that sodding bikini shot when they introduce me.'

'I'm going to make a phone call.' Tess shot off the sun lounger and almost sent Lola and Ellie crashing to the ground as the end that she'd been sitting on sprang up in the air. 'I'll probably have to go into work this evening, but I forgive you.'

The two girls rearranged themselves and sat back down. Lola prodded Ellie in the side. 'You're really brown, you know,' she said apropos of nothing, as if Ellie being really brown wasn't a good thing. Lola preferred to look as if she'd just been laid out on a mortuary slab. 'Will you promise to lay off the self-tanner between now and tomorrow, otherwise you'll look like you've been Tangoed?'

'But it's TV! I don't want to look washed out by the studio lights.'

'You don't want to look like a drag queen either,' Lola insisted. She assumed a martyred air. 'Maybe I should come with you as your personal make-up artist. I'd love to have a crack at Jeff Jenkins . . . Beneath that bland day-time TV exterior, he's meant to be an absolute sex monster. Dick bigger than a French stick.'

Ellie clapped her hands over her ears. 'You are *so* not coming anywhere near the *On The Sofa* studios tomorrow. And thanks, now all I'll be able to think about when I should be concentrating on my interview is how big Jeff Jenkins' knob is.'

Lola looked entirely unrepentant. 'Well, it beats imagining the audience in their underwear when you get nervous.'

Camden, London, 1987

Everyone was making demands on her. On one side there was Sadie and Carol. On the other side was Billy. But they were all united by a common purpose: to snatch Velvet away from Ari and install her in the beautiful nursery in Golders Green with the handmade cot and rose-sprigged wallpaper, and never give her back.

Velvet should have been the most demanding thing of all, but she wasn't. She'd stare up at Ari with big, trusting blue eyes in a way that made Ari fall apart.

Billy was furious when Ari brought Velvet back to the playwright's house instead of handing her over to Carol, but Carol would get to spend the rest of her life with Velvet so the least she could do was let Ari have a measly six weeks. Not that Carol saw it like that.

Billy was furious that even the playwright's Japanese girlfriend was besotted with Velvet and invited mother and daughter out of their third-floor suite of rooms to ply them with expensive baby clothes in return for cuddles.

He was furious that Ari was breast-feeding and eyed Velvet jealously as she clutched onto her mother, as if Ari's breasts were for him alone. 'Why can't you bottle-feed her, Ari? It's the nineteen eighties for fuck's sake.'

He was especially furious that Velvet slept in the same bed as them, in between them, and that Ari couldn't give him her undivided attention like she used to because Velvet needed her undivided attention too.

But Ari was furious with Billy too. Furious that he still hadn't fallen in love with his daughter when loving Velvet was the easiest thing in the world.

When the six-week deadline slid by and Velvet was still with them, Billy didn't shout. And when Carol came round almost every day and demanded what she'd been promised, he watched with an impassive face as Ari gave her sister reason after reason why now wasn't a good time.

'Of course you can have her, but the thing is she's a bit chesty at the moment.'

Or, 'I just haven't had time to see the lawyer.'

And even, 'The health visitor says I need to breast-feed her for at least three months. At least!'

Billy didn't say a word but he arranged for the playwright's girlfriend to babysit Velvet and he took Ari to dinner at the Russian restaurant in Primrose Hill. Ari tried not to twitch or to look as if her mind was miles away, or not miles but five hundred yards down the road and across the square where Velvet might be left unattended or have developed colic or was perhaps simply crying because they'd never been parted.

She tried to focus on Billy, who was smiling at her in the soft candlelight. He looked so beautiful that it was hard to remember that most of the time his face was split with a sneer.

They ordered borscht, then stroganoff, mopped up with dark rye bread, but Ari could hardly eat. Finally Billy pushed their plates to one side so he could take her hand.

'You know I love you, Ari,' he said. 'You know I've been waiting for you.'

Ari knew what was coming. She stroked her fingers along the rigid line of his knuckles. 'I'm still here. I haven't gone anywhere.'

Billy shook his head. 'You don't love me any more. Not like you used to.'

'I do love you, but now I love Velvet too. It's not like people just have a set amount of love to dole out. It doesn't work like that.'

'But we had a deal. You promised, and I get that your hormones are through the roof, but Ari, we were heading somewhere. We're not going to get there if you take your eyes off the prize. When was the last time you even picked up your guitar?'

The solution was simple. She wondered why'd she never thought of it before. 'It doesn't have to be either or. I can have it all,' she said, and she laughed because it was so obvious now. 'Why can't I have Velvet and fame, if it will have me, *and* you?'

Billy's face darkened and Ari realised too late that he didn't want to be third on her list of priorities, and actually he wasn't. But Billy hated being in second place too. 'You can't have it all,' he told her bluntly. 'You either love me completely, and that means that you give me all of yourself, or you don't love me at all.'

She wasn't going to keep Velvet, but Ari had never counted on Velvet being part of her, so that losing her would be like losing a limb. Worse. People managed without arms or legs, but once Velvet was gone, Ari would be fractured and the kind of broken that couldn't be made whole again. She loved Billy – she did – but he was never going to be enough to fill the void that Velvet would leave. When Velvet was gone, Ari still wouldn't be able to give all of herself to Billy, because her heart belonged to her daughter now.

'Two more weeks.' It was a desperate plea. 'Let me have two more weeks with her.'

Billy didn't shout or swear or cause a scene. He stood up, pulled two grubby ten-pound notes from his pocket and put them on the table. 'Me or the kid, Ari,' he said, and then he walked out.

Chapter Thirty-one

The next morning, as she was driven to the *On The Sofa* studios on the South Bank, the size of the male co-host's penis was the very last thing on Ellie's mind.

Despite the air conditioning in the car, Ellie could feel sweat dotting her forehead and her upper lip. She had three white dresses in the garment bag draped over her lap. Tess had said to bring options, and she was worried that even with repeated applications of a so-called invisible antiperspirant she'd have unsightly yellow marks under her arms. She'd have to remember to keep her arms at her sides, but in a natural way. Not a stiff, shop mannequin way.

She and Tess had also come up with a list of talking points: Ellie had no problem with Billy Kay or any member of his family and was very sorry that they'd had their lives disrupted. She was just a hard-working young woman who wanted to get on with her life. And she had a really funny but completely untrue anecdote about dressing up as a four-pack of Kleenex Velvet loo roll one Halloween, because Tess said it was essential to make the audience laugh at least once. Probably, Ellie'd have had more luck in memorising her talking points if she was giving them her full attention instead of wondering if she should call Ari. Not to apologise, not yet, but she wanted to hear Ari tell her that she could do this, that she'd rock it out and that she had her blessing.

405

It had been twenty-four hours since they'd last spoken. They'd hardly ever gone so long without even a phone call before. Ellie was pretty sure it had happened only once when she'd had laryngitis. But she was still furious with Ari, years and years worth of fury, and she couldn't handle another row before her TV debut.

She wiped her sweaty forehead with her equally sweaty hand. It wasn't just nerves that was making her glow and giving her an insistent, nagging throb between her eyebrows. The endless weeks of sticky heat had given way to a humid, airless day. Thunderstorms were predicted, even though there wasn't a cloud in the sky. They'd predicted thunderstorms before, which hadn't amounted to anything more than a light breeze, but this morning the city was simmering like it was about to come to the boil.

'Would you mind turning up the air con?' Ellie asked the driver, struggling to make herself heard over Talk Radio, then she settled back on her seat. Could she make it to the studio without throwing up?

It was a relief when her phone rang, but it wasn't Ari. It was David.

She was tempted not to answer, but then Ellie thought of how it would feel to hear his voice. So polite, so proper even when he was talking utter filth. There was absolutely nothing he could say that she wanted to hear, other than, 'I'm sorry for all the heinous things I put you through. I was wrong, and I've found a way for us to be together.' This was never going to happen so she answered with a snippy, 'What do you want?' to let him know that she might be taking his call, but she wasn't taking any nonsense.

'Ellie?' There was the beat her heart skipped. 'Don't do it.'

'Don't do what?' she asked, genuinely confused. *Don't live your life without me in it. Don't forget to floss before bed.* There were so many possible don'ts.

'Do not do the interview that you're on your way to do.' It sounded like he was whispering.

'What makes you think I'm on my way to an interview and what makes you think it's any of your business?' she snapped.

'Please don't do it. You have to trust me on this.'

'Trust you as my father's legal representative or trust you as the man who's happy to shag me as long as nobody knows about it?' Ellie had to whisper herself because even with Talk Radio on, she didn't want the driver to hear, then maybe mention it to someone from *On The Sofa* in the staff canteen.

'That's not fair. How about you trust me because—'

'Because what?' she demanded. 'Because . . .?'

'I have to go,' David said abruptly, then he was gone and the car was pulling in outside the TV studio.

Ellie was so spooked that it took three attempts to undo her seatbelt and the driver had to get out and open the door for her. She hadn't even had time to take more than two steps on wobbly legs before a young man with extravagantly coiffed hair, dressed in a very tight, very blue suit hurried out to meet her.

'Velvet?' He didn't even wait for an affirmative reply but gathered her up in an exuberant hug. 'I'm Zach. I'm one of the researchers from *On The Sofa*. I'll be looking after you. We're so psyched that you're here.'

So, this was one of Tess's arch nemeses. Ellie could tell why. She also wondered what the opposite of psyched was as they swept past Reception and down a long corridor, the walls painted a zingy lime green and dotted with photos of the great and good and also the not so great and not so good.

'Do you mind if we don't get the lift? I'm *so* claustrophobic,' Zach said, ushering Ellie through another set of doors to a stairwell. 'It's only a couple of flights up.'

They reached the third floor and apparently it was still 'only a couple more flights', when Ellie panted, 'I thought Tess would be here.'

'Oh, she's around,' Zach said vaguely. 'Anything you need, just ask me. We all want you to love your *On The Sofa* experience. We'll get your make-up done, give you a little pampering session, then we'll try on some clothes. You're a size six, right?'

'I'm a size eight,' Ellie gasped in panic. 'Sometimes I'm a ten. Tess told me to bring my own outfits.'

'Oh, no need to worry about that.' They were on the fifth floor. Zach opened another door and eyed Ellie's garment bag. 'Why don't I look after that for you?'

Ellie tightened her grip. 'That's OK,' she said sweetly, though a distant alarm bell was going off in her head. 'I really would like to see Tess, please.'

'I'll find her for you,' Zach said as he galloped down another corridor, Ellie scurrying to keep up with him. 'Look! It's your very own dressing room!' A door was thrown open and Ellie was hustled inside. 'Even Pippa Middleton didn't get her own dressing room. She had to share with a girl from *EastEnders*.'

Ellie knew when someone was trying to sell her a bridge, but she smiled tightly at Zach, who muttered something about having to see a man about a dog (she hoped she wasn't the dog in that scenario) and left her alone.

There was a counter lined with mirrors adorned with lightbulbs, which made Ellie feel a bit showbusiness, but also even more panicky as she parked her vanity case and studied her face for open pores, blackheads and any stray eyebrow hairs that needed eradicating before she was HD ready.

There were also a few limp-looking, garishly hued frocks hanging from a clothes rail. Ellie was having nothing to do with them. She unzipped her garment bag and carefully hung up the three white dresses she'd brought with her. She didn't want to look too virginal, that would really be pushing it, but they'd look good against her tan and wearing a crisp, white dress was the quickest way she knew to becoming her own heroine and finding some semblance of calm.

Suddenly Zach reappeared with two women. One of them was lugging a huge make-up case with her and the other had a few more garish dresses over one arm and a carrier bag full of shoes that looked like they'd come from somewhere that advertised itself as 'a one-stop shop for all your stripper needs'.

'So, this is the lovely Velvet, and this is Elaine and Mercedes who are going to make you look even more beautiful,' Zach exclaimed.

Elaine was make-up, Mercedes was wardrobe and was already pulling out a skimpy red dress that was slashed down to *there* and hocked up to *here*. 'This would look great with your colouring and your long legs,' she said, holding it out to Ellie reverentially like it was this season's couture.

'No, thank you,' Ellie said politely. 'I never do legs *and* cleavage.' She also didn't do clothes so thin and shiny that they'd go up in flames if they came within ten metres of a lit match.

'What about this one, then?'

Another dress was held up for Ellie's inspection. It was neon pink and would have been a great look if she were a podium dancer in an Essex nightclub.

'Why don't you slip one on so we can see what it looks like?' Zach suggested. 'I know they might seem a little—'

'Cheap?' Ellie asked. It wasn't often she could arch an eyebrow, only when she didn't think about it too hard, but her left eyebrow was sweeping up now.

'Bright,' Zach said. 'They'll really pop under the studio lights.'

'I think I'll end up popping out of them, and before the

watershed too,' Ellie said with a fixed smile to show that she wasn't being a bitch. 'I'll be more comfortable in my own clothes.' She waved a hand towards Mercedes and her clothes rail. 'I've also got my own shoes. I have narrow feet and weak ankles. I'm very difficult to fit.'

Ellie had a whole cacophony of alarm bells ringing in her head now. David's phone call was taking on a new significance, She was meant to be here to be portrayed in a flattering light, not dressed up in tacky clubwear.

'Why don't we make a decision about the clothes later? Let's sort out make-up,' Zach said with the same ingratiating jolliness.

Sorting out make-up involved Ellie shying away as Elaine came at her with thick foundation five shades darker than her skin tone, or false eyelashes or vampy red lipstick, or said cajolingly, 'What about a nice smoky eye?'

'I don't think that's appropriate make-up for daytime TV,' Ellie kept saying, though Zach and Elaine both insisted that anything lighter would fade out under the studio lights. 'I want to see Tess.'

Zach was still mouthing platitudes when Tess finally responded to Ellie's increasingly frantic texts.

OMG!!! So, so, so, so sorry. New producer wants ratings up. Lara & Rose Kay been booked too. Totes stitch up. I'm locked in an office. Think U should walk.

Ellie's first instinct *was* to walk. It was her second, third, fourth and fifth instinct too, but then she thought about her half-sisters in the very same building, just a few metres away, prepping for their turn on *On The Sofa* to sing their same tired song: We're sad. We're devastated. She's a no-good little tramp. Her mother's even worse. We only want to protect our precious, precious baby brother. And have we mentioned that we're guest presenting some lame show on ITV4?

Ellie was here so she could finally tell her side of the story. But it wasn't a story. It was the truth. Lara and Rose might have Georgie Leigh to brief them and David Gold to be utterly scheming on their behalf, but Ellie wasn't entirely inexperienced. She was friendly and personable, and if she could flog thousands of pounds worth of art to arrogant Russian oligarchs or uppity R 'n' B artists or vicious trophy wives and have them add her to their Christmas card lists then she could sit down on a sofa for twenty minutes and make the studio audience and the wider public like her too. How hard could it be?

Ellie snatched up the jar of Ponds cold cream that Elaine had dumped on the counter. 'OK,' she said. 'I am really trying not to be a bitch but if I do this I am going to do it wearing my own clothes and a flattering daytime make-up look. If anything goes on my face that I don't like, then I'm bringing out the big guns.' Ellie waved the Ponds cream threateningly. 'If you persist in trying to force me to do anything that I'm not comfortable with, then I'm going home.'

Zach actually wrung his hands. 'But, Velvet—'

'Look, I chose On The Sofa for my one and only interview because I thought you'd show me a little respect and some understanding. Please don't let me down,' Ellie finished with a brave smile, which drooped slightly at the corners because was this what David meant when he'd said that she used a smile to get her own way?

If she did, then it worked, because Zach backed off immediately. 'We just want you to be happy, Velvet.' He smiled brightly and rubbed his hands together. 'Why don't I get you coffee and a muffin?'

It wasn't going to be the world's most auspicious TV debut, Ellie thought as she picked up the remote control to switch on the TV that was mounted to the wall.

'Oh, let's see if Homes Under The Hammer is on,' Mercedes exclaimed, and snatched the remote away so Ellie couldn't see how the interview was being trailed. Would Lara and Rose go on before her? Or would she get

411

first crack at warming the audience up? These were questions that needed answering, and even if she couldn't have face time with Tess, at least they could text.

Have decided 2 stay. Wearing white Whistles dress & will try to b myself. Any more tips?

Ellie got changed into the white broderie anglaise shirt-waister with the full skirt, which she'd been wearing at Glastonbury the first time she'd met David Gold. She wasn't sure if that made it a lucky dress or an unlucky dress, but she could still feel the phantom touch of his hands on her arms as he'd steadied her, see the quirk of his lips as he'd smiled, and her face flushed in a way that had Elaine coming at her with a powder puff as her phone pinged.

OMG Ell! Walk! Go! This is a car crash and U R going 2 end up DEAD!!!!!

The alarm bells upgraded to a full sixteen-siren roar, with flashing lights and an arse-clenching feeling like the end of the world was well and truly nigh.

Ellie eyed her garment bag, then resigned herself to leaving her other two frocks behind. Same with her vanity case, even though it contained about a month's salary worth of product. 'I need some fresh air,' Ellie said, forcing the words past her constricted vocal chords. 'I'm going to pop out for five minutes.'

Elaine and Mercedes looked at each other, then at Ellie, who tried to assume an expression that was appropriately nervous rather than utterly hysterical. 'I think the room next door has a window we could crack open,' Mercedes said, because even the make-up and costume department were ready to fling her to the lions. Or were desperate to keep their jobs. Whatever.

'Look, I'm not—'

'Velvet! There you are!' Zach was back without the promised coffee or muffin. 'Shall we start walking?'

It was time to come clean. 'I might as well tell you that

412

I'm bailing on you,' she explained as they set off at a fast trot. 'None of this feels right, you know?'

'You're nervous. That's completely natural,' Zach assured her, as they got into a lift, even though he'd pleaded claustrophobia. Obviously, he'd wanted to avoid Ellie coming face to face with Lara and Rose without a camera to record the meeting for posterity, she realised. 'Jeff and Angie will put you at ease.'

The lift doors opened and, hand on her elbow, Zach guided her through two sets of double doors, then a long, long corridor. 'The thing is, Zach ... well, I'm not convinced I'll be portrayed in a positive light.'

Zach made an ouchy face as if Ellie had mortally wounded him. 'We're all thrilled that you're here,' he said, dodging the issue. 'And it must feel really good to know that you can get your point across after all those *terrible* things Lara and Rose Kay have said about you in the papers.'

'Yes, but what—'

'I bet it made you really angry. Furious.' Ellie was just about to turn a corner, but Zach ground to a halt so he could take her shoulders and look deeply into her eyes. She was starting to hate him in a very special way that she'd hardly ever hated anyone before. 'I would have been furious. And your poor grandparents. I saw them in the paper and they looked really sweet and kind .'

'Yeah, well they are,' Ellie agreed, not sure why Zach felt the need to bring this up right now.

'But they also look very, very old. You must have been so frightened that all the revelations and all the mean things people like Lara and Rose were saying would give them heart attacks and then, well, they might die.'

Ellie was appalled. 'Oh my God! Why would you even say something like that?'

But she knew why he was saying it because Tess had told her that one of the least savoury elements of her job was to sometimes babysit guests and get them suitably riled up/tearful/hyped (delete where applicable) before they went on.

Which was why Zach was saying, 'Just the thought of your grandparents not being there for you must be heart-breaking. Do you feel like you might cry?' he asked hopefully.

'This interview is not happening.' Ellie turned on her heel in order to leave so it couldn't happen, when a woman dressed all in black with a clip-on mike came barrelling round the corner.

'There you are,' she said to Ellie with a bright smile as she looked her up and down. 'Not at all what we were expecting.'

'Talking of things that weren't expected—' Ellie began, but the woman had one of her arms and Zach had the other and he was still talking about her grandparents' untimely demise as she was marched around the corner so fast that her feet didn't make proper contact with the floor. They came to yet another set of double doors and these ones had a red light above them that said 'On Air'. Ellie found herself being pushed through them and onto the set of *On The Sofa*.

Camden, London, 1987

Billy was a stone-cold bastard. Ari had always known that, always known that her love wasn't enough to change him, but she'd still wanted him. Even now, she ached from the want of him.

Besides, she could never be the kind of mother that Velvet should have, which was why Carol was taking her at the end of the week. Or the end of the month. Then it was halfway through the next month and Ari hid behind the curtains when Carol banged on the door and the playwright's girlfriend pretended that Ari wasn't there.

Ari couldn't go out much in case Carol was lurking in next door's bushes but it was April, the promise of sun in the air and it wasn't good for Velvet to be cooped up, so Ari fashioned a baby sling out of a leopard-print cardie and stepped outside.

Velvet's big eyes were wide with wonder at the world and it was all Ari could do to watch where she was going because Velvet was endlessly fascinating. Ari spent hours marvelling at all the miraculous parts, from tiny toenails to the startling mop of curls, which made up her perfect baby.

It was Camden and it was Ari back in her big hair and big heels. She was stopped every five paces by an old friend, an acquaintance, someone she used to be in a band with. They all cooed at Velvet and Velvet cooed back at them. Then they all smiled and laughed and told Ari how lucky she was.

When they bumped into Chester, Velvet managed to get one fat arm out of her swaddling and waved at him. It was humbling to watch the look of slavish adoration that lit up his face as he ever so gently stroked Velvet's cheek. 'She's beautiful, Ari,' he said in a reverent whisper. 'She's a little princess, isn't she?'

They went to George & Nicky's for a fry-up, and when Ari took Velvet out of her sling, Chester scooped up the baby and kissed her as she gurgled with delight.

'Don't get too attached, Chester,' Ari said softly. 'My sister's taking her. I'm not cut out to be a single mother.'

Chester covered Velvet's tiny ears before he said, 'Bullshit, Ari. You're cut out to be whatever it is that you've set your heart on.'

Chester insisted on taking them to Gateway to buy groceries and nappies. He even wanted to go to Argos to buy a pram but Velvet was getting fretful, so instead he gave them a lift back to Primrose Hill.

Velvet was incensed when Chester drove off. She arched her back, stiffened her limbs and threw up all over Ari. The playwright had been making vague threats about rent but when Ari bumped into him in the hall he took one panicky look at the vomit-laden pair and gestured upstairs. 'You've just this second had a visitor.'

Billy! Ari knew that he'd come back because, despite everything, he loved her and if he loved her, then eventually he'd learn to love Velvet. But standing in their room, a discomfited look on her face, was Georgina Pratt.

'Oh, hello,' she said, when she saw Ari. She gave Velvet, who was still screaming, a horrified glance. 'Yuk! Has it been sick?'

Velvet spat up another flurry of puke by way of reply and Ari managed to catch it in her hand. Motherhood had given her an entirely new skillset.

'What are you doing here, Georgina?' she asked as the girl followed her into the bathroom. Ari filled the washbasin with lukewarm water and efficiently stripped Velvet, who protested every inch of the way. 'As for you, madam, stop bitching.'

'I'm sorry about what happened before Christmas, throwing the drink at you. And I wanted to see the baby.' Georgina peered over Ari's shoulder as she plonked Velvet in the basin and washed her down. 'Can I hold her? I've never held a baby before.'

Icy fingers scrabbled their way down Ari's spine but she let Georgina take her, showed her how to support Velvet's head. Velvet loved nothing more than someone new smiling and talking nonsense at her, so she quietened down and looked at Georgina expectantly.

'I could keep an eye on her if you wanted a shower,' Georgina offered.

There was something about Georgina that had always felt off to Ari. Like, underneath the doughy, dumpy, Billy-worshipping exterior there were darker forces at work, but she was covered in sick. There was even sick in her hair and under her fingernails.

'Would you? Take her into the bedroom and sing to her. She loves that. I'll be five minutes.'

Four minutes later, when Ari turned off the shower she heard Velvet's angry bellows, like she was being tortured. Naked and dripping wet, she rushed from bathroom to bedroom to find Velvet dumped on the bed, from where she could easily have rolled off and crushed her skull.

'Georgina!' she screamed, as she scooped up Velvet, spooking her and making her cry even harder. 'Shhh. Shhh. I'm not mad at you. I could never be mad at you.'

Ari sat down on the bed and did all the things that Velvet loved. Rubbed her face against her daughter's fat belly, blew her kisses, raspberries, even played Little Piggy on her starfish hands, until Velvet nestled her head in the crook of her neck.

Ari patted soothing circles on the baby's back and thought about maybe taking a nap too, then she noticed that a whirlwind had swept through the room.

A whirlwind called Georgina Pratt, who had gathered up every single one of Billy Kay's possessions and spirited them off. Every last guitar pick and pair of socks, and the two tartan laundry bags that contained the demo tapes and notebooks that charted the beginning and the during and the painful end of Ari and Billy.

Chapter Thirty-two

Oh! It looks much smaller than it does on TV, was Ellie's first thought. Then: why is everyone so mad at me?

Ellie was standing at the back of the room and gazing out, not onto the famous *On The Sofa* set with its two huge red sofas, but into the audience, which was a sea of angry, hostile faces all looking at Ellie as if she'd gone round to each of their houses and murdered their children and pets.

The urge to cry was sudden and very strong, but the woman with the mike had her arm in an uncompromising grip and Ellie was being yanked forward, as Jeff Jenkins stood up and said, 'And now here to answer these claims is Lara and Rose's alleged half-sister, Velvet Underground!'

Ellie was led to a high stool. Apparently she didn't even merit a sit down on one of the famous sofas and for some reason she was clambering on to it in an inelegant scramble and sitting there patiently while a stagehand shoved his hand down the front of her dress so he could attach her to a microphone.

She couldn't tear her eyes away from the audience. There was one pugnacious-looking woman, sitting five rows back, who kept pointing at Ellie and shouting something that Ellie couldn't hear – probably just as well.

'Velvet?'

'Huh? What?' She turned to the nearest sofa where

Angie Drake and Jeff Jenkins were sitting. 'What?'

Jeff Jenkins didn't seem as nice and smiley as he usually was. Even pretty, giggly Angie was frowning at Ellie. 'You seem quite surprised by the audience's reaction,' Jeff said. 'How does it make you feel, Velvet?'

Like, I want to get into the foetal position and rock back and forth. Ellie blinked at him. 'Um, it's Ellie. My name's Ellie.'

'Have you changed your name because of the press attention?' Angie asked.

Ellie shook her head. 'No. I've always been Ellie.'

'Does this kind of reception make you wish you'd never sold your story to the papers?' Jeff Jenkins wanted to know and Ellie stared at him in dismay because if they couldn't even get *that* right.

'I didn't,' she said, but she was drowned out by jeers from the audience.

'You did! Because all you and your mother care about is fleecing money out of our dad,' cried a voice, and Ellie's gaze finally swivelled to the other red sofa set at a right angle to Jeff and Angie's sofa. Sitting on it were Lara and Rose Kay.

She was in the same room as her two half-sisters and suddenly Ellie was trying to remember how to breathe, hands clinging to the edge of the stool as she gawped at them. Lara was the taller, fiercer-looking one and Rose was softer and somehow droopier, as if maintaining her size-six figure was a feat of endurance. They both had a Royal Borough of Kensington and Chelsea air to them: long buttery limbs, long buttery hair and an air of discontent on their pretty, pouty faces.

'We always knew you'd go to the papers over Daddy's little mistake,' Rose said. She was sniffing and had a tissue clutched in her hand, which she very carefully dabbed under each eye so she didn't smudge her make-up. 'Daddy might have strayed that one time but your mother threw herself at him.'

'It wasn't like that at all . . .' Ellie risked glancing at the audience because they couldn't be buying any of this bullshit, but one look at their rapt, intent faces and it was clear that yes, they were buying this.

'I can't even look at a paper or a magazine without seeing you in it,' Lara said haughtily. 'Falling out of your clothes. It's so undignified. You have no integrity.'

The sheer nerve of them – Sadie would call it chutzpah – rendered Ellie speechless. As if she was having an out-of-body experience, she could see herself perched uncomfortably on a stool, forehead scrunched up and showing quite a bit of leg. She tugged down the skirt of her dress and, as Lara patted Rose's knee in a sisterly gesture of support, Ellie felt herself getting angry.

It was good. The anger was good as long as she didn't let it take complete hold. 'I haven't done anything wrong,' she said in a voice that sounded a little stronger.

'How you can sit there and lie like that?' Lara gasped, turning the fake indignation all the way up to eleven. 'What is wrong with you? You're, like, a sociopath.'

Ellie didn't know what was wrong with her either. She was on live TV, for better or for much, much worse, and she had to do something rather than sit there with a face full of gormless and take everything that was being thrown at her. She was better than this. She was a fucking people person and she'd spent days in David Gold's apartment (she hoped that he wasn't tuned in to *On The Sofa* right now) watching nothing but daytime television, and it wasn't *that* difficult to get the audience on your side.

She could do this. She had no other option.

'All right, all right,' she said, more as a direction to herself than anyone else, then she forced herself to lift her head, pin her shoulders back and look Lara and Rose right in their pretending-to-cry faces. 'I came on the show to set the record straight so will you please let me do that, OK?'

She didn't wait to find out if it was OK, but plunged on. 'I know you only have my word for it, but my mother never asked anything of Billy Kay. Not a thing.'

'No, that's not true,' Lara interjected. 'Not a week went by when there wasn't a phone call or—'

She sounded so convincing that Ellie found herself wondering if she was the one that had got her facts wrong and then she remembered that she hadn't. 'My mother and Billy Kay were together for a year. It was well documented at the time. Then he left when I was three months old and he went back to your mother. I'm really sorry that you're still hurt by that, but you can't have a year-long affair with a married man if the married man isn't willing,' she said. 'There was no other contact after that. No phone calls. Not even a birthday card.'

Ellie let that sink in. The audience seemed unsure, Lara and Rose were worriedly whispering to each other, Angie Drake was doing her listening face and Jeff Jenkins was obviously getting directions from the producer in his ear. Ellie hoped the producer was saying, 'Let her speak! I'm sick to death of the other two.'

'When Billy went back to his family, he wasn't famous, but he got famous pretty soon afterwards, yet Ari never took him to court to ask for maintenance. Despite what you might have read, my mum has principles even though when you're a single parent money's always tight. New shoes, a school trip, a supermarket shop; whatever you have doesn't last very long.'

There was the very faintest murmur of agreement. 'It's obvious that you love your mother, but she hasn't been a very good role model, has she?' Jeff Jenkins said, and it took every ounce of muscle control she had for Ellie not to leap off her stool and smack him. So, Ari was a single mother, big whoop. If that was the worst they had to throw at Ellie, then they were going to have to try much harder. Statistically speaking, a good half of the audience were either lone parents or had been brought up by a single parent, and they needed to join her team.

'No, she wasn't a good role model,' she agreed equably, and she saw Ari's face, as familiar as her own, smiling that crooked, wryly amused smile. Whatever deeply buried anger and resentment Ellie might have harboured towards her mother was no match for the love that she had for Ari. No matter how bad things were, Ari was the constant in her life, the person she could always turn to. It had ever been so. No matter how inadequate Ellie had felt sometimes, she'd always been good enough for Ari.

'She was an excellent role model,' Ellie explained for the benefit of the peanut gallery. 'Sometimes she'd have up to five part-time jobs, but she was also the cool mum who was in bands and knew loads of interesting people. And somehow she never missed a single school sports day or a PTA meeting.' There was so much more to say. That Ari had taught her about Patti Smith and the suffragettes, showed her how to play 'Heart Of Glass' on the guitar and told her that she was beautiful but that it was more important to be clever and funny, and that she could be anything she wanted to be. She'd stuck inspirational Nora Ephron quotes on the bathroom mirror and though it killed Ellie not to be able to share that with the *On The Sofa* audience, she needed to keep this simple and direct. She paused and it seemed as if the audience were leaning forward eagerly. 'Though sometimes I wished that she didn't turn up for school sports day or parents' evening in a leopard-print catsuit, but whatever.'

There was laughter at that. Not sneery, cackling laughter either. It could be that the tide was turning in Ellie's favour. Lara Kay obviously thought so because she pointed a stiff finger at Ellie. 'Well, she couldn't have been that good a role model when the papers are full of stories about what . . . how . . . well, that you're a bit of a slapper, quite frankly.'

422

Even Rose looked shocked and there was a gasp from the audience like they were clutching their collective pearls, and surely Lara wasn't allowed to say the word 'slapper' before the watershed? And . . .

'That's a really hurtful thing to say,' Ellie said. 'Especially when the papers print stories that aren't true and—'

'Well, you would say that, wouldn't you?' Rose shrugged sheepishly, like her heart really wasn't in it. 'You might pretend that they've made up the stories but there's no smoke without fire.'

Ellie opened her eyes as wide as she could. 'So, the stories in the papers about you shoplifting and Lara sleeping with her best friend's boyfriend were true, then?' she asked in faintly scandalised tones.

'No! That's not what I meant!'

'There were actual quotes from the actual guy you were seeing about your actual sex life!' Lara reminded Ellie furiously. 'Actual pictures of you in your underwear.'

A ripple of excitement went through the audience. Angie Drake smiled nervously, eyes darting between the two sisters on the sofa and Ellie on the stool of shame. Jeff Jenkins realised that he had to take control of this situation. 'To be fair, Velvet, Lara does have a point.'

Not from where Ellie was perched, but she was committed to this now. 'Let me be very clear. I did not sell my story and I certainly did not use my new-found fame to make vast sums of money by giving interviews to the papers and signing up to pose in bra and pants—'

'That was a legitimate modelling job.'

'Will you let me finish?' It was the 'don't fuck with me' voice that Ellie didn't know she was capable of until it came out of her mouth when Muffin was being absolutely impossible or Ari was about to embark on some ridiculous scheme. It was the voice that could even stop Vaughn in his most autocratic tracks. Lara Kay settled back on the sofa with angry huffing noises. 'If I'd wanted to sell my story – which I didn't and don't and never have done – then I would probably have done it when I was working insane hours in awful jobs to fund my degree. Have you ever cleaned the men's loos of a pub after last orders on a Friday night?'

It was a rhetorical question but Angie and Rose both shook their heads.

'Well, I have, and it's character-building. Or that's what my boss used to tell me.'

The audience were definitely Team Cohen now. Before she could lose their interest or Lara and Rose could make it all about them again, Ellie spread her hands wide. 'I don't want to be all "woe is me" but the last two weeks have been awful. I've had my privacy stripped away from me, my grandparents, my mum, my friends have been door-stepped by the press; I'm not even sure I still have a job; and I know it's a bit rich to sit here on a prime-time TV show and moan about press intrusion, but I wanted people to be able to see the real me.'

'Do you really expect people to believe that you didn't pose for those photos?' Jeff Jenkins asked with a sceptical look to camera. Ellie would never have believed he'd be such a tough crowd; he had always seemed so charming on TV.

'When you're followed round all day by photographers, they take hundreds of shots and use the one picture when you're stretching up or bending over or—'

'. . . like, sometimes it's really hard to get out of a sports car with your legs clamped together,' Rose Kay offered eagerly. 'I've had photographers lie on the ground to try and get an upskirt picture. They're disgusting.'

'Right, well, there you go,' Ellie said, and Rose beamed at her. It would have been churlish not to smile back. Ellie managed a tight grimace as Rose was poked in the ribs by her sister, who then turned the full weight of her venom back at Ellie.

'Like, that bikini picture wasn't papped. It was posed!'

It was impossible for Ellie not to roll her eyes. 'What is your problem?'

Lara quivered with outrage. It had to be exhausting to maintain that level of outrage for so long. 'You are! The things you've done to my family. You should be ashamed of yourself.'

It was time to wrap this up. Ellie could tell that from the guy who was standing behind the camera making winding motions, and Angie was sitting up straighter, looking right to camera and smiling . . .

'I'm not ashamed of anything,' Ellie said quickly. 'What have I done that's so wrong apart from dating an absolute creep and not having tighter security controls on my Facebook photo albums? If that's what I'm guilty of then so is every other twenty-six-year-old woman in Britain, am I right, ladies?'

Ellie wasn't sure she could pull off an Oprah-esque 'am I right, ladies?' but the *On The Sofa* audience were clapping and there was even an excited, 'You go, girl!' from one of the back rows.

'Ellie, you're handling this so well,' Angie Drake pronounced breathily. 'But before we break, how did you feel when you found out you had a half-brother?'

The question caught Ellie unawares like a punch to the stomach, so she wasn't capable of dissembling. 'I was . . . I am kind of shocked.'

'Especially when Charlie's grown up knowing his father. It must have been very hard for you not to have a dad. Is there anything you'd like to say to Billy Kay?'

One of the cameras zoomed in on Ellie. If it got any closer, she'd have a good case for aggravated assault. But it was hard not to tear up because for most of her life she'd thought about what she wanted to say to Billy Kay. Even a month ago she'd have tried with all her might to forge some connection or bond with him. But that was a month ago, and this was now.

'He might have been there at my conception but it takes more than that to be a dad.' There was one single, unprompted tear teetering on her bottom lashes. 'Anyway, who needs a father when you have grand-parents and aunts and uncles, cousins and amazing friends?' Just the thought of Chester gave the unshed tear the push it needed to start a slow trickle down her cheek. 'So I don't feel like I ever missed out by not having a dad. Not even a little bit. In fact, I feel lucky and blessed that I've spent my entire life surrounded by people who love me.'

The audience were actually getting to their feet and cheering, but it was less to do with Ellie's *tour de force* performance and more that a producer was making frantic arm movements to get them to stand up and applaud wildly.

As Jeff Jenkins asked the *On The Sofa* viewers to tune in at the same time tomorrow Ellie was helped down from the stool. Someone shoved a wad of tissues into her hand as she was hurried from the set.

Once Ellie had finished dabbing at her eyes and blowing her nose, she realised that the someone was Tess. 'I'm sorry it turned into such a bloodbath.'

Ellie peered over Tess's shoulder to the *On The Sofa* set. Lara Kay was screaming at one of the producers. 'Have you been fired for giving me the heads up?'

'They decided that Zach was expendable after he did such a rubbish job of prepping you.' Tess smiled beatifi-cally. 'New producer's going too for sullying the *On The Sofa* brand. You know, when Lara Kay called you a slapper?'

'It will be etched into my memory until the day I die,' Ellie said truthfully, because she wasn't in that place where she could joke about what had just happened. She didn't think she'd ever get to that place. 'I can't believe you'd want to carry on working here. It's a pit of vipers.'

'No, it's really not,' Tess insisted. 'Usually it's fluffy and extremely non-controversial, which is why our phone lines are jammed and Slappergate is trending on Twitter. Look, I am sorry, Ellie . . .'

'I know you are and you did try to warn me.' It hadn't been Tess's fault, Ellie knew that, but she wasn't ready to let the subject rest. 'So how did my interview get derailed when you were meant to be looking out for me?'

'I'm not exactly sure. When I got in at eight thirty this morning, everything had changed. Apparently, the new producer took it upon herself to contact Billy Kay's publicist to see if he'd come on so you could have a touching televised reunion.'

'God, no!'

'And it turned out that Billy Kay's publicist was a real piece of work,' Tess said, just as there were the sounds of a commotion behind them and Ellie looked round to see Georgie Leigh storming onto the set from the other direction so she could yank a still-screaming Lara Kay to one side and seize the producer by her shirt.

'That was not what we agreed!' Georgie was dressed all in black this time, still dripping with gold jewellery so her bangles jangled furiously as she all but shook the hapless woman, who was trying to say something but not getting very far. 'Who coached that little tart? When I find out who it was, I'm going to end them!'

Tess and Ellie both cowered behind one of the stage flats. 'Now I understand how my interview got derailed,' Ellie whispered. 'That's Ari's deadliest enemy.'

They watched as Georgie unhanded the producer and pushed her away. She did a keen-eyed sweep of the studio, her gaze coming to rest on the flat behind which Ellie hoped she was obscured from view.

'The only other time I met her she was really nice. Overbearingly, creepily nice,' she hissed to Tess. 'I think the homicidal threats are actually preferable. You know where you are with homicidal threats, don't you?'

'Let's get you out of here,' Tess decided, and she bundled Ellie out of the studio, down several miles of corridor, and deposited her in a tiny airless room with a desk, chair and a flipchart. 'I'll grab your things and order you a car. Be back in ten minutes.'

Camden, London, 1987

Carol started crying as soon as Ari arrived at The Coffee Cup in Hampstead, wheeling Velvet in the new pram that she'd bought with the proceeds from selling her second favourite guitar.

'You're keeping her, aren't you?' Sadie asked. When Ari nodded Carol cried even harder.

Eventually she stopped crying and once she'd dried her eyes, she stood up. There was a hardness in her eyes that hadn't been there before. 'I will never, ever forgive you for this,' she promised.

Ari was sorry for hurting Carol, the kind of sorry that couldn't be put into words. She did try but Carol turned her face away.

'I never want to see you again. What you've done . . . You *promised* . . I didn't think it was possible to hurt this much,' Carol said in a choked voice, and Ari knew how she felt because she knew how much it would destroy her if she didn't have Velvet.

'But I am sorry, Carol.' The words weren't ever going to be enough, but when Ari went to place a hand on Carol's arm, her sister reared back as if she had dipped her fingers in hydrochloric acid. 'I just never knew that I'd love her like this.'

Sadie stood up too. Ari had never seen her quite so furious – close to it, but she'd never reached the summit before. Nice Jewish girls didn't have babies out of wedlock. Or if they did, they certainly didn't brazen it out instead of having the child

429

adopted by a lovely, kosher-keeping couple or the older sister whose life was blighted by the curse of infertility.

'You are a selfish, selfish girl. Don't come crawling to us when you've changed your mind, and don't think you'll get a penny from us either. You're on your own, Ariella,' were Sadie's parting words, as she swept majestically out of the café, Carol trailing behind to send one more agonised but venomous look in her sister's direction that would haunt Ari for years to come.

They'd left a pot of tea and a round of raisin toast behind and Ari wasn't proud. Also, she was hungry and had one pound, forty-seven pence to last until she could get a job.

For one fleeting second, she wondered if she'd done the right thing by her daughter. All she had to give Velvet was love and Ari was never very good at loving people.

Well, she was just going to have to get better at it.

Chapter Thirty-three

Tess wasn't back in ten minutes and Ellie had nothing to do but mull over her first and last TV appearance, because she was never doing that again. Not even if BBC4 begged her to present her own series on Modernist Art.

She'd wanted to appear dignified, but she'd used her 'bitch, please' voice, badmouthed Billy Kay, even though she'd been adamant she wasn't going to stoop that low, and she'd cried. It might only have been one tear, two at the most, but crying on television . . . she was never going to live it down.

It was more than that. The secret place inside her heart that was reserved for just a handful of people had been exposed to the entire nation. You always had to hold something back, but Ellie had given it all away and she felt hollow now. Empty. As if while she'd perched on that stool, in front of the harsh lights and the all-seeing cameras, her soul had been scooped out like the flesh from an over-ripe avocado.

'Car's here,' said a cheerful voice, and Ellie looked up at a woman who wasn't Tess, who had just opened the door.

Ellie was reunited with garment bag, vanity case and handbag, and on reaching Reception was also presented with a huge bouquet of pink roses and lilac hydrangeas 'From all your friends at *On The Sofa*. We'd love to have you back. Any time,' said the woman who wasn't Tess. Ellie wanted to say she'd rather eat her own spleen but

431

mumbled that she'd love to before she was shown into a people carrier.

There was no driver, not that Ellie minded. She was already retrieving her phone and scrolling through a multitude of messages from people who she wouldn't have believed watched daytime TV. Most were cheer-leading variations on the theme of *You rocked it, babe, and your hair looked fantastic*, apart from Lola who wanted to know: *Did U get a look at Jeff Jenkins' knob? Bigger than a baguette?*

It felt good to giggle though it swiftly became a gasp of fear when Ellie saw she had a text from Vaughn. Vaughn didn't usually do texts, but he'd also sent an email and left a caustic voicemail message requesting Ellie's presence in his office 'before end of business today. By which time I might not be quite so angry with you, but don't count on it, Cohen.'

She'd been half inclined to ask the missing driver to drop her at the gallery, but now Ellie wasn't sure. She could go home because she hadn't been home in weeks, but technically she always thought of Ari's tiny, cluttered flat as home. Ari, however, was the one person who hadn't left any messages, even though she was the one person that Ellie most wanted to talk to.

She was angry with Ari for withholding and Ari had to be angry with her for raking up the past, but whatever they'd both said had to be unsaid because Ari was her mother and her best friend and they belonged together. They *had* to get through this latest, gut-churning upset and Ellie wasn't going to let the day finish without making up. After all, Sadie insisted that it was bad form to let the sun set on a quarrel, though Ari always pointed out that Sadie was physically incapable of apologising to anyone for anything.

Ellie was just wondering if Ari was at work today and might be persuaded to take a long lunch when she heard

432

the boot slam shut. Then both passenger doors opened and two people got in on either side of her so Ellie was forced to slide to the middle of the seat.

'Sorry. Could you budge up just a little more? You're sitting on my seatbelt,' squeaked a voice to her left. Ellie stared in horror at Rose Kay, who was suddenly sitting next to her.

'For fuck's sake!' Lara Kay was on Ellie's other side. 'Now you're trying to take our Addison Lee car as well.'

'I was here first,' Ellie said icily. 'Why don't you get out of *my* car?'

'Three to Clerkenwell,' the driver clarified as he started the engine.

'I'm not going to Clerkenwell,' Ellie insisted, as Lara tutted and made a big show of shifting so that no part of her or her gorgeously soft and squashy Chloe hobo bag was anywhere near Ellie. 'There's been a mistake.'

'Three to Clerkenwell,' the driver repeated. 'Velvet, Rose and Tara.'

There was a predictable explosion on Ellie's right. 'It's Lara with an L! Lara!'

'She gets that all the time,' Rose told Ellie. 'Tara or Sara. Even Cara and Mara.'

'Shut up!' Lara snapped. She was the most foul-tempered person that Ellie had ever met. 'Don't talk to *her*.'

The three of them settled back in silence. The nagging pain from before was now hovering around Ellie's temples. She didn't have the energy to argue with the driver. She pressed her fingertips to her forehead and was grateful when Lara demanded that the driver turn up the air conditioning.

'I tried to find you on Facebook loads of times but I didn't know you called yourself Ellie now,' Rose said, smiling timidly as Ellie looked at her in surprise.

'You knew about me before? You knew about me?'

Rose nodded. 'When we were little and we were being naughty, Mummy used to say, "I bet Velvet isn't so badly behaved." Then she'd pretend to ring you up and ask if you wanted to come and live with her after she'd sent us to a home for naughty girls.'

Ellie could only stare in disbelief at Rose, whose eyes were fixed resolutely on her face. 'Really? Wow.' She couldn't even begin to take in this information or that the Honourable and chilly-looking Olivia had a sense of humour.

'It's all a bit surreal, isn't it?' Rose was so close now, she was almost in Ellie's lap. 'You've got our old nose.'

'If you don't shut up, I'm going to slap you,' warned her elder sister. She gave Ellie a cursory glance. 'Mummy made sure our noses were fixed as soon as we were sixteen. They used to be big and bent like yours.'

When it came to body defects, all Ellie's energy was taken up with minimising the effects of small tits and frizzy hair. The slight kink in her perfectly average-sized nose barely even registered, so she failed to rise to the bait. She had a feeling that getting people to rise to the bait was Lara's *raison d'être*.

That wasn't important right now, though. 'You've known about me for years, but you still didn't have a problem spouting all those lies in the press.' Words failed Ellie for a moment and she could do nothing but twitch her limbs in sheer, restless rage. 'You sat in that studio and looked me in the eye and banged on, once again, about how you'd been torn in two by the revelations that you suddenly had a half-sister. Oh, I'm sorry. My mistake. An *alleged* half-sister.'

There had been a time in the not too distant past when Ellie had always kept a firm grip on her emotions. Now she actually had Rose Kay gingerly patting her arm in an attempt to calm her down. 'Look, Ellie . . . do you mind if I call you Ellie? It's weird 'cause in my head I always think of you as Velvet . . .'

'Oh, call her what you like,' Lara sighed, like it was her lot in life to be the older, meaner sister. This time, though, the look she gave Ellie was more curious than cursory. 'You don't look like a Velvet.'

'Nobody does. It's a ridiculous name. That's why, as soon as I could talk, I insisted on being called Ellie.' Ellie turned back to Rose. 'So, you were just about to explain your part in my downfall.'

'It was nothing personal,' Rose assured her, her pretty face drooping downwards in dismay. 'When your ex started hawking his story round, it was just really good timing because the *Chronicle* had found out about Charlie and were going to run with that story. Charlie's only nineteen and he's really shy and he hates a fuss. It would have been torture for him.'

Lucky Charlie. He had the entire Kay clan, and all their minions, working tirelessly to protect his precious privacy, so Ellie couldn't really find it in her heart to have much sympathy for him. Especially when she'd been sacrificed to keep him safe. Still, at least the Kays cared about something other than making money.

'And Billy was putting the finishing touches to his greatest hits,' Rose continued, blithely unaware that she'd just disproved Ellie's theory that the Kays weren't all bad.

'It's a retrospective of his career.' Lara begged to differ. 'There's even going to be a collection of his most iconic photographs at the National Portrait Gallery.'

'And he's going to do his first stadium tour in years. It's very exciting,' Rose added as if she expected Ellie to feel the same unconfined joy as she did. 'Billy swore he wouldn't do a greatest hits . . .'

'God give me strength.'

'. . . or a stadium tour, but he has a massive tax bill. It is beyond massive.' Rose held her hands apart to indicate the enormity of just how much her father owed Her

Majesty's Revenue and Customs. 'And, well, I know it sounds a bit . . . um, what's the word I'm looking for?'

'Evil? Exploitative? Despicable?' Rose seemed sweet, and if the circumstances had been different . . . But they weren't different. Rose and her sister were not good people. Good people didn't lie and cheat and cash in on other people's misfortune. 'Any of those words suitable, or should I keep going? Bad enough that my ex-boyfriend shops a completely bogus kiss-and-tell to the papers, but the pair of you, your family, your publicist, your fucking lawyer, have made it a million times worse. You've just about buried me and I've barely been able to claw my way out.'

'I think you're overreacting a little bit,' Rose said hurriedly, snaking out a hand like she was going to pat Ellie's arm again, then snatching it back when Ellie bared her teeth. 'We didn't know you, and we just figured . . . Georgie said that you'd make some money from selling your story and doing modelling jobs or some reality TV so it was win-win. How were we to know that you weren't that sort of girl?'

She wasn't that sort of girl, and when they'd realised that, then they'd thought they could play her for a total fool.

'You couldn't understand,' Lara said coolly. 'You haven't grown up in the public eye. You don't know how these things work. Billy is an artiste. He's an icon, he can't be held to account. Normal rules don't apply when you're a creative genius.'

She said it with a completely straight face as if she'd drunk the Kool-Aid. It was like trying to reason with a Scientologist, 'Billy? Don't you call him Dad, then?'

The two Kay sisters laughed. 'As if! How weird would that be?' Lara looked much friendlier when she smiled, not that she was anyone Ellie wanted to be pals with.

'He says that anyone can have a dad, but only we're

lucky enough to have Billy Kay as a father,' Rose explained and before Ellie could make gagging noises, Rose suddenly burst into tears.

'Oh, for fuck's sake, don't do that.' Lara reached round Ellie to slap her younger sister on the arm. 'What the hell are you crying for?'

'Don't slap her!' Ellie stroked the red mark on Rose's arm and it suddenly struck her that she was touching her own flesh and blood, someone who shared the DNA in her that wasn't Cohen DNA. It was one of those big moments that she'd remember for the rest of her life, like her first kiss, or the time that one of Ari's friends fixed it for her and Tess to meet Shane from Westlife, or the look on David's face when she'd told him to fuck off. So it made no sense that Ellie felt nothing more than slight concern that someone sitting next to her was crying. It was entirely unsettling, because family was family and she loved hers; grandparents, cousins, even maybe Aunt Carol, but Rose, and especially Lara, made her feel nothing more than a nagging unease. Maybe that was only to be expected after the latest round of revelations. 'Your sister's right. There's nothing to cry about.'

'But you're my sister too and now the three of us are together for the first time,' Rose said, leaning towards Ellie as if they needed to hug.

Fortunately, the car had come to a stop and the moment was gone.

Rose and Lara scrambled out. Ellie sat there for one confused moment because they were outside the offices of Wyndham, Pryce and Lewis. Then she got out too.

After she'd collected her bags from the boot, she turned to Lara and Rose, who were hunting for a tissue. Ellie opened the side pocket of her Mulberry, and presented Rose with a pack of pocket wipes. 'I'm not going to say it's been good to meet you because it's actually been incredibly upsetting.'

'Oh, come on, it wasn't *that* bad,' Lara grudgingly conceded. 'But it's not like we're going to be friends, is it?'

'No, it's not.' Ellie didn't feel any regret about this mutual decision, but Rose, who was still sniffing and hiccuping, wrung her hands in protest.

'But we said we were sorry . . .'

'No, you didn't . . .'

'Well, we are, and we could start by being Facebook friends,' she protested snottily, as if she was working up to weeping again. 'We hardly have any family.'

'What about Charlie? What's he like?' Ellie asked, because how could she not?

Rose frowned as she considered Ellie's question. 'He's lovely but he's very quiet. It's really hard to know what he's thinking.' She went almost cross-eyed as she tried to think of something else to give Ellie. 'But he can be really silly sometimes. He loves watching *You've Been Framed* and he makes a really good chilli.'

There was a painful twinge in Ellie's heart as she processed this handful of facts. Made a tiny space in there for a half-brother that hadn't existed forty-eight hours ago. 'He sounds really nice,' she said to Rose.

Lara folded her arms and sighed. 'Charlie looks a lot like Billy, and Billy loves that. It means Charlie gets a free pass and that's why sometimes he behaves like a spoiled little shit.'

Coming from Lara Kay that was quite the ringing endorsement. 'But you must have grandparents and cousins and—'

'Not really. Billy doesn't speak to his family, and so—'

'Rosie! Stop over-sharing!' Lara hit Rose with her bag. 'Don't start crying again.' She turned to Ellie, who was watching this display of sisterly love with a bemused expression. 'This is why we went with the heartbroken angle. She can cry on cue. She cries all the fucking time.'

438

'I don't.' Rosie scrunched up her face. 'I do, but I can't help it if I'm sensitive. Why can't we be friends on Facebook?'

It was going to be easier to give in, Ellie decided. Then she could toddle off into the sunset. Not that there was any sun left. The sky was leached of all colour and appeared closer than normal, as if it was pressing down on the tall city buildings. It was still bloody hot, though. Ellie tugged at the bodice of her dress, which was sticking to her, and looked at Rose, then at Lara. 'Facebook friends, but limited profile. That's all I'm prepared to offer, and even that's pushing it. OK?'

They nodded.

Lara gestured at the offices behind them. 'We'd better go in.'

Ellie should go and make up with Ari, then persuade Vaughn to reinstate her with immediate effect.

First, though, she couldn't help but stare at the shiny gold plaque that said Wyndham, Pryce and Lewis. David would have looked at the plaque that morning as he pushed open the heavy wooden door; eyes shadowed, lips tight because he was still sore about what had happened in Paris. Maybe he regretted what had happened in Paris, but then David didn't do sentimentality, Ellie thought bitterly to herself. Still she choked on her next breath when the door suddenly opened.

Her shoulders sagged as a young man in his early twenties, wearing a suit that was slightly too big for him as though he was hoping to grow into it, hurried down the steps. 'I have to go,' she said to Lara and Rose, who were repairing the damage done by Rose's crying jag with the aid of spit-slicked tissues. 'I'll see you around.'

'Everyone's waiting in the conference room,' the young man said, and Ellie was grateful he was interrupting what might have been a slow and torturous goodbye.

There wasn't time for kisses or hugs, which was a relief,

439

just half-hearted waves. Lara and Rose turned in one direction, Ellie the other, but the young man touched her lightly on the arm.

'Miss Cohen? Are you not coming in with us?' he asked with some surprise.

Ellie was equally surprised. 'Was I meant to?'

He nodded. 'It was why we asked the car to bring all three of you from the TV studios. Oh, sorry, was that awkward?'

'A little bit,' Ellie said, playing for time as she tried to decide if she did want to go inside. Inevitably, there'd be lawyers who'd threaten her with all sorts of dire legal stuff for saying what she'd said on telly. Then again, David was behind that door.

Ellie imagined the rest of her life would be spent replaying the handful of memories that were all she had to remember David by, until those memories would be so threadbare that she wouldn't be able to trace the warp and weft of them any more. Seeing him again would hurt, but missing the chance to see him would hurt even more, so Ellie followed Ben Wyndham, a direct descendent of the original Mr Wyndham, into the elegant Georgian town-house, up an ornately carved wooden staircase and down a panelled corridor. Ellie wanted to hang back, turn back, but instead she forced herself to smile at Ben Wyndham as he held a door open for her and she walked into a room.

Ari was sitting on an ancient leather sofa, which was something of an anticlimax.

'You all right, hot stuff?' Ari asked, as if they'd spoken only a couple of hours earlier. 'Thanks for making me sound much, much cooler than I really am when you went on the telly. That was a bit of a bunfight, wasn't it? Are you OK?'

'Don't ask. How are you? Are you OK?' Ellie asked as she heard a muttered apology from behind her, then the door closing. 'And what about us? Are we OK?'

'We are always OK,' Ari said stoutly. 'But I have to say, Ellie, even though I hate fighting with you, will you believe me when I say that the things I didn't tell you were for your own good? Trust me on that. Please.'

Ari glanced up at Ellie, who was still hovering by the door, and smiled. It was a poor excuse for a smile. Though she had on full warpaint: flicky eyeliner and trademark red lipstick, hair pinned in an elaborate series of waves and coils, Ari had looked better. With dark circles under red-rimmed eyes that even heavy foundation couldn't conceal, for once she was showing every one of her forty-eight years, and Ellie hated seeing her like that; hated Ari's forced, shamed smile as if she expected her to start shouting at her. Ellie *had* tensed when Ari, once again, shied away from the dark truths of her past, but suddenly that didn't seem as important as sitting down on the sofa next to her mother and taking her hand.

Ari's hand was freezing, though the temperature on the old-fashioned thermometer on the far wall was in the high eighties. 'Everything will be all right,' Ellie said. She wasn't sure how to make it all right, but statistically speaking it would be all right sooner or later. Ellie squeezed Ari's hand instead. Ari returned the pressure. 'Anyway, Mum, what are you even doing here?'

Clerkenwell, London, Present Day

Only for Ellie would Ari be sitting in a tiny anteroom in the offices of Wyndham, Pryce and Lewis after getting a phone call from some lawyer who pleaded with Ari to be there 'for your daughter's sake'.

Even though Ari was angry with Ellie for trying to prise out secrets that might destroy the pair of them, it was the kind of anger that walked hand in hand with fear. Ari's been looking out for Ellie her whole life, protecting her from harm, shielding her from evil, so there is absolutely no way she is going to let Ellie walk into the offices of Wyndham, Pryce and Lewis on her own.

As it is, Ellie has got her own stuff going on right now. She's been on television and she's been crying, and when she talks about Chester, her pretty face crumples again and again. She looks up at the ceiling, takes a deep breath, and tries yet again. 'I always hoped you and Chester would get together one day, and I know it's not going to happen now, but you have to make things right with him, Mum.'

'I will,' Ari says, and she means it. She feels the loss of Chester right at the centre of her being but it still doesn't compare to the time she lost Billy Kay.

Ari's been thinking about the time that she lost Billy Kay quite a bit over the last few days.

'All I ever wanted was Chester as a dad,' Ellie says. Her chest heaves and usually Ari vows to avenge whoever's hurt her daughter, but this time she's the one to blame.

442

Ari smooths back Ellie's hair. Her beautiful curls are kicking back in but she won't share that with Ellie, it always makes Ellie cross and makes Ari sound like Sadie. 'We don't always get what we want, sweetie,' she tells her instead. 'In fact, sometimes, what we want won't do us any good.'

'Chester said that he's missed out on so much by loving you,' Ellie says and she shrugs apologetically, because there's no nice way to say what comes next. 'And so have you, Mum, by still being in love with Billy Kay. You could have let yourself love someone else, if you hadn't been waiting for him. He wasn't waiting for you – wasn't waiting for us – was he?'

'He wasn't,' Ari says, but she hasn't been waiting for Billy all these years. Not in the way people think. Ever since she saw pictures in the paper of this Miranda, and her son, who looks like a tenth-generation copy of the real thing, she's slowly been coming to terms with the fact that some time over the last twenty-six years, she stopped loving Billy. The weird thing is that she doesn't really hate him either. There was another reason why she'd been so driven. 'You have to understand that ever since he left, I've always measured my happiness, my success, against whether I could bear to see Billy again,' she tells Ellie. 'I was always sure that one day we would see each other again. Still am. We have unfinished business.'

Ellie points at herself. 'Yeah, sitting right here.'

'No, not you, my little narcissist. It's not always about you.'

'Then what?'

There are some things that Ellie doesn't need to know. Christ, Ari goes hot and cold and feels as if a platoon of ghosts have walked over her grave at the thought of some truths coming out. Truths that she and Ellie might not be able to come back from. But there are other truths that Ellie is probably old enough to deal with. 'Music things,' Ari says vaguely. 'Copyright issues. Won't bore you with the details.'

'Does he owe you money?' Ellie's eyes narrow. 'Did you write some of his songs on that first album? You know, Tom always says—'

Ari knows what Tom and Tabitha and Chester and, God, even her brother-in-law Sidney say about the songs, about how many millions are hers by rights, but they could never understand that when they eventually met again, Ari had wanted to face Billy as his equal.

'What I wish is that I hadn't spent years chasing this elusive dream that I was going to make it,' she says to her daughter. 'That I'd become famous and fêted and my songs would mean something to generations upon generations so I could show Billy that I didn't need him, that I was better off without him.'

'Well, that's crap,' Ellie says sharply enough that Ari looks at her in surprise because there's a new edge to her daughter that Ari hasn't seen before. 'The fact that you never gave up on your dreams, that you never settled, is amazing. It's inspired me my whole life. *You've* inspired me.'

It's all getting too saccharine sweet. Any moment, Ellie might break into the chorus from 'Wind Beneath My Wings'. Ari nudges her. 'Yeah, well, it wasn't so inspiring when you were a kid and I was trying to soundcheck at some dive in God knows where, and you wouldn't stop nagging me for a bottle of Coke and a bag of crisps.'

Ellie nudges her back. 'OK, just so you know, it's not so inspiring either when you insist on climbing up on a speaker stack and I'm terrified that you'll break a hip.'

'You little bitch!'

Ellie looks at her with those dark eyes that technically she inherited from Billy, except Ellie's are always warm, always twinkling, full of love, except now when they're swollen and glassy with unshed tears. 'Do you regret having me?' she asks baldly. 'Your life would have been different if I hadn't been in it. I mean, you could have really focused on your music. You could have been famous . . .'

'No!' It might be Ari's turn to cry. 'No! Don't you get it, Ellie? You are the love of my life. Sometimes I wish things had turned out differently, but I don't even want to think what my life would be like if you hadn't been in it.'

'But . . .' Ellie gestures at nothing. 'Your dreams might have come true if you hadn't had me.'

'They were just dreams. But you're real.' Ari takes Ellie's hands and places them over her heart. They don't often have chats like this, talk about their feelings, but it's important that Ellie knows this before it's too late. Before she confronts whatever's waiting for them in these offices. 'I'm not the best mother in the world, I know that. There were lots of things I should have done, should have given you, but you've always been loved, Ellie. You don't even know how much you're loved.'

'I do,' Ellie says, and she does burst into tears then, and Ari cuddles her and promises her that everything will be all right.

After a while Ari makes Ellie blow her nose, tells her to do something about her make-up and she wonders if she shouldn't just hustle her daughter the hell away from here, but then some grey-faced, grey-suited lawyer comes in and says that they're ready for them in the conference room.

Chapter Thirty-four

They were shown into another wood-panelled room with portraits of doughy old men on the walls. Lara and Rose and a gaggle of young blondes were seated at one end of a large conference table, a couple of starchy-looking men in suits gathered down the other end talking to Olivia Kay, who seemed remarkably smiley for someone whose husband was a serial philanderer and, by all accounts, a total dick.

Then Ellie wasn't paying any attention to Olivia because David walked into the room and he looked stony-faced, which was when he looked his best – apart from those few times when his eyes were all pupil and his jaw was clenched as he thrust inside her. Ellie blushed a bright, rosy red as David strode to the head of the table, ran his eye around the room and settled on her.

Everything else – people, furniture, fittings, ugly portraits – ceased to be, and it was just her and David.

Then David looked past her, as if Ellie wasn't even there, and folded his arms. 'Before we get started, if you're not related to either a Cohen or a Kay or employed by this firm, you need to leave,' he said coolly. There was a brief pause, then the blondes seated on either side of Lara and Rose got up and left.

'Oh, but Georgie's on her way over,' Olivia Kay said with a bright smile. She looked remarkably poised in white trousers and a crisp navy blouse. She also looked as if no one ever said no to her. 'She's one of us.'

'Only family,' David repeated in a voice that made every single hair on Ellie's body stand to attention. 'I have to insist.'

'Have I ever mentioned that I hate lawyers?' Ari groused under her breath. She had, many times. 'Is that a Wyndham, a Pryce or a Lewis?'

'Sshh! Stop talking, Mum.' Ellie gave Ari's hand a warning pinch as David turned and glared at both of them. Ellie glared back just to show that her feelings hadn't changed since their showdown yesterday morning.

It was just that her feelings were complicated. Her head was thinking of the hurt he'd inflicted and the hurt that was yet to come if she let him back in her life, but her heart was thinking, oh God, it's his stern face. I adore his stern face.

'Now, nobody is leaving this room until we've reached a resolution,' he said grimly. He wasn't looking at her any more, or Ari, or Lara and Rose. Or even Olivia, who was leaning against the wall and more interested in her BlackBerry than David's stern face. He was looking at a middle-aged man in dark glasses, wearing a blue suit with a purple pinstripe running through it and a Ramones T-shirt. His hair was a preternatural blend of silver and white and styled in an Artful Dodger cut, which looked odd, though it probably photographed well. It was a man that Ellie had barely noticed as she'd squeezed past him to sit down.

It was Billy Kay. Her body gave a quick painful jerk of recognition, then she was unable to do anything. Couldn't even keep holding Ari's hand with suddenly boneless fingers as she stared at Billy Kay, who was steadfastly looking at . . . it was hard to know *exactly* what he was looking at as he was wearing shades indoors.

So strange that she hadn't noticed him because her attention had been focused on David. Even in a room

447

full of people, David was the only person Ellie could see.

Except now. It was creepy to keep staring at Billy Kay. Ari said something but Ellie didn't hear her. She barely even registered Rose Kay's shocked giggle as she saw where Ellie's attention was riveted.

'This whole business needs to be brought to a swift close.' David's voice pierced the miasma that was clouding Ellie's senses. It was a relief to turn her head and watch him pace up and down. 'Enough is enough.'

'But, David, Billy has his retrospective and tour coming up,' Olivia demurred with a tinkling little laugh. 'There wouldn't be much point in going ahead if there was no publicity campaign in place.'

'In light of the *Chronicle*'s latest scoop, I think it would be wise for all parties to curtail any press activity. Or maybe I should make all of you write out a hundred times, "I will maintain a dignified silence."' He smiled without even trace amounts of humour. 'It's time to close ranks, if only from a legal standpoint. After the hacking scandal . . .'

David talked about the Leveson Inquiry and how the Kays' right to privacy would be seriously eroded if anyone knew that they or their representatives might be placing false stories in the press. He used lots of long words, which Ellie usually found quite a turn-on, but today he might just as well have been talking Dolphin.

To her left Billy Kay was a shadowy dark presence with tendrils snaking out towards her, ready to reel her in, so she kept her gaze fixed on David.

Then David stopped talking and went into a little huddle with Olivia Kay and his crabby-looking colleagues. There was a lot of whispering and gesticulating, then David shrugged, his shoulders flexing though the view was obscured somewhat by his grey suit jacket. Ellie stared at him like a thirteen-year-old girl greedily gazing at her crush. No wonder Ari was giving her the side-eye.

But if she wasn't looking at David, then she was forced to look at Billy Kay. He was staring down at his hands, adorned with chunky silver rings. Lara said something to him and he took a long time before he answered her with a terse monosyllable.

'For goodness' sake. Really? *Really?*' David turned away from the huddle and one of the other men stepped forward.

'Miss Cohen?'

'Ms Cohen,' Ellie and Ari said in unison, which made David smile faintly.

'Ms Cohen, junior. Our client is keen to effect a mutually agreeable settlement. May I ask exactly what you require in order to facilitate this?'

Ellie looked at him blankly. Then she turned to Ari, who shook her head as though she didn't have a clue either. 'What?' She sounded unbelievably stupid. 'I mean, can I have, like, um, some clarification, please?'

The two older lawyers and Olivia Kay regarded Ellie coolly, then went back to their huddle, David joining them when Olivia tugged lightly at his jacket sleeve.

He was the first to emerge from this new caucus. The atmosphere in the room was tense and stuffy, and everyone seemed to be watching David as he walked to a small desk to fetch pen and paper and wrote something on it.

'Is this clarification enough?' he asked. He leaned across the table so he could push the paper towards Ellie and she caught the citrussy hint of his aftershave.

She hooked the paper with a fingertip and pulled it closer; the marks on it blurry and indistinct. Each time they swam into focus, Ellie would blink and they'd go back to being hieroglyphics again.

Then she heard Ari say, 'Fuck me,' and the next time she looked down, Ellie could read the figures quite clearly.

Five hundred thousand pounds was written in David's

immaculate copperplate script. Obviously the massive tax bill hadn't completely wiped out the Kay coffers and they were still able to scrounge together some loose change.

In terms of sheer numbers and weighted to inflation it recompensed Ellie for all the things she'd missed out on when she was growing up. Not just the everyday burden of food, utilities and new shoes but the ballet lessons she'd desperately wanted. Clothes that hadn't been bought from one of Camden's many charity shops. The school trips she'd missed because Ari was too pigheaded to ask Sadie and Morry for cash, which they'd gladly have given.

She wanted to say very calmly, 'Shall I give you my bank details so you can transfer the funds, and will I have to pay tax on it?' Of course, she did – she was only human – but she didn't *really* need compensation for all the things that Lara and Rose and even Charlie had been given, while she'd gone without. Despite the lack of funds, Ellie's childhood had been rich in other ways. There'd been trips to the V&A, the National Portrait Gallery and the Science Museum. Long summer afternoons playing rounders and picnicking in Regent's Park. Dancing like a wild thing on the stage while one of Ari's bands had been sound-checking. Most importantly, there'd been more love than one little girl knew what to do with.

The only thing missing, the one thing that she'd really wanted, was sitting at the other end of the table and still ignoring her from behind his Raybans.

Ellie glanced at Ari just to be sure. Ari made her feelings obvious with another squeeze of her daughter's hand. 'No!' Ellie said flatly. 'How rude!'

Lara and Rose nudged each other. The lawyers looked as if their flabber had been well and truly gasted. But David didn't miss a beat. 'Seven hundred thousand pounds, not a penny more,' he said coolly. 'That's what's on the table.'

'I don't—'

'It's offered without prejudice and on the understanding that you and your mother will sign a confidential agreement that clearly states that you have no claim on any further monies from my clients, who accept no liability for any of the events that may or may not have resulted in this settlement.' He sounded so bored, like this whole business was beneath him and that he'd much rather get back to his office and draw up a few watertight contracts so some dumb teenagers with a newly minted recording contract would sign their souls away. 'Furthermore, you will never talk to any media organisations or post anything on any social media sites even tenuously related to the Kay family.'

'You mean you want to buy me off and hit me with a gagging order at the same time?' Ellie queried. She rested her chin on her hand and tried out her most piercing stare on Billy Kay. 'You can't even look at me, can you? Look at me!'

'Hey, easy tiger,' Ari said softly. She took Ellie's hand again, hidden by the table, and stroked the thundering pulse with her thumb, the way she always had when Ellie was younger and needed to calm the fuck down.

He, Billy Kay, moved. Rested his hands flat on the polished table top and glanced in Ellie's direction. 'I'm looking at you, Happy?' His voice was sour and sharp like vinegar. It made her die inside a little.

He *was* looking at her now, but as if Ellie shouldn't be there. Like she was a minute speck of dirt on a clear, smooth surface.

As she sat there and he sat there with his dark glasses and his sharp suit and silly hair and mocking sneer on his face, Ellie realised that her life had been great precisely because Billy wasn't in it. Lara and Rose were flawed and a bit fucked up. They didn't have any family. Didn't seem to have much in the way of friends. All they had was money. They were obsessed with it, and not in the honest

451

'if you want the good life, then you have to work bloody hard for it' Cohen way.

Ellie couldn't bear to look at Billy Kay any more and inevitably because her heart was the brains of the operation, she went back to looking at David. He raised his eyebrows, then was still; wasn't going to give anything away.

They should have been the two most important men in Ellie's life and in a really dark, terrible way they were. Because they were taking it in turns to destroy her spirit, to try to make her as cynical and bitter as they were.

Both of them were hopeless, but Ellie still had hope. 'I don't want anything from you,' she said, eyes sweeping round each Kay, her shadow family. 'I absolve you of any responsibility towards me. I'll sign whatever you want.'

Ellie stood up on legs that were much more shaky than she would have liked. 'You've spent all my life pretending that I didn't exist, that I was some shameful secret marring your rock 'n' roll back story, then you drag me out when it suits you so you can pimp your digitally remastered back catalogue.' Shoulders back, chin up. 'Well, you don't deserve to have me in your life.'

When Ellie stepped out from behind the table, it felt like she had only recently learned how to walk. She waited until she was almost at the door, before she turned and she couldn't look at David any more, but she could look at his colleagues. 'Just give David that senior partnership already. Put his fucking name on the shiny plaque outside.' It was one of the three worst moments of her life, but she could still manage the moxie to give a hollow little laugh that was pure Bette Davis in *All About Eve*. 'Believe me, he really went the extra mile to get it.'

Clerkenwell, London, Present Day

Ellie makes a spit-and-sawdust speech that's pure gumption, because she's her mother's daughter, then she storms out. The lawyer, the tall, intense one with a voice like knives who's been gazing at her daughter with a dumbstruck expression when he thinks no one is looking, storms after her. Ari can hear them shouting in the corridor outside.

Ellie never shouts.

I'm too old for this shit, Ari thinks.

They sit and they wait and wait for the other lawyer to come back.

The atmosphere in the room is so thick you could cut it into individual slices. Ari doesn't want to be here with these people. The past is always something she feels guilty about, and yes, she does feel guilty for what she put Billy's women through. Though it doesn't compare to how they'd suffered at Billy's own hands as he moulded their souls until they were as misshapen as his.

It's obvious the other lawyer isn't coming back. Before Ari can make her excuses, Billy's daughters get up and go without a backward glance. There's a cough and the other two suits, who have been deep in conversation, approach her.

Ari can have the money, same terms and conditions. Isn't she a lucky girl?

She's been waiting for this moment for half a lifetime. She should be word perfect as she slowly and deliberately scrunches up the piece of paper. Then she turns to Billy. 'You think this even begins to compensate me for advances and back royalties, digital rights, licensing? Not even close. Not even in the same ballpark as close.'

No one looks confused, because they all know what he did, and Ari thought she was long past this but the anger feels like corrosive acid running through her veins.

Billy takes off his shades. Ari holds her breath. She doesn't want to fall again, but his eyes are dead and cold. Not a spark left in him. 'I don't know what you're talking about,' he says so calmly that she can't quite take it in. 'Sweetheart, back then you only knew three chords and started every song with the "Be My Baby" drumbeat.'

Billy sounds so supremely unbothered by her accusation that Ari's rendered mute. She'd been expecting defensive bluster, shouting even, but not flat denial.

'You did. You know you did,' she says helplessly, because she's waited three decades for this showdown and this is not how it's meant to play out.

'Dear Ari, you're embarrassing yourself,' Olivia says coolly, but Ari can see how her hands shake before she folds her arms and tucks them out of sight. 'Please don't.'

'I should have known this was about money.' Billy stands up and walks towards her, and the lawyers and even his doggedly devoted wife cease to exist. It's just her and Billy. Ari stands up too and he sidles up close in that snaky way that had always got Ari in a panic that he was going to kiss her. Or that he might not. 'If you wrote those songs, then how come you never wrote anything that was half as good as them since? Huh?'

Ari wishes she knew the answer, but Billy does apparently.

'I get it, darling. I get why you're mad, why you're flinging accusations around,' he says, his breath caressing her ear, arm stealing round her waist. 'It was your decision, Ari. You chose the kid over me. You chose her over the music. I tried to tell you that you were never going to get anywhere if you were stuck with a baby who demanded every single thing you had to give. I warned you.'

So this is what people mean when they talk about

epiphanies. This is her eureka moment! Ari actually raises her eyes as if she expects to see a light bulb going off above her head. 'No, she didn't,' she says and she's laughing because it's so obvious now. 'It was you. You sucked me dry and after you went, I was empty. Ellie didn't ruin me, she saved my life.'

'Whatever,' Billy says, and he turns away as if Ari isn't amusing any more. She's boring and Billy never got on well with boring. But Ari's not done yet.

'Anyway, what kind of man makes the mother of his child choose between them? A really shoddy excuse for a man, that's who. Jesus, your ego was always the most constant thing about you.'

'It wasn't about my ego.' He's angry now; it's the first real emotion he's shown. 'I left because you didn't love me enough.'

He sounds like a lost little boy. Ari can't bear to see him so diminished. She glances over at Olivia and something fleeting passes between them. It's not hate on the other woman's face but resignation – acceptance, even – because she put Billy first and she stood by her choice and wasn't going to let Ari judge her for it. 'Billy.' Ari sighs his name, because she's wasted too much time being angry with him. 'No one could ever love you as much as you need to be loved.'

'No, you mean, you couldn't. You're not capable of loving anyone.'

'That's not true. Not any more,' Ari insists, willing away the tears. 'I'm full of love.'

'You never even wanted her,' Billy says, spite making the words sting. 'You would have had an abortion if I hadn't talked you out of it. Then you tried to fob her off on your sister. I think *that* would ruin her life, if someone told her.'

This man tried to destroy her for having the audacity not to love him to the exclusion of everything else. Fine. Ari can take it, but Billy isn't going to destroy Ellie, simply to punish her for being chosen over him. Ellie should never have to doubt how much she's loved.

'I did love you back then but I never trusted you,' Ari says, folding her arms and looking straight at Billy. He's put his Raybans back on but Ari knows she has his full attention. 'You might have the reel-to-reels we recorded but sometimes I ran a tape straight off the mixing desk. Gave them to Tabitha to look after.' She shook her head. 'And Georgina only had five minutes to clear out that room. She didn't think to look in the summerhouse where there were half a dozen of those Black 'n' Red Notebooks that we wrote lyrics in. Come on! When you rerecorded the songs, you must have realised you didn't have hard copies of all the lyrics.'

A muscle in Billy's cheek gives an involuntary spasm. Ari thrills to the sight of it. 'You're bluffing.'

Ari grins. Suddenly her heart feels light. 'You'll never know. Just don't come near me or mine again.' She shakes her head. 'You're not capable of understanding that if I lived my life a hundred times over, I'd always choose Ellie over you. Always.'

Ari knows that she's never going to see or hear from Billy again and that's reason enough not to look behind her as she walks out of the door straight into the path of Ellie's lawyer.

Chapter Thirty-five

Ellie wasn't even halfway down the corridor when she heard the door open behind her and, before she could quicken her pace, David had caught up to take her arm.

'Don't touch me!' It was a shriek.

'Ellie . . . what I said in there, I *had* to say it.' He didn't even care that she was trying to bat him away with her handbag. 'I was doing my job.'

'What? You were just following orders? Do you even know how that sounds?'

David obviously did because he scowled, then closed both arms around her to prevent the damage she was intent on wreaking, and marched her down the corridor to an office, its door wide open, which he slammed shut after them.

It was a fancy corner office panelled in gleaming dark wood and shelf upon shelf of leather-bound books. David pushed her down into one of two stiff-backed chairs in front of the huge desk, which was empty except for a computer and a telephone. He didn't even have a pen tidy or an in-tray and an out-tray, because he was a cold-blooded, heartless drone.

His hands were still on her shoulders and Ellie pulled her bag close like a cushion she could cuddle for comfort. Now that she wasn't trying to cause him physical damage, he stopped touching her.

The only thing worse than David touching her was

when he wasn't touching her, which made no sense, but then, everything that had happened today had been completely senseless.

David grabbed the other chair, turned it round and pulled it so close to Ellie that when he sat down, their knees bumped. 'You should take the money,' he said in a low voice. 'He owes you that much, doesn't he?'

Ellie wanted to smack her forehead in despair. Or his forehead. 'I don't care about the money.' She exhaled slowly. 'I don't care about him. And I especially don't care about you any more.'

David looked her steadily in the eyes. 'I don't think that's true.' His voice didn't waver. 'You wouldn't be so upset if you were indifferent to me.'

'I didn't say I was indifferent,' Ellie argued, clutching her handbag even tighter to her chest. 'I said that I don't care about you any more.'

'Apart from the first time we met, you've always known what I did for a living. Unfortunately, my job requires a certain amount of dissembling,' David said levelly. Ellie hated when he was like this: cool, watchful as he mentally weighed her up, like he was predicting her next move before she even knew in which direction she was heading. Sometimes she wished that he'd lose his temper and have a good shout. Recently she'd become a big fan of having a good shout.

'Those people in that room, they've corroded your soul.' She wasn't even trying to hurt him now, but to warn him before it was too late, though deep down she knew that it already was. He was too far gone and she couldn't save him. There was a good reason she'd sworn off saving men from themselves. 'The things they make you do should be beneath you.'

He recoiled a little. 'I have tried again and again to protect you,' he protested.

'No, you've been trying to protect your clients and your

458

own career path,' Ellie scoffed. 'None of it was for my benefit.'

David suddenly reared up and grabbed her seat back so he was there, right up in her space, close enough to kiss, not that he looked as if he wanted to kiss her. 'I haven't been protecting my clients, I've been protecting you *from* my clients.'

Ellie screwed up her face in contempt. 'You've got a funny way of showing it!'

'I'll admit that I was determined to think the worst of you. I saw that scene with Richey. And when I read his story in the papers, well, it was obvious you had absolutely no self-respect.'

It was Ellie's turn to flinch. 'I'm not like that!'

'I know. I should have realised it from that first meeting at the Wolseley, but I told myself that you'd eventually run true to type. That you could deal with being papped and tabbed because you were in it for the money and the glory. But you confounded me every time I spoke to you.' He sighed. 'For fuck's sake, you even paid your own hotel bill! Then that first evening at my flat, I saw who you really were.'

Ellie remembered that evening too. She'd tried to be calm and reasonable but had ended up red-faced and indignant. She was sure she'd shouted at him and had generally been everything that she always tried not to be. 'Like I keep saying, you met me when my circumstances redefined extenuating,' she said.

'That evening it was painfully obvious your life was coming apart at the seams and I bore most of the responsibility for that. You didn't even whine that much,' he said untruthfully with a soft little smile that Ellie wanted to return; wanted to more than anything.

'I seem to remember whining quite a lot, actually,' she reminded him.

He shrugged. 'You could have whined more than you

did. I got the measure of you that day and the more I got to know you, the more I liked you. And the more I liked you, the more I wanted to protect you.' David shook his head and Ellie was hanging on his every word, until she remembered.

'Was it protecting me when you didn't tell me about Charlie!' The betrayal hit her anew. 'He's my brother!'

'I couldn't tell you! You don't even know the half of it. The things I could tell you . . .' He swallowed hard as if he were pushing away the words. Words that would probably break her but she wanted to hear them anyway.

'What things?' She couldn't help the hand that crept up to touch the taut line of his jaw. 'Tell me!'

'I can't. I won't. Not to protect him,' David captured her hand, which was still on him, and held it tight, 'to protect you.'

There were so many things that Ellie wanted from him but pity wasn't one of them. 'Because you feel sorry for me?' She snatched her hand back. 'Oh God, I'm *your* lame duck!'

David's face creased in confusion. 'What are you talking about?'

'You feel sorry for me! It's so obvious now. It's like Ari. She doesn't tell me things that I have a right to know because she thinks I won't be able to cope. You're just the same. I'm a fully functional adult. I don't need you to protect me. I can handle some hard truths and I can look after myself.'

'Maybe Ari doesn't tell you things that she thinks might hurt you because she loves you?' David suggested softly. He hadn't gone back to his chair but was squatting down in front of her. 'Maybe I'm in love with you too.'

It was enough to make Ellie's heart go pitter-patter had her heart not been weighted down with a heavy burden. She wanted to believe that love would conquer all and they'd kiss and the screen would fade to black, but you

460

couldn't let yourself fall in love with someone who only wanted part of you.

'Last time I checked I was still Billy Kay's daughter and you were still his lawyer.' Ellie wished that she didn't sound quite so bitter; it didn't become her. 'Tell me, what's changed since we had this same conversation in Paris?'

David rested his hands on her knees and tried to stare her down. 'We can do this,' he said earnestly. 'We just have to keep my job and my clients separate.'

'It's not going to work. I never want to see that man again, but he's my father and I'm done with hiding that side of myself away.' Ellie put her hands on David's shoulder and leaned forward until their foreheads were touching. 'If you say you love me, if you want me in your life, then it has to be all of me. All or nothing.'

'Nothing is ever that straightforward.'

'It is if you let it be,' Ellie insisted. 'I'm not going to be your lame duck.'

'Why do you keep going on about ducks?' It was hard to be exasperated with someone when you were forehead to forehead, so they broke apart.

'I deserve so much more than what you want to give me.' Ellie stood up but David was now resting on his haunches as he gazed up at her. 'We can't have any kind of future because you're caught up in a filthy business. Why can't you see that this job, doing the dirty work for men like Billy Kay, is eating away at all the good in you? Stealing it bit by bit. I will try to save you because it's what I do but I'll end up destroying myself in the process.'

David bowed his head as if he was a penitent seeking redemption. 'Then you don't love all of me either, do you?'

Ellie kind of did. That was the problem and that was why she was heading for the door, while the fire was still in her belly and she had the guts to walk away.

*

She half expected David to come after her again. No, she *wanted* him to come after her and tell her that she was wrong. That he could change. That they were worth fighting for, but he didn't and soon Ellie was standing outside the offices looking up at a dense grey sky that bulged with the threat of rain.

On the street it was humid, as if the whole city was stewing inside a pressure cooker. Ellie ducked into a Pret across the road for a sandwich and ate it in the back of a black cab as she tried to come up with a plan to save her job.

She'd have all the time in the world to think about David and all the 'couldas shouldas wouldas' but only about ninety minutes tops to placate an angry boss, so she concentrated on stoking the fire in her belly so it didn't splutter and fizzle out. Twenty minutes later she was marching up to the door of the gallery and pushing it open with such force that it crashed back on its hinges and made Inge, sitting behind the reception desk, jump in her chair.

'You frightened the life out of me!' she snapped in a very un-Inge-like way, rearranging the papers on the desk that had got muddled up during her panic attack. She looked up. 'Oh! Is it really you?'

'Of course it's me! Who else would it be?' Ellie asked. She sounded cross too, but that didn't last long because Inge was almost vaulting over the reception desk so she could fling her arms around her.

'God, I've missed you so much! Promise that you'll never go away for so long again.'

'I wasn't gone *that* long.'

'Two weeks!' Inge rested her head on Ellie's shoulder. 'It's been awful.'

That made Ellie almost smile. 'Did you actually have to put in some hard graft?'

'So much hard graft!' cried a voice and then Piers was hugging her from behind. 'Don't ever leave us again.

462

Vaughn has been horrible. Like pre-Grace horrible.'

'He fired Muffin for sending a painting to Burkina Faso when it was meant to go to Buenos Aires,' Inge explained, which to be fair did sound like a sackable offence. 'He called her terrible names and he threw that little miniature Damien Hirst skull that he uses as a paperweight at her head.'

'Really?' Ellie gently disengaged herself from the group hug. 'Is he very angry with me too?'

'The angriest,' Inge assured her. 'Piers and I were watching *On The Sofa* on the computer and we were so engrossed . . .'

'You were *amazing*,' Piers breathed. 'Not at first. You kept opening and closing your mouth like a blowfish, but then you were amazing and your hair looked very shiny. Though you really can't pull off an "Am I right?" You're not sassy enough.'

'Thank you for that constructive criticism,' Ellie said, and the fire was fizzling out because Inge and Piers were so pleased to see her and she hadn't realised how much she missed them or the gallery. Which reminded her: 'So, Emerging Scandinavian Artists, was it a sellout? How many orders for the Perspex bicycles?'

'Lots,' Inge said helpfully. 'Lots and lots. So, anyway, when you were on *On The Sofa*, did it look as if Jeff Jenkins was well endowed?'

'Yes, did it? I heard he's packing a monster in his chinos.'

'Piers! That's disgusting,' Ellie said and then she giggled, which meant that her blood was no longer up and Vaughn would make mincemeat of her, call her terrible names too, and not only follow through on her sacking but refuse to give her a reference. It would be a major victory if he didn't throw any art at her. 'Is Vaughn . . . y'know . . . ?'

'He came up behind us when we were watching and you know how he gets that weird tic in his cheek when he's stressed?'

Ellie nodded. She knew it only too well.

Inge folded her arms. 'It was going like a jackhammer.'

'He swore,' Piers added with relish. He always enjoyed the novelty of not being the person who Vaughn was swearing at. 'Said he was adding a new clause to our contracts that we were never to speak to any media outlets without his written permission but it didn't apply in your case 'cause you were already sacked.'

'He said you needn't bother working out the rest of your notice.' Inge shrugged apologetically. 'But you are coming back, aren't you? Because with you and Muffin both gone, I've been really stretched. It's been hellish.'

Inge didn't look as if she'd been stretched. She looked as languid and swan-like as ever, but Ellie wasn't in a position to allay her fears. Not when her own fears were far greater. 'Is he in?' she asked heavily.

'Yes. It's his last day in the office before he takes the rest of August off. He was meant to leave at lunchtime but he's been waiting for you,' Piers informed her. He gave Ellie a pitying look. 'Grace even popped over a couple of hours ago to find out what was keeping him.'

'Oh God.' This was the worst day of her life. This would be the one she remembered when time and distance made all the other worst days recede. 'I'd better get this over and done with then.'

'Don't leave us,' Inge said forlornly as Ellie started the trudge up the stairs to Vaughn's office. She was tempted to skulk in her office, and check that no one, like Piers for instance, had messed it up in her absence, but every second she dawdled was another second for Vaughn's temper to escalate ever higher.

'Come in.' Vaughn's summons was as sharp as her rat-a-tat-tat on his office door.

He was sitting at his desk, staring at his laptop screen, hand fisted in his hair, and didn't even look up as Ellie stood uncertainly by the door.

464

'Sit,' he barked. This obviously wasn't going to be an informal chat on one of his comfy white leather cubed armchairs. It was going to a bollocking administered while she sat on the very uncomfortable, very rare, wire mesh Marcel Breuer chair, which would probably snag on her broderie anglaise dress.

By her estimation, Ellie sat there for a good five minutes without Vaughn acknowledging her presence, which was certainly a theme for the day.

Ellie had been here before. Not often. Only once when she'd been outbid at a very important auction. Vaughn had given her the silent treatment for eleven agonising minutes until she'd nearly cried from the sheer anticipation of the impending telling-off. Piers had once sat in this very spot for twenty-three minutes. But instead of feeling cowed and liable to prostrate herself on the floor and beg for mercy, Ellie could feel the righteous anger spark up in her belly once more.

She was so over men and their utter inability to behave like normal, rational beings. The game-playing! The sneakiness! The double-speak! Compartmentalising their feelings until they were so tucked away, they couldn't find them any more.

Enough!

'You know what? I refuse to be sacked,' she said. Vaughn's head jerked up. He tried to glower but Ellie had taken him by surprise and it lacked its usual ferocity. 'I don't accept my dismissal. I rescind it.'

'You can't rescind it. It's legally binding.' Vaughn had now succeeded in knitting his brows together. 'You've dragged down the good name of my gallery and you went on that awful television show. What did I say to you before the opening?'

'You said a lot of things.'

'Never complain, never explain,' Vaughn repeated grimly. 'You did both. And if I hadn't already fired you, I'd be firing you right now. You have no dignity, Cohen. You should be ashamed of yourself.'

When he was being this objectionable, Ellie really had to remember why she wanted to continue working for him. 'I love my job and I'm good at it—'

'You're not that good at it. You knew absolutely nothing when you first arrived here,' Vaughn said loftily. He was enjoying himself, which was actually a good sign. Ellie didn't doubt he was furious with her, but if he'd been *really* furious, his voice would be a flat, ominously quiet weapon that could inflict all manner of pain. 'You were nothing without me, you'll be nothing again.'

'I'm not going anywhere.' Ellie crossed her legs and folded her arms to show that she was serious. 'The fact I went on TV doesn't affect my ability to do my job. You trained me up and promoted me because you recognised my talent and—'

Vaughn yawned. 'Is this going to take much longer?'

'Are you going to give me my job back?' Ellie sounded metronome-steady but her heart was racing as much as it had been when she'd stepped onto the *On The Sofa* set earlier or clapped eyes on her father in the not-so-loving flesh for the first time ever. Today was sucking beyond all measure.

'No.' It was brutal and uncompromising. It was fuck off and don't ever darken my doorstep again. There was nowhere left to manoeuvre. Except . . .

'Fine,' Ellie said, folding her arms, furrowing her brows and pursing her lips in a way that Lola always described as her epic bitchface. 'Whatever. I know a really good lawyer and I have an excellent case for unfair dismissal. Excellent. You think the good name of the gallery's been damaged by me standing up for myself on live TV, well, just wait until my case makes the papers.'

Vaughn was doing some epic bitchface of his own.

'What's got into you, Cohen? Whatever it is, I don't like it.'

'Well, I don't like being sacked because of a situation that wasn't my fault and was an utter living hell, not that you cared about that. My dismissal was unjust and unreasonable.' Ellie breathed out through her nostrils like an angry dragon. 'I refuse to be treated like that.'

'If I'm such a beast to work for, I'm surprised that you still want your job back.' He made a big show of looking at his watch. 'So, was that everything?'

It was Vaughn at his most bloody-minded. Ellie wondered if she did actually want her job back. Oh, but she did. She so did. Vaughn had taken a chance on her, seen something special in her and he'd taught Ellie everything she knew about buying and selling art. But he hadn't taught Ellie *everything* she knew, which reminded her . . . 'I think so. But before I go, I just want to show you something,' Ellie said, unzipping her laptop case and pulling out her iPad.

'What? The showreel for your glittering new career as media whore?' Vaughn asked nastily, but everyone knew his bark was about twenty-seven times worse than his bite.

'No, if you won't reinstate me solely because you refuse to admit you were wrong to fire me in the first place, then I wanted you to see the first clients I'll be representing as an independent art dealer,' Ellie said, 'I'll have to find gallery space, probably in East London, but it'll be exciting. You know how much I love a challenge.'

Vaughn raised his eyebrows. 'Just what the world needs. Another jumped-up gallery girl thinking that they have what it takes.'

Ellie held up her iPad to show Vaughn the film she'd shot of Claude and Marie's trees in all their drooping, paper beauty. Then she showed him their timelapse movie of a forest through the seasons. 'What do you think?' she asked anxiously, because this wasn't part of the scene they were playing. He was her boss, her mentor, and when it came to art, she valued his opinion above all others.

'Interesting,' Vaughn murmured. All of him was still, but if he'd been a dog his ears would have been on high alert and his tail would have been wagging joyously.

'I know I'm getting ahead of myself but I can just see the Turbine Hall at Tate Modern transformed into a magical wood, can't you?'

'Maybe.' Vaughn steepled his fingers. 'It would also work well at the Guggenheim.'

'Well, that's something to consider after they've made the Turner Prize shortlist,' Ellie agreed. 'So, I'll be back at my desk tomorrow morning, usual time. OK?'

'Why don't you want to set up on your own?' Vaughn was looking at her with a grudging admiration that had to be killing him.

'I haven't quite finished picking your brains,' Ellie said as she turned off her iPad, because Vaughn wasn't going to sack her and they were back in that place where he was borderline mean to her and she gave him only borderline attitude. 'And I'd really miss Piers and Inge.'

'Do *not* start getting mawkish or crying, Cohen. Even I have my limits.'

She wasn't planning on doing either of those two things. Not in front of Vaughn, anyway. 'Do you want an update on obscure French Surrealists and female painters from between the wars before you go on holiday?' she asked.

It was another hour, and many phone calls from Grace, before Vaughn left the gallery, after many dire warnings about what would happen if they forgot to set the security system.

Ellie waited until she'd watched Vaughn's car disappearing out of the mews, then she shut the gallery door and turned to Piers and Inge, who were doing the final sweep. 'I don't want to go home just yet and I don't have any paparazzi following me so I'm going out to drink huge quantities of alcohol. Who's in?'

Piers said he'd love to but Monday night was his one alcohol-free night of the week, and Inge wasn't that keen either.

'Maybe one really quick drink round the corner?' she suggested as Ellie chivvied the pair of them out of the door. 'It's definitely going to rain. The BBC said so!'

'You won't melt,' Ellie insisted. 'Come on! Today has pretty much chewed me up, then spat me out. If you've missed me as much as you said you had, then you *have* to come drinking with me.'

All she wanted to do was to wipe the day from her memory, and not even the part of the day that featured a baying TV audience or her father barely able to summon up the energy to speak to her. She wanted to erase the picture etched in her brain of David on his knees as he said he was halfway to being in love with her.

Ellie longed to rush back to the offices of Wyndham, Pryce and Lewis and tell him that it was OK. She was ready to be loved by him and compartmentalised the rest of the time. Except it wasn't OK, it wasn't even a little bit OK, so alcohol was the best way she knew to temporarily erase some of the pain. She also needed to know that she wasn't alone – she had people who accepted her wholly as she was, and would even hold her hair back when she threw up from too much vodka. Tonight, she needed a support system, whether her support system liked it or not.

Inge was far too placid to put up much of a fight. Piers capitulated once Ellie agreed that he could go back to his flat and change while she and Inge made their way to a bar in Hoxton that did killer cocktails. En route Ellie rang Tess and Lola and her cousins and the friends that she absolutely knew for certain hadn't tried to sell her out to any news organisations.

Tonight she wanted to get back to being the girl she'd been before all this had started.

Clerkenwell, London, Present Day

His name is David Gold and he says that, despite his better judgement, he's in love with her daughter.

They're not words designed to warm a mother's heart, and Ari is no exception, but they end up drinking gin and tonics in a pub tucked away behind the Inns of Court.

'She doesn't want to be with me,' he says *yet again,* and now he's more mopey and less intense, he seems nicer. But he made Ellie lose her temper, and he's a lawyer, and though Ari loves Ellie to pieces, even she's starting to get bored with how much this guy keeps banging on about her.

'Well, if she doesn't want to be with you, then what can you do?' Ari asks briskly.

'I hurt her, that's what I did,' he says, and puts his head in his hands. 'I tried to play her. And I should have told her about Charlie, about the songs Billy stole.'

'You knew about the songs, then?' Ari asks with a snarl because she wants there to be no ambiguity about this.

He inches his bar stool further away. 'Of course I do. There's been a contingency plan in place ever since Billy signed the recording contract.' He stares down at his glass. 'We never had this conversation, but if you have the stomach for a fight, if you're brave enough, you have an excellent case against him.'

Ari has white-knuckled hands around her glass and she's not sure if she's going to throw it in his face. 'So what else do you know that you haven't told Ellie . . . *yet?*'

'I don't know what you're talking about,' he says. For a lawyer, he's a terrible liar.

'You know everything, don't you? You know where every single one of Billy's victims is buried,' Ari muses, and he doesn't deny it. 'What do you mean by "a contingency plan"?'

He ducks his head, even though Ari still hasn't thrown anything at him. 'Your sister wrote to Billy several times after the adoption fell through. She was very upset.'

Ari nods. 'Upset doesn't begin to cover it,' she says. She's amazed that she can even talk when her heart is in her mouth. She can't even be angry with Carol. It wasn't until she'd got pregnant with Louis using IVF – though they used to call it having a test-tube baby back then – that Carol forgave Ari. Not forgave her, but maybe accepted why Ari had behaved the way she did. 'What did she say in her letters?'

David Gold looks her in the eye. 'She repeatedly mentioned your intention to have the pregnancy terminated. They're all on file in my office.'

The room tilts wildly around her, floor rushing up to meet her, ceiling falling down on top of her. Ari can hear a rushing in her head and she thinks she might faint, or that the shame might swallow her whole. Deep in her bones she knows that Ellie would probably forgive her for this one terrible transgression, because surely Ellie must know just how fucking much she's loved. But Ari still can't forgive herself. Didn't really know what love was back then until Ellie showed her how . . .

His hand on her arm brings Ari back to the ugly present. 'Not a day goes by when I don't regret what I almost did,' she says in a voice gone rusty.

'You have to understand that I'm not protecting *him*.' His face twists into something ugly for a brief moment. 'Protecting Billy Kay is a very unfortunate side-effect of protecting Ellie. She loves you very much, that will never change. She could deal with this, all of this but, quite frankly, I don't see why she should have to.'

Maybe this lawyer guy isn't so bad after all, Ari thinks just as

Ellie rings. Ari can tell when Ellie's faking it until she makes it. She's trying to sound perky and peppy as she asks Ari if she has the garment bag containing her boring white work dresses that she left behind and she wants Ari to meet up with her and her friends. 'Please come,' she says. 'Piers is wearing lederhosen. It's the most ridiculous thing ever!'

Ari glances over at David Gold, who's sitting there trying not to listen to Ari's side of the phone call. He doesn't seem like one of Ellie's lame ducks, one of her pet projects. He was more dangerous than that: he is someone who could really hurt her.

'. . . we're at that bar in Hoxton Square, underneath the Thai restaurant. Hang on!' Ellie is shouting at her friends. 'It's called Happiness Forgets. Symbolic, much?'

Ari agrees that it is, and agrees that she might see Ellie later, then hangs up and turns to David Gold. 'When you love someone, your first and last instinct is to shield them from anything or anyone that might do them harm.'

He nods gravely. 'I know.'

'But there are times they're going to get hurt and there's nothing you can do to stop it. Especially when you're the person who might end up hurting them the most.'

'That file, the letters, I'll make it all go away. As though it never, ever happened.' David Gold takes Ari's hands as if he's taking an oath. 'You don't have to worry. It will be all right. I promise you.'

Ari mouths a thank-you, can't do any more than that no matter how much she wants to, and they sit there in silence for a good minute, her hands in his. Then someone pushes past them and the moment becomes awkward. Ari pulls away and almost smiles. 'Look, I can't say I'd be happy to have a lawyer in the family, but David, you're Billy Kay's lawyer . . .'

'I know. I know. Believe me, I know,' he snaps.

This relationship is doomed, Ari is sure of it, but he loves Ellie, and Ari has to trust that she's done a good enough job raising her daughter that she'll be able to give as good as she gets.

'Will you please tell me where Ellie is?'

Ari hands over the garment bag, gives him the address of the bar and warns him that if he so much as makes Ellie shed one single, solitary tear she knows a man who'll break his legs.

Chapter Thirty-six

By the time Ellie and Inge reached the tiny bar on Hoxton Square, just across the road from the White Cube gallery, Tess and Lola had already arrived, scored a table and ordered a round of Tom Collins.

After the Tom Collins, Ellie had a Ward Eight – rye whiskey, lemon juice and grenadine – which made her pull faces as she determinedly drank it down. Then she moved on to a Tantris Sidecar, a deadly concoction of cognac, calvados, cointreau, Chartreuse and syrup with more lemon, and third time was the charm.

Everything was soft focus in the dimly lit room as Ellie blearily looked around. Most of the people she'd called had turned up, even on a Monday night when the BBC said it was going to rain, because these were the people who were always on her team. Once Billy Kay and *On The Sofa* had been discussed for all of five minutes, Emma, Laurel and Tanya wanted to talk about a girls' weekend in New York before Rosh Hashanah to find some really fit single, Jewish men ('I mean, there have to be *some*') and was Ellie interested? Lola had an interview for a part-time job as a taxidermist's assistant, Tess had been given her very own in-ear microphone that afternoon and offered a permanent contract, and everyone else wanted to talk about how Portland was the new Brooklyn.

The world was carrying on same as it ever did.

'Hello you,' said a voice, and Ellie looked up from

pensive contemplation of her empty glass to see Laetitia, one of Lola's friends, smiling at her as she brushed something off her shirt. 'You're having a bit of a rough month, aren't you?'

'Roughest month ever,' Ellie agreed. Her speech was ever so slightly slurred but her senses were still razor sharp. 'Is that . . . are those . . . you're wet! Is it raining?'

'It's like something from the Old Testament,' Laetitia said, holding up a damp strand of hair for Ellie's inspection. 'I got here just before it really unleashed.'

Ellie nudged Tess, who was sitting next to her and talking animatedly to one of Inge's male flatmates about something that involved having to stroke his arm a lot. 'It's raining,' Ellie said. 'Can you believe it?'

'About bloody time,' Tess said, without even looking up. Laetitia had gone to get a drink, two Japanese girls were taking a preening picture of Piers for their style blog and the cousins were all transfixed by the screen of Laurel's iPad.

No one noticed when Ellie slipped out of her seat and up the scarred wooden stairs. She had to flatten herself to the wall to make way for two sodden people who seemed to think they had right of way, then she was opening the door.

The rain was coming down in a gushing fall of fat drops that bounced on the pavement on impact. Ellie stepped over the fierce stream of water sluicing into the gutter. The five seconds it took to take those five steps outside was long enough to soak her. Her white dress, even her bra and pants were drenched, feet slipping in her wedge sandals, but as she stood there, arms outstretched, face turned upwards, it felt like a fresh start.

The dirty hands of the Kay family had left smudgy grey fingerprints all over her, and the rain was washing them away.

The rain also melted the tears that were streaming

down her cheeks. Crying because she had to let go of those childish dreams of the father who never was, and the father that there could have been, but mostly because Ellie knew that every man she ever loved would always be a little bit less than the man she'd walked away from this afternoon.

She'd done the right thing, so why did it feel like the end of everything that was good?

Her grief was interrupted by the shrieks of two girls as they ran across the square, ducking this way and that as if they could dodge the drops. Ellie wiped a wet hand across her wet face, her make-up all but a faint memory by now, sniffed and was just about to worry about what prolonged exposure to rainwater would do to her straightening treatment when she saw a figure walking slowly through the sheets of driving rain.

She squinted as the figure came towards her. He was shielded by a behemoth of an umbrella so his suit was absolutely bone dry, as was the garment bag draped over one arm.

He stopped when he was within five metres of Ellie and said something that was lost in the dirge of the deluge.

'What are you doing here?' Ellie yelled, closing the gap between them so he could hear her. 'How did you know where I was?'

'Ari told me,' David said. He stared at her in disbelief. 'You're absolutely soaked.'

Ellie shook dripping rats' tails of hair out of her face. 'Never mind that. Why would Ari tell you where I was?'

'Because when I told her I was in love with you, she took it better than you did.'

Ari's track record when it came to affairs of the heart was pitiful, so Ellie wasn't going to let her mother's opinion sway her.

'Nothing's changed,' she said. David was so close that she was now standing under his huge record-